THE BLOOD TRIALS

THE BLOOD TRIALS

BOOK ONE OF THE
BLOOD GIFT DUOLOGY

N. E. DAVENPORT

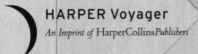

HARPER Voyager
An Imprint of HarperCollins Publishers

THE BLOOD TRIALS. Copyright © 2022 by Enishia Davenport. All rights reserved. Printed in Canada. No part of this book may be used or reproduced in any manner whatsoever without written permission except in the case of brief quotations embodied in critical articles and reviews. For information, address HarperCollins Publishers, 195 Broadway, New York, NY 10007.

HarperCollins books may be purchased for educational, business, or sales promotional use. For information, please email the Special Markets Department at SPsales@harpercollins.com.

Harper Voyager and design are trademarks of HarperCollins Publishers LLC.

FIRST EDITION

Designed by Angie Boutin
Title page background image © Vidady/abode.stock.com
Circular ornament © Andrey/adobe.stock.com
Map illustration by Nick Springer

Library of Congress Cataloging-in-Publication Data has been applied for.

ISBN 978-0-06-305848-4

22 23 24 25 26   LSC   10 9 8 7 6 5 4 3 2 1

For my mother, who always encouraged me to dream
the biggest dreams and fight fiercely for them

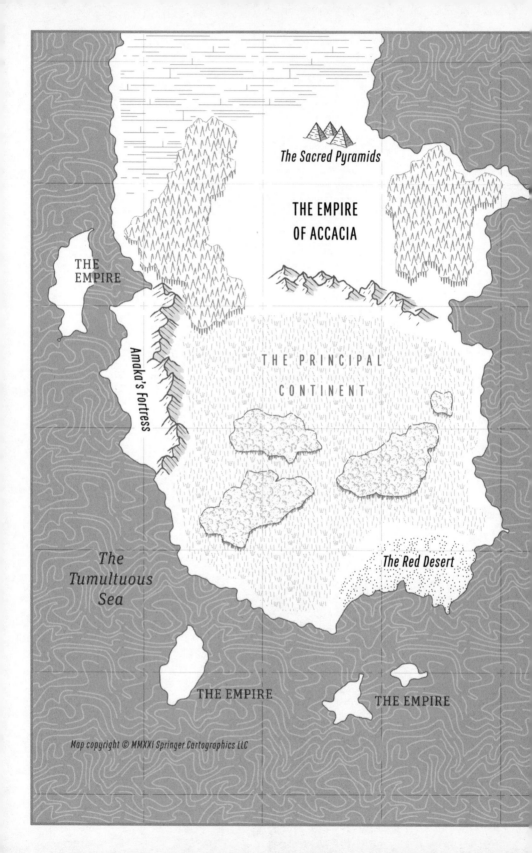

THE
BLOOD
TRIALS

1

I SLAM THE SHOT GLASS down on the table. The amber liquid stopped burning on its way down my esophagus three swallows ago. I'm on my sixth shot. I think. I blink, and the room tilts. I cling to the latest shock of euphoria that floods my system. Triple-distilled Mareenian whiskey with legalized boosters is a glorious thing.

I don't wipe the miserable look that steals onto my face in time.

My friends glimpse it.

"You good?" Selene asks.

I snicker at the irony. Usually, I'm the one looking after her when we're partying.

"We should call it quits," Zayne slurs. He stands up, adamant, only to sway and flop back onto his barstool.

Selene snorts into the ale she's been sipping alongside the shots. "Lightweight."

She's not wrong. Zayne is only drinking so much tonight to indulge me. I insisted we celebrate with one last hurrah before Commencement in the morning busts up our trio. *And they leave me behind.*

Selene and Zayne will be declaring Praetorian, throwing in their bids to become two of the most fearsome and respected soldiers of the Republic. I'm not declaring anything. I'm doing what the psymedics who conducted our exit evals suggested and taking a year off. It's been three months since my grandfather's death, and according to the professionals, I'm still struggling at finding healthy ways to cope. Unprovoked brawls have become my friend. I've stopped attending most classes and combat-training blocks, filling that time with parties and drinking.

I grip the edge of the table, cursing the fact that while I still have a nice buzz, my euphoria is gone. The extra, numbing punch that boosters pack is fleeting, *until you reach a certain threshold, and then the boosters drop you into oblivion.* Oblivion is what I'm seeking tonight. The crooked room means I'm almost there.

Our waitress, a petite girl with red hair a shade lighter than Selene's, saunters up to the table. "Can I get you another round?" Her green eyes framed by short, dark lashes don't stray from Zayne. She's been eyeing him all night. She angles her body so he gets an eyeful of her cleavage.

He grins, taking notice and flashing twin dimples. "Sure, *Leslie.*" The way her name slips off his tongue is both an assertion and invitation. Selene and I roll our eyes at the same time. Zayne's ash-blond hair, blue gaze, tanned complexion, and boyishly handsome features make him more than attractive. They make him gorgeous. He knows it, and every girl he comes across knows it.

Leslie blushes while nibbling coyly on her bottom lip.

Ha! She's coy, my ass. The slow way Zayne's half-lidded eyes rove over her curves is exactly the thing she was angling for each time she came over.

"What time does your shift end?" he says.

She pauses, pretending she has to think about it. "One."

"I'll wait on you. Escort you home."

I roll my eyes again.

She blushes redder and emits a breathy "Okay."

"Drinks," I butt in with the demand. "We'll take two more rounds."
Two should get me to where I want to be.

"How about *one more* and we call it quits?"

I stare at Selene like she's sprouted horns. "Since when does Selene
Rhysien, party girl of our academy class, cut a night short?"

She and Zayne exchange a look. I bristle because the look is about me.

"Commencement is tomorrow," Zayne says, slipping into his usual
rule-following form. "We all need to be coherent, upright, and not nursing head-splitting hangovers in the morning. It's probably wise to cancel
the drinks and head to the barracks."

Fuck *that* noise. I hiss in a breath at the pounding that kicks up
in my head. The tilted room starts spinning. A glum, victorious smile
twists my lips. "I think it's too late for me to avoid any of that." I laugh
like it's no big deal. "It's not like tomorrow is as important for me as it
is for you guys.

"Bring two more rounds only for me," I tell Leslie, in case I need an
extra push over the ledge. "My friends do need to be done for the night."
I, however, don't. Who cares if I make it to Commencement at all? I
won't have family present eager to see me graduate from Mareen's most
prestigious academy, and there's no grand next step for me afterward.

"You need to be done too," Selene says without the tact Zayne used.

Our waitress watches the exchange awkwardly.

"Let's compromise." Zayne, of course, is ever the diplomat. "We all
have another round together then we all leave together."

I glare at him.

He and Selene stare back at me, an unyielding and united front.

"Fine," I lie, already thinking of ways to skirt the promise. "One
more round, since apparently it's gang-up-on-Ikenna night."

Leslie smiles in relief, then makes her escape.

"For real, Kenna. We're *all* leaving. I'll drag you out of this bar if I have to." Selene gives me a humorless look that tells me *You know I'll do it.*

"Okay," I say, exasperated. "We all leave together to get some rest for a Commencement ceremony that will mean nothing to me and everything to you." Bitterness drips from my words. It shouldn't. The psymedics' recommendation is a good thing. It allows me to keep numbing the pain by shirking all duty and indulging in reckless shit for the next year.

Embarking on my personal grand adventure early, I look around for Leslie, willing her to hightail her ass back to our table with the next round.

She reappears not a moment too soon.

I swipe up the full shot glass she sets down in front of me and toss it back. A new high instantly hits. The euphoric numbness lasts longer this time, perching me on the ledge of oblivion but not yet pitching me over. My stupid system is purging the alcohol and boosters too damn fast.

I nod toward Leslie, who's taking the drink orders of rowdy Praetorians at an adjacent table. "Weren't you planning on going home with Miss I'm-pretending-to-be-coy-but-I'm-game?" I ask Zayne, trying to maneuver out of the promise my pushy friends muscled me into making.

But I don't really care about his answer the moment I recognize the people at the table she's serving. I instantly wish I hadn't looked over at the Praetorians, because it blows my high and sends me sprawling back from the ledge on my ass. The tiny symbol emblazoned in gold above the left breast pocket of their maroon dress coats marks them as belonging to Gamma cohort.

Grandfather's cohort.

One of the guys sees me watching his crew. He salutes me with a raise of his glass before downing its clear contents. His chestnut-brown hair is buzzed half an inch longer than an induction cut. He has dark-cobalt eyes and a leanly muscled, powerful form shown off by the way his dress uniform is specially cut to his body. The tip of an inktat peeks from under the stiff white collar of his coat. He's attractive, but it isn't his good looks I'm staring at. It's the wretched Gamma symbol. An ache blooms in my chest, and treacherous, unbridled thoughts of everything I've lost pummel into me like steel-fisted blows. My grandfather. Our plans for my future. My friends come morning. I don't just need to be back on the ledge again, I need to be careening over it. But to do that, I'm going to have to stay in the bar and engage in a fresh bout of heavy drinking.

Which means ditching these two before Commencement.

I need another shot.

"Isn't your father expecting you at home tonight?" I remind Selene. Her father is a Tribune, one of the fourteen powerful generals who sit on the Tribunal Council and help govern Mareen. His rank places her family among the great war houses of the Republic, and it's a long-standing tradition for their children to spend the night at home instead of the barracks on Commencement Eve. At dawn, breakfast feasts will be held by all the war houses in honor of their graduates, who will undoubtedly declare and be confirmed to the venerated Praetorian rank. I should be returning to Grandfather's residence tonight. He and I do not hail from a war house, but I should be waking to an intimate breakfast between the two of us in the morning.

Instead . . .

Selene shrugs. "He'll get over it. I'll be at Rhysien Manor by sunrise. If he wanted me in residence overnight so bad he would allow you and Zayne to sleep over with me. I'm not letting you stay in the barracks alone."

I curtail a wince. After tomorrow, I won't be a cadet anymore and I'll have to move out of the barracks. The only other place for me to go will be Grandfather's vacant apartments. I will be passing many nights alone then.

I lash out, mustering a bravado I don't feel. Snorting, I say, "I can't believe you wasted your breath asking." It's true—her Tribune General father would never abide me or Zayne sullying any of his private dwellings. I'm not the right skin color, and Zayne doesn't have the right pedigree. But she's not her father, and she doesn't deserve to bear the brunt of my fear and anger. It's my baggage. Not hers.

Selene opens her mouth to say something in defense of her father then snaps it shut. Consternation creases her forehead, and she's about to speak again when she's cut off.

"You're Amari's get." The derisive voice comes from behind me. Already disgruntled, I swivel to face whoever it belongs to and glower at the dark-haired male with a gold Alpha insignia stitched into his maroon dress coat.

I return a sneer as contemptuous as the one he's giving me. "No shit."

He towers over me with a superiority that's meant to intimidate. Smug arrogance due to his rank makes him dismiss the threat laced through my stare. He's confident he can kick my ass. I'm confident he can't. I was reared by the best combat mind Mareen has ever seen.

And I want this fight way more than he does.

The smile that carves onto the bastard's chiseled face is cruel. His features are flawless. That fact is about to change if he doesn't march away from my table. The temper Grandfather jumped through painstaking hoops to help me tame is running hot. Since his death, I haven't bothered much to keep it in check. What I'm hurtling headlong into doing is a million times brash and stupid.

It's the perfect way to top off the night.

You're better than this, Ikenna. Rise above. Be smarter. Those like us have too much at stake. Grandfather's cautioning voice sweeps through my mind. I ignore it because if he really cared, he'd still be here. He wouldn't have let himself die.

Zayne grabs my arm when I push back from the table. "Let it ride. He's a Praetorian."

Selene presses her mouth into a hard line. She doesn't warn me to let things go. She doesn't urge me on either. But the ire in her gray eyes and her clenched jaw says she wants to. She really, really wants to.

Zayne is right. What the hell am I doing? My response isn't normal for a green cadet fresh out of a martial academy. Even the northern one. Praetorians are the deadliest, most specialized soldiers of the Republic. Biochips enhance their already extraordinary skills. The implants elevate them from lethal to nearly unopposable. Me fighting the jerk runs too great a risk. I take a calming breath, letting better sense prevail for once.

The Praetorian's grin spreads wider. "Listen to your friend. Stay seated and stay in your place, akulu." He spits the slur at me. It's a word that benignly means the color black in the Khanaian tongue of Grandfather's paternal people. When Mareenians speak it, though, it oozes their disdain and prejudice against those with darker skin.

And even that I can ignore. I've heard it so many times I let the slur roll off my back.

His eyes tighten from my lack of reaction. "It's a damn good thing the Legatus Commander died so early," the fucker drawls. "Otherwise Mareen would have been stuck with an akulu occupying its highest office for decades longer. It's a disgrace. Your grandfather was filth. I'm glad he's dead. A full-blooded Mareenian is Legatus now, as it always—"

I lose it. One minute I'm perched on my stool trying to stay calm. The next my chest is heaving and my pulse races as my muscles tense for a fight. I surge to my feet as the spike of adrenaline surges through my blood. Call me whatever you want—sticks and stones and all that. But my indignation on Grandfather's behalf blinds me to all sense of reason.

I strike out, faster than a lowly cadet should be able to move, catching the Praetorian off guard. I revel in the satisfying crunch of bones beneath my right knuckles. Blood spurts from the asshole's nose. I rear back and punch him again in his broken septum. He wails, a sound you'd never expect to hear a Praetorian make, as he flies backward. I'm on him before he can pick himself up from among the fallen table and bar stools. I drive punch after punch into his pretty, porcelain face.

It's better than the boosters.

Arms lock around me and drag me away. I assume it's Selene or Zayne. I crane my neck to see that it's neither. Another Praetorian from the asshole's cohort is holding me. I struggle against his steel grip. His buddy finally peels himself off the floor with a grunt.

Asshole Number One glares at me through the eye that isn't swollen shut.

I give him my best smile.

He steps toward me. He brandishes a combat-grade dagger in each hand. I laugh at the display that's meant to terrify me. It's an unhinged sound that's sped a dozen miles past mad.

"Let her go!" Selene shouts behind me.

The noise of a scuffle tells me that she and Zayne have leapt out of their seats, and I look to see that a couple of the Praetorian's Alpha cohort buddies are restraining them.

"So, this is how it's going to be?" I throw over my shoulder to Asshole Number Two, who has my arms pinioned behind my back. "You're going to hold me in place while your dickhead friend carves me up because otherwise he couldn't beat me?" I spit on his gleaming white shoes.

I stare back at the Praetorian I attacked, refusing to cower.

"No. It's not." The Praetorian from Gamma cohort who saluted me steps between me and Asshole Number One. "Let her go, Chance," he says to the guy holding me.

"Fuck you, Reed. Stay out of this. It's got nothing to do with you."

Reed rolls his shoulders then widens his legs into a basic combat stance. "I disagree. She's Verne Amari's blood, and the Legatus Commander was a Gamma man."

Eight other Praetorians from Alpha cluster to the left of me. In response, the four from Grandfather's cohort that had been sitting at the table with Reed crowd around him. Gamma is outnumbered. I assess the one girl and four guys—five guys including Reed—and something about the way they all hold themselves, with the absolute confidence of coiled predators ready to strike, makes me put my money on their team despite the odds. Gamma cohort has a long legacy of claiming some of the fiercest and most lethal Praetorians. Also, the proudest.

The bastard holding me grunts something unintelligible under his breath, then shoves me at his buddy. I stumble forward from the force of it. "Just the two of them then. Since she thinks she's tough enough to take on a Praetorian, they'll settle this the way we do. One on one. Bitch got the drop on my man because he hesitated. Radson didn't want to hurt her."

If that isn't the most ludicrous load of shit I've ever heard. I didn't get the drop on him. I didn't sucker punch him. I'm simply faster. And probably stronger. And as well trained, if not more so. Grandfather made sure of it. I've been undergoing Praetorian-style strength conditioning and combat training since before I entered the academy.

The Praetorian in Grandfather's cohort, Reed, looks at me with a raised eyebrow.

"It's okay," I say, brazen. "I got it." I motion to Radson's swollen left eye and broken nose. I'm a cadet. I'm nowhere close to his rank. I'm also so much more than that and good ol' boy Radson decided to fuck with me on the right day. I smile at Radson while motioning him forward. Feeling the severe strain of my cheek muscles, I know I appear a little psycho. Maybe I've finally gone off the rails. Maybe today is the day that the psymedics warned me would come if I didn't properly grieve. I can't think straight, my emotions are whacked out, and good sense shattered to pieces about a minute ago when I took a swing at a Praetorian in a bar full of onlookers.

"Kenna, this is insane," says Zayne, straining against the guy still holding him.

"It is." Selene agrees with him, but the tone of her voice says she wants somebody to kick the Praetorian's ass in the worst way. The guy gripping her forearms holds them so hard purplish bruises darken her chalk-white skin beneath his fingers. She kicks at him, but with lightning quick reflexes, he darts his left shin back and out of reach. It doesn't deter her. She keeps fighting to inflict some kind of damage. She wants me to do the same.

Radson holds his combat daggers in a white-knuckled grip. He angles the pair straight at me. He's livid, and his ego took an armored transport–size bruising. He's itching to soothe his male pride. Too bad for him, that's not how things are about to go down.

"Without weapons," Reed says. "Otherwise, we're not doing this. She doesn't have any, and it won't be a fair fight." Actually, I do. I'm *always* armed. I just haven't felt the need to reach for them yet.

Radson looks to Asshole Number Two, Chance, who seems to be acting as Alpha cohort's leader.

He smirks but nods to Radson.

Radson drops the daggers.

I don't wait for him to reach me and throw the first punch. I close the distance between us and hammer a side kick to his upper torso. I lighten the force of the blow so I don't crack a rib that could puncture a lung. Punctured lungs collapse and his biochip won't circumvent a mortal wound. I'm not so far gone that my aim is to kill him. That would be more than reckless. He's one of the Republic's precious soldiers. It would be signing my own execution sentence. Though the raging inferno in his eyes makes it clear he means to kill me, I have to content myself with the fact that his ribs will ache like a bitch for weeks even with expedited healing.

He doesn't allow me to land a second kick. He hurls four punches at me in rapid succession. I dodge each one except the last. A right hook crashes into my left shoulder. It snaps out of socket. I shove aside the searing fire that explodes up and down my arm.

He attempts to inflict maximum damage and ram another punch into my dislocated shoulder. I dodge it, wrenching to the side and sweeping my leg out in a wide arc. He's so focused on my upper body that he forgets to monitor my legs. I sweep his out from under him and he crashes to the floor. He springs back to his feet without the aid of his hands.

There are about seventy people in the bar in addition to the waitstaff, but none of them are going to get in between Praetorians fighting. They don't have a death wish. Most of them stand around ogling the fight and casting pitying looks my way, despite the fact that I'm the one winning.

Radson and I circle each other, reassessing and recalibrating. Grandfather taught me that everyone has a tell. Radson telegraphs his movements by shifting his weight to the side he's going to strike with. He prematurely tenses the muscles he's going to use. I shoot forward before a left hook can splinter my jaw and gift him a vicious roundhouse kick to the chest. Needing a good, cathartic fight—something that petty brawls with my academy peers hasn't given me—I hammer kicks to his stomach, left hip, and knee. Bones pop and he curses as he falls to the ground.

He struggles to stand. He heaves himself a quarter of the way up before his shattered knee gives out. When he falls down, he stays down.

Sensing movement behind me, I spin around to the Praetorian that grabbed me when the fight first started. I recenter my weight, remaining light on the balls of my feet. He throws a punch that never connects.

Because Reed blocks it. "It's over, Chance."

Chance growls at me around Reed's formidable stature. I meet his eyes with an unaffected, bored stare, goading him into fight two of the night. Fight one was the best time I've had in months. My blood is still whooshing in my ears, adrenaline is at a peak, and the electric current of something much more dangerous yet thrilling surges in my veins.

My death gleams in Chance's eyes. Praetorian cohorts operate as fiercely loyal units, and I kicked his friend's ass and embarrassed him in the worst way. Allegiance to his cohort demands he answer that with retribution.

He's welcome to try.

I crack my neck, ready to fight the whole of Alpha cohort in one night.

Reed gives Chance his back and faces me. "Walk away. Go home."

Home. I inwardly flinch at the word, though he could mean the barracks as much as Grandfather's apartments.

"Kenna, let's leave." Selene touches my elbow. Zayne appears at my other side. I guess the Alpha cohort assholes restraining them finally let them go.

As much as I want to fight the entire world, I let them pull me toward the exit. Standing in the bar among the Gamma cohort team, Grandfather's old team, and hearing the word *home* on Commencement Eve opens up a devastating dam of grief that threatens to drown me. I *should* be going home. I should be spending the night at Grandfather's apartments, dressing for Commencement in the morning with his help, and being escorted to the ceremonial hall by him. But he won't be at the apartments, and he won't be at Commencement. Selene will be among a legion of family. Zayne's labourii parents will be in town from the Southern Isles to see their son become the first in their family to declare Praetorian.

Nobody will be at Commencement for me.

Selene emits a shrill whistle once we're outside the bar. "I know the Legatus Commander taught you some killer moves, but damn. I don't think I've ever seen anybody move like that. Not even him, the times he conducted our training sessions. You were quicker than Praetorian-quick."

I grimace as she, Zayne, and I crowd onto a steel bench curbside to wait for the public craft Zayne hails on his Comm Unit. I didn't mean to show off like that. Because while biochips give Praetorians extraordinary abilities, something detested by the Republic confers my abilities. With my high completely worn off, the full weight of what I did crashes into me. I didn't get tangled up in some dumb squabble with a fellow cadet. *I fought a Praetorian.* And I put a good extent of my skill level on display. The Praetorians and everybody else in the bar are going to be talking about how fast and with how much prowess they saw Verne Amari's granddaughter move. Grandfather would be incensed. Igniting that kind of talk is the opposite of everything he taught me.

In places like Mareen that suffer no love for the Pantheon, people like you survive by laying low in plain sight.

It's the second time tonight his voice rings in my head. This time, it's laced with censure. I'd been fully responsible for myself for all of three months, and I was already massively screwing up. I catch my shoulders slumping inward in shame and straighten them. Grandfather's ghost doesn't get to lecture me or make me feel further like shit.

I study the scarlet spots staining my hands, navy cadet jacket, and white pants. I'm positive all of the blood is Radson's. I still inspect my knuckles for cuts because I really was an idiot tonight. *Magic signatures are left behind in the blood,* that nagging echo of Grandfather's voice scowls at me.

A sleek, silver bullet train zooms by on the skyrail that runs from the inner sector of Krashen City out to the capital's commuter quadrants. I let its soft susurration drowned out the rest of how Grandfather would berate me. The sky sprawling above the train is cluttered with clouds that are a fitting oppressive gray. Peeking between them are bright constellations that add splashes of color yet do nothing to make me feel less bleak. The constellation that shines directly above me— Krashna's Sword, comprised of ten indigo-blue stars—finishes Grandfather's lecture that I don't want to hear. Krashen City is named after the ancient god of war that the Republic once patronized then eventually denounced. When it did, Mareen also culled all citizens bearing any blessings from the gods.

All such citizens they knew about.

Our public craft sidles up to the curb. Zayne and Selene stand. I lumber to my feet a moment later. A door made of one-way glass slides up as we approach the craft. I duck inside and slide all the way over to the opposite end of the plush burgundy seat so Selene can climb in next and Zayne after her.

"Your destination is Krashen Military Base—Cadet Barracks. Precise time in transit is five minutes," a robotic female voice informs us as the craft zooms away from the curb. It angles upward into the drab sky and carries us toward the skytowers in the distance. Erected from precious obsidian and refined glass, the base's skytowers are monuments to Mareen's military strength. They stand sentinel over the Republic's great capital city. They were originally raised in tribute to Krashna and are a stark contrast to the monochromatic, single-story, silver flats of the inner sector that were built centuries after the Tribunal Council renounced the god.

I eye one particular tower that twists into the air in a helix shape.

"Adjust destination to the Tribune General residences on base," I direct the craft.

"New precise time in transport is seven minutes," it responds back.

"We're staying at the apartments tonight?" Zayne's slim eyebrows shoot up in surprise. I haven't set foot inside Grandfather's apartments since his death.

"*We're* not. I am," I say as plainly as possible. "Thank you both for being so supportive, but go be with your family," I tell Selene, "and go enjoy your waitress," I tell Zayne. "I promise this isn't about me trying to drink myself into a stupor," I add before either can protest. In a rare moment in which I allow myself to be vulnerable, I openly share my misery with my friends. "Spending tonight by myself is the last thing I want to do. But as hard as today is, Commencement tomorrow is going to be harder when the option of passing nights in the barracks with you guys is torn from me. I think I might fare better if I go ahead and rip the bandage off before I'm more of a mess."

"I understand." Selene's voice is soft. She scoots closer to me and hooks her arm through mine. "Are you sure about us not staying though?"

"Because we can," Zayne says. "But if what you want is to be alone, we will respect it. We're here for you and whatever you need to cope better."

Selene frowns at him, but then nods.

"I'm sure." I'm not sure at all. However, I insist to them that I am. They'll be moving into the Praetorian Compound tomorrow without me and embarking on a new life. I need to get used to doing things without them. And they need to get used to not having to babysit me.

I WALK OFF the elevator and down the hall with confident steps, but once I arrive at the entry to Grandfather's apartments, my hand shakes as I raise it to the biolock, where a beep confirms I've passed the first security check. I almost snap my eyes shut so I can't pass the second. I force myself to stare into the electric white laser so it can scan my retinas. The second beep sounds. The palladium doors slide apart to reveal a too-quiet interior, and all the oxygen vanishes from the hall because I'm back to being ridiculous.

I stand in the hall of the skytower that contains the Tribune General residences frozen in place. *You can do this, Ikenna. It's your living space now. Walk inside.* The pep talk fails to get me moving.

I startle at the fall of footsteps on my side of the door. I turn in the direction of the elevator. A man with astute green eyes, matte brown hair shorn into a brush cut, and skin the same olive hue as Zayne's stalks toward me. The elevator slides noiselessly closed behind him. Like the entry door, it requires submitting to a double set of bioscans. Aside from me and Grandfather, Rudyard Brock is the only other person with clearance for the three private floors that Grandfather's residence spans. I face Brock with a scowl, making a note to revoke his unrestricted access.

"What are you doing here?" I'm too irritated at his presence to address him with a deference befitting his Tribune General rank.

Instead of answering me, he nods toward the open doorway. "Let's go inside."

"Why?" I say, automatically defensive. Brock was to my grandfather what Selene and Zayne are to me. He is also the Tribunal Council's Spymaster, with eyes and ears everywhere. I bet he's already heard of my bar fight and tracked me here to upbraid me.

"It is Commencement Eve. I thought we'd honor the tradition of spending the night with family. And we also need to have a chat." He says the last part neutral enough. But his mouth tightens at the corners and his eyes widen a fraction. That expression is the look Brock gets when he's disappointed about something. Well, he can take his current disappointment and shove it up his ass.

I want to be childish and demand that he leave. These are my apartments now, after all, and I don't have to tolerate anyone inside them who isn't welcome. But Brock deserves more respect than that, even if his insistence on trying to play a surrogate parent is too much.

I sigh and wave Brock inside. I enter behind him, trying very much not to trail him like a sullen child about to be scolded. Regardless of the respect I owe him, I am kicking him out if he goes too far.

As soon as I enter the great room, my eyes snap to the three wooden crescent moons that hang on the wall above the palladium door. Grandfather nailed them there. He never shunned the Khanaian arm of his heritage and embraced many of its customs instead. Hanging crescent moons on Khanaian lintels supposedly grants protection when leaving and returning home. Those moons afforded no such thing to Grandfather. He died in his bedroom, under their watch. Instead, they probably damned him.

I make a mental note to take them down. Clearly, they're useless.

Brock points to the sofa upholstered in gold Mareenian silk. It's an antique with silver, claw-footed legs, and Grandfather, a man who enjoyed the luxuries he worked his ass off for, paid a fortune for it. "Have a seat, Kenna," Brock says.

Only four people on the whole planet of Iludu call me *Kenna*—well, three now. Selene, Zayne, Grandfather, and Brock. Grandfather raised me from birth, and Brock was there as his wingman for most of it. Since Grandfather's death, I've pretty much pushed all of his efforts to be supportive away. And his using that name grates on me.

I cross my arms and lean against the wall. "I don't need a stand-in for Grandfather." It's something I've had to remind him of often in the last few months. And, okay, maybe I've been being petulant and immature, but Brock thinks he can tell me how to grieve, and that is not a thing he gets to do.

"Are you sure? Someone has to look after you in Verne's absence, since you insist on landing yourself into all the trouble you can find." His voice is terse, but he makes a good effort to keep most of the ire from it, which is why I don't kick him out—yet. "A *Praetorian*, Kenna. For the Republic's Sake, you got into a bar fight with a *Praetorian*? Oren Radson could have killed you."

No, the fucker actually couldn't have killed me, but Brock doesn't need to know that. Grandfather kept his confidence about many things, but the Pantheon-blessed gifts I harbor wasn't one of them. The aberration might have been too much for even his brother-in-arms to abide.

I motion down the length of myself. "I survived the fight intact."

A long-suffering stare is his answer to that. "You've spent the last three months trying your level best to demolish all you've accomplished at the academy over eleven years of training. Are you proud of that? Because Verne wouldn't be. You've worked so hard to have the top marks to be able to declare Praetorian tomorrow, and your stunt tonight could've fucked it up."

Okay, now he's getting dangerously close to being shown the door. "It no longer matters if I make Grandfather proud, does it? He isn't here. Just like you weren't there, tonight. I was defending myself in the bar. That asshole came for me first." Yet, as hard as I try—all the indignation I feel—I can't shake all of the nagging shame his words produce. I also can't shake how his reference to Grandfather makes my throat constrict and ignites an acute pain in my chest. He's right. Grandfather would be embarrassed by my behavior. Grandfather trained me better. Grandfather raised me better. I *should* be better. Stronger. And yet, I'm not, and I have no idea how to be.

And here's Brock, a living reminder of all that.

"I understand your challenges, Kenna," he says. "But you must be smarter. Stunts like tonight place a target on your back. Don't give your enemies more ammunition."

I almost laugh at the speech coming from him; he has the Republic's sacred trinity of legacy, lineage, and pale skin. What does he know about targets on backs? "I don't need *you* to tell me the tight line I'm walking with Grandfather gone or the added scrutiny I'm under. I've lived with people hating me for who I am my whole life." It's a hatred that's bullshit. But Mareen's bigotry is so ingrained, especially among the upper strata of society, there's nothing I can do except deal. Or leave, which I refuse to do, because the Republic is my home. I have a right to exist here and make a life here just like everyone else.

"Without Grandfather around, things will get worse regardless," I continue. "I'll have a target on my back regardless. It'll magnify if I declare Praetorian, which is why I'm not." There. I said it. The real reason why I'm not going out for the rank Grandfather and I always planned for me to achieve. *Because I don't know if I can handle it. Because I don't know if I'm competent and capable to take care of myself without him.* It was easy to be confident about *everything* with him around.

Without him, it's brutal—and terrifying.

Brock stares at me like I stabbed him. "What do you mean you aren't declaring?"

I meet his incredulous stare that says I've lost my mind and hold firm to my decision. "I'm taking a year off, as I'm sure you know my exit eval suggests." Of course he knows. He hasn't been able to help himself when it comes to keeping tabs on me.

Yet this news seems like it's genuinely surprising to him. "Like fuck you are. You're declaring Praetorian like Verne wanted," he says with steel. "And even if he didn't want it, I wouldn't let you shit away your life with that misguided decision. You're too good for anything else." His tone blasts the absolute authority of a Tribune General that leaves no room to do anything other than fall in.

Except I've already carved out that room in my heart—I'm done with being ordered around. I bristle. "You don't get a say. It's my life. I'm not looking for your approval or input."

"Deference, Kenna," he says low. "I've had enough of you ignoring decorum." His warning to proceed with caution holds a lethal edge, reminding me that he might have had a hand in raising me, and he might be like family, but he's still one of the mightiest men in the Republic whom most people wouldn't survive fucking with on a good day. I have to give it to him though. His restraint is impeccable. If he were Grandfather, my ass would've already been handed to me for the gross disrespect. It's what makes the Republic what it is: adherence to these strict social rules that I want to pitch into the void yet are thrust upon us from our youth. If anything truly made me Mareenian, it's this idea of snapping to when I hear the word "deference."

It's only an idea, though, especially in this moment. So I widen my stance and cross my arms. Yeah, it's stupid, but I'm still feeling particularly reckless tonight and I can't help myself.

A muscle in his jaw ticks. If I were anybody else, I probably wouldn't inhale my next breath. But this is Brock—he's here because he genuinely thinks he knows what's best for me, and believes he's looking out for me. It would be sweet if it wasn't the total opposite of what I wanted right now.

Quietly, he says, "If you don't become a Praetorian, it won't stop people in Mareen from confronting you. You're lost without Verne. He was your dagger and shield. Hell, he was the whole Republic's dagger and shield—mine, too, so many times. So I get that. There are days I feel adrift without him. But throwing away Praetorian rank is not the answer. It won't do what you think it will. It'll only increase your vulnerability to attacks, not lessen them. If you're a Praetorian, you'll have a lot *more* protection. Both internally from your cohort and politically. Only a Praetorian can challenge or kill another Praetorian—both traditionally and because of skill—and the law states there always has to be a verifiable and valid reason. So once you hold the rank, your pool of enemies that can actually strike out and harm you in any significant way shrinks."

I snort. I can't help it. "I kicked the guy at the bar's ass. Obviously, I can handle myself without the rank. I don't need its supposed protections."

He looks me over head to toe with intense scrutiny. His mouth settles into a thin, disbelieving line. "Did anyone intervene?"

I want to scoff and laugh that I didn't need a damn person to intervene. I would've been good even if all of Alpha cohort decided to fight me. Or if Radson had wanted to use his knives. But that's not a wise thing to confess. So, I swallow my pride and give him a person. "A guy named Reed. He's in Gamma. He stopped the fight before it got out of hand. I think because of Grandfather. He spoke of him like he knew him personally."

Brock's stare sharpens. "*Darius Reed* approached you and spoke to you?"

"Yes," I say, confused as to why he's locked onto the fact with such interest. "Why is that important?"

"No reason," he says coolly. Too coolly. My curiosity about the Gamma guy immediately heightens. It already sticks out as strange that he did insert himself in the middle of my altercation. I might be a fellow cohort member's kin, but I'm not Praetorian myself, and Praetorians don't involve themselves in non-Praetorian business. It's one of their codes of decorum.

"What's up with Reed?" I press.

"If he places himself in your path again, you need to be careful."

"You say that like he's a threat. But he took my side at the bar."

Brock's expression goes completely flat. "Maybe."

I push off the wall. Brock is insufferable. "Stop being cagey. If you think he's a threat, I want to know why."

Instead of coming clean, he walks over to the marble wet bar—no respectable Mareenian dwelling lacks one—against the far-right wall and pours himself one of Grandfather's aged whiskies from a crystal decanter. I think how I can use another drink, but Brock will not be amused if I ask him to pour me one.

He takes a sip of the liquor, then places the glass on the bar. He motions to the sofa again. "You're right. You are owed an explanation. Sit down and I'll give it to you."

I comply with his request this time—at least it will get him talking—and plop onto the sofa.

He looks at me hard. "Whatever we discuss does not leave this room. It stays strictly between you and me. Do you understand? Rhysien's girl and the Southern Isles boy do not hear of this."

"Got it." My mind races with what he might say if he's explicitly made Selene and Zayne off-limits. I can't fathom what it could possibly be.

He joins me on the couch. Showing a vulnerability I've never seen him display before, he scrubs a hand down the front of his face. He instantly looks a decade older than his sixty-four years. Whatever is going on with the guy from Grandfather's old squad, it's heavy.

"I don't believe your grandfather died of a failed biochip like the official Tribunal autopsy states."

"What?"

"I'm almost sure he was assassinated."

His words reach my ears distorted. Warped. I couldn't have heard him right.

"Why do you think that?" Shock makes me choke out the question. I thought this was about Reed. What he just admitted was the last thing I expected to hear.

"I've suspected it since Verne died. At sixty-five, he was as strong, healthy, and infallible as soldiers half his age. The biochips we received as Praetorians mean us old men get to live well into our mid-hundreds. Failed biochips sometimes happen, but a malfunction on the scale that causes a heart attack is exceedingly rare. It occurs in one in five thousand implantees. And those who die from *that* are even rarer—one in fifty thousand."

I know the statistics. I'd shouted them at the autopsy medic I'd demanded to speak with, swearing he was incompetent. He'd assured me he made no mistakes. The cause of death was indisputable.

But it isn't that lying bastard I'm pissed at when I leap from the sofa. "Why did you wait to tell me? It's been three months! Three months of me believing a lie about Grandfather's death. Three months of me not knowing he was *murdered*."

"Because you haven't been in the best frame of mind," Brock snaps back. "I was giving you time to get yourself back together, and you never did."

"I was grieving," I sneer.

He looks back at me, saying nothing.

I check my temper, because this has turned too important to lose my shit.

"You think Tribune Generals sanctioned the assassination." It's not a question. And it's the only reason he'd mention keeping this from Selene.

His curt nod sets my heart hammering. But the affirmation isn't exactly a surprise. More than half of the Tribunal Council begrudged Grandfather's appointment to Legatus Commander. War hero or not, it was hard to swallow an akulu man claiming only half-Mareenian parentage ascending to the highest rank in the Republic. Grandfather dying because of their prejudice plunges the blood in my veins to glacial temps. Then the ice thaws, bubbling into a violent volcano.

Those motherfuckers.

Grandfather hadn't died from a malfunctioning biochip. He'd been murdered by his own Council. The Council he'd kept from being slaughtered by winning the war against the invading Accacian Empire and its Pantheon-blessed Blood Emperor.

"Which ones?" I ask. "I want to know exactly how the assassination was executed and who precisely was involved. All of Mareen's Tribunal Council except you or a small, cowardly few?" I wipe the moisture pricking my eyes away. Grandfather didn't deserve this. He was a good man. A loyal man who served the Republic for over forty years. He fought and bled and warred for four decades for a people who never wholly loved him back. "You're going after them, right? Tell me you're working to charge them with treason and to make those responsible pay." The words are coming from me in a rush; I'm not even worrying if he responds. My voice is hoarse. Pleading. It cracks from the raw anguish, the pure fury. I spring from the couch. I need to be up and moving and preferably *hitting* something. I bury my fist in the wall. It doesn't feel nearly good enough.

Brock stands and clasps my shoulder. Frustration and guilt twist his features. "I wish I had those answers to give you. Someone in the Tribunal almost certainly ordered Verne's death, but I don't know who."

"You're the fucking spymaster."

"Which is why this is so dangerous. If *I* don't know, then what does that tell you?"

I blink at that.

"What I do know is that the only way Verne dies is if someone close enough to him killed him, and the only ones who could do that would be—"

"Praetorians," I finish for him. "Is Reed a suspect?" He has to be if Brock warned me to be cautious of him.

"Yes," Brock confirms.

"Where is he on the list? The middle? Near the end? At the top?" The fact that he helped me out in the bar doesn't mean a thing. He could've been doing it to cover his ass—or to get close to me for some other reason related to Grandfather's murder.

Brock's features pinch like he doesn't want to say. He rubs his forehead. "He's the prime suspect. As leader of Gamma, he worked closely with Verne on a lot of initiatives, and Verne had a meeting with Reed on his calendar the day he died. They met in the apartment two hours prior to his death. Please don't fly off the handle and do anything reckless with that information. Trust me to deal with things."

"Like you trusted me only to tell me about Grandfather's death three months later?"

"Exactly," he says. "Because I knew you'd want to do something rash." He rubs the space between his eyes. "Perhaps you not declaring is all for the best. Reed is also set to be a part of the senior Praetorian team that will transition the new class."

That news has the opposite effect than I'm sure Brock hoped. I seize onto that knowledge. There was already no way in hell I was sitting back and doing nothing, but now I have added incentive to do what I decided the second he told me a Praetorian killed my grandfather. "I'm declaring Praetorian," I tell Brock. "Damn whatever fears or shitty feelings I had toward it before. I want the rank so I can help you. If I'm a Praetorian, I can investigate, too, which will be useful, since you're a Tribune. If you do too much poking around yourself, it could scare whoever's guilty into triple-checking they've covered their ass and sweeping any trail that might lead to them clear. But if I do some poking around, I'm the akulu girl that people always dismiss."

"I was afraid you'd say that." Brock cocks his head, assessing me. "This is serious business, Ikenna. I wanted you to declare Praetorian because I want the best for you. But with that aim, it becomes infinitely more dangerous."

"You think I don't know that? You think I'm *scared?*"

"I think you *should* be. Your recent antics will get you killed. If you do this, there can be no more wallowing in grief. No more hotheaded stunts." Doubt that I can clean up my act clouds his green stare. But the months I've spent fucking up were because I thought I had no purpose. And that's as much his fault for not telling me the news sooner.

I'm ready to move forward now.

"I know I've been a mess. I promise that's over."

He continues to look unconvinced. "You must understand that a declaration and confirmation by the Tribunal doesn't make you a Praetorian. Acceptance by your fellow Praetorian Guard and invitation into a cohort makes you one. After Commencement, senior Praetorians will put you through challenging trials. They will test your mettle more than your academy instructors and classes ever did."

I cut him off. I don't need all the pretty warnings. "I know of the trials. I can survive them."

"You think you know, but you really don't. The trials are designed to exert every effort to break you, and you are already demonstrating the ease with which you crack under pressure." I flinch at the observation put so baldly. The fact that he feels that way means I've been spectacularly fucking up and doing Grandfather's memory so much disrespect.

We are forged by adversity. We are tempered in perseverance. We are Amaris.

This time, when Grandfather's voice sweeps into my mind, I welcome it. I seize onto it and let it shake me free of the foolishness of the last three months. *We are as strong as Khanaian steel,* I say to myself alongside Grandfather's whisper. *We do not bend. We do not break. We do not bow. We do not yield.* It was his mantra. One of his first lessons . . . and one of the first things I abandoned after his death. It is time to start embodying it again.

I draw myself up to my full height, needing Brock to believe in me. "I am Verne Amari's granddaughter. I won't break."

"For your sake, I hope that's true." His response is a kick to the teeth. "If you're going to insist on snooping into who killed Verne, which I don't advise, but you're stubborn, remember that whoever did it has to be a formidable opponent. So, if you do find proof or any sort of evidence at all that points toward somebody, bring it to me *first*, and I'll keep you in the loop on my end too. Do not act rashly no matter what you uncover. Understood?"

"Affirmative," I say, and snap off a salute, assuming the proud mien of a soldier, of one of Krashen Academy's best. I let Brock see the old Ikenna, the girl I was before he turned up at my barracks to tell me Grandfather was dead and my universe collapsed.

I let him see the lie he wants to see.

He studies me for a long moment; then, he returns my salute. He nods at this version of me approvingly. "Now, that's the Ikenna Amari I know. *That* is Verne's granddaughter." I stand up straighter, making myself a promise to do what I told him I would, which is get and keep my shit together. Because it's the only way I'll have the competence to accomplish my real reason, the reason he doesn't need to know, for declaring Praetorian.

"I really appreciate you coming by," I tell Brock. "But I need to be alone to process and get my head together before the morning."

At first, I expect a refusal. Brock has gotten good at playing mama hen. But he only offers me a curt nod. "That's a good idea. Everything you've found out tonight is a lot. Try to get some rest, too, if you can. Tomorrow is a big day. I'll see you at Commencement."

Grandfather was murdered. Grandfather was murdered. Grandfather was murdered.

It's all I can think after he leaves. The truth thunders through my whole being, and my anger explodes fully uninhibited.

It's like an inferno, a molten blast that roils through me. It's swift, torrential, and all-consuming. I can almost feel my blood heating, scorching my veins. I don't try to curb the rage. I let it flow through me, crisp and sharp and cleansing. I let it hone my focus to a dagger-sharp edge because after I declare tomorrow, I plan to do more than help find proof. I plan to use my Praetorian status to get close to Darius Reed, confirm that he's guilty, then kill the piece of shit.

I think back to the bar. How *dare* he speak Grandfather's name tonight? How dare he talk like he owed Grandfather allegiance? A deep-rooted, visceral outrage ignites inside me alongside the fury. Reed owes me a kin debt, and I *will* collect it. I don't give a damn how formidable he might be or how dangerous. He could be the best Praetorian in the Republic, but he hasn't yet gone up against me.

His days are numbered.

2

"HOW DID WE GET DOWNGRADED from the crap academy barracks?" Selene sweeps an insulted gaze around our new digs. It's a tiny, windowless room with a steel door, two small beds, a narrow dresser for us to share, and a slit in the wall that'll spit out fresh maroons—the standard, unadorned fatigues we wore in the academy.

Our lackluster lodgings *are* a surprise. The base's Praetorian compound is nearly as ritzy-looking as the Tribune General apartments. It consists of an imposing skytower that is one gargantuan tessellation of interlocking four-pointed stars, the Republic's national symbol. It's topped with a maroon spire, sprawls as wide as it stretches high, and is all smooth angles, sloped roofing, and opaque panes. The inside of the compound we marched through was just as immaculate and gleaming as the outside until we took a shaft down to the subterranean level as our instructions directed.

Into this dark, underground bunker.

"I gather," I say more to lift her spirits than mine, "that this is only temporary. Once our transitioning is complete, we will get permanent accommodations ground-side that better suit you."

She looks around again and shudders. "I hope so. Praetorians cannot live like this." Selene is tough as nails, but she's also a creature of comfort. "I'm not sure people that aren't *prisoners* can live like this."

I walk over to the beds with four feet of cramped space between them. "Do you have a preference?"

"Screw you," she says at my smirking expression, and puts her stuff down on one of the beds.

She studies her nails that always have a fresh coat of polish. The color depends on her mood. Today, she's sporting plum. It's a confident, bold color that says she's feeling on top of the world. Even though we're underneath it at the moment. That's Selene. A dichotomy of many things. She's as fierce as she is materialistic and as concerned with the color of her nails and her striking beauty as she is with knowing fifteen different ways to kill a person with her bare hands.

"Knock-knock." Zayne leans against the open door.

"Can you believe this?" Selene asks.

He grimaces. "I can. We declared and were confirmed as Praetorians. Except we're not. Now the actual Praetorians have to place their stamp of approval on us. I'm guessing all of this is part of the transition process."

"You mean the hell we're about to endure," I say. "We might as well call the hazing ritual what it is."

"Can't get much closer to hell—literally—than where we are now," Selene grumbles, then groans and flops on the bed with her bag. Assuming that's the one she's claimed, I sling my duffel off my shoulder and drop it on the one to my left.

"Damn Praetorians and their initiation rites," she mutters. "Maybe I should have declared administratee. At least I'd be in cozy accommodations and not getting the shit beat out of me."

"Don't forget the fun little survive-or-die situations they'll be throwing at us."

She groans louder.

Zayne offers Selene a wry smile as he plops on the bed beside her. He bops her chin. "Buck up."

She jabs him in a spot beneath his second and third left ribs.

"Ow." He massages the spot that's been tender since he broke the bones during a sparring exercise three years ago.

"*Buck up*," she mocks. Selene straightens out of her slouch. "Whatever," she says, then rolls her shoulders like she's readying for a fight. "Let the torture games begin."

Zayne looks down at his Comm Unit. Other than the report-for-duty instructions, we've received no other communication. "I wonder when it'll all start."

"They likely won't tell us," I guess. "They'll let us get nice and comfortable, drop our guard, then blindside us with some shit."

"No matter what," Selene says, staring intently at Zayne then me, "we get through this like we got through the academy. Together. I have something for you, Kenna." She reaches over Zayne and grabs her duffel from the foot of the bed. She pulls a small white box from one of the side pockets. As she holds it, splotches of pink splatter her cheeks.

"What's that?" I stare at her and the box, curious. Selene never looks sheepish about anything.

"A graduation present for you," she answers awkwardly. "I . . . sort of had it made . . . after your grandfather died because I knew . . . but then you decided not to declare and . . ." Okay, now I really stare at her bewildered. She never gets tongue-tied over anything either.

"What's in the box?"

She tosses it to me. "Just open it."

I lift the lid and immediately understand why she's so flustered. Nestled atop a velvet cushion is a small silver medallion with the four-pointed star of the Republic etched onto its flat surface. The pendant hangs on a slim chain. The necklace is identical to the one fastened around her neck. Such pendants are worn by Praetorians of legacy lines and gifted from one family member to another on Commencement Day. It's a distinction I would've been given by Grandfather after I declared.

"Even though Legatus Commander Amari is gone, you still have family around," Selene says softly. "I wanted to make sure you don't forget that, and receiving one of these is a thing you've been looking forward to since we were, like, ten."

"Eight," Zayne chimes in. "You two have been harping about those medallions since Indoc Year." He rolls his eyes, but there's no real rancor in it. His tone is as uplifting and tender as Selene's.

I wave the box at him. "Did you know about this?"

He shakes his head. "Nope. That's all Selene."

I turn to my best friend, who has always been more like a sister. "I . . ." I stumble over finding a sentiment that's adequate. I settle for simply saying thank you.

"I'm glad you told the psymedics to shove their recommendation. This is where you belong."

"I'm glad too," says Zayne. "What changed your mind?"

I mostly keep a straight face. We've never kept secrets from each other. Now I must keep a huge one. I wonder at what Selene will do if her father does turn out to be one of the Tribune General conspirators. She doesn't suffer delusions about his shortcomings, but she's close with him, and she loves him in spite of them. Which is why I can't answer Zayne's question entirely. I can only give them half of the truth. The part I arrived at last night while my anger and fury wouldn't allow me to sleep.

"This is what Grandfather wanted for me. I wanted it, too, before he died. After the bar, I did some reflecting, and didn't like what I saw. So, I did this for me as much as I did it to honor his memory and his dreams for our family. He was a first-generation Praetorian. I can be a second generation. If I have children and one of them is Praetorian, the Amari name will evolve into a legacy line."

My surname was handed to Grandfather by a Khanaian father, robbed by shitty racism of holding any rank higher than labourii. Mareen allows transplants from ally nations but keeps them at the lowest rungs no matter their achievement. It was Grandfather's greatest ambition for our family to burgeon into a venerated legacy line and eventually a war house after a few esteemed generations. He groomed my mother for that. He groomed me for that.

It's a thing I'm positive the assholes who took him from me aimed to stop. In fact, it might be the chief reason he died. With me about to graduate and declare, he was getting one step closer to becoming more than the war hero to whom the Republic was forced to hand the Legatus seat.

They do not get to succeed. I won't let them get what they must ultimately want. They don't get to see the Amari name, *my name*, fade into obscurity. I refuse to let them. I'm taking what they thought to deny my family. I'm snatching the Praetorian rank *I deserve*. The rank I endured eleven years of brutal training blocks and ass-kickings and broken bones and pushing myself *past* my physical and mental limits to earn the marks to have a chance at. If for nothing else, then as a grand *fuck-you* to those who want to see us exterminated for no other reason than how we look and the heritage we bear. I've worked too hard for the same bigoted shit that took my grandfather from me to take my goals from me too. I survived the academy, *and I thrived*, to force a respect nobody can deny me, regardless of who I am. So while I have other reasons, I'm not lying to Zayne right now either.

I'm no longer prepared to throw what I've fought for away.

I loop the legacy pendant around my neck, fully settling into the conviction.

"Maybe we'll all end up tapped for the same cohort," Selene says, excited. "I know you'll be gunning for Gamma, Kenna. My father will be pissed, but I could do Gamma. He has my brothers in Epsilon to pacify him."

"I'd be honored to be tapped for Gamma," Zayne says. "They're the cohort with the highest moral fiber. If Alpha tapped me, I'd tell them to go fuck themselves."

"Agreed," Selene says. "Not that any of us in the room meet those purist assholes' criteria anyway. Zayne is a southerner, I'm a girl, and Kenna's Mareenian pedigree isn't potent enough."

"I definitely want Gamma," I say. An invite will place me that much closer to Reed if I don't get to him during the trials.

Selene grins. "Then it's settled. We all gun for Gamma."

"What does it matter? If you don't pledge Alpha, you're trash regardless." I know that voice. I hate that voice.

Caiman Rossi, top cadet in our graduate class and golden boy of the Rossi War House, pokes his smug face into our room. His father is Haymus Rossi, our new Legatus Commander.

Greysen Hunt, Caiman's bootlicking sidekick, stands in the doorway too. Greysen isn't the scion of a war house, but he is a Praetorian legacy kid, probably here hoping for the same thing my grandfather did—a way to get his family closer to being a war house. We should be in the same boat, but of course we're not, because he's an asshole.

He looks me up and down with disdain. "I can't believe the Tribune Generals let another akulu ascend to Praetorian."

I let the insult ride. I promised Brock and myself I could keep it together. I'm here for a purpose, and it isn't to get into more petty fights.

Besides, I've already kicked Greysen's ass seven times before.

"She hasn't ascended yet," Caiman quips. "She still has to pass the trials. Watch yourself, Amari." He gives me a blinding, shit-eating grin. "You don't belong here. Somebody might take it upon themselves to reverse the majority confirmation vote Brock maneuvered and remove you."

"And somebody might reverse your stupid face. You're such a fuckboy," Selene says. "Get out."

Caiman sneers down his aquiline nose at Selene, who's still sitting on her bed. "I'm the son of your Legatus Commander. I can stand where I want."

"You're the son of a whore and can stand there as long as you kiss my ass."

Caiman's golden eyes flash, but he only allows the tell that Selene's jest strikes deep to linger for a nanosecond. Then he laughs, running a hand through his flaxen hair with all the arrogance of a war house scion bearing the porcelain complexion of a northern-born. "At least my mother stuck around to raise her children."

Selene is about to retort when Corbin Enzo, a buddy of Zayne's, joins the party.

"Brilliant comeback, Rossi," he deadpans as he shoulder-checks Caiman when he passes by him. "Excuse me," he says with feigned politeness as Caiman stumbles out of the way. Enzo crosses muscled arms over an impressive chest and leans against the dresser beside the door. I almost expect the shoddy furniture to buckle under his weight.

Enzo is a decent guy in a prepossessing package. Like Zayne, he's an example of someone who won the genetic lottery without the assistance of gene manipulation. "Anybody up for a little celebratory fun?" he says in his usual easygoing way. "I'm hosting a craps game to pass the time until our Comms light up with something exciting and this thing kicks off."

"I'm in," Selene says, ignoring Caiman now. "It'll likely be the last chill time we get until the trials are over."

"I think I'll sit it out," I say. I'm not here to party.

Selene shakes her head. "Nuh. Uh. If I'm going, you're going. I'm not leaving you behind to keep dealing with *The Dumbass Show*."

"I'm not wasting my night sticking around here and informing losers how much they suck," Caiman scoffs. "I was just stopping by to remind you three real quick in case you forgot: Don't let being here go to your head. You're still trash." He pushes off the doorframe and saunters away.

Greysen hangs near the door, unsure what to do for a second, before following after Caiman like a good little puppy.

Enzo shoots two middle fingers at their backs. "Caiman is going to be insufferable now that Daddy dearest is Legatus Commander."

I clutch my chest in mock astonishment. "You mean more than he already is? Caiman has been a pain since we were eight, marching around the academy like he owned the place simply because his father is rich and powerful."

"Attitudes like Caiman's are so typical of scions," Enzo grumbles. "No offense, Selene."

"Gee, thanks," she says with false sweetness.

"It is why Tribunes should not be allowed to hold the rank," Enzo says. "We started elevating Praetorians without war house ties because it keeps the Republic stable. It is an office that needs to be above Tribune General power struggles and politics."

He doesn't need to convince me—I'm Grandfather's kin and I've lived it firsthand. It is a lesson Mareen learned decades ago when a civil war erupted between war houses and the crippling instability made it possible for Accacia to invade us. Haymus Rossi, head of the most prolific and powerful war house—due to its assload of Praetorians— wormed his way into the Legatus seat by capitalizing on the public's fear that Grandfather's death might give Accacia the confidence to launch a repeat assault. Which . . . is a hell of a motive to take someone out.

He *has* to be on Brock's list of Tribunal conspirators. He's certainly on mine.

"Maybe we should all just murder Caiman and his father. We'll be doing the Republic a favor while putting ourselves out of our misery." Selene eyes the space Caiman vacated like she can't think of a thing that would bring her greater delight.

At the moment, I can't either.

Enzo cracks a dry laugh. "That's not a bad idea." On the heels of it, his mood lightens. "So who's ready to come lose a fuck-ton of credits?"

"Didn't *you* lose a small fortune to *me* last time we played?" Selene only slightly speaks in hyperbole. He handed her over a good eighty thousand.

Enzo winks at her. "Let's put something else on the table this time."

She smirks. "Not gonna happen." It's clear what he means by his faux-leering look. They used to have a thing, but Selene broke it off when, according to her, real feelings ruined the thrill.

"I'm coming," Zayne says. "I am not missing you two duking it out." Zayne doesn't have their wealth to shit away, so he never plays himself. I don't think he's ever been jealous, though—he's the kind of person who just enjoys the company of others.

I, on the other hand . . .

"I'm for real hanging back," I tell Selene. I'm supposed to be getting my act together, not giving Brock proof that I'm the same out-of-control Ikenna.

"What's up with you, Amari?" Enzo asks. "Why don't you want to come?"

"The trials are serious." It actually is a good excuse. "Deadly. Pseudo-partying on move-in day isn't the smartest idea."

"Who are you and where did you stash the Ikenna from the last three months?"

"*Enzo.*" Selene hops up from the bed, crosses the room, and smacks him upside the head.

To Enzo's credit, he looks like he wants to kick himself. "My bad. That was a cruddy thing to say. I know you've been going through it. I would be too."

I wave his apology off. He's good people. "It's cool."

"If you don't want to go, I won't either," Selene offers.

"Neither will I," Zayne says.

"Aww, come on," Enzo protests. "It won't be a celebration if you're *all* missing. I'm inviting our whole Krashen crew. I also invited some people from the other academies. It'll be good to mingle with fresh prospects." He wiggles his eyebrows Zayne's way.

"You're a pig," Selene lets him know.

He laughs. "Don't act like you don't think the same way about guys."

"I'm a girl. It's different when I do it."

"That's sexist."

"No, it isn't."

It is, I think, but don't say anything. Though their fling only lasted a few months, they've never stopped flirting with each other, and it's actually amusing to watch it.

"Whatever you say, *Donya* Rhysien." He dodges the next swing Selene takes at his head.

"Do you want to end up in your family crypt early?" she asks viciously. With her mother gone, and her father unmarried, she technically is the Donya of Rhysien War House. But only someone who likes missing teeth points that out. Any reminder of the title that saddles her with the chief duty of churning out scions makes her see red.

"It's good to have you here with us," Enzo says to me while taking a jab to the shoulder from an irked Selene. "You're a fellow Praetorian I'd want at my back."

"Duh, who wouldn't," Selene remarks, cooling it. "Kenna is badass. She's beat the shit out of you how many times in combat class? I think she even marred Rossi's perfect, highest-exit-marks record a time or two."

"Six times," I correct her. "But who's counting."

Truth is, I shouldn't have done so. That's easy to say in hindsight, though. Because there were a few times when we were much younger—and before Grandfather succeeded in getting me to wrestle my temper under control—where I slammed Caiman Rossi on his high-and-mighty, I'm-the-best-in-this-training-class ass.

Clearly triggered, Enzo rubs between his pectorals. We were paired during the hand-to-hand combat part of our Commencement tests, and I *might* have bruised his breastbone. "Don't remind me." He winces good-naturedly. "Although, speaking of kicking ass, I heard about your brawl with an Alpha Praetorian. How are you standing upright? Damn, girl. You stay showing the majority of us up. Did your Comm Unit track the fight stats? What were your average strike and dodge speeds? What was the force behind your landed hits?"

He's so eager, I'm taken aback. His zealous questions are proof I was an idiot in the bar. How rampantly is that story spreading?

"It didn't track anything," I say casually. And it's true. Having that feature on would be stupid. Telling Enzo my estimation of my stats would be stupid too.

He shakes his head. "That's a pity. I would've liked to know them." They'd be interesting to all of the Tribunal Council as well. Too interesting. Which is why my Comm Unit is disabled from tracking any hard stats on me.

"All I want to know," Enzo continues harping, "is how did you beat him so bad when you don't have a biochip yet?" Which was precisely why I shouldn't have won the damn fight. It's also precisely why I should have never gotten into the fight in the first place.

It's why I need this conversation over.

"Genetics," Selene answers for me. "The Legatus Commander had skills. Biochips and good training alone don't best the Accacian, Pantheon-blessed Blood Emperor. If that were the case, the Aggression wouldn't have ravished us for five decades and slashed our forces in half."

Enzo looks me over appreciatively. "True. Those are some mighty superior genetics. Where can I get what you have?"

"Well, you're not sleeping with me, if that's what you're asking. I'm not getting murdered by Selene."

Zayne bursts out laughing, and Enzo reddens. Before it can devolve any further, our Comm Units beep at the same time. I could kiss mine for the interruption.

Entry floor. North wing common room. Six minutes. Wear your maroons.

Selene curses. Enzo turns giddy. Zayne springs from the bed.

I crack my neck.

The trials are about to start. Adrenaline pumps through my veins at the knowledge. Whatever the senior Praetorians are planning to throw at us, I'm ready for it. There's too much at stake for me to fail.

3

WE'RE GREETED BY A BUFFET spread, a fountain of sparkling wine, and a droid-tended bar when we enter the common room.

I look around dumbfounded.

"Did we report to . . . a mingler?" Zayne looks as stupefied as me.

Enzo looks around and laughs. "Looks pretty much like it."

A humanoid droid glides up to us. It carries a serving tray full of pink shooters that hiss smoke. "Would you like one?" it asks in a tone whose cadence and intonations are damn close to human-produced speech.

"I don't trust it," I say. "Something about this whole thing feels off. If they were throwing us a mingler, why not convey that in the reporting instructions, why have us wear our maroons, and where the hell are the senior Praetorians? It's only us new confirmations in the room."

"Oh, it's likely a setup for sure," says Enzo. "I'd bet on it. I'm thinking they're gifting us a party tonight and intend to throw the first trial at us at the ass crack of dawn in the morning. Catch us off our game.

It's what I'd do if I was hazing a new class." He rubs his hands together, smiling deviously. "I admire their tactics."

"Should we cut out then?" Zayne asks.

"I say we stay. If this is a Last Supper sort of deal, we might as well enjoy it before the muck starts." Selene swipes a shooter from the tray, knocks the candy-scented stuff back, and her gray eyes go glassy from the boosters.

"I wouldn't down too many of those if Enzo and Ikenna are right," Zayne cautions.

She sniggers. "Who do you think I am? *You?* I'll still be in perfect shape with a couple."

Enzo shrugs. "Same, so fuck it. We gotta eat, and wash it down with something, right?" He grabs a shooter off the tray too.

I mean, I get his and Selene's logic, and I'd totally follow suit if I hadn't vowed to get and keep my shit together.

"Would anyone else like one?" the droid prompts. "They're quite delicious."

"No, thank you," I tell it. Zayne does the same, and it slides away.

Around us, most everyone else seems to have made the same decision as Selene and Enzo. People are starting to relax, pick up drinks, and load plates down with food.

"That looks yummy." At first, I think Selene is talking about a dish on the buffet table. But I see her finger points in the opposite direction. She ogles a tall guy with dark hair and darker eyes slouched against a wall across the room, because of course she does. When is Selene ever not scoping out guys, no matter the situation? Honestly, I admire her skill and dedication to staying laid without hiatuses.

Poor Enzo suddenly finds somewhere else to be, stalking away and taking Zayne with him.

The guy Selene has in her crosshairs is surrounded by a small cluster of folks. They're an obvious tight-knit group, and you can tell they're southern Mareenians by their thicker accents that carry—all of their vowels are pronounced in a rougher manner—and by the olive tint to their skin. Which means they're all from the Southern Isles Martial Academy, since non-northern-borns have to test into Krashen or attend their regional school as cadets.

The Southern Isles guy catches Selene pointing at him and offers up a crooked grin. She crooks a finger toward herself, calling him over.

I shake my head. "I envy the fact that you can think about sex right now."

"Listen, if I have this one last night before hell kicks off, I'm making the most of it in case the trials force an ungodly long break from good dick. And he looks like an exceptionally fuckable—and rideable—specimen that can tide me over."

I can't deny her claim. The guy has a sexy face, chiseled frame, and dimpled chin that further enhances his aesthetics.

She points to the buddy he left leaning against the wall. "He's yummy too."

"He is," I agree. He's about six feet of a trimmed, athletic physique, deliciously tanned skin, and a nice ass (or so I assume from his thick thighs and sharply cut hips). I'll have to get a peek behind him to confirm that though . . . I sigh.

"I'll pass. Gotta start things off right, and for me, sex would be the opposite of that."

She bumps my shoulder with hers. "I'm proud of you." Then she gives me a wicked grin. "Don't worry. I'll be debauched and reckless enough for the both of us tonight."

I howl. I can't help it.

"Hi," Selene's newest toy, whose neck is free of a legacy pendant, says smoothly when he reaches us. "I'm Dex."

"I'm Selene." She makes her name sound like pure sin. "This is Kenna."

Dex gives me a polite, quick hello and turns his full attention back to Selene. And just like that, she's snagged him. Not that he ever stood a chance.

"You're from the Southern Isles, obviously," she says, looking him up and down in a slow perusal. He pushes his broad shoulders back and puffs out his chest, happy to let her.

She likes him, but I don't. He's too pretty and he knows he's too pretty. It isn't the same as the smooth way Zayne wields his good looks around women. Dex seems noxiously vain, and I'll be happy to get away and leave Selene to her mission as soon as I can.

So, it's a surprise when, turning toward me, he asks, "What was it like to be raised by the Legatus Commander?" He doesn't spit out Grandfather's title with derision or hatred. He utters it with reverence and admiration. It gains him a couple of points his vanity lost him.

"It was . . ." I'm unable to voice anything about how it was to be raised by Grandfather. He was the Legatus Commander to everyone else. To me, he was and always will be the sole parent I've known. He was my protector, my caregiver, and my safety net. While he was alive, I didn't have to be afraid of anything—not even discovery of being Pantheon-blessed. Because to me, Grandfather in his full Legatus Commander uniform and pelt could slay any monster. He'd cull any threat.

Except the one that killed him.

"I don't think I'd be able to articulate a response either." Dex's words break into my struggles. "The Legatus Commander, despite his mixed origins," he says awkwardly, then clears his throat, "is a legend. I wish I were alive and a Praetorian in his cohort during the time of the war. I would give my left nut to have seen the supposedly immortal Blood Emperor stare down his own mortality."

Selene, who has other plans for that left nut, doesn't seem too happy that he's talking to me instead of her. She's about to say something when my Comm Unit dings with a message that cuts into her glare and Dex's tirade against Mareen's long-standing enemy. I silence and delete the message without reading it when I see the face of its sender.

Selene leans over, already bored of Dex, and eyes my Comm Unit because she's nosy. "You're still ignoring—"

I slice her a look. She better not say his name and detonate that very personal grenade in front of a stranger.

"How many times has he reached out since . . . you know?" She means Grandfather's death.

My Comm Unit dings again with a second message from the person in question.

Selene's interest has Dex leaning across her to steal a look at what's stolen her attention from him. It makes me sway back to disliking him. She can be nosy. He can't. I don't know him at all.

I swipe the person's image off my Comm Unit before Dex can get a good look at his face. I make a mental note to finally go into his contact card later and block all notifications.

In fact, I'm wondering if I can do that now—finally leave the party and go back to my room—when a male voice that isn't Dex's cuts into my thoughts.

"Excuse me?"

I raise my head to see the guy Dex left behind. "What?" I grumble, irritated at the person who keeps blowing me up.

Dex's friend grimaces at my response. "I'm sorry. I didn't mean to bother you. It's just . . ." He rubs the back of his head.

I see Dex watching him, amused, and I glare at them both. What the hell is going on?

"You finally worked up the courage to haul your ass over here?" says Dex. "You missed me asking about the Legatus."

His friend looks disappointed. "Oh."

Dex is being a jackass, though, because I never actually said anything about Grandfather.

"You're an admirer of my grandfather too," I muse more to myself than either of them. It's weird getting this kind of response to him. I'm used to prickhead remarks and racial epithets like in the bar.

Not . . . nervousness. Or reverence.

Dex's friend rubs his head again. "Um, no." He blanches. "I mean, yes, I am. But no, that's not why I came over. I . . . err . . . walked over because . . . well . . . I'm an admirer of *you*."

I stare at him, dumbfounded for the second time in one night. I laugh. He's joking. He has to be freaking joking.

His face burns red. He looks mortified. "Oh!" I say. "You're serious?"

"Verne is a legend," he sputters, "but when I got here, word is your skills might surpass his. I overheard some Krashen folks talking about a fight with an Alpha Praetorian. Said you beat the guy up pretty good. Said he could barely match your speed and technique. I thought it'd be cool to meet you and give you your props. And I wanted to ask how in the hell the great Verne Amari trained you to be *better* than him combat-wise, if that part of the talk isn't being exaggerated?"

"I—" shit. Now, my fight is getting around to complete strangers from outside of Krashen. I play off how nervous and absolutely terrified that makes me with a cocky but good-natured bravado. "Training with him from the time I could walk has its perks. Grandfather was a master in combat arts, and any master's aim is for the student to surpass them." I hope that's enough for this guy and Dex to pass on and at least give the talk about me some sort of logical and safe explanation.

"I'm awed," the guy says. "I'm Torin, by the way. It's nice to meet you."

Before I can respond, an ear-shattering siren blares. The overhead lights wink out, drowning the room in darkness.

I'm not rendered blind like my peers. My eyes adjust to the pitch-black and focus past it to see a yellow odorless gas spraying down from the ceiling. Wheezing and strangled coughs erupt around me. I try to keep my breathing even and not inhale a sharp breath. My lungs still fill with the gas. They burn like they're being singed from the inside out. Selene doubles over, sputtering and gasping for a breath of fresh air she won't get. I latch on to her and haul her upright. Several people have already thudded to the ground. Zayne's and Enzo's eyes are a watery mess across the room. Torin is on his knees struggling to stand back up. Dex slumps against the arm of the chair he'd been sitting on moments earlier to keep himself on his feet. His hand clutches his chest as he controls his breathing the best he can, taking in only slow sips of the contaminated air. Huge gulps or normal breaths will wreak maximum havoc.

His stock in my eyes once more goes up some. But we'll worry about being friends later.

This was a setup, just as I thought. But not in the way we imagined.

Which was stupid of us.

They won't catch me being stupid again.

I position my body into a fighting stance, heart thudding, waiting for what comes next—because I know the gas is just the beginning.

Senior Praetorians swarm the room. Half of them barrel through an archway near the bar. Their counterparts vault over the bannister of a staircase. They move with ruthless speed and vicious agility. Black masks cover their faces. They're dressed in combat-grade black tactical gear. This isn't for show—the Praetorians don't waste time launching their assault.

If it weren't for my gift, they'd be shadows weaving silently in the darkness, like I'm sure they are for everyone else under siege while their eyes take more time to adjust.

I shout for Zayne to look out for the officer creeping up behind him before spinning to my right and blocking a right hook from an attacker. The impact of the blow reverberates up my left arm. It's hard enough to shatter bone. I'm lucky—or Pantheon-blessed—it doesn't. He hurls blow after blow. I block them, but even with my considerable speed and skill I don't get in a punch of my own. A second attacker joins the fray. I mark the familiar set of his broad shoulders and upper bulk and become damn sure it's Darius Reed. *Good.* Relishing the opportunity to bash his face in even though I can't kill him just yet, I throw myself into the fight with a special viciousness. Reed turns out to be faster and more relentless than the first officer I engaged. I barely manage to hold my own against the two of them. The first spins out of reach of my roundhouse kick that should have unhinged his jaw and faces off with Dex, leaving me to Reed. I quickly scan the common room. About thirty new graduates lay on the ground. Some are clutching body parts bent at wrong angles. Others gush blood. A lot are motionless.

I turn my attention back to Reed in time to jerk to the right. My left shoulder is knocked back from the jab. I make a growling sound low in my throat and—realizing I can't keep playing defense—launch myself at him. We hit the ground with me on top. I keep the leverage for all of half a second before he uses his bulk to reverse our positions. Powerful thighs straddle my hips, pinning them in place when I buck against his weight to throw him off. That doesn't work, so I yank the knife concealed on my right hip free. I see the surprise in his eyes when they catch the blue glint of Khanaian steel. He wasn't expecting me—or anybody else in the room—to disobey the ban on personal weapons during the trials. Well, I don't expect to be murdered my first day, so I'm glad I ignored that little rule. I don't hold back the irreverent snort. Even if my life wasn't in immediate danger, I'd have had the knife: I've carried the blade on my person since Grandfather gave me the one out of his pair as a birthday gift when I was ten. I wasn't leaving it behind.

And I'm not showing Reed the weapon so he can admire it. The Praetorians aren't pulling their attacks. In fact, I think they're trying to kill us all, and if this is a life-or-death combat trial, it's the perfect opportunity to slaughter Reed sooner rather than later. The reasons Brock gave me for his suspicions are good enough as proof of guilt, so I'm not about to pass it up. Without hesitation, I move to bury the knife in Reed's chest.

I thrust up fast. He dodges me faster. It's my turn for my eyes to widen in surprise. Very few people move quicker than me when I'm not holding back. The knife nicks his left arm instead of sliding into his heart. I stab out with it again. His hand grabs my wrist in a punishing grip. My bones groan beneath his fingers. I brace for the blinding pain that will erupt when he tightens his hold and shatters the fine bones of my wrist. It never comes. Instead, he uses his free hand to pluck the knife from my fingers. In my astonishment, I'd stupidly let my grip go lax.

"You weren't issued weapons," he growls. "The trial's hand-to-hand."

"Fuck that," I spit. "You all have biochips. And poison gas." It's a good reason for my actions. I would've tried to stab the motherfucker even if it wasn't about a kin debt.

"You're supposed to figure out how to maneuver around it, *aspirant.* That's the trial."

"Then the knife was genius," I snarl, and shove him off me.

I jump to my feet. He's on his before I'm on mine. Another knife, taken from its place at my back, is in my hand. I took Brock's warning about Reed and the trials to mean I needed several. If Reed's surprised, he doesn't show it this time. "A fight is a fight," I say unapologetically. "Besides, if you're as good as Praetorians *claim* to be, little old me using a weapon against you won't matter." I shrug, like the knife in my hand is no big deal. I also pull a Selene move and bat my eyelashes. The gas is mostly dissipated now. It allows me to heave in a deep breath, letting my chest rise then fall. He's a man. So, either the explicitly wanton body language will throw him off focus and make him stop thinking with the head attached to his shoulders or it'll automatically remind him that I'm supposed to be weaker and more fragile than him. I can use either effect to my advantage.

Except he doesn't take my bait. He bursts into action a tick after I do. We collide in a fury of punches, blocks, and kicks. When we break apart, I'm heaving for real this time. My lungs are screaming for oxygen. It seems I was the one who did the foolish underestimating. I held nothing back and still failed to outpace or outmaneuver him.

I scrutinize Reed more sharply. How can he move that fast? His skills whisper at more than Praetorian training and the advantage of a biochip. I'm also suspicious about *where* he learned to fight like he does. His fair skin, pin-straight hair cut short, and light eyes make his

Mareenian heritage clear. Yet the way he fights in the style of Xzana, a Khanaian combat art, is so fluid, precise, and mesmerizing, it's as if he learned it from a Khanaian master. If we weren't in the middle of trying to kill each other, I'd demand to know if he was personally trained by Grandfather. Brock said they worked closely together. If Reed killed Grandfather, and Grandfather trained Reed when he's never trained anybody else other than me, then Reed betrayed him on a gut-punching, lowest-of-bastards level. The possibility makes me want to drive my knife into the asshole's eye as soon as I can get an opening. I want to do more than kill him. I want to *hurt* him. I want to make him suffer.

Unfortunately, neither of us gains the upper hand. We're circling each other, trying to figure out a weak point to strike at, when lights flood the space. He immediately straightens his body. I don't drop my guard, but I don't attack. A modicum of sense cuts through my bloodlust, and I manage to rein it in because I surmise the surprise combat trial is over. Outside of it, I don't have a good reason to destroy Reed in a room full of people.

Keeping him in my periphery, I search out Selene and Zayne among my transition class that's still standing. I find Selene near the bannister. There's a cut above her left eye and she's nursing an obviously broken right arm. Zayne is near the back of the room. He's more banged-up. One eye is swollen shut, blood oozes from his left ear, and he sways on his feet. I see Enzo, Torin, and Dex sporting nasty injuries, too, but they're also on their feet.

Roughly two hundred new graduates are strewn across the floor. Twenty-four senior Praetorians took them down in minutes. If this test didn't terminate after a predetermined time, our whole group might be down. As much as it galls me to admit it, if our fight had gone on longer, Reed might've taken me down, which is no small thing.

The transition officers snatch off their masks. Reed, who is still standing close enough for me to stab in the throat, looks me over coolly now that he's unmasked. A hardened, indecipherable expression steals over his face. I can't tell if it's a challenge, a threat, or something else altogether. Whatever it is, I give him my own savage look back, and mine is unmistakably homicidal. *You're fucking dead*, it says, and I let him take that as me being disgruntled about our tussle instead of what it's really about.

Aside from Reed, I recognize a second Praetorian among the officers from the debacle at the bar. Chance, the bastard from Alpha cohort who tried to hold me in place while his buddy pummeled me. Fantastic. I have two confirmed jackasses to deal with during the trials.

Chance stands beneath the bannister, not far from Selene, scanning the room, smug. His gaze stops in its tracks when it locks on me. A slow, sadistic smile blooms on his face. "Just because you were declared Praetorian and were confirmed," he says, striding forward to the center of the room, "that by no means makes you a Praetorian." His decree is an echo of Brock's, and Zayne's from back in our quarters.

Chance's sneer zeroes in on me like a heat-seeking missile. "Or in one particular case, just because you made it here because of who your family is, that damn sure doesn't make you one of us." I don't think he realizes that literally applies to almost everybody gathered in the common room.

Or maybe he does. But he's focused on me. So I stare back, defiant.

"If you haven't figured it out by now, I'm your lead." When Chance says it, his mien is cocky, exuding a mocking, superior swagger. The other officers are the same. He's talking to the entire room but directs that bit of info especially my way. Then, his eyes snap away from me, and he stabs a finger at Reed. "That's your co-lead."

What the godsdamned hell?

This has to be some kind of cosmic, not-funny joke. The combo couldn't be any worse for me. *Fuck. Fuck. Fuck.* I almost erupt with hysterical laughter. I was haughty, and Brock was profusely right about the danger of the trials, in all the ways we thought *and* in a much different way. If I'm not careful, these trials could end with me in my family crypt beside Grandfather because Chance likely wants me dead from when I kicked his boy's ass in the bar, and Reed just made it clear that he's gunning for me, too, for whatever reason. I look at the aspirants expired on the floor. These trials would be the perfect way for both of them to end me without any suspicion.

Silently, Reed crosses to the far-left wall. He touches the screen of his Comm Unit, and a projection of all the new graduates' names appears against the wall. Our names are in bright orange and arranged into columns against a black backdrop, lending the arrangement the look of a scoreboard. About one-fifth of the names are crossed out. The number matches up with the number of people who are down.

"Take a good look at this board," Reed says. When he addresses our whole class, his voice rings out across the common room. Like Chance, it has a quality that carries. Unlike his co-lead, it demands total respect and your absolute attention. They're both equally grating. "Fifteen hundred of you across our four martial academies declared Praetorian," he states. "One thousand and seven of you got Tribunal confirmations. Of those one thousand and seven, eight hundred and six of your names are left in orange without a strikethrough. We will weed out the remaining weak among you with the same cutthroat, meticulous efficiency that we demonstrated tonight."

He gestures to the fallen portion of our class. "The first cuts—the ones who didn't get Tribunal approval—got off easy compared to what's coming, because they aren't dead. Those two hundred with lines through their names? They're getting off easy too." I look down and notice most of them are starting to stir. It's probably why Reed didn't stab me when he took my knife from me—this wasn't a test to the death. Interesting.

Reed continues. "At least they're spared the suffering we're going to put you through. Truth is, I'm shocked there aren't more of you on the ground. You collectively failed to demonstrate the most basic of critical thinking attributes in a hostile situation. You knew coming into this there wouldn't be a welcome party. And yet you walk into one and weren't suspicious? I'm disgusted. There is no reason, or excuse, for you dropping your guard in this common room. Or anywhere. No real Praetorian isn't constantly on guard. We shouldn't have been able to take you by surprise. You should be embarrassed that we did. You are not here to have a good time. You aren't here to be comfortable, and you damn sure aren't here to be pampered with parties like Donyas."

"That's your Death Board," Chance says, pointing to our names. "It'll be projected on the walls of all common rooms, the mess, the lecture dome, and in the halls of your quarters. The only things you'll be able to do without seeing it are wash your asses and sleep. Or have your name struck through—because dead men don't see. It'll get updated after every trial and keep a running list of those among you who only marginally suck."

Marginally suck. Does he think he's clever? And the pomposity of Reed . . . oh, the transition officers really are assholes.

"This is the one trial you get to fail and keep your miserable lives intact!" Chance shouts. "One thing I will not tolerate during my transition process is lackluster performance that proves you aren't fit to call yourself a Praetorian. And if you aren't fit to hold my rank, then you aren't fit to live. As of this second, every last one of you are scum on the bottom of the transition teams' boots. Common soldiers, administratee, labourii, artizans, and anybody else not Praetorian are that. You, you sorry lot, are Praetorian *aspirants.* You want the title? The rank? The prestige? The privilege to continue breathing air? You pass the trials. All of them."

When he finishes, Reed taps the Comm Unit strapped to his right wrist. "We're ready for you," he says into the device.

Four women hurry through the entrance carrying large metal briefcases. They wear the white coats of medics. They cross the room, stepping over the bodies of aspirants, and lay the briefcases atop a long table below the staircase in the back of the room. The medics prop the briefcases open to reveal dozens of syringes filled with a green serum.

"Line up," Reed orders us, jabbing a finger at the table. "The serum will temporarily confer the benefits of a biochip. You'll need the added durability and accelerated healing for the remaining trials."

I file into the rightmost line forming in front of the medics' makeshift stations.

"That one's getting too long. Move to your left," Reed orders as he's walking by, overseeing the process.

I grit my teeth, chafing at taking orders from him, but I do as I'm told because I don't have any other choice.

Zayne steps into the line behind me. Selene brings up the rear.

"Are you okay?" I ask him over my shoulder.

He winces. "No. I feel worse than I look."

"Well, you look like hell."

Dex is three aspirants ahead of us in line. He receives a shot in his bicep. The medic uses the arm not hanging limp at his side. He moves aside and Torin, trailing blood, takes his place.

"I bet your new admirer would love for you to kiss him better later," Selene says over Zayne's shoulder. "You can be his sex goddess and he can worship you properly."

Zayne makes a strangled noise in the back of his throat that I do not appreciate. "Who? Kenna? She'd be more like some scary-ass war god."

Apparently, both of my friends are comedians right now. If they weren't so banged-up, I'd punch them.

I step up to the medic at the head of our line instead of deigning to respond. She's a short, slender woman with blond hair streaked through with silver. I present her with my right bicep. This isn't my first injection of a serum, so anxiety at allowing my skin to be nicked doesn't spike. I've been getting yearly repro-shots since twelve to avoid bleeding for days at a time every month. The medic jabs a fresh syringe into my bicep. A stinging coolness radiates around the entry site. It spreads down my arm. The tips of my fingers tingle with the sensation as the needle withdraws. The needle is thin enough that no more than a tiny drop of blood beads up on the surface of my skin. The medic wipes it away with a cotton swab drenched in antiseptic. I track the swab as she tosses it in a biohazard bin, an ingrained reaction. The concentration of antiseptic was more than enough to dilute the magic signature in such a minuscule amount of blood, but I'm always going to be sure.

"Today tested combat," Reed tells us after all aspirants have received injections. "The bioserum will have the brunt of your injuries healed by sunrise. Your next trial comes then. It'll test agility and stamina, and I promise, you'll need to be in top form. We're meeting on the lawn at dawn. See you then."

"Thank us for the shots," Chance says. "They *might* get you through what's next."

I LIMP INTO my room beside my friends. Despite the injection and my Pantheon Blessing, everything throbs with the ache of getting my ass kicked.

"I hate Reed," I grumble. "And that fucker stole my knife."

"You mean the knife you weren't supposed to have?"

"That isn't the point."

I shoot Zayne a murderous glare when he cracks a laugh. The effort costs him. He sucks in a sharp breath. "Ha!" I say to be petty when he grabs his side. "That's what you get."

But the exertion of energy costs me too. Black swims across my vision. I throw my hand out to brace myself against the wall.

"Are you all right?" Zayne asks.

It takes me a second to gather enough strength to answer, "Yes." Though even as I say it, I can't peel myself off the wall.

"Are you sure?" Selene looks at me with growing bewilderment.

And now I'm not sure.

A fresh bout of dizziness makes the room lurch. I collapse to the floor, gasping for air. Pressure explodes in my chest. It leaves behind an acute tightness that makes me terrified I'm suffocating. Paralysis seizes me, and for several long, terror-stricken moments my limbs won't obey my commands to move. My lungs won't obey my commands to suck in oxygen. Then, I feel the pulsing warmth of my Pantheon Blessing flaring to life. As it floods my veins and my entire body, the bizarre symptoms ease. I gingerly push to a sitting position. Selene and Zayne, who've dropped to my side, help me onto the bed. I sag against it, drained. The fatigue isn't altogether alien. When my Pantheon Blessing heals me, it usually leaves me some level of fatigued. But I'm weak like I've never been before. I'm so exhausted all I want to do is curl into the bed and sleep for days.

"What the hell was that?" Selene scans me like she can figure it out simply by virtue of her scrutiny.

"I don't know." What I do know is I can't stay upright. I lie on my side. My words come out sluggish as I describe everything I felt. I skip over the part that has to do with my Pantheon Blessing being the reason I'm now in the bed instead of still sprawled on the floor.

"Do you think it was the fight? Your face-off with Reed was brutal. It could be some kind of internal damage that the serum isn't working fast enough to heal." Selene lays a helpless hand against my cheek. "Maybe we should get you to a medic. You need to be checked out."

"I'm fine," I assure her. I might share her concern if I didn't have a self-healing gift. More likely, the weird episode was an adverse interaction between the bioserum and my gift. It's possible that my Pantheon Blessing didn't like the dose of the serum competing with it. No matter what, the last thing I need is to have someone poking around inside of me.

The problem is, I probably *should* go to the medic. It felt like I had a heart attack. But that's ludicrous. I'm only nineteen and my Pantheon blessing means I will easily live upward of two centuries without the life boost from a biochip. A heart attack makes no sense.

Yet Grandfather should've lived many more years, too, and he had a heart attack. My thoughts rattle inside me at the implications of that. My mouth turns dry when I recall his cause of death.

His *official* cause of death.

Maybe the lack of oxygen for those seconds is affecting my head, or maybe it's delirium setting in from the exhaustion that makes me think how Grandfather's heart attack would've been an easy thing to mimic with the right bioserum. And if those who murdered him wanted to get away with killing his akulu granddaughter aiming to become a Praetorian so they can fully extinguish the Amari name, then injecting me with the same bioserum after a combat trial would be a very smart, very inconspicuous way to go about it—they could pass it off as a genetic defect. If Reed killed Grandfather under Tribunal orders, the treacherous bastards involved could've instructed him to kill me, too, via the scheduled bioserum injections and not the preceding supposedly lenient trial, where it would've stuck out if I were the only one who ended up dead.

I don't want to go down this wormhole, but it's too late. Because now I can't shake that maybe my injection was different from the one everyone else got. My injection could have been meant to be lethal.

It could've been a hit.

Perhaps I'm being paranoid, making connections where there aren't any. Aspirants die all the time in the trials, after all, and the battle with Reed *was* vicious. Like Selene pointed out, I could've gotten more banged-up than I realize and the collapse I suffered could have been the result of some internal havoc that's been healed. But there's also the niggling observation that our fight had seemed personal for Reed as much as for me. He came at me with too much intensity to simply be an agent carrying out orders to terminate me. So even if there isn't a tie back to the Tribunal, something *is* up with him. Could he have had a reason to go after Grandfather and then me independent of the Tribunes? I can't confirm his motivations right now, but I can confirm one thing.

"Was there a cool tingling at your injection site?" I quietly ask my friends.

Selene answers, "No."

"It was like a pinprick of heat," Zayne says.

Selene nods, verifying my suspicions are right. Not necessarily who tried to kill me, but that something was definitely wrong about the serum I received.

I go rigid on the bed. My fingers dig into the mattress as fury washes over me at the certainty that Reed—either on his own, or under orders from my grandfather's murderers—almost certainly tampered with my injection. He was the one who called the medics into the room, and he redirected me to a specific line. That can't be a coincidence. I'm positive it was done on purpose.

And he wasn't acting alone.

Terese Akkhad, I hiss inside my head. That was the name stitched on the white coat of the medic who administered my shot. There were dozens of identical syringes in the storage case she carried into the common room. She would've needed to know which one was marked for me and its purpose so she didn't deliver a deadly injection to the wrong aspirant. It's not much to go on, but it is a starting point to investigate what happened to me and if it's connected to Grandfather's murder. It's a bonus that a medic is much easier for me to get at than a Praetorian.

I want to leap off the bed and go track down Akkhad immediately. But I know I can't sneak out of the compound to find and interrogate the woman working with Reed tonight. For one, there's no way Selene and Zayne are letting me out of their sight after my episode. The only way I'm leaving the compound is if they're escorting me to the med tower to be checked out . . . which might not be a bad ploy *if* I could be sure Terese Akkhad was on duty in the tower this late and *if* I could shake my friends and go alone. But they're both too damn stubborn for that. And even if I could convince Selene and Zayne to let me go to the med tower across base alone, there's the fact that my energy remains mostly sapped.

Tomorrow. I have to resolve to go after the medic tomorrow when I've recovered from the energy drain and my friends don't feel the need to stay fused to my side.

So, I just have to survive tonight . . . and whatever Reed and Chance throw at us in the morning.

4

"ATTENTION!" YELLS REED THE NEXT day. For the festivities, he's donned battledress. A breathable black shirt with a maroon stripe that slants across the front of his chest clings to his torso. His cohort insignia that marks him as part of Gamma is in gold on another, smaller stripe running horizontal along his left shoulder. The shirt is paired with combat-grade black tactical pants.

The most important thing he's wearing, though, is a bored visage that says he isn't impressed with us.

It's the exact same uniform as the rest of the haughty officers—two senior Praetorians from each of the twelve cohorts—before us.

My aspirant class straightens already stiff-backed postures as we stand on the lawn outside of the compound. The sky overhead churns storm-black. If Mareen hadn't quelled all its Pantheon-blessed, I'd swear it was a thing that was done on purpose to kick off the first full day of the trials. At least the absence of a sun dulls the morning heat of the Torrid Season.

We've assembled in order of Commencement rank, from highest to lowest accumulated marks. My poor performance during the last three months aside, I occupy the twenty-ninth spot and the first of the fourteen tight lines we are gathered in. Grandfather and I were always careful that I not stand out too much; I couldn't be too skilled. However, to survive the martial academy and the games of rank, race, and nationalism that pervade all levels of Mareenian society, I had to be better than average, because my mixed heritage leaves me straddling the line of "other." And it's not just race—I'm one of the only three girls assembled. Selene is twenty bodies down the front line from me, and the remaining girl, from Dex's Southern Isles crew, is near the head of the line behind me.

Chance, who stands beside Reed, curls his lips back in distaste at us. "Females especially do not belong in my form. It's simple biology. You're physically inferior and too delicate." He's an Alpha prick—with all that word conveys—so of course that's his position. Although most of the other cohorts hold the same bullshit belief. It's why his fellow officers look at us with a similar contempt, except for two. The same cool, detached expression rests on Reed's face, and the lone girl among the officers is stone-faced.

Chance takes a step forward, and there's unmistakable menace in the movement. "Walk now," he tells me, Selene, and the other female aspirant. "Or I will break you quickly and then I will end you quickly. Or maybe I'll do it slowly and really have some fun. We'll see." He jerks a thumb toward the female officer. "Or," he says with a chuckle, "you might be like Dannica and survive your transition. But ask her sometime what it took to do so. I think she might've preferred dying."

I hate bullies. I really godsdamned do. Too bad Reed stopped the bar fight before I got to beat the shit out of Chance too.

The girl, Dannica, keeps the same steel expression at Chance's statement. Her hair is dark with a slight kink that persists in the severe fish-tail braid it is pulled into. Her eyes are violet, and her nose is slightly wider than the lean, aquiline shape of most Mareenians' noses. She looks almost like she has whispers of Khanaian heritage somewhere in her ancestral tree. Some throwback genes that made an appearance in her. Bearing a kink to her hair and that wideness of her nose, she can't be the result of in-vitro gene manipulation if she has Mareenian parents. No two Mareenians would select a child to look like she does. In addition to her sex, her appearance is also likely why Chance took a dig at her.

While she doesn't give off a reaction to it, Reed does. The whip of violence that cracks through his blue stare is so swift I might've missed it if I wasn't already keeping him in my sights. I look between him and the girl, musing about the nature of their relationship. A gold *Gamma* symbol glitters on her shoulder too. They're cohort brethren, and I also wonder if they're more than that from the intensity of his response to Chance's taunt. I file the observation of their closeness away in case the intel is useful later. Then I give the bulk of my attention back over to the immediate threat. Chance, who has begun a slow walk down the length of our formation.

"Me, my team, and this process do not give a shit who you are, what legacy line you come from, or what war house produced you," he informs us. "I will eliminate every bitch-ass, good-for-nothing, waste-of-space one of you who fails to pass muster. That's the point of these trials. You gotta make the cut with nothing except your own grit, your own fortitude, your own skills. Because these trials do more than make Praetorians. They shape the future and fabric and power distribution of Mareen. These trials are where common folk achieve a level of wealth and influence that'll otherwise evade them their whole pathetic lives. Legacy lines are fractured and forged, and war houses either retain power, see it diminished, or enjoy an immense swell—sometimes war houses can even be shattered. That's what being in a Republic means:

merit over blood. And beyond and above that is a fact that is much more crucial . . ." He stops walking and pivots on his heel to face us full-on. He points at the flagpole in the center of the lawn that's flying two banners. One rests at half-staff; it's swathed in the maroon-and-gold colors of wartime. The other flaps at the top of the pole and dons the maroon-and-white colors of peacetime. "The positions of those can change at any minute. The Republic has enemies. Praetorians don't just fight those enemies. Praetorians turn the tides of war. Praetorians win crucial battles and force retreats. Praetorians keep the Republic a sovereign state. We aren't here to fuck around."

It's almost rousing, for all its patriotism. But it's also patronizing, misogynistic, and full of shit. *Merit over blood.*

Please.

Why would the color of my skin matter, then? Or my gender?

What an absolute tool.

Following his declaration, Chance brandishes a sundisk, a small weapon with a sharp-edged perimeter that can slice through bone like it's silk. He rolls it across his knuckles as casually as if it were a coin. "I'm feeling generous today. I'll give you the grace of a warm-up before we really kick things off." The sundisk comes to rest between his thumb and middle finger. "Duck," he says. The guy, a legacy from Krashen three bodies uprank of me, doesn't react to the order fast enough. The sundisk embeds in his right shoulder then detonates. The microblast takes out a chunk of flesh. He wails in agony.

"You're messing up my damn form with that whimpering and piss-poor reaction time," Chance barks. "Shut the fuck up or the next sundisk embeds in your chest."

All eight hundred and six of us go on high alert once the terms of engagement are made clear: namely, that engagement is always imminent. Reed tried to warn us last night, but this somehow makes it realer—it's probably the menace and glee that play across Chance's face. I brace to be the target of whatever Chance will fire at us next. His weapon of choice this time is a blaster. He holds it in one hand and a fresh clip of UV bullets in the other. He jams the clip into the gun and takes aim at our form. The blaster travels slowly past each one of us on the front line. Chance takes his time, chuckling at our shot nerves. He sweeps the blaster down the line, up it, then back down it again. I tense each time he nears Selene or Zayne.

"Duck," he finally says. A shot cracks through the air. A guy near the center of the line drops to the ground. He doesn't move. The bullet slammed into his torso. "You're not dead, so haul ass up," Chance hollers at his latest victim. "The shot was clean. Don't insult me."

My hearts stops thudding in my chest. We've all taken numerous clean shots in the academy. They don't do any lasting damage because they miss all the vital bits, but they still hurt like a bitch.

"Duck," Chance orders again. I drop to a crouch. The top of my head burns from how close the bullet grazes by. "That wasn't a clean shot. Good thing your reflexes aren't as lacking as your lineage."

"You motherfucker!" Selene screams down the line. "You tried to kill her!"

"I gave her a test, Rhysien! And you're out of pocket! Fall the fuck back in!" The blaster is aimed at her, but I'm not really processing that.

Because she was right—the asshole *did* just try to put a bullet between my eyes.

"Are you going to stay in the dirt, Amari, or get your sorry ass up?" Chance turns the glower meant especially for me on the whole line. "The Praetorian Trials will be administered over the next six weeks. From here on out, there is no going back for any of you. Either you move forward as Praetorian Guard or you fail out of the trials—and from now on failure *is* death, if I didn't make that clear with this fun little exercise. Praetorians are the deadliest, most highly trained, most skilled of Mareenian soldiers. What's the creed of a Mareenian?"

"*Duty! Discipline! Endurance! Valor! Obedience! Honor!*" the line shouts to him.

"Throw that shit away," he shouts back. "Combat, Survival, Strength, Strategy, Nerve, and Resilience is the creed of a Praetorian. Your grit will be tested in each area. How bad do you want the rank I hold? Not all of you will come through on the other side as one of us. Most of you will fail. If you think I'm kidding, do some research. See how many Praetorians there are. And consider how many pledge each year.

"I am not joking. Your life is in your hands—whether that's a future as a Praetorian or in a body bag is up to you. Personally, I don't care if it's the latter. In fact, it is my singular mission over the next six weeks to see to that outcome, because I don't want weakness next to me when I'm on a mission. If the whole of you die, so be it. A new crop will replace your pitiful, unworthy asses next year and we'll add numbers to our ranks then. Maybe. Only the best, only the strongest, become Praetorian. The rewards are high, so our standards are high. Our expectations are higher. To be Praetorian is to be unbreakable. Unbeatable."

I almost snort. I beat and broke his buddy in the bar. If that guy is one of the best, then this scare tactic has nothing to do with me. Given the situation, though—and the sensation of the bullet going past my head—I have enough discipline not to let my reaction out. I catch Reed looking at me. It's the first time he's done so on the lawn. Previously, whenever his gaze has traveled toward my spot in the form, it's slid past me like I don't exist. Now his hard stare is fixed on me, and it's so dark it's night-blue. His eyes hold a glint of censure.

The desire to snort dies away completely because how fucking dare *he* rebuke *me*. If I could breathe flames, I'd melt that insulting look off his snake-ass face. Along with his skin and bones.

A crack of thunder splits the air and the skies join in on our torture. I forget Reed for the moment and curse. We only get a few good downpours during the Torrid Season. Of course, the cosmos decided to gift Mareen with one of those today.

Chance slides a delighted smile to the transition officer on his right.

"Rain is perfect weather for stamina conditioning. Don't you think, Nero?"

The senior Praetorian who wears a *Beta* symbol on his battledress grins like a fiend. "I sure do. They can roll in the mud like the worms they are."

"Two hundred or three?" Chance asks offhandedly.

"Four," Nero chuckles.

"You heard your Third. Drop and give me four hundred!" Chance sloshes his boots around in the water that's saturating the lawn. "If your chin touches mud, I slam a sundisk in your spine. Welcome to the Trials!"

The first two hundred burpees are a breeze. The next hundred Chance counts off are doable, but intense. It's the last one hundred that might do me in. Even I have my limits. My legs and arms burn like they're on fire. By number three hundred and ten, they wobble. When I go to the ground for the push-up part of the burpee, my chin comes two inches away from brushing the standing water that's accumulated. A boot to my back prevents me from heaving myself all the way up. It grinds into my kidney, crushing the wind out of me from how bad it hurts.

I strain against it. It bears down on my back harder. Nero's face appears in my line of sight. "Your lead transition officer wants you to fail. You can give up now, and he'll oblige you a quick death, or you can be stubborn and die painfully. You don't get a choice after today."

If Nero is eye-level with me and Chance is busy counting off, I have no clue who's trying to break my back. Great. The bastard has enlisted a whole team to help him harass me.

"Fuck you and him." I lower myself, then thrust hard against the boot weighing me down. A quick glance at my surroundings informs me I'm not the only one they are tormenting like this. Reed has his boot crushing Zayne's spine. The one female officer is doing the same to Enzo. All of our transition team has their foot on somebody's back. I'm just extra special and got two hecklers.

We get to the four hundredth burpee and Chance tells us to hold the position when we're level with the ground, trapping us in a plank.

"For how long?" Torin groans. His arms tremble.

"For as long as I fucking want. Somebody is going to drop. We are not leaving this lawn until one of you do."

We hold as long as we can, but then Torin collapses. My heart rams against my chest. *You should've conserved your energy instead of asking the useless question, you fool.* I don't know him well. Really, I don't know him at all. But our conversation during the mingler meant he wasn't just someone nameless to me, and he seemed decent. So it hurts a little more.

Chance produces a sundisk without batting an eye. "Anyone else care to do the honors?"

Nero, our third in command, volunteers.

Chance throws him the sundisk. He snatches it out of the air. He stalks to the doomed guy from the Southern Isles and shows us all that Chance wasn't bluffing when he promised to slam sundisks in our backs if we dropped during conditioning.

The rest happens in slow motion. Torin doesn't get the chance to scream, whimper, or even plead for his life before it detonates. A hole is blown into his back. Blood and chunks of flesh splatter the lawn, Nero, and two aspirants nearby. Enzo is one of them. He's turned green. The other aspirant outright vomits. He isn't the only one who hurls. It's the first time that the majority of us has seen death so up close and personal, let alone one of our class.

"Don't you dare move!" Nero shouts. "If you can't take seeing death, how are you going to be a Praetorian?"

I grit my teeth, wondering if I can feel my arms anymore, or if I feel my arms too much.

The whole time, I'm thinking Torin could've been any one of us. *He could've been me; I came damn close to dropping too—I just might anyway.* He could still be any one of us since the trials are only getting started. If this is today, what the hell will the remainder of things bring? My pulse whooshes in my ears with the question, and I see the same question plain in the twisted terror on the faces of all my peers too.

It's a gut-wrenching shock to my system. I think it's the same for all us aspirants because everyone stares at what's left of the body with open horror. Chance was right about one thing during his speech—we all have our reasons for entering the trials and being determined to see them through, no matter the cost. And we all went into them knowing the danger, the peril, the deadly way they're conducted. But what just happened with Torin is so much more than a lethal test. It's vicious and savage and barbaric and gruesome. It's fucked up and twisted and warped and so wrong. They could have let him walk out of here. They killed him instead.

I guess the logic is they're training us to defend Mareen, and if we go to war, war is gruesome. War is ugly and bloody and messy and fucked up and twisted too. But that's different. This isn't war. Torin wasn't an enemy combatant. He was a classmate. An innocent kid with tired arms. A citizen of the Republic whose customs just got him murdered.

And the way Nero did it, smugly and cheerfully, like the shit was a euphoric rush and like he relished it. Chance gave the order with the same sick glee. The rest of our officers aren't any better. They're a bunch of superior assholes too. They've all had their feet on our backs. Now they stand stoic and unflinching and expressionless. It's all wrong on so many levels.

I spot Dex, Torin's friend, across the lawn not too far from his remains. Several emotions play over his face at once. First, there's utter devastation. Then grief. Then fury. Finally, he hangs his head—all while staying in position. I think that last one, the resignation, is the worst. I glare at Chance and Nero standing shoulder to shoulder. The two of them deserve the death Torin just got.

It's shitty, but I thank the gods it wasn't Selene, Zayne, or Enzo. If it were one of my friends, I wouldn't have been able to stop myself from unleashing hell on the lawn.

"Now, get your asses up and run the perimeter of the base twice," Chance orders. "*Please* lag behind the pace your officers set and let me have some more fun."

It's not easy for us to comply—the Praetorians are biochip-fast, and they don't dial back their speed when they run with us.

THAT NIGHT, I sit at a table in the mess with Selene, Enzo, and Zayne, monitoring every entrance, archway, and window. I don't trust any of our transition officers now. As Chance promised, the Death Board is projected on the wall behind the serving line, and it's been updated. Five more aspirant names have a strike through them—Torin's, plus the four Chance and Nero took out during the run.

Staring at it, I dimly remember that I'm supposed to be seeking out the medic when I get a respite, but today was hell. Mentally, physically, and emotionally. Now that conditioning is over, I've got nothing left. As much as I hate it, I have no choice but to delay going after Akkhad at least by another day.

"Remind me again why we're here?" Enzo says, picking at his food and drawing my attention back to my battered friends. He spears a scalloped potato with his fork, eats one bite, then sets the fork back down on his plate. "I don't have the stomach for this right now." He pushes the plate to the middle of the table.

I think most in our aspirant class feels the same way. I do for sure. We were dismissed to the mess for our first meal since dawn, but nobody is really eating.

"I don't think I'm likely to forget the sight or sound of a sundisk blowing apart flesh anytime soon," says Selene. She didn't even bother to grab food from the serving line. The officers gave her and the other girl in our class as hard a time as they gave me. She's hunched over the table, rubbing a broken left collarbone that the bioserum is working to mend. The skin surrounding the break is swollen and purplish-blue.

Enzo gingerly touches her elbow. "How do you feel?"

She jerks away. "I'm fine. Don't treat me like I'm more fragile than you are."

"I'd walk." Zayne hasn't stopped staring at the Death Board since we entered the mess. "I don't need the prestige and I don't care about any elevation in status. I don't need to be rich either. I swear I'd walk if it wasn't for my parents. They need this. I'm doing this for them. They can't keep . . ." Visible hysteria chokes off his words. He's shell-shocked.

I squeeze his shoulder. "We know." His parents are labourii *and* from the Southern Isles, which the Republic as a whole mostly ignores in terms of funneling resources and infrastructure to. The string of fiercely independent islands are still being made to pay for not falling in line with the rest of the nation when the Tribunal ordered a complete disavowal of all beliefs and customs having to do with the Pantheon.

Zayne rasps a laugh. "I left home for nothing. When I tested into Krashen, the only reason I came was to work toward the Praetorian rank so I can turn the generous stipend that comes with it over to my parents, and it's likely all been for nothing. The way things are going I'll end up dead before these hellish trials are over and my parents will still live in piss-poor conditions and starve anyway."

"I *can't* die," Enzo says, staring at the Death Board now too. He jabs a finger at it. "My name has to stay on that board without a line through it. If I die, then the duty falls to one of my siblings to become Praetorian so our legacy line doesn't break." He shakes his head vehemently. "I don't want Vasa, Geo, or Remi anywhere near these trials." Although he says this, he's shifted to looking at the Death Board like he already sees his name crossed out. Zayne and Selene gaze at it in a similar way.

"Hey!" I slam my hands down on the table to get their attention. "If we think we're already defeated, then we are dead already. Our asshole officers have won. *We can do this.* We can get through this. None of us would be sitting here if we weren't capable of it. It'll be grueling and hard, and completely terrifying if today is anything to go by, but not impossible. We can best those fuckers."

We have to. For as much as I need to take down Reed and anyone else who killed my grandfather, I know that will be a lot harder without these three.

Zayne gives me a salute with no heart in it. "I hope you're right, Kenna."

"I need some fucking liquor," Enzo mutters.

"I need a good lay," Selene says. "Several of them, in fact, after today."

When Enzo turns to face her, every last feeling he has for her shows on his face. I can guess where he's about to go with her, and it's a path he's so going to regret venturing down. I'm already insulted and furious on Selene's behalf. So much that I want to hop over the table and strangle some sense into him before he can open his mouth. *Fucking men.*

"Don't," I say, in warning.

The big idiot ignores me. "*You* actually don't have to be here. You should—"

"Me walking away isn't an option," Selene snarls. Of course, it isn't an option for her, and Enzo should know that. If she leaves the compound, then she has to move into Rhysien Manor, and she'd rather face death than what'll come with the relocation.

Enzo clenches his jaw. His lips press together in a grimace, as if he's wrestling with whatever he wants to say next. I have high hopes that he'll apologize and smooth over his mistake for all of only a few seconds because then he sighs and says, "Fuck, it. You can shoot my balls off for this later. But I need to say it because if I don't and something happens to you . . ."

I shake my head. Even if he had a good point that didn't make him seem like an overbearing, obtuse ass of a male at the moment, it's an argument he can't imagine he'll win. It'd be easier to pick up a mountain range and move it than to change Selene's mind about anything after she's made it up.

"Spit it out," Selene says tersely. "Get whatever you need to off your chest."

He thrusts a hand through his hair. "You can't delay fulfilling what it means to be a Donya forever anyway. You already know that all you're buying yourself is two to five good years, at max, before your father forces you out of active duty, and then you have to do what you're running from regardless. So, given what we saw happen on the lawn, what's the godsdamned point? One of those poor, unlucky bastards could've been any of us. *One of them could've been you.* If you walk, you're at least ensuring you keep your life and that you live a long one."

"Go to hell, Enzo. What you're speaking of isn't any kind of life I want. It's not even a life worth living. So, I'll stick with this alternative, however short it lasts, thank you, because at least it's a life I chose."

"I care about you, that's all," Enzo responds softly. "I can't live with seeing you die."

"Umm, do you two want some privacy?" Zayne asks. "Kenna and I can leave." He stands to do exactly that, because it's clear *he* wants them to have some privacy so he doesn't have to listen to this get any worse.

I stay parked where I am. There's no way in hell I'm leaving Selene to this face-off alone.

"No, sit down," Selene snaps. "This convo is about over."

"That's your problem," she says to Enzo. "This isn't about you and what you can't live with. It's about me and what I can't live with." She slices a withering look down the length of him that he absolutely deserves. "I already have one male that lords over my life. I will not have two. I wouldn't expect you to understand this because you're a legacy male who's always enjoyed the privilege of some control over your life and you always will, but I refuse to go be cooped up in Rhysien Manor playing Lady of the House. I refuse to be chained to an arranged marriage with some virtual stranger my father feels is of suitable stock, then be expected to churn out babies for him afterward, only to then see some of those babies have to go through this same shit and maybe die and break my fucking heart. I won't be reduced to nothing more than a scion-making broodmare locked in a gilded cage while my father gets to keep playing war house head, my brothers get to keep playing Praetorian and fucking whoever they want, and my new husband gets to keep doing whatever the hell he wants too. Me becoming Praetorian *won't* be a two-to-five-year delay. You should have more faith in me and know me better than that. Not that it's any of your business or that I owe you an explanation, but I hate being underestimated, so fuck you for that too.

"Besides, I plan to make this permanent with my war house in its current predicament."

"I—" Enzo starts then shuts the hell up like he should've done from the start and actually begins to think about what Selene might have in play.

The predicament Selene refers to is Rhysien War House coming up one short of the ten Praetorian scions it needs to produce every generation spanning twenty years to retain war house status. Selene becoming a Praetorian fulfills the quota. Sure, she has two younger cousins who can fill the tenth slot eventually before her generation ends, but the oldest is still a cadet two years out from Commencement, the youngest is five years out, and neither of them are sure things. Their marks are nowhere near Selene's marks at the academy.

I do Enzo the favor of connecting the dots between the info he already knows and what he never bothered to ask before declaring Selene needed to give up the trials. "Our girl can likely skirt becoming Rhysien War House's Donya in more than name indefinitely." I throw Selene an appreciative look because her scheme is brilliant. "Especially if she further manipulates things to her advantage and makes sure her two younger cousins keep with the trend of shitty marks."

Selene pops her lips, smug, because she's already been triumphant in her plans. "Staying out of the crucible of the trials and enjoying a long, cushy life as a scion with the status of our house secure isn't a hard sell to pampered, rich boys if it comes with the right added bribes."

"Oh," is all Enzo can manage to say.

"I can handle myself," Selene asserts.

He gives her a tortured look. Then finally says, "I hope you're right. I hope we're all right in thinking that, because after conditioning . . . I don't know if I can handle myself. And that was the first day. Hell, I don't know if any of us really can. Or if those who stumble through this to the end will make it by sheer luck."

Although I tried to bolster everyone's confidence before, the bleakness in Enzo's words—the grim, raw way he says them, with utter totality—forces me to acknowledge the daunting truth of them. That skill and an iron will alone might not get us through this because we're up against tougher, more seasoned, and more relentless opponents. And given that, how in the hell do we find a path to the finish mark other than stumbling through things and praying we don't die? The panic and terror that gripped my friends as they stared at the Death Board finally seizes me. Because before this conversation, I kept thinking how there's no way I'll fail. Between my skill and my Blood Gift, I'm as powerful as any Praetorian—if not more so.

But it's not about that. It's about the fact that they have a sociopathic commitment to culling our numbers, and the ability to grind us—even me—into dust just from sheer exhaustion if nothing else.

It feels like being doused in subzero water then shocked with a high-voltage stun gun. I grab for my usual defense mechanism and try to fit back on an armor of bravado—I look for something to say in response to Enzo's observation that's chock full of it—but nothing comes. Because now I can't shake the petrifying, unnerving possibility that sheer boldness and strength—the two things I've always depended on to pull me through tribulations—won't get me through everything that comes next. They barely got me through today and the previous night. I was so sure going into the trials that Brock's warnings about them were overkill, especially for someone like me. But after today . . . nothing about the Trials is what I thought it would be. They're more ruthless and more brutal than I imagined. I can't lose my friends in these trials, and I don't want to lose my own life in them either. And yet . . . I might not have the power to stop it.

5

THE NEXT MORNING, A SIREN blares through our quarters before dawn. The transition officers forgo dispatching reporting instructions to our Comm Units. Instead, the bastards run through the halls banging on our doors, leaving drones behind to zoom in and drop flamespitters when we open them. The small metallic sphere that clatters to the floor of my room hisses and erupts in a spray of fire and smoke. I cough, snatch my sleep shirt over my mouth, and run from the room in the shirt and cotton shorts. Selene does the same in a nightdress. The metal floor of the hallway is cold against my bare feet, but I can't afford the delay retrieving my boots will cause. Smoke is spilling out into the hall from every direction. Without a protective mask, the risk of suffocation is high.

"Rise and shine, princesses." Of course he uses a gendered term as an insult. "Did you sleep well?" The voice that taunts us over the siren isn't Chance's. It's Nero's. "I did. Four hours is a luxury in the field.

Your lead officer wants your asses in the dome. It's time to take you to school. Follow the drones."

The drones zoom off. We have to sprint to keep up with them, and with the smoke, they're barely visible, making it difficult. They ascend stairs. Twenty damn flights.

We hustle into a circular room that's built identically to the lecture domes in the academy. Observer benches rise from floor to ceiling in a spiral formation. We take seats closest to the presenter's pit at the very bottom.

And wait.

It's the first thing we learned at the academies: we are on the instructor's time. We sit, quiet and attentive, using the respite to gather our breath and our wits.

The latter is a bit harder, knowing that more of us might die today.

The officers' sick Death Board spans the wall we face. Taunting us.

The transition officers leave us waiting in the lecture dome for more than two hours. Outwardly I'm patient, but inside I'm seething—this is precious time I could've used to find Akkhad. For everyone else, it's precious time they could've used to sleep longer after yesterday's exhaustion. Obviously, the officers are aware of the latter. They want us to be half-delirious from lack of sleep for the next trial. They also apparently want us to be hypothermic, because the dome's air vents are blowing subzero temps.

"The lead for our class is a real jerk," Enzo says when our wait time is creeping up on hour three. Some aspirants remain silent, terrified to agree. Others laugh while shooting nervous looks down at the presenter's pit, where Chance can pop into existence at any time.

"I like him," one particular suck-up says. He makes sure his voice carries for any transition officers listening. "He's only doing his job. They have to make sure we're tough enough to hold the rank."

"They can do that without killing us," Selene chimes in.

"We won't have the luxury of performing without the pressure of life-or-death when we're in the field," Suck-Up says. "The trials are for our own good."

"Yes, having sundisks slammed in our spines or being burned alive in our rooms is for our own good." I can't help the snark. I'm irritated about being half-dressed, shoeless, and cold.

Caiman offers up his opinion: "Going through hell is also supposed to bring us together." He slings his arms across the shoulders of Greysen to his right and Petre, another one of his academy buddies and a fellow dickhead scion, to his left. "Well, the majority of us. Some of us will never belong."

"What the hell is your problem? Why does me being in these trials bother you so much?" *So much for my outward patience.* Chance, at least, has a semi-good reason. I beat his man in public. If our positions were reversed, I'd be nursing a petty grudge too. But that's Chance. Caiman, on the other hand, has all of Mareen at his feet, and he's *always* been preoccupied with me.

Maybe he has a crush on me?

"*You're* my problem, akulu," he shoots back.

Maybe not.

"You think the world is supposed to bow to you since you're so uber special because of your grandfather. You've gotten all of the benefits of being a scion of a war house without having to work for it. My family bled generations over for me to have my status."

If I wasn't wedged between Selene and Zayne on the bench, I'd fall off it. He was literally trying to throw what I charged him with back at me. *I'm* the one riding someone else's past commendations? It's so preposterous it's laughable.

"My grandfather bled for me to be sitting here. If I remember correctly, he bled for the entire Republic. But even if that wasn't true, I bled to be sitting here. I went through eleven brutal years at a martial academy, same as everyone else. I got bruised, battered, and drilled the same as everyone else in preparation to serve the Republic."

"Yet everyone else couldn't fuck off for three months and end up in the trials. I wonder how you did?"

"Oh, fuck you. Are *you* accusing *me* of nepotism? You, Golden Boy Rossi, who gets everything handed to you because of how powerful your war house is?"

He shrugs. "Like I said, my family bled for generations for the privilege. Led a coup against one vile god and fought a worldwide war against all of the Pantheon to earn the right to be called a war house. Your kin are Khanaians. They were busy being pampered by Kissa and sheltered from what the rest of the gods did to Iludu during the Pantheon Age."

"The Khanaians helped lock the gods away in the end," I snap back. "My grandfather was also half-Mareenian."

"Perhaps, but you're less than half. You are more Khanaian than Mareenian. That makes you more of an abhorrence than he was."

"My grandfather was proud of his Khanaian half. I am too. If you don't like it, that's your problem."

"You're both embarrassments to the Republic."

"How? Verne Amari and his kin suffered alongside and fought with yours during the Pantheon Age. *He* fought the Blood Emperor one-on-one. Everyone knows about his legacy, but morons like you always conveniently overlook it. Are you really this stupid, or do you just spew the garbage handed down from your father? I've always wondered. I'd rather be an embarrassment than someone whose entire function is to be a clone."

For the briefest moment, his veneer of arrogance thins. Then he is applying a fresh coat of his trademark stupid, pretentious sneer. "Whatever, Amari. I wouldn't expect you to understand how being an heir to a war house works."

Is that an insult? I wonder if the Rossis specifically breed wit out of their children. I'm about to retort when a voice calls out, *"Hello, losers."* We hear Chance before we see him.

The floor of the presenter's pit has slid open. A podium rises out of the gaping hole. All twenty-four of our transition officers, in casual battledress and looking well rested, stand atop it. The drones lie in an inert line along the front edge of the podium.

"Did you sleep well?" Chance asks. "I did. Got three whole extra hours." The podium stops moving. The juvenile teasing flees from his demeanor. He straightens his posture. Steel threads through every inch of his mien. "DO YOU KNOW YOUR HISTORY?"

We know this exercise from the academy. We leap from our seats, snap to attention, and shout, "Yes, Praetorian Chance. We do."

"We'll see. The stakes if you don't are higher than the running that academy instructors made you do. You're locked in here. The drones activate and drop micromissiles that will splatter everyone's guts on the walls if it takes me longer than three seconds to hear a *thorough, correct* answer from any one of you. Praetorian Reed is your drill chief."

Chance steps back among the cluster of transition officers, and Reed steps forward. "At ease," Reed tells us before he begins the drill session.

"Don't relax too much," Chance interjects. He touches a finger to his Comm Unit, and the drones lift off the podium. They whiz up out of the presenter's pit. They come to a hover above our heads.

Reed tosses the first question at Selene: "When were the original Praetorian cohorts founded, Rhysien?"

"The year 3245, Before Pantheon Expulsion," she rattles off.

"Rossi, name the original ones."

"Alpha!" he yells proudly. "It was the first, most lauded, and most accomplished. Theodolphus Rossi, Mareen's first and most esteemed Legatus Commander, led the initiative that formed it and the rest of the original—"

"I didn't ask for a boast of your genealogy tree or for you to compose odes of praise to Alpha. I asked for the names of the original cohorts. Just a list, Rossi. The inability to achieve brevity is a shortcoming that could get you and your cohort killed."

Despite who it comes from, I enjoy Caiman's dress-down immensely.

Caiman turns red in the face. He isn't used to superiors not heaping praise on him. Even when he screwed up or came up short in lessons, our academy instructors found a way to say something positive. But he doesn't hesitate, which almost ruins my happiness at his misery. "Alpha, Beta, Gamma, Delta, and Epsilon were the firsts," he grinds out.

Reed moves on to another aspirant. "Why were they founded, Dulsiner?"

Selene's almost-hookup, Dex, and the Southern Isles girl exchange frantic looks.

"One second left," Chance shouts.

"Which one of us were you addressing? Me or Bex?" Dex scrambles to say. From their names, I know they are twins. Mareen has specific naming conventions for multiples.

"Time's u—"

The girl, Bex, starts spouting an answer. "The original cohorts were founded when Mareen's first Legatus Commander ushered us out of the chains of patronage to the god of war. We rejected his war-gift in preference of autonomy. The men of the first Praetorian cohorts were warriors who were exceptional fighters and strategists without being Pantheon-blessed. The cohorts were formed to fight against Krashna, who refused to relinquish rule over Mareen."

Reed accepts her answer. "When were the rest of the cohorts formed, Drake?"

Zayne jumps up. "When the Accacian emperor began instigating conflicts on the Minor Continent eighty years ago. Having annexed all of the Principal Continent under the Accacian flag, he turned his sights across the Tumultuous Sea. Mareen, Khanai, Lythe, and the Free Microstates to the far north represented the one remaining corner of Iludu he hadn't yet conquered. Cohorts Zeta through Omega were formed in preparation for Mareen to be capable of mounting a victorious resistance against the Blood Emperor when the skirmishes he provoked escalated to full-scale war."

Reed levels a grim gaze at the whole of us. "Verne Amari, our forty-fourth Legatus Commander, won the War of Accacian Aggression that eventually came. Barely. The Blood Emperor and his legions wielded a blood-gift so powerful, we could not do what the original cohorts did with the god of war and beat the gifts of the Pantheon with tech. A third of our people were massacred." He waves his hand and drone-captured images from the war illuminate the curved walls and ceiling. The projections give the effect of being under the dome of a planetarium, but we're gazing up at atrocities instead of the stars.

Holographs of the Memorial Monuments erected in the northern, southern, western, and eastern regions of Mareen rise up out of the floor in front of us. The names of Mareenians who died in the war are lasered into the quartz slabs. There are scores and scores and scores of names.

"Accacia didn't wage a war against us; they carried out a slaughter," Reed continues. "The Blood Emperor vowed to eradicate every Mareenian for the slight of refusing to submit to his self-proclaimed Pantheon-blessed reign. He promised us there would be no Mareen left when he wrestled from us that which the gods promised him but we would not give him willingly. He'd make it a scorched, barren ghost state that belonged to his empire. He nearly made good on the vow."

A solemnity falls over the room. Mixed into it is a quiet rage that I share and understand wholeheartedly. The Blood Emperor is a monster and the reason my mother is dead.

"Our major cities, bases, and ports fell to Accacia," Reed says, and the domed ceiling shows the eastern and northern cities ablaze, the western and southern ports painted crimson, their crystalline blue waters shimmering red, and bases in three of the four cardinal points reduced to rubble. "Our great Krashen City burned along with the rest. Only Krashen's base withstood the siege, and it, too, came close to falling in that last battle. The combined might of Mareen and its allies could not withstand the vastness of Accacia's forces. The entire Minor Continent drowned in blood during the war." The dome ceiling above reflects this, no longer limiting the havoc it shows to Mareen. The war crimes the Blood Emperor and his legions committed across all sovereign nations of the Minor Continent bear down on us. The history depicted is too horrific to stare at for long—and it's not as if we haven't heard all this before.

"One man's prowess turned the tides and led Mareen to a victory that ended the war. That man is no longer around, and Accacia will take advantage of it. It is merely a matter of time before its Blood Emperor ignores the peace treaty that he's enjoyed playing fast and loose with since Verne Amari forced him to sign it. Another war *will* come. That is why each year's class of neo-Praetorians undergoes trials. Yes, they are grueling. Yes, they are hell. Yes, they can rob you of your life. But they are also critical to your survival and, more important, Mareen's survival. Common soldiers do the work of the front lines. They clash with armies. They fend off enemy soldiers in ground and air strikes. Praetorians do the work of special ops. We execute the missions that require skills above and beyond what the average individual is equipped with. The missions that take out critical players, critical units, or critical resources. It is we who will either win or lose a war for the Republic. If we fail an op in wartime, if we aren't good enough, or strong enough, or smart enough, or calculating enough, or ruthless enough, we will be responsible for the Republic seeing the devastation it suffered during the last war with Accacia."

Reed gives us this speech to impassion us. To motivate us today after Chance gave us his speech to intimidate us yesterday. I see through his rhetoric . . . and yet, it works. My peers stand as one at the conclusion of it, straight-backed and proud without having been called to attention. I stand along with them. My aspirant class radiates an iron determination to conquer the trials. Yesterday, we were all groaning about them. Fearing them. Today, they are welcomed. Everyone has become eager to prove themselves courageous, capable, and the kind of soldier Reed said was crucial to the Republic's persistence. As our co-lead, Reed exudes a righteousness and a magnetism that easily trap everyone in his orbit. It makes the aspirants also eager to prove themselves to *him* after his speech, because it's difficult not to automatically trust him, like him, and feel a bit mesmerized by his presence.

Oh, he is good.

Really good. He would fool me with the act, too, if I didn't already know better. If I'm being honest with myself, he *did* have me fooled in the bar. It shows me another facet of what I'm up against with him and how hypervigilant I'm going to have to be around him.

The room answers with fervor when he shouts, "What is the creed of a Praetorian?"

"*Combat, Survival, Strength, Strategy, Nerve, and Resilience!*"

He calls, "What is the creed of a Mareenian?"

My class responds with equal zeal as before. "*Duty! Discipline! Endurance! Valor! Obedience! Honor!*"

He salutes us, satisfied.

I try to discern what his play is with keeping to the charade. On the surface, it seems that he and Chance are two different people with opposing aims during this transition. Chance instructed us to throw the Mareenian Creed away. He wants to indoctrinate us to see ourselves as supreme. Individuals who are above the average citizen and better than them. Reed supposedly wants us to see ourselves as a part of the whole even as we are a separate, vital component with a duty to safeguard the rest. It would be an admirable mission and make it obvious why Reed belongs to Gamma cohort.

If he wasn't full of horseshit.

Grandfather had a similar philosophy. Most Gamma Praetorians do, because of Grandfather. That's what bothers me so much: Reed is only pretending to embody that; he can't really uphold such beliefs if he murdered the very man who instilled the principles he spouts in Gamma, who made it his life's work to remake the Republic and instill these values throughout all of the cohorts and Mareen—even if the change was slow-crawling.

And now, literally, dead.

It's this that actually stops me from jumping up and trying to strangle Reed right now. Because there's no way he acted alone—the desire to keep Mareen from realizing my grandfather's dream would be a powerful motivation for the Tribunal. It was no secret most Tribune Generals, war houses, and Praetorian cohorts have vehemently resisted the changes Grandfather tried to push. Mareen is stubborn in its traditions and its elitism as much as in its bigotry—which, I am realizing, is all part of the same thing. A lot of people among the upper veins of society would not have taken kindly to Grandfather's vision for change.

So, this could be about two things: their hatred for him because of his lineage *and* animosity toward him because of his policy initiatives—which Brock said Reed worked closely with him on. Maybe Reed was a plant from the beginning. Someone charismatic who was handpicked and groomed by Tribunal conspirators to get close to Grandfather, earn his trust, pretend like he embodied everything Grandfather believed in, and then murder him.

It's a sequence of events that makes perfect sense, and it provides a reason for why Reed is keeping to the noble act. Pivoting toward scum so soon would be an instant red flag for someone like Brock, who already has reason to suspect the possibility of foul play and might be scrutinizing everyone's actions in the wake of Grandfather's death to confirm it.

Keep playing your little game. I hope it makes you complacent. That way, it will be easier to kill you.

"Tomorrow, you will have your Survival Trial," says Reed. "It will test your prowess and cunning against things imbued with power from the gods." For the rest of my class, enthusiasm instead of dread ripples across the room at the forewarning he grants us. Personally, it barely moves me at all. I stare at Reed not with the utter regard and reverence that everyone else does—I don't have it in me to muster the pretense after the dots I've connected—but with a placid face so I don't give away all the different ways I'm imagining slaughtering him.

Bloodlust hits me for the Tribunal conspirators too. It sinks its teeth into my gut, twisting savagely, when I think of the considerable time and effort and manipulation it would have taken to move Reed into place as Grandfather's mentee, to set Reed up to earn his trust, and then for Reed to wait for an opportune time to assassinate him. The guilty Tribune Generals would've had to be plotting against my grandfather for a long, long time to accomplish all of that. Reed might be the hand that executed him, but they are the brain that came up with this idea, the arm that maneuvered him into place, and the finger that pointed him at Grandfather and pressed the button to detonate the death blow.

Which all means I'm not stopping with Reed when I collect my kin debt. I want them dead too. All of them. I want everybody who was involved to pay. I want them charged and found guilty of treason, but I'm not going to wait if that doesn't come as quickly as I want. No matter what, I will be their executioner's blade. I will be the arm that kills them like they were the arm that killed my grandfather.

"You're dismissed to the mess. Conditioning is back on the lawn in three hours," Chance says, cutting into my thoughts. The way he steps up and in front of Reed to announce it makes clear the grievance he can't quite keep out of his tone at being upstaged.

I study the two of them with interest. This is the third time there's been some sort of animosity between our lead and co-lead, when you'd expect those positions to present a united front. Which means whatever the source, it's a deep-rooted grudge that both parties still carry if they can't wholly put it aside to conduct the trials.

It's another bit of information of potential worth I file away about

Reed. Maybe I can wield it to my advantage when the time comes and somehow use Chance to strike at Reed.

For now, I stand and approach Reed in the presenter's pit while the rest of my class files out of the room. I clutch my left shoulder and make a good show of wincing as I do it. The lull we're granted for the rest of the day is the perfect opportunity to go after Akkhad in the med tower. But first, I need to exhibit a good reason for leaving the compound and going there.

If he can put on a good act, so can I.

"I'd like to request release to the med tower," I say when I'm standing in front of Reed. "I think I've got a sprain from conditioning, and I want to have it checked out before the Survival Trial."

As he looks my shoulder over, his brow furrows like he's actually concerned, and I really want to punch him in the throat because the hell he is. He tried to kill me.

"The bioserum isn't healing me for some reason," I say to add validity to my feigned injury and to watch his reaction to me referring to the serum. Not that I think he'll reveal he knows anything—which he doesn't. He keeps the same worried expression in place, fucker, but it was worth a shot.

Keeping up the noble act that I banked on, he gives me a nod of permission. "Go get it looked at."

"DO YOU HAVE an appointment scheduled?" a receptionist asks me when I arrive at the med tower. She sits behind a glass welcome desk beside five other colleagues.

"No," I say to the middle-aged woman. She wears the white-and-gray fatigues of the Medcorps rank.

"Do you need treatment or are you here to see an admitted patient? If it's for treatment, there's about an hour's wait."

"I need an examination," I answer. "I was sent over from the Praetorian compound. I'm one of the aspirants."

Her demeanor automatically becomes more ingratiating. She sits up straighter, snaps off a salute. "Of course. I can get you seen right away."

"Is Terese Akkhad on duty? I'd like to request her as my medic." I pitch my voice low so I'm not overheard.

"Let me check." Her fingers fly over the touchscreen computer that's embedded in the glass desk at her workstation. She frowns then looks up at me in apology. "I'm sorry, Praetorian. Medic Akkhad is unavailable."

"Will she be on duty later today or tomorrow? I can come back."

"Is there a reason it needs to be Akkhad?"

Shit—think fast, Kenna. "She's treated me for this issue before," I lie, "so I just figured it'd be easier for her to get this looked at."

The woman nods, even as her face pinches in consternation. "I . . . I am very sorry. Medic Akkhad is out on extended leave. Do you have an alternate request? I'd be happy to accommodate it. Or I can recommend someone?"

Double shit. The events of yesterday and this morning cost me valuable time. If the serum Akkhad dosed me with was meant to be lethal, then her extended leave is no coincidence. My appearance on the lawn after the injection would've made it clear that Akkhad botched the kill. And when that was discovered, any shrewd person involved in treason would've tied up the loose end she became. I needed to get here sooner.

I need to get better at this spy shit, and quickly.

"It's all right," I say to the receptionist while cursing myself for not thinking of that before now. I should've been smarter and thought of a way around the delays. "I'll come back another time."

I take my time returning to the compound. On the slow walk over, I run a search on my Comm Unit for all public records on Terese Akkhad. The first results it returns are useless. She's a forty-three-year-old who graduated from the western martial academy with unremarkable exit marks and a lackluster class rank. Post Commencement, she completed her specialized medic training at a rural hospital in the western territory of Mareen, then worked there for ten years before being promoted and reassigned to the med tower on Krashen Base. As I near the Praetorian compound, I'm about to give up hope that the search will return anything significant. But stubbornness makes me plant myself on a bench that's adjacent to the front lawn and keep combing through hits. I click on an engagement announcement that contains Akkhad's name. I gape down at my Comm Unit's screen. *Akkhad* is the medic's born name.

Rhysien is her matrimony name.

The engagement announcement is for Terese Akkhad and Winton Rhysien. They were married twelve years ago, right after the promotion that landed her on Krashen Base. Winton Rhysien isn't one of Selene's brothers, and he can't be a close uncle or cousin because I've never heard the name before. The man must be a distant relation. This discovery rocks me all the same. I sit on the bench numb. An armored transport whizzes by, and its soft trail of noise sounds like a roar. Brock warned me that Selene's father might be involved, but a part of me wanted him to be wrong. The engagement announcement provides only a tenuous link, but I'd be stupid to dismiss the fact that the medic who gave me the deadly serum has ties to the Rhysien War House. It can't be a coincidence. When you're dealing with scheming Tribunes, *coincidence* holds little meaning. And it all adds up to one thing.

My best friend's father tried to kill me.

I fidget with my Comm Unit as I sit on the bench, not wanting to consider what Sutton Rhysien's involvement means for my friendship with Selene, or how it might affect it. I've met the man. I've had dinner at his house, attended parties there, both with my grandfather and for Selene. When someone is like your sister, often it makes their parents like your own. I never quite had that with Sutton, but then again, I don't know if *Selene* ever quite had fatherly affection from him. Still, she's never spoken of him with anything but respect, and often with love. So it's hard to dissociate that connection from the one I've just made about him trying to kill me. Blood being thicker than water and all that.

If there's someone who gets that, it's me.

Which means that this is something I have to face. I'd be lying to myself if I said it changes nothing. The truth is that it could change so much. It makes things so messy and complicated that it could change *everything*. It could destroy our friendship. I could lose her. The prospect terrifies me—I can't imagine life without her. Certainly can't imagine a good life without her. Yet there's no way I can pretend like I never uncovered the link and let things go. So I compartmentalize. I lock my worries about Selene away and focus on only the issue at hand: her father. First, I'll deal with Sutton Rhysien, then I'll figure out where that leaves me and Selene.

But I'm definitely going to be sleeping a little less easy next to my Rhysien roommate.

With stiff fingers, I type in a new search of public records using the name *Terese Rhysien*. She has a Krashen residence listing on base and a second one out in the southern sector, where the war house manor homes and smaller mansions owned by individual scions are located. I copy the off-base listing to an encrypted storage bin on my Comm Unit and clear the search results cache.

As much as confirming Selene's father's guilt is like a kick to the teeth, the gold lining in all of this is if Terese is married to a scion, then she likely isn't dead. To keep the Republic stable and the war houses' constant power grabs from descending into violence that could lead to a second civil war, scions and their spouses are afforded heavy protections. So if this is a massive conspiracy, Sutton, Reed, and anybody else would be hesitant to outright kill Terese, because a thorough investigation would then need to be launched to look into her death, and they'd want to avoid that. Which means the opportunity to track her down might still exist.

I won't make the same mistake I did the first time around. I'm going after her today.

I check the time on my Comm Unit. I've only used up an hour. I still have two left before today's conditioning session starts. That's plenty of time to take a public craft out to the southern sector and see if Terese is hunkering down there.

A WOMAN TOO old to be a daughter and too young to be a parent answers Terese Rhysien's door. She's dressed in brown skirts, a cream blouse, and a dark-green shawl. She looks startled to be receiving a visitor. "May I help you?"

"Is Terese Rhysien home?" I ask genially.

She looks me up and down, taking in my maroon fatigues and the unmistakable color of my skin. There aren't many places in Mareen where I can go and not be recognized, so I wait for her to connect me with the images she's seen on holoscreen newsreels. When she does, her mouth forms a silent O.

I'll take that over a sneer.

"I was seen in the med tower by Medic Rhysien a couple days ago, and I have a follow-up question that I really don't want to go over with another medic except her. But the tower told me that she took an unexpected leave of absence and can't be reached by Comm Unit. Is she home?" The explanation for me turning up on the doorstep is flimsy, but it can't be disputed by Terese if she isn't home, and if she is, well, then it won't matter anyway because I'll have verified what I came for.

"I see." The woman continues to peer at me. She pats the low bun her hair is pulled into. "My goodness. I—I'm sorry. I'm flustered that *you're* on my doorstep." She presses a hand to her chest. "I mean, Lady Rhysien's doorstep. I beg your forgiveness, again. I'm Vivi, the housekeeper. Would it be terribly out of place if I say I'm so very pleased to make your acquaintance? Your grandfather worked to improve conditions and wages for labourii a great deal. I know it's not much consolation, but I'm so grateful for everything he did, and just wanted to let you know our Republic lost a good leader. Perhaps the best leader we've ever had." Her cheeks flush. "I guess I have to ask your pardon thrice. I'm rambling, and that's not what you asked at all."

"You don't have to apologize," I say good-naturedly. I automatically know that I'll get further with the woman if I treat her with the common decency and respect most labourii don't receive but should. "I'm sure my grandfather would be gratified to hear his ideas had even some effect. Now . . . Lady Rhysien?"

"I'm so sorry. She isn't home."

"Is she in the city?"

"No, she and her husband departed for Hyacinth with no return date."

So, she is alive, at least as far as her housekeeper knows, and she's vacated her Krashen house for the western city that's Rhysien War House's seat of power.

I smile warmly. "Thank you for your time. I suppose I'll just have to pick a new medic." I frown. "Though I do hate turning all my personal details over to a brand-new stranger." The lie should cover my tracks. It's definitely something a war house scion, a powerful legacy, or the family member of a former Legatus Commander might be concerned about. The upper ranks only played nice with one another on the surface. It was always smart to closely guard any secrets or details of weaknesses.

The woman gives me a sympathetic nod. "I can imagine." But she's also a good servant, and doesn't give me more about her lady. I can respect that.

I'm also glad the visit isn't a waste. I now know Terese's home is vacant except for the housekeeper, who should be easy enough to get around when I go back to search it—houses have studies, and most studies have in-home computers. Terese's computer should be synced to her Comm Unit and a cloud storage drive, like the norm. With any luck, I'll find some sort of concrete evidence among one of those three things. She had to have received a directive to show up at the compound and target me. She also had to have received communication that the serum failed and that she was to leave the city. If she was involved with the dosing of Grandfather, there might be orders involving that as well. If something incriminating is on her drives, there's no question that it'll be locked behind passwords and encryptions. But that's a sort of proof too.

And I can get around those if I need to.

Not a waste indeed.

WHEN I RETURN to base, I have enough time left to stop by Grandfather's apartments. I drop into the chair in his office, and what I need to search Terese's drives is right where it should be. I grab the highly regulated, highly illegal mining chip out of the side drawer of his desk and pocket it. Then, I go over to the curio cabinet beside the desk because there's something else in the office I want. My eyes go immediately to the spot where the mate to the knife Reed swiped should rest.

It's empty. The blue steel dagger isn't there.

Where the hell is it?

It can't be anywhere else in the apartments. Grandfather was set in his habits, to a fault, and he's kept that dagger in the curio cabinet for as long as I've been alive. That dagger *was* in the cabinet before his death. I saw it with my own eyes when I visited him at home two days before he died. If the blade is missing from its place, that means it was stolen. Given the timing of when it was lifted, it's not a far leap in logic to conclude that the person who took it is the same person who made the quiet, clean death in Grandfather's office look like a heart attack.

Darius Reed has both *my knives.*

He probably swiped Grandfather's as some sick kill trophy. Blue steel is highly prized, and there's maybe only a dozen blades circulating outside of Khanai. As furious as I am that he'd have the audacity, I'm also fucking elated. If the blade is in his possession, that proves he's the killer. It isn't all the evidence I need—I still need a kill order or some other smoking gun—but it'll be a solid start.

I smile, thinking about finding Reed with the dagger. Because the weapon he stole is going to be the exact thing I gut him with, both literally and metaphorically. So, in addition to searching Terese Rhysien's home, I also need to search Reed's apartment in the compound. The latter will be much harder, though. I'll have to evade detection by Reed himself as well as the slew of in-residence Praetorians aside from any of our officers who might be around.

Not to mention my fellow aspirants. And my friends.

And Selene . . . who I'm already starting to question as a friend, which is like a punch to my lungs.

I shake off that feeling and sit back down at Grandfather's desk to test out a theory of how I might break into Reed's quarters. Every last Tribune is arrogant to a fault. That pomposity might mean Grandfather's murderers didn't bother to wipe all the access codes of a dead man. Hoping that's true, I turn on Grandfather's computer and navigate to the Tribunal's secure record files. An encrypted screen pops up, along with a password box.

I punch in the random sequence of five letters and four numbers Grandfather made sure I knew, and it gets me into the files. A joyless smile twists my lips because of the reason I have the code in the first place—insurance. Grandfather gave me the codes in case something exactly like this happened to him. He wanted me to be able to do whatever I thought needed to come next.

I do not sink into the fresh grief and misery that crashes into me when I consider this. I shake it off because there's too much I've got to do. Grandfather doesn't need my sorrow. He needs me to expose what really happened to him and make sure the people responsible don't get away with it. Not just for revenge, although that's driving me pretty hard. But because Verne Amari genuinely cared about the Republic and—more important—*all* the people in it. People like Vivi, and Zayne's parents.

This is so much bigger than me.

And this knowledge grounds me . . . and makes me want to take out these motherfuckers even more.

I copy layouts of the compound's upper level to my Comm Unit, along with the floor and exact location of Reed's apartment. The Tribunal's conceit is about to get me Reed, and Reed can be another avenue I use to get to them.

6

"ARE YOU SURE YOU DON'T want to come to the card game?" Selene slides her hands out of the mini lacquer applicator in the center of her bed. She inspects the fresh coat of flirty pink polish it applied for imperfections. "It'll be good for you to get out of the room and do something not related to our possible impending deaths. If I need it, you *definitely* need it."

"I'm good. I'm exhausted. But have fun and don't bleed Enzo's pockets too dry."

"I won't. I took him up on that offer to put something other than credits on the table this time," she drops casually.

I almost fall over the side of my bed, and it isn't from my exhaustion. "You're breaking your rule?"

She shrugs. "I don't know what tomorrow will involve, but Reed made the coming Survival Trial seem heavy. Sex relaxes me and puts me on my A game. Plus, in the event he, or I, don't come out on the other side . . . this last moment will be nice. I guess."

Oh, my girl *tries* to be flippant, but her ass is totally transparent.

Which is why it's so hard to think she knows anything about her father's complicity in Grandfather's death.

It's what makes all of this so hard.

That's not the reason I'm begging off, though. I yawn, too tired to really give her a hard time about breaking her rule for Enzo or point out what that means. Our second day of "conditioning," aka Chance's torture fest, lasted until after sundown. Strong or not, I was pushed to my limit—especially since I'd used my mealtime to snoop—and now I lie down in bed and pull the sheets up to my shoulders. The hard mattress beneath me feels like luxury. My eyes cross from heaviness. "At least squeeze in a few hours' sleep between rounds with Enzo."

She throws me a wicked wink as she hops off her bed. "Fuck today. Sleep tomorrow."

I half groan, half giggle, delirious with the need to become unconscious. "That's a butchery of the Praetorian motto."

Whatever she says I don't hear.

I WAKE TO the feeling of my arms pinned against the mattress. My eyes pop open to a familiar tousle of blond hair, gloating golden eyes, and an obnoxious leer. I don't hesitate—I knee Caiman in the groin and dig my elbow into Greysen's neck. Greysen coughs, clutching at his windpipe and gulping down air. I should have crushed it. Then his attempt to breathe would be futile.

I don't have time to regret it though—Caiman reacts with lightning speed. I roll to the side before the blow hurtling toward my jaw lands. I immediately hop to my feet and jump from the middle of the bed to the floor. I face Caiman and a recovered Greysen.

"How the hell did you get in here?" I snarl. The door is programmed to open for my handprint and Selene's.

"The ex–Legatus Commander is no longer around to protect you," Caiman answers darkly. "You should have declared a rank more befitting of what you are. Faded into obscurity and let the name Amari die."

"Are you delusional? Even if I did declare something other than Praetorian, that would never happen. The name Amari will always be synonymous with the man who saved the Republic's ass."

"You're a disgrace to the rank." He spits at my feet. "Your grandfather was a disgrace to the office of Legatus Commander."

He sounds exactly how the Alpha cohort dick did at the bar. "I get it. He saved our country. He was leading it toward a better place. You hate him because of that. And me. Me, mostly because of my skin color, but also because I remind you of the fact that none of your 'pure' families could stop the Blood Emperor. Real fucking original. Try forming a thought independent of what your father and the rest of the assholes in the Republic think."

He reddens at my accusation but has the wherewithal to sputter, "The truth doesn't need to be original."

Did he seriously just say that corny shit? "Get out." I don't yell. I say it calm and collected, trying to keep my cool but also keeping my stance loose, my eyes taking in everything.

Caiman smirks. Greysen does the same. Like Caiman, I'm pretty sure there isn't an original bone in Greysen's body. He exists to be a carbon copy of the friend he worships.

"Not that you've ever had any authority, Amari, but you especially don't right now," Caiman says.

"Akulu," Greysen adds.

"It's sad that's the only thing you can think to call me. You should get more creative. Or get a thesaurus—that's a book full of synonyms.

Do you know what synonyms are, Greysen?" I shake my head. "'Akulu.' So stupid. The slur stopped hitting its mark eight years ago." When you've been called something all your life, either out loud or in people's heads, at some point the insult loses its serrated edge.

But they didn't come for an etymology lesson or to learn how to spew better insults. They both take a step forward at the same time. I don't take a step back. What I want to do is take my own steps forward. Several of them in fact. Instead, I exercise the discipline and restraint I didn't in the bar and stay rooted to the floor.

"What are you going to do?" I can hazard several guesses, but I want to see if I can talk my way out of this.

No such luck—Caiman brandishes a double-edged combat-grade Mareenian knife that he snatched out of the holder strapped to his side. "The Legatus Commander is dead. Maybe his kin should be dead too. Maybe when Selene stumbles back in after getting screwed by some guy with a garbage pedigree, she should find you like your Grandfather found your akulu whore mother. Her throat was slit from ear to ear, right? How many stab wounds was it? Eleven? Twelve? No, thirteen. Her body lay cold and dead for a day in a pool of blood before Verne found his daughter. That's one thing the Republic should thank that godsforsaken heathen Blood Emperor across the sea for. He knocked the great Verne Amari back down a few notches."

No . . . he didn't just say that.

Because at the mention of my mother, a topic I never discuss, the thing inside me I've been holding tightly coiled snaps. I forget the promise I made to my grandfather. To Brock. To myself.

The palm of my right hand smashes into Caiman's nose. It spurts blood. Greysen's hand clutches at my right elbow. Or rather, it tries to. It barely grazes it before I'm spinning around and my heel is connecting with his gut. As he doubles over, I bring my leg back and quickly drive it up again, my knee smashing into his chest. Greysen collapses to the floor, groaning and grabbing at cracked ribs. I drop to a knee and deliver a jab to his right temple. He's out of commission, which should make this easier.

Kill them. Kill them. Kill them.

The wild insistence rides me. I know it's my Pantheon-blessed gift igniting in my blood. I shake it off. I can't kill Caiman Rossi. Greysen, I could probably get away with by claiming self-defense. His father isn't a Tribune. If I kill Caiman, my death is following close behind.

An uppercut to my chin makes stars explode around the room. Caiman sweeps his left foot out in a move I anticipate a split second late. My back smacks against the floor first. The back of my skull thuds against it two seconds later. Blinding pain splits my skull, my vision blurs, and two Caimans stand over me instead of one. He drops to the floor and covers my body with his, pinning me in place. Fire lances through my left shoulder when Caiman's knife stabs into it.

"That's one," he whispers into my ear.

Another lance of fire. This time above my right breast. "Two."

A third lance. My side. "Three."

Black blinks in and out across my vision. I take a chance and lurch my head forward toward one of the Caimans, satisfied with the crunch of my skull against his already-broken nose. His weight lessens as he grunts. My knee connects with his balls, and as he gives me a little room, my fist does the same to his stomach. I shove him off me and push to my feet. He's on his feet just as fast.

I blink, not expecting him to get a second wind so quickly. Shit. I thought I had time to make it to the door. He should have been knocked out of commission for at least a *little* bit with my headbutt/crotch-kick combo.

I don't have time to dwell on it, though. More pressing is the question: What am I going to do about him now?

I can't injure him much more than I already have, and I definitely can't kill him. I'm bleeding and tangled in a situation I don't see a clear way out of. The one thing I'm pretty sure of is that one of us probably isn't going to leave here under their own power—Caiman isn't just going to call a truce and walk out of my room.

As we stare each other down, more than my death blazes in his eyes. An all-consuming, raw fury stoked by blind bigotry rampages like a wild animal across his face. "One of us isn't leaving this room alive," he says. "And I sure as hell am not about to be the one who dies."

I already thought that, you unimaginative son of a bitch.

"Yeah, well, it's not about to be me either." I crouch into a defensive stance, rolling my shoulders and shifting my weight to the balls of my feet so I can strike out with brutal speed and accuracy if he charges at me.

I am so fucked because now there is only one way out of this, and if I take that path, I risk exposure. But if I don't, I have to kill Caiman if I want to survive, and then I'm dead anyway.

Do it! My Pantheon-blessed gift roars.

And this time I listen to it.

Both my blood and Caiman's blood are mixed on my skin. That's all I need.

I lock eyes with Caiman. The force of the bloodlink I establish between us knocks the breath from my lungs. It's worse for Caiman—his gold eyes turn vacant. His muscles go slack. I slap my hands against my knees and hunch over, sucking in breaths and forcing my trembling body still. I need to finish this, then take care of all the blood. There's too much of it leaking from me. The magic signature will be massive. I peer up at Caiman. I wince at the absence of consciousness behind his eyes. I've reduced him to a mindless puppet. *My* mindless puppet. The Blood Emperor of Accacia is notorious for this stunt. I shudder at the comparison to Grandfather's mortal enemy. *I am not him,* I tell myself. *I am not the monster who slaughtered half a continent, murdered my mother, and tried to kill me in her womb to strike at Grandfather.*

But I am going to use his power.

"Leave," I tell Caiman through stinted breaths. "Go to your room and go to bed. Take Greysen with you. When the two of you turned up here tonight, I kicked your asses and then you retreated because you decided to save your miserable lives. When you wake up and the bloodlink has faded, you will remember exactly that."

With jerky, robotic movements, Caiman crosses the room, heaves an unconscious Greysen over his shoulder, and exits.

I slide to the floor instead of rushing to the bathroom, bury my head between my knees, and vomit. I've never used my abominable gift like that before. I feel like death. The gods never give without exacting a price. Using their blessings takes a toll. The tremors wracking my body won't stop. I need to get to the shower. I'm covered in too much of my own blood, and I need to dilute it before the magic signature turns into a beacon. The Tribunal has a Pantheon-blessed lodestone enhanced with homing intelligence in the Pinnacle Tower. It was the one Pantheon-blessed thing they didn't exile from Mareen when they decided high-tech weapons and combat augmentations was Mareen's new doctrine. Now that I've used my power like this, it's only a matter of time before the beacon catches wind of my magic and the Praetorians come, not to train me but to kill me.

Fear and anxiety suck all the air from the room, leaving my chest burning and on the verge of exploding. It takes everything to push past it, and then all my remaining energy to crawl to the bathroom and turn on the shower. I heave myself under the cold spray of water. It's agony. So is the screaming panic in my mind.

I need to get back to the room. Need to drench the bedroom with water to dilute my blood. Need to scrub everything clean. Need to . . .

Need to not slip into oblivion from the rapid blood loss that's going to damn me.

"KENNA. KENNA. KENNA, wake up."

Selene's voice is distorted and far away. My mind drags itself awake, hovering in a state between reality and fog.

Hands shake my shoulders. A mattress is beneath me. I passed out in the shower. *My blood.* I'm fucked . . .

"Come on, Kenna, wake up. I need you to wake up." A pause. "There was so much blood. I don't know what happened. If you hear me at all, wake up. I patched you up the best I could." Her voice drops to a whisper. "Your skin . . . it's burning up. Blood kept pouring from your nose. It was a lot of blood, Kenna. I probably should have gotten help. I probably should still go get help. Yeah, I should. Okay. I'm leaving to do that. I'll be right back. Hang on."

I jerk fully alert and shoot up to a sitting position in the bed.

My shirt has been stripped away. White medgauze covers my neck, chest, and side. The regeneration salve on the bandages itches like a bitch. I dig my fingers into the mattress so I don't scratch at anything and reopen wounds.

Blood. There was too much blood left in the room before and I've been bleeding more since. I wipe at my nose. It's dry at the moment. The sheets around me are clean. So is the floor beside the bed. "Where is it?"

Selene looks at me as wild-eyed and frantic as I stare at her. "Where is what?"

I jump up. My legs tremble. I steady myself against the bed. "My blood on the floor, where is it? The blood from my nose, what did it get on? What did you clean my blood up with?"

"I . . . towels."

I grab her arm. "Selene. Where are the towels? I have to dilute the blood."

"Bathroom. The towels are in the bathroom."

I rush to the bathroom, grab the bloodied towels off the concrete floor, and throw them in the shower. I don't start breathing easier until water rushes from the shower head and soaks them. I should burn the towels. It's safest and smartest to burn them. Grandfather always burned the things I bled excessively on. I can't do that down here. The smoke detectors will go off in the close confines and my doing it outside on the grounds will look suspicious.

Selene watches me from the doorway. "Why do you need to dilute your blood? That's a ritual the Accacian blood-gifted perform." Her quiet voice isn't accusing. It's taxed with worry.

"It's—it's also a Khanaian superstition. Sorry, I just freaked. I'm okay," I assure her. "I'm good." I say it again because she doesn't look anywhere close to convinced—whether about my excuse or that I'm okay, I'm not sure.

"You had three stab wounds. You were passed out in the shower. What happened?"

I laugh without mirth. "Golden Boy Caiman happened." I touch a hand to my tender side. I know without removing the medgauze that my wounds are nearly healed because of my blood-gift. I sag against the glass pane of the shower, staring at the water swirling red with my blood. A constant stream of crimson seeps from the towel and down the drain, taking some of my tension with it.

"Kenna," Selene says hesitantly. "Do you have the blood-gift?"

"Yes," I heave. I could keep denying it, but for some reason that feels wrong, even with what I think I know about her father. In fact, it feels *right* to tell her. Which makes me feel better—like I haven't lost her.

There's also the fact that there's no other truly believable explanation for what she just saw me do. The former excuse I slid her was paper thin. Khanaians have no such rituals, and if they did, Mareen would make it its business to know about it, educate its citizens on it, and train us to be extremely vigilant with the neighbors mimicking blood practices.

"Did the Legatus Commander have it? The gifts were generational." I see Selene grasping to put pieces of an outlandish puzzle together in her mind. Her eyes widen at the conclusion she comes to and she doesn't cover up the automatic revulsion in time.

"No," I grit out. "He didn't have a trace of Accacian blood."

"Then where did you get it from? Was it—" She knows we don't talk about my mother or the circumstances surrounding my conception. Except now, of course, we are.

It was simple enough, really. Grandfather's elevation to Legatus Commander meant he could afford gene manipulation and a surrogate carrier. Without needing a wife, he gave himself a daughter who was like him. Part Mareenian and part Khanaian. He'd create a fifteenth war house of Mareen with the Khanaian blood that the Republic had used to limit what his own father could become. However, my mother went rogue. Or, as I like to think of it, she was human. So she had a child the common way, one whose genome wasn't spliced and mapped prior to conception.

Me.

"I suppose from whoever my father is," I say. Though he never let it show toward me, I imagine Grandfather was furious about my blind origins. I guess it worked out in the end, though, because the random genetic die that got cast gave Grandfather what he wanted anyway. A grandchild to carry on the Amari name who was as remarkable and matchless a scion as one from any war house. It's why he didn't resent me having the gift and the heritage of his hated enemy. My mother's transgression helped his cause.

It just wasn't helping me right now.

"You think your father was Accacian?"

"All evidence points to it. Grandfather's father was full-blooded Khanaian and his mother was full-blooded Mareenian."

I wait for the condemnation to darken her gaze. For revulsion to cloud her face like it did when she'd thought Grandfather had Accacian lineage. It will hurt, but I won't fault her for it. The Accacians *are* our enemies.

Instead, she looks at me with pity, and I can't decide if that's worse. "How?" she asks. "I mean I know how. But *how?*"

I'd have liked to know the same thing. Grandfather always refused to give me details—I'm guessing he knew very little to begin with—

and you can't extract information from a dead woman. "Your guess is as good as mine. Grandfather thought it'd be better for me if everyone thought my darker coloring came from a Khanaian father."

Selene walks into the bathroom and sits on the commode. "That makes sense. The Accacians are despised. You would have been despised too."

She's right. People knowing of my Accacian lineage would have subjected me to even greater prejudice. Hatred in Mareen for the Accacian emperor and the aggressions he committed against the Republic before, during, and still after the war runs deep. And yet, she doesn't despise me right now.

"You're taking this all relatively well."

"Well, duh. How else would I take it? What would I do?"

I meet her eyes. Her expression shifts from bewilderment to hurt. She comes over to the shower and takes my face between her hands. "You didn't think how I feel about you would change did you?"

I look down at my bare feet, too raw and exposed to keep looking at her. She has always had my back and I've always had hers. But my Accacian heritage is different from all those other times and every other thing that makes us different. "It could have changed things," I admit into the terse silence.

"No, it couldn't," she says, seething.

She's pissed, angry enough that I swear I see mini flames spark in her gray eyes that match the color of her hair.

She pulls me into a hug that crushes me against her chest. "Nothing could cause me to stop having your back and being your best friend. If you told me your blood-gift comes from the Accacian emperor himself, my reaction would be the exact same."

I wince from the force of her embrace.

She jumps back. "That was stupid. Sorry. Did I hurt you?"

"I'm still tender. That's all." Since my secret is out between us, I peel away the medgauze at my side, then do the same with the gauze at my neck and chest. I show her the knitted-together skin beneath the thick coat of clear regeneration salve in all three spots. My skin is the pinkish-brown of newly generated epithelial cells. The bioserum I was injected with after the first trial would've healed the stab wounds on my side and neck, but not the mortal one to my chest.

If she had been unsure before, the proof is now standing before her. It's one thing for her to *hear* of the gift I have and not recoil. It's another thing entirely for her to *see* it.

Her eyes widen at the mended flesh. She raises a tenuous hand between us and then drops it at her side. There's no mistaking the slight shudder that ripples over her. I understand it, but I can't curb the sharp hurt. My best friend, *my sister*, might not detest me, but she is terrified of my abilities, and that's equally as painful.

And now I worry that I made a mistake telling her . . . and that hurts most of all.

7

"HOW LONG HAVE YOU BEEN up?" asks Selene.

I pause in my task and turn around to find her sitting up in bed. Although I showed her proof I was good as new last night, she watches me like I'm still injured.

"An hour." I wait while she considers me after a night's sleep, after her panic over my wounds has subsided and she's thinking rationally again. I brace for the full-blown disgust that didn't come last night—or even just for things to stand awkward between us after that shudder.

She cocks an eyebrow at the cache of weapons—blaster guns, knives, throwing stars, sundisks, flamespitters—spilled onto my bed. "Did you rob the armory tower while I was asleep? Are you planning a coup? If so, I'm in."

My smile is goofy. Huge. Her wiseass crack lifts a million tons of pressure from my chest. No matter what happened last night, we're still solid. We're still *us.* "You're hilarious. No—droids delivered them with the suits." I point a double-edged throwing knife at her combat-grade black microprene suit hanging from a hook on the wall. I'm wearing mine.

I slide the knife into my left boot, pick up its twin, and slide it into my right boot. Two blasters sit in holsters at my sides. A third blaster—a fifty-caliber Desert Phoenix—gets concealed at the base of my spine beside a knife with a wickedly curved blade. Sharp and pointy toys are more my thing, but the Desert Phoenix is a beauty. It has a six-inch barrel, is light as sand, and the recoil is nonexistent. It's a semi-automatic, self-loading, magazine-fed masterpiece in precision that only gets issued to Praetorians. We got to play with them once during marksman training in the academy, and I've had wet dreams about carrying my own ever since. For the first time since I got here, I'm actually a little excited to become a Praetorian for reasons other than revenge.

I tuck several throwing stars, sundisks, and flamespitters out of sight along my body. I'm weighed down with the best weapons Mareen has to offer, and yet I feel light, mostly because I'm missing the weight of Grandfather's blue-steel Khanaian blade. Its absence feels like I'm missing a limb. Reed has it, and Reed is going to return my shit to me, *both blades*, before this is all over.

It's only a matter of whether I pry them out of his hands or back—or blow a hole in his head with my new Desert Phoenix.

"Why do you look all homicidal and the sun isn't even up?"

"I was thinking about Reed and my knives—*I mean knife.*"

Selene cackles.

"It's not funny."

She laughs harder until she's wiping her eyes. "But it kind of is. He's really under your skin. Is this about the Combat Trial? Are you pissed because nobody has ever bested you like that before?"

She's still chuckling. I snatch a pillow off the bed and hurl it at her face. "And nobody *has* bested me. He definitely didn't. It was a draw." It doesn't matter if time running out on our fight was the reason. "Since we're on the subject of people *under* our skin though—let's talk about you and Enzo last night, *rulebreaker.*"

She stops laughing. *Ha!*

She grabs her Comm Unit off a small table beside her bed, pointedly ignoring me. "It's almost sunrise. Guess I should get up."

I let the Enzo thing go—for now—and toss her the microprene suit. "You should."

She studies her nails after she catches it. "These should definitely be black today. I'm feeling murderous too. Particularly toward Caiman and his lapdog." She eyes me again. "You positive you're okay?"

I peel down the high neck of my suit. I show her that the flesh at my neck is back to its normal dark brown, without a scar in sight. "My chest and side look the same. I feel great. Let's go kick some ass."

Mollified, she smiles and slides out of bed, stretches, then disrobes. The uniform fits her lush curves tight as a glove. The supple, durable, high-tech material it's made from can withstand UV bullets, knife slashes, flames, and frigid conditions as low as negative 90 degrees Celsius. Which means if I find myself stranded in the coldest place on Iludu—like the Ice Wastes, with consistent temps hovering around negative 80 Celsius—I'll survive. For a little while, at least. I turn the collar of my suit back up, shuddering. I really hope that's not where we're headed for this next trial. I fucking hate the cold.

Selene pads over to my bed and eyes the weapons. As I buckle on three more knives and another gun, she gets to work concealing a mini armory against her body too.

When we step out into the hall, the fucking Death Board stares us in the face. The senior Praetorians are really trying to screw with us going into this thing, because it's plastered along the length of the walls and the ceiling in repeated copies. It flickers between the accurate version with 801 names without a slash—we didn't lose anyone to day two of conditioning—and a version where some new names are crossed out . . . and a third where all of our names are crossed out. The mindfuck works.

Selene and I, and everybody else, amass in the hall to head upstairs. We stand paralyzed, rooted to the floor, and staring at it. The absolute silence that persists might as well be a death knell. It douses whatever high spirits we might have mustered. The three versions of the board continue to flash back and forth. Then the one that shows everybody as dead remains fixed on the walls.

"Take a good look." Chance's voice comes over the speakers. "This could be reality. In the trials, in a skirmish, or in a war. That fact is what the second trial is about. If you want to live, you're going to have to do more than earn the right. You're going to have to endure hell and come out on the other side whole. Expect your numbers to be slashed in the triple digits. Any of you can perish."

I don't know who reaches for whom first. All I know is I feel the brush of Selene's hand, and our fingers lace together.

She squeezes my hand. "We get through this . . ."

I squeeze hers back. "Like we got through the academy."

"Together."

"Together."

"PUT THEM ON," Chance orders us aspirants as our transition officers pass out red velvet hoods.

"Remember what I said in the dome," Reed says as he hands a hood to the aspirant on my left. "Be smart. Think critically. If you can do that, you'll stay alive."

Chance scowls at his words of encouragement. I think he'd scowl at his mother telling him good morning.

Reed holds a hood out to me. I snatch it from him and slip it over my head. His rough-callused hand bands around my arm. He marches me forward, and it takes everything in me not to panic that he's so close to me when I'm so vulnerable. But he won't kill me, I don't think, in cold blood with witnesses around.

"I want my knife back," I let him know.

"I want to be Legatus. Sometimes we don't get what we want. That blade is contraband. It's mine."

He is so full of shit. And the fact that he mentioned the Legatus like he didn't murder one . . . it's taking all my willpower to keep my hands from his throat.

"How is it contraband when you all just gave us a stockpile of weapons?" This has nothing to do with the rules of the trials and we both know it.

"We *lent* you weapons and *permitted* their use today. Yesterday, possessing one was contraband. It was in your report-for-duty instructions. As was the command that you obey everything we tell you."

I bite the inside of my cheek to keep from saying something reckless or smashing my fist into his face. I want my damn knives, but I know it's not the time. Yet.

"Watch your step," he mutters right before the ground slopes.

I'm pondering what he means by that when shrill, early morning sunlight penetrates the velvet fabric of the hood as we exit the compound. The Torrid Season heat warms my face and neck beneath the hood by several suffocating degrees. I hear the low, idling hum of a grounded stealth jet, and we stop moving. The trademark purr tells me it's an eighth-generation GH-17—a sleek, chrome beauty outfitted with enough firepower to level a city in seconds.

Reed leads me across the pavement and up the jet's loading ramp. The echoing cavern of a cargo bay greets me. I wish I weren't blindfolded so I could marvel properly at the masterpiece of stealth, speed, and perfection. I've never seen one up close. A GH-17 can turn invisible with the press of a button and circle the entire planet in less than twelve hours.

I'm marched out of the bay and into more silent surroundings. Misjudging the height, I plop down into the seat Reed guides me to. I hear the commotion of more aspirants settling into seats around me.

The GH-17 is spacious enough to tote a small militia. All us aspirants plus the officers fit comfortably.

A while later, my spine slams against my seat as the jet takes off. I listen to the whirring of its twin engines for an indeterminate amount of time, musing at the irony that the jet's design isn't a feat that Mareen can claim. Khanai is king of air and space, and the Republic forks over tons of credits and weapons tech in exchange for the superior jets. I'm infinitely smug about that. The Republic believes people who look like me are so inferior, and yet without our engineering *and* combat-arts brilliance—since Mareenian combat training borrows from Xzana principles too—the Republic's great military would be hobbled.

My pride drops a peg when my stomach dips during a quick descent. The aircraft plummets toward the ground, then pulls up short and smoothly slides to a stop. The hood is snatched from my head, and I finally get a chance to take in my surroundings. My glee is cut short when Chance steps into my line of sight. His dull blue eyes light up like a prank is about to happen that only he is privy to. His pink lips curl up in a grin. "You're with me, Amari." He yanks Dex's hood off, Caiman's, Greysen's, Petre's, and the hood of one other aspirant who used to hang tough with Caiman when we were cadets. I groan. Great. I have to contend with Caiman and his asshole friends while trying to stay alive during whatever this trial is.

"Move out," Chance orders.

Refusing to have Caiman and crew at my back, I wait for the four of them to fall in line behind Chance before I move. I descend the ramp behind Greysen and in front of Dex.

Anybody would know where they've taken us at first glimpse. Onei's Expanse is one of the Wonders of Iludu, and there's no other forest on the planet like it. I've seen dozens of drone-captured vids of the unclaimed wilds that sprawl between the Kingdom of Khanai and our onetime ally, the Federation of Lythe.

Trees that stretch to the sky with ash-white bark and jewel-black leaves spread out, a vast sea around me. The forest is named a wonder for the trees' black leaves and glittering fruit of the same color but also because of something else—the something that makes any excitement I might have felt at having my hood off dissipate rapidly. I feel the sinisterness in the dense, sticky air as we step onto the amber soil. Low-lying bushes and shrubs with leaves that glimmer the same onyx as the ones on the trees cover the forest floor. My stomach kicks into somersaults. I might've preferred to be dropped in the Ice Wastes. The same ancient stories that recount the times the gods walked the planet and doled out gifts during the Pantheon Age—the ones my grandfather insisted on telling me—warn that Onei's Expanse suffers no trespassers. The forest itself is said to be a living thing—a vengeful deity of the Iludu Pantheon trapped in forest form.

And this is where they drop us.

"Like the rest of your counterparts, you're trekking through this hellscape for four days," Chance says, a sense of glee on his lips and in his eyes. "The trial is to survive Onei's Expanse. Outgoing and incoming signals from your Comm Units have been jammed except for the locator signal so we can track you. If you exit before your time is up or desert your group, you fail the trial and forfeit your life. Praetorians aren't cowards or deserters." He strides back to the stealth jet chuckling. Before he boards, he turns to us wearing a pure, wicked look. "By the way—you've also gotta retrieve the head of an Accursed while you're here. Prove to me you've got the balls to hold my rank."

I gape after his retreating form, and a quick glance shows similar feelings of incredulity. What he's asked is impossible. He really has made good on his promise to try his damnedest to ensure we all die. Because if we survive Onei's Expanse for four days (and that's a big *if*), there is no way in the gods-created hell we're surviving an attack on an Accursed.

Why not just kill us at the base and save everyone the trouble of all this pomp?

The jet's ramp whizzes up into its underbelly. It zooms off to drop the next group in another section of the forest. I watch it leave until it disappears from view. Selene and Zayne are aboard the jet. My friends are being carted away from me. Carted to their deaths. The urge to run in the direction the jet vanished and track them down courses through me, even though that task is as impossible as hunting an Accursed for his head. Onei's Expanse is vast enough that we could all wander its maze of trees for a year without bumping into one another. I look at the lot I was chosen to endure this trial with and sigh—I'm positive the sick choice was intentional. I assess Dex. I might have an ally in him.

Or I might be all by myself.

"What do we do?" Petre asks.

"Survive," Caiman says with an inflated bravado that I'm positive Onei's Expanse will soon rip to shreds.

Right on cue, a furious howl as unnatural as the feeling of the forest itself shakes the trees. The howl echoes again, angrier than before.

"Let's move," Caiman says, throwing a look at the thick foliage. Whatever the source of the howl is, the flora is concealing it well. But it sounds close. "We aren't going to survive this piece-of-shit forest by dicking around for the next four days."

Neither will we survive it by following a dick.

It's not that I disagree with his idea that we move, but I'm not committing myself to his leadership either. My boots crunch against dead leaves that have turned from onyx to coal black. I've strategically placed myself at the rear of the group.

"Do you have a plan other than for us to traipse around and pray we don't die?" I ask Caiman.

"*You* might need prayers. I don't. My top marks will see me through this."

Does he seriously think the fact that he graduated with good grades is going to keep him alive out here? "What are you going to do: use your report card as a shield? Will those top marks see you through the hunt of a dangerous subhuman beast without discussing a plan? One of them has the strength to tear through a horde of us, and guess what? They travel in *packs*."

"She's right. It's smarter to form a solid plan up front," Dex says.

"Nobody asked you, southern boy."

"Nobody didn't ask him either," I say, but Caiman is already ignoring both of us.

Damn Chance to the deepest level of hell for giving us orders to stay together and making me have to work with this arrogant piece of shit. This trial would be less of a godsfuck if I could simply go it alone.

I'm sure there's a lesson there, but right now the only thing I care about is being alive in four days.

That may not be in the cards, though. A whiff of dirt and sap and rot and ruin stings my nose. Caiman and company pick up the smell too. Dex is the last to react, and I can't help but worry for him—he needs to be quicker with his instincts. He smashes a heavy boot into fallen leaves, making a loud crunch.

He needs to be a lot fucking quieter too.

"Don't make another move," I whisper lower than the soft wind that rustles the trees, the same breeze that's bringing more of the noxious odor that's making my eyes water.

Dex turns his head, careful not to shift the weight of his body to make more leaves crunch. He raises a quizzical eyebrow at me.

I slice my head to the left, not daring to speak the word "Accursed" aloud. We're not ready to face the pack that's near. We don't have a plan to survive them. We don't have a plan to isolate one. We don't have anything other than confusion and bickering, and right now the one thing I'm sure of is that rushing into that particular fight half-cocked will get us dead.

Yet we all stand frozen—even me. Bowel-loosening terror unites us. We scan the trees that camouflage the creatures, their skins blending perfectly into the forest so they can better stalk trespassers. Recorded histories purport that the Accursed were once Lytheian men who fool-ishly petitioned Onei, goddess of the hunt, for immortality. She granted their wish by changing them into soulless creatures confined to prowl-ing and patrolling the forest for eternity. Now they're prowling for us, with their ash-white skin as hard and rough-textured as tree bark, their onyx-dark eyes, stone-smooth bald heads, and unbreakable bones all nearly as ancient and as powerful as the Expanse itself.

Or so the legends go. Either way, I don't think they're going down easy.

The breath I've been holding expels as I register the pungent scent is getting weaker not stronger. They were close but are now moving away from us. I shudder, but gather myself quickly, with just the slightest bit of guilt. I'm glad they're leaving, but not if what drew their attention was Zayne's or Selene's group. *That's irrational*, I tell myself—the Prae-torians would have dropped us leagues apart to further fuck with us.

"Are we following after them?" Greysen asks hoarsely. His tone begs for the answer to be no.

Petre and Brylin, the fifth member of the group I'm stuck with, look to Caiman for a decision.

"What do you think, Ikenna?" Dex asks.

"Who cares what she—" Greysen begins.

"Shut the hell up so I can think," Caiman interrupts. He's rattled. The nearness of the pack this soon after our drop has blasted a hole in that bravado he stepped into the forest with.

"If we go after them right now, we're dead," I say. "We need to lure one away from its pack. The five of us might be able to best a single Ac-cursed if we attack him in a concerted effort. It's easy to work one into a mindless frenzy if it scents human blood." *I got top marks, too, Caiman.* "We can use that to our advantage."

"That's an okay plan," Caiman concedes grudgingly.

It's a terrible plan; it still means going up against the Accursed, but it's a damn better one since his ass can't counter with anything else.

"How do we draw one away from the group?" Dex asks.

"I don't have an answer to that problem yet."

Nobody else can offer a solution either.

Caiman uses this lull to his advantage. "We move, for now," he says, resuming control. "We can figure it out while we put distance between us and this clearing. We've lingered long enough for our human scent to be all over the place."

I don't disagree. The forest swarms with creatures Onei created to have a hunger for humans, and the Accursed are only one of them.

WITHOUT BEING CLOSER to an answer about how to fulfill our hunt, we trudge through the godsforsaken forest until the little sunlight that squeezes through the black canopy disappears. Strokes of moonlight from Iludu's triplet moons—crescents tonight—paint the understory in silver ribbons. We stumble across a small glen free of the trees that crowd the rest of the Expanse.

Caiman steps into the center of it and turns in an assessing circle. "We stop here and rest. We'll have a wide-open view of anything that comes at us."

I give him my most incredulous look. "And it will have a wide-open view of us."

Caiman ignores me and sets to work assigning us jobs.

"That's not a good idea," I advise when he tells Dex to get a fire going to light the clearing better.

"Nobody asked you, Amari."

"And again, I didn't ask you to ask me. I'm *telling* you—a fire won't only endanger your miserable life, it will endanger mine too. Onei's creatures are drawn to heat and flame."

Greysen hawks up a wad of snot and spits on the ground. "You sound like one of those old Khanaian Sight-Gifted hacks that still fear myth and magic and the fucking Iludu gods. We bested those bastards a millennium ago. We proved man and tech beats magic and divinity. We can start a fire and deal with whatever it draws."

Of course he wasn't squawking that tune when Onei's Accursed were a few feet away. But time—and distance—makes fools of us all.

Great fools, in Greysen's case.

"I don't care what I sound like. We're not starting a fire. I'm not being torn apart by whatever was emitting that howl earlier, or something else for that matter, just so you and Caiman can stop being scared of the dark."

"Fuck you, Ikenna," Greysen says. "You're not the leader here."

"You're not either. And neither is Caiman. I don't remember Chance assigning one of us the position."

"Oh really? Who is going to challenge that?" Caiman looks around at the others, who will all defer to him. He's a guy; I'm a girl. He's full Mareenian; I'm not. His father is Haymus Rossi and the new Legatus Commander; my grandfather is dead.

And even though this is about survival and common sense, it's almost as if those things are working against me right now.

Dex rubs the exposed tanned skin on the back of his neck. "Given the old stories of the forest and its goddess, I don't think a fire is such a good idea either."

Caiman's eyes darken at Dex's disagreement. "Tough shit. I'd rather be attacked by something that I can see than something I can't. You two are welcome to find another place to pass the night if you don't agree."

"You're an idiot," I tell Caiman. But I can't go. If I separate from the group, the transition officers tracking my Comm Unit will know. And if I stay with the group, I'm dead too. Caiman in his stupidity is determined to see that we all are. I find a boulder sticking out of the ground and slump against it.

"I hope whatever is out there kills you guys first, so it's too full to eat me," I mutter.

Once Greysen and Petre get the fire going, I slide a knife from a sheath in my sleeve into the palm of my hand. I roll its hilt between my fingers, sure I'll need it before the night is over. I glare at the blaze, seeing all of our demises in the dancing, laughing flames. The gleeful things mock our inanity, the flicker ruining our night vision.

Caiman slings a small sack off his shoulder. I curse myself for not thinking about food along with weapons when he takes out energy bars and tosses one to Greysen, Petre, and Brylin.

He waves the bar he keeps for himself at Dex, punishing him for siding with me.

Clearly someone—probably Chance, or maybe dear old Daddy—tipped him off with details of our second trial.

I didn't think I could hate him more, but my stomach grumbles at the sight of the bars, and I'm glad it's low enough for only my ears to hear. I wouldn't give fuckboy Caiman the satisfaction. I survey the trees that line the edges of the clearing and recall everything we passed on the trek here. There was nothing remotely edible. The black, golden-stemmed fruit hanging in the trees would kill me with one nibble.

"You look tired," Dex says to me

Hell, I am. I thought I was doing a better job of not letting it show. The excessive use of my blood-gift and then the considerable damage that same gift worked to heal is running me down. The few hours of sleep I snatched after Selene patched me up wasn't enough. Plus, my senses have been on hyperalert since boarding the stealth jet, making things worse, to say nothing of the adrenaline of the closeness of the Accursed and whatever lies out there for us now. I've been running on nothing but fumes, and now that I'm sitting down, I can barely keep my shoulders from slumping. If I close my eyes, I might sleep the entire four days we're stuck in the forest.

Maybe being eaten alive doesn't hurt as much if you're already asleep.

"I can take first watch," Dex offers. "Keep an eye out for Expanse threats and our asshat mates."

I arch an eyebrow at his chosen swear. "That's one I don't hear every day."

His laugh flashes the dimple in his chin. "You would if you grew up in the Southern Isles. We have all sorts of colorful terms."

I laugh, too, thinking of Zayne. I hope he and Selene are okay. I start to ask Dex if he knew Zayne before the martial academies, but I stop myself, as it's unlikely. The Southern Isles consist of seven large barrier islands and three smaller tidal ones, each with its own distinct flair. It would be like someone asking me if I knew a random Khanaian. So instead I ask, "Which isle are you from?"

"Which one do you think?"

I smirk, but play along as a way to keep myself awake.

"Are your parents fisherpeople?" If they aren't, I can rule out Isthel, Zayne's home.

"No. Nice question though. Shoot me another one." He yawns. We both need this game.

I think over what to ask next.

"Did you attend weekly temple as a child?" The people of Mysine are among the few left in Mareen who haven't abandoned worship of the gods. They attend temple every week in hopes that should the gods ever return, they'll be looked upon favorably. Not that they would be. If the gods do come back, nobody on Iludu is escaping their vengeance.

"I didn't. But my parents have a healthy respect for the Pantheon." That tidbit doesn't narrow things down much. Although they were in the minority, scatterings of people across Mareen chose not to completely ignore the gifts, curses, and lessons left by the gods when the Tribunal Council's anti-Pantheon mandates swept through the Republic.

"Do you have a betrothed?" Everyone from the wealthiest to the poorest arrange their marriages on Riall.

He shudders. "No."

He isn't from Isthel, he isn't from Mysine, and he isn't from Riall. That leaves four large isles and the three small ones. I decide to run through the remaining barrier islands first. Yves is discounted when he tells me hunting for sport wasn't a part of his childhood. Boris is crossed off when he reveals he doesn't have a diehard love of sundisk hockey.

"Sweet, smoky, or spicy?" I finally ask.

He scowls.

Ha! I've trapped him with my question. The Isle of Cara is infamous for smoking everything that's a food; the people of Tinure prefer their meals seasoned sweet (who in the gods knows why); and the peoples of the short string of three tidal islands add so many peppers to their dishes, Grandfather always returned with heartburn that ravaged him for a week when he visited.

"You have to answer the question." I cross my arms and wait.

"Smoky," he says.

I grin, victorious. "You're from Cara."

"I am," he answers proudly.

"I've visited Cara often. We have a family home there. My grandfather's mother was from Cara."

"I know," Dex says, suddenly sheepish. "She was a dressmaker like my mother is. I know near everything that's public knowledge about Verne Amari. He is an inspiration. He came from labourii parents and the quaint Southern Isles like me and ended up a Praetorian and the Legatus Commander. If you don't mind me asking, how did his Khanaian father and Mareenian mother meet to produce him? I know mixed marriages are common in Rykos, but they are unheard-of everywhere else in the Republic." He asks it as respectfully as one could ask such a thing, so I decide to answer, if only to keep the convo going and keep myself awake.

"My great-grandfather relocated to Mareen as a young man because the old Tribune General of Brock War House offered him a small fortune if he quietly worked in his employ. He was a seventh-generation bladesmith, and few individuals could design a finer personalized blade. That isn't public knowledge because Brock War House didn't want him being poached by other houses." Grandfather's pair of blue steel daggers—which I still need to get back from Reed—had been forged for him by his father before he departed for Krashen Academy. His father was also a Xzana master and Pantheon-blessed with a metallurgy-gift, but that's knowledge nobody needs to have. "My great-grandmother was the private dressmaker to Donya Emmaline Brock, and that's how she and my great-grandfather met." Brock doesn't have a wife or daughter, so his mother is still their war house's Donya despite Brock having moved into his father's Tribune General seat.

"Ah," Dex says. "Can I ask one more thing I'm curious about?" The way he says it slyly and probingly automatically makes me leery.

The guard I had lowered slams back up. "What?" My stare is glacial.

He rubs the back of his neck at my changed mood. "Uh . . . I've just been wondering . . . when I first met you and Selene . . . on your Comm Unit that day . . . I saw . . ." He fidgets in nervousness. "Never mind."

Clearly he glimpsed who was on my Comm Unit's screen during the mingler-turned-ambush. If I don't address it, he'll continue to draw his own conclusions, and that may get out of hand. "You saw the Khanaian Crown Prince," I supply for him.

He continues to rub the back of his neck. "Yeah. How do you know him? Well, I mean well enough for him to be sending a direct message to your Comm Unit."

"We're lovers."

"What?"

I sigh, then laugh quietly. "No, it's nothing like that. We're childhood friends. I sometimes accompanied my grandfather on his diplomatic visits to our ally's kingdom when he visited to make sure our alliance held strong. He wanted me to be as familiar with my Khanaian heritage as I am with my Mareenian heritage. The Crown Prince was my playmate while my grandfather and his father talked trade and defense."

"You're friends with royalty? Is there anything about you that isn't spectacular?"

"Loads." He should've seen me in the bar on Commencement Eve and for the three months prior to that. He wouldn't be looking at me so amazed—unless he's easily impressed by public intoxication. "I am not special," I assure him. To prove the point, I add, "Technically, you've been chummy with royalty too. Selene is Mareen's equivalent to aristocracy. She's a Rhysien war house scion."

He turns from looking amazed to lovesick at the mention of Selene and their brief flirtation before things went to hell with the trials. "I really like her. She's not the stuffy, nasty, pretentious person I expected for a war house scion and its Donya. She's cool."

I jerk a thumb toward Caiman Rossi. "You mean she isn't like him."

He chuckles. "Yeah. That."

I take pity on him and give him a hard look. It's better he hear it now than fall in love with my friend at some point and get his heart broken later. "I adore Selene, and she is wonderful. The best, in fact. But she doesn't do anything other than casual. You should know that if you're thinking about trying to start something up with her. She always tells her hookups that going in. If you end up being one, listen to her. She means it."

Of course, there's the recent developments with Enzo . . . and whatever the hell last night was for them. But that's none of Dex's business.

His lovesick demeanor turns positively crushed, but I won't apologize. "Thanks for the warning. Why is that?"

That is a topic that isn't up for discussion in any way. So all I say is, "It's not my thing to tell."

Despite all the interesting turns our talk is taking, I yawn.

Dex nods at me. "Seriously, you can trust me. Get some rest. I promise I'm one of the good guys. Maybe if you tell Selene that when we get back, she'll give me a real chance."

"Not likely." My eyes droop closed. I pry them open. "And Mareenian soldiers don't entrust strangers with their lives."

"They're also shrewd and should know when to recoup their strength to fight the next day. You're my only lifeline out of this trial, Amari. If you die and I'm stuck with Caiman and his gang, I'm boar-fucked. If for no other reason, you can trust me to watch your back because of that."

"There's no way I'm interested in watching a boar fuck you from behind."

He laughs, and I'll admit I find his swearing choices interesting. Okay, I like Dex a lot more than the first impression he made back at the compound. Maybe he is a decent guy and maybe I *can* get a few moments of rest.

A sound, not like the howls from earlier—a fiercer, angrier, more vicious growl—cracks through the air like thunder. It obliterates all thoughts of sleep. I drop a second knife into my free hand and stand. Dex brandishes a Desert Phoenix. Across the glen, Caiman, Greysen, Petre, and Brylin have blasters in hand.

I see the glint of eyes first. Multiple pairs of gold orbs glow among the trees. One set narrows on me. An unnatural call, low and fierce, ripples up from the creature's belly. They're not Accursed, but I'm not sure that's much of a relief. Instead, sleek, muscular sabines with thick, indigo-blue, oil-slick fur emerge from the trees. They stride toward us slowly and purposefully on powerful legs built to support their massive bodies as much as they are built for speed. Their crushing jaws are packed with teeth. Canine sabers extend from the top row past the big cats' chins.

"Put the blasters away!" I shout to the group. "You need steel." Dex is the only one who listens. "Seriously—do any of you know shit about this forest?" Grandfather made me learn everything that academy training lacked about the footprints the gods left behind. Suddenly, I'm glad that he did. It might help me out of this current peril.

If the shitheads I'm stuck with stop being morons.

"Sabines are divine, nearly immortal animals," I grit out. "A bullet shattering their skull won't be enough to put them down." That's because the wound will knit itself closed as quickly as it is inflicted. Piercing the heart that beats in its chest cavity—which is hard to get to with a blaster—or decapitation are the only two ways to kill the preternatural cat. Sabines, like the forest and its Accursed, are masterpieces of Onei.

So of course, Caiman and his miserable friends keep blasters trained on the beasts, and I run out of time to try to make them listen.

There are four in the pride. The largest one runs a long, pink, bristled tongue over the pointed edges of its saber teeth. It peels its lips back as if to smile, assuring me I'm about to be dinner.

I'm fucking honored.

I crouch low and wait for the creature to make its move. I *am* surviving this goddess-cursed forest. And if by some chance I don't, I won't be felled by a godsdamned haughty-ass cat.

I run toward the sabine at full speed and drop to the ground, sliding between its legs and narrowly missing the massive paw it swats at me. Past its claws, I shove a knife into its fleshy underbelly. Triumph turns to ash as the blade misses the heart and scrapes the breastplate. I yank my knife free and scramble to my feet. I spin around to face it down as it roars, the cat no longer remotely amused. It lunges for me with wide-open jaws. I dart to the side and out of its path.

"Amari!" I spin around to the sound of Dex yelling my name.

Another sabine is sailing through the air straight at me. I drop to my knees, and it sails over me. Dex collides with it, and I turn my attention back to the first sabine I engaged with.

It rushes me. I don't dodge its razor-sharp teeth fast enough this time. They close around my forearm and clamp down. One of its teeth slices into my skin. It goes through one end and sticks out the other, skewering my arm. Pain explodes from my elbow to my fingers. It's so bad my eyes cross and my vision turns blurry. It takes every ounce of strength I possess not to writhe in its hold. Panting, I swing my free arm around and sink my knife into the side of its neck. Once. Twice. Three times. Four times. Five times.

Somehow, in all this, I don't cry out.

Hot blood spurts out of the artery I've hit and sprays my face. What's coating my lips seeps between them and into my mouth. The blood is bitter and tangy . . . and I don't mind the taste. It carries a power in it that feels like choking down thunder and lightning when I swallow. I'm just not sure it's enough. I don't stop stabbing. The sabine has me pinned and if I let up, I'm dinner.

It roars, raises a paw with clawed talons that's bigger than my head, and slams it into my chest. The microprene suit shreds. Sharp splinters of pain shoot through my lungs. I wheeze, gurgle blood, and I know that fragments of broken ribs are puncturing vital organs.

The sabine retracts its tooth from my arm. My knees buckle.

The beast preens over me, licking its paw. It's a victorious predator playing with its food. I look up at it harried and wild, and a feverish sweat breaks out over my entire body at the certainty that I'm dead. A primal scream of denial sticks in my throat.

A cry comes from my right and Dex is leaping onto the sabine's back and shoving a knife into its right eye. It rears back, bucking him off, and turns to face him, snarling.

It's one of the bravest things I've ever seen, and also the stupidest. The beast tears into Dex, ripping bloody chunk after bloody chunk out of his torso. His screams are silenced when it rips into his throat. I taste bile along with the blood that seeps from my mouth. The sabine leaves what amounts to a pile of shorn meat and flesh behind. Even Dex's face is gone.

All for a few extra seconds of my own life.

Onei's creature swivels to me, eyes wild and glowing red except for the black of its pupils. It takes a step toward me, then its muscles lock tight. Its nostrils flare. Its eyes narrow to tiny, agitated slits. The sabine takes another step. Powerful leg muscles lock up again. It roars in fury, jerks to one side as if yanked on by some invisible chain, and then sprints across the clearing. The creature disappears into the trees. Its pride members stop their assaults and follow. I'm in shock—what in the gods' names is going on? As I lie on the ground, bleeding, a small thought seeps into my mind: what the old stories say must be true. The ancient power of Onei prevents a sabine from taking down two kills at once. A pride being bound to its leader must also be true. It means we're safe for now.

I start to asphyxiate on blood.

I lie on the forest floor unable to heave myself off the ground.

"Should we help her?" The voice is Petre's. His boots are inches away from my head.

"We should leave her here." That voice is Greysen's.

"What if someone finds her?" Two fingers touch my neck. Caiman's. "She isn't dead yet."

"Who the fuck is going to find her?" Greysen.

"There are other teams out here." Caiman again.

"Chance dropped them at the opposite boundary. Our instructions were to make sure the akulu bitch didn't return to the compound, regardless of how she fared in the forest. This is the easy way to do it. In her condition, she's as good as dead. She won't survive the night and the forest's creatures this injured. The blood would literally be off our hands."

"Do you think I care about blood on my hands?" The disdain in Caiman's voice is chilling. "I'd rather make sure. My house never half-asses ops. Grab her legs."

There are grunts and then I'm heaved off the ground. The jostling sends fresh stabs of agony through my chest that knocks me unconscious.

When I battle back to semi-lucidity, wind is battering me as I fall. I hit . . . something. Water. I think. It could have been steel for how much it hurts. And even if it is water, there are plenty of rocks to bludgeon my body. I sink beneath the rapid current. Water floods my lungs. Gravity drags me down.

Down.

Down.

I fight against the desire to just drown and kick against the pressure of all the water pressing down on me. My entire body writhes in pain as I do, but I know pain. Pain I've dealt with. I can't go out like this. I won't die like this. I have too much left to do. I need to get through the trials. I need to prove who killed Grandfather. I need to kill them.

Can't kill anyone if I'm already dead.

With everything I have left, I somehow reach the surface. I breach it, but it isn't enough. I'm in the middle of a river and the bank is so far away. Impossibly far. The current slams me against a boulder, and whatever breath I might have gained is knocked from me. I claw at the rock, trying to hold on and not get swept farther downriver. My fingers slip. The current takes me. I slam into a second boulder. A third one. The impacts keep adding their damage to the havoc wreaked by the sabine. By whatever the three assholes did to manhandle me to the river in the first place. Black creeps into the edges of my vision. The lucidity I clawed my way back to is slipping away. I fight to remain conscious. A deep, innate knowing warns me if I black out this time, I'm not waking back up.

Ikenna—you have to fucking fight.

I know this. Yet it doesn't make things easier. The river takes a treacherous turn and the current sweeps me around the bend. I have no way of knowing where I'm going, as it's still barely light out. In a desperate effort, I reach out for the low-hanging limb of a tree stretching out from the bank. I grasp it, but grab a twig that's too skinny. It snaps.

Fuck the gods.

I grab for a sturdier branch. With my left hand, I hold on with my last ounce of strength. With my right hand, I grasp an adjacent thick branch closer to shore. I surprise myself each time a part of my body responds to what I ask it to do. I heave myself a little bit closer to not drowning. Lifesaving branch by lifesaving branch, I make my way toward the bank with excruciating slowness. Finally, I let go of the last limb and collapse onto damp sand.

Gasping, I want to sleep, but it's a thing I can't do. I battle the blackness back again and try to assess the situation. First thing is clear: I made it out of the river Caiman threw me in. I feel pretty confident I'm not going to die on dry ground. My body has a different opinion, though. Because even while I should be healing, neither my blood-gift nor the bioserum is repairing my injuries fast enough. My eyelids grow heavy. It feels like a palladium door weighs them down.

Live, I command myself.

Live.

Survive.

I don't know why I think there's a chance I can actually obey myself.

Because Amaris are as strong as Khanaian steel, Grandfather's stern voice says. It grips me and refuses to let me go. I cling to it. I use it to hang on to life for a few seconds longer. *We do not bend. We do not break. We do not bow. We do not yield.*

We do not let pretty-boy assholes leave us for dead.

I drag my eyes open, ready to do what I need to in order to keep living, then wish I had stayed in the river.

Bare feet rest beside my temple. Their ash-white skin is muddied. The toenails are jagged and yellowed. They curl downward, looking like they belong to some animal. The feet are attached to ash-white legs that are just as dirty. A tattered loincloth is wrapped around the person's waist. They're naked except for that. More muddied, dirtied, skin rests above the loincloth. Onyx-dark, slitted eyes stare down at me. The Accursed's lips stretch across his face in a facsimile of a smile. It's hideous and chilling. Horror whisks away my scream. Standing over me are four of his kin. I try to scramble away, but I haven't regained enough strength. I don't think it would have mattered. The Accursed stoops down, digs bony fingers into my arms, and plucks me up as if I weigh nothing. He slings me over his back. I gag on the putrid smell of rotting flesh. Drowning in terror, I reach for my blood-gift. It doesn't flare to life. Nothing answers my call. Not even an ember.

Without my blood-gift, can I truly be alive?

I must be. This is too horrific an ordeal for me not to be. I've been decent, mostly, in life. The Pantheon wouldn't condemn me to suffer this special hell.

So I am alive then. And for some reason, I don't have my blood-gift. I don't know if it's because it's depleted from keeping me alive, twice, in so short a time or if the magic of the forest has something to do with its absence. Even Pantheon blessings have their limits. Either way, the damning consequence is the same: There's no hope of me getting out of the Accursed's clutches with my blood-gift gone—and I don't know when it might recover.

Still, I'm a fighter. That's how I was trained. So I beat my fists against the once-man's back. It's a futile effort, but I do it anyway. The Accursed keeps striding forward unfazed, carting me away from the river, the rest of his hunting party bringing up the rear.

I guess Caiman and Chance got their wish after all.

8

THE ACCURSED TOSSES ME INTO a pen. It's rudimentary, built from ash-white pikes staked into the ground. Five identical structures are situated around me. Ice crawls down my spine at the sight. I gape in horror at my surroundings, a shiver overtaking me as I process the level of reason reflected by creatures I thought operated on the basest, crudest of levels.

The pen adjacent to me holds an enormous she-wolf, another of Onei's creations. The canid's carnelian pelt is missing patches and is matted with blood. She wails the bemoaning yowl of a wounded animal and licks at a bare patch on her side that is oozing. She shoots a savage look at the retreating form of the Accursed who carried me to the campsite. He disappears into the hut the rest of his pack entered when we arrived. A howl rattles the bars of the she-wolf's pen. It's distinct yet familiar, and I realize the howl we'd heard when first dropped in the forest was hers.

I'm not getting answers from her, though, so I turn to the pen that faces mine. It holds a brown-haired fellow aspirant whom I don't know personally. He didn't graduate from Krashen Academy, so he isn't out of the North, and his porcelain skin is too pale for him to have been reared by the Southern Isles Academy. He squats in the corner of his pen in a dirtied microprene suit, straining to pry two bars apart with his bare hands.

"Have you made any progress?" I ask.

His laugh is without mirth. "Shit, no." He slaps the bars. "This is fucking useless. Did they strip you of weapons too?"

"Yes." I scrub a hand across my forehead. "They took my Comm Unit also."

He tries his best to keep his face hardened, to keep the sheer panic that has every muscle locked tight from stealing onto his features. I realize he's trying to be a soldier of the Republic. To muster a bravery he doesn't feel. It's impressive for as long as it lasts, but for a moment the mask slips. His blue eyes radiate a sheen of terror and his pinched features crumple into an utterly hopeless array. "I wasn't aware the fuckers operate with such high intelligence. The officers could've warned us about that. My group went after this pack and they fucking ripped through us. It was carnage. I'm the only one that survived."

Yes, they could have. And they *should* have. I am completely unsurprised that they didn't. They're assholes. What bothers me more was how little of what I had learned at the academy made sense either. It's like the Republic *wanted* this secret too.

That is too deep a hole for me right now. "Who dropped your crew?"

"Nero." His jaw clenches when he speaks the name.

"Were Selene Rhysien or Zayne Drake with you?" I force the question out. Part of me needs to know, and another suddenly cowardly part of me doesn't want to hear his answer.

My heart stops slamming against my sternum when he says no.

The strong stench of rotting flesh tears my attention away from him. The five Accursed emerge from the hut. Two of them cart a human-shaped mass. The person has been skinned from head to toe, reduced to a hunk of pink, bloodied meat. They carry the body to the fire that simmers nearby and spit it, like you would a pig. One of them jams the pole into the corpse's mouth, works it through the body cavity in a way that makes me clutch my own stomach, and then the pole juts out of the corpse's ass. I fight a wave of nausea as the body is lifted onto wooden columns on the sides of the fire with notches for the spit to drop into. An Accursed takes hold of a crude handle attached to the spit. He turns it, rotating the body slowly.

My stomach lurches. "Is that . . . is that one of your crew?"

The boy's answering nod makes bile burn the back of my tongue.

The human muscle and sinew crackles and sizzles as it chars, but it's the smell that's truly awful. It assaults all my senses at once. It's equal parts broiled calf meat, corrosive sulfur, sweet cerebro fluid, and acrid fumes from incinerated organs. The odor is suffocating. Cloying. So thick and rich I can taste it. I don't think my nostrils will ever not burn with the mephitic scent. I'll never eat anything close to grilled meat again.

I double over and retch. I haven't eaten since before we left the compound, so thankfully there isn't anything in my stomach. More searing bile is what comes up. And I can't stop it from spewing out once it starts. A human is being cooked less than ten feet away from me.

"I have to get out of this pen!" the aspirant shrieks, finally losing it.

"Agreed," I rasp. I take a deep breath, make sure nothing else comes up, and scramble from my sitting position to a crouch. The pen's ceiling is too low for me to stand up straight. I scan the bars that lock me inside. A makeshift door is fastened closed with a rope. A rope that could be cut if I had a fucking knife. I feel for one of the knives I weighed my suit down with, even though I know every last one of them is missing.

For some reason, I think about Reed and my other knives at that moment.

"It's useless," the aspirant says in an echo of his previous words. But they're softer this time. They fall from his lips as a hushed acceptance of his grisly death overtakes him. He slumps to the ground, staring at what used to be his teammate being blackened and slow-cooked over the fire.

"Don't look at that!" I snap my fingers in his direction when he doesn't respond. "Hey! Look at me! Not that!"

"And how the hell do I not smell it?"

I don't have an answer for him. But one thing at a time. "Start by looking away. Now!"

When he still doesn't seem to hear me, I thread the command in my voice that our instructors at the academy yelled orders at us with during drills. *"Aspirant, look at me."*

He drags his gaze from the awful scene before us to my pen. He's broken out in a sweat, and his porcelain skin has turned as bloodless as the ash-white skin of the Accursed. "We will get out of here," I promise him. "I will get you out of here. Stay with me."

He nods, but then he buries his head between his knees and weeps. He ceases to be a soldier of the Republic. The facade of a Praetorian aspirant disintegrates. He's just a scared young man trapped in a peril he can't see a way out of.

I can be exactly the same, but I refuse.

Think, Ikenna. What's the maneuver? What's the way out of this? I pass the rest of the night trying to answer that question and come up with nothing.

IN THE MORNING, the Accursed lift the cooked human off the fire, slide the spit out of him, and set him on the ground. The five of them grab hold of a body part. Two grab the legs, two grab the arms, and one holds the head. They pull at the same time. The body parts tear away without sickening pops. That's how tender the meat and bones have become. It's the worst thing I've ever seen—and also the most fascinating. I can't look away. They feast with a ravenous hunger. The one body between five Accursed is devoured quickly, and they turn voracious eyes toward the pens where they've got extra morsels.

Two from the pack prowl to the pens. They stop between mine and the other aspirant's. As they survey us, their bald heads swish back and forth in a sinuous, boneless way that any creature with a spine shouldn't be able to achieve. The one nearest my cage, the one who carted me to the campsite, grunts, tilts its head to the side, considering me, and sniffs the air in front of me. He closes the distance between himself and my cage. Every step he takes forward makes my heart crash against my chest harder. He stands directly at the door to my cage, and I plant my feet in the dirt. I will not scramble away or retreat. I will not go out like a coward. Hobbled without my gift or not, the fuckers are not carting me to the fire without a struggle. At least, as much of a struggle as I can put up. *Even without my gift, my training is solid*, I reason, and try to latch on to the belief that, no matter how slim the odds, I might be able to fight my way free. I roll my neck, loosen my shoulders, and sink into the offensive Xzana stance that's most optimal when you're facing an opponent with more mass and more power behind it. I eye the Accursed. I'm not sure how quick they run—nothing we learned in the academy about them told me that—but maybe, just maybe, I can strike out as soon as he opens my cage, knock him off guard, and run like hell. And it might be a totally idiotic thought. But I'll be doing something instead of merely rolling over and dying, which I will not do.

The Accursed reaches out a hand, and I'm ready to either fight while getting away or fight while dying. Instead of opening the cage, he reaches in through the bars and his fingers curl around my pendant and yank it off. What the hell? He stares at it like the shininess has him enraptured. He brings it to his nose and sniffs it. He flings it to the ground. He looks my way, sniffs into the cage as if scenting me, and swings his attention to the other aspirant.

Weird.

I stare after him stupefied. I don't have time to consider the bizarre behavior because he's quickly snatching my comrade out of his cage. I seem to have gotten a pardon, however brief, while the other aspirant is chosen as the heartier meal.

His bloodcurdling screams are repeated kicks to my gut after I promised we'd make it out of this horrendous ordeal alive. He dissolves into a sobbing, trembling, shrieking mess. Every part of me goes hollow. Numb. Or it wants to. But I'm not dead yet, and I've never been weak, so I shout and yell and scream at them to let him go. Despite my damn power being absent, I reach for my blood-gift again. I try to will it to life through sheer force of will. My efforts are fucking useless. Like before, my gift doesn't ignite beneath my skin. It sits inert, as if I don't possess it at all. More than anything, that's what scares me, even as I watch help-lessly as my comrade is dragged to the roasting spit. A snap of his neck silences his screams. Then the once-men set to work skinning him.

THE ACCURSED'S APPETITES are sated after their second feast. It makes me the lowest form of shit to breathe any relief about that. I sit in the dirt, watching after the once-men as they disappear back into their wood hut.

I've got to find a way free before they decide they're hungry again. Roast Ikenna is *not* on the menu.

I don't take my eyes off their dwelling once they amble inside. I stare at it, watching, waiting. I try to be rational. To think through the situation, think through my training. But nothing trained us for this. And so much of what made me the soldier I am is my blood-gift, and it's nowhere to be seen. Calmness turns to hyperventilating, reaching over and over again for a Pantheon Blessing that isn't there. The sun crawls below the horizon, and Iludu's three moons inch into the sky. The glow they cast drapes a red translucent shroud over the entire forest. The clearing seemingly glows with a natural bioluminescent light that's the color of freshly spilled blood. It's beautiful and horrific, and enough of a distraction to my thoughts that I pry my eyes off the hut. I turn to the sky and look at the moons. They're sleek waxing crescents, and they blaze a brilliant crimson. I rasp out a dry laugh. Blood Moons amplify the power of those who bear the blood-gift. Of course a trio of them would be present in the sky while my gift is suppressed.

Squinting up at the moons, I call to my blood-gift for the hundredth time, even as I have no faith it's going to matter. I *need* it to answer. It's the only way I'm getting out of this pen.

Please . . .

Something ignites.

A small kernel of it tries to spark. But as quickly as that tiny portion flares, it sputters out. Like a fizzle of current that doesn't quite have enough juice. My blood-gift falls completely silent, so I reach for it again, trying to force that starter current into something stronger.

The door to the hut creaks open, and the blood in my veins hardens to ice. All I can do is stand frozen and stare at the hut, waiting for the Accursed to step into view. The blood-gift—the secret I was never supposed to use—failed me when I needed it most. It's there, I can feel it's there, but it's refusing me. I'm not sure I believe in fate, but it feels like the Pantheon is trying to tell me something.

Namely that this is it. It's my turn.

I've imagined my death a thousand different ways if the Tribunal ever discovered my blood-gift, but I never imagined I'd die like this. Alone. In a cage. Or rather, just outside a cage in the middle of a goddessforsaken forest. Powerless and at the hands of monsters who see me as a midnight snack.

Only one of the Accursed emerges instead of the whole pack. It isn't the one that carted me away from the river. This one's bald head is narrower. His lean nose a bit more slender. His cheekbones sharper. His eyes are oval-shaped and wider than his brethren's. He looks at me in the pen, then turns away and treks off into a grove of trees along the western edge of the campsite. I let loose a breath. I have to slap my hands against my knees to stop them from trembling—both my hands and my knees. I lean against the bars, thanking the cosmos for this reprieve while carrying the grim knowledge that I won't get a second one unless I can find that spark of my blood-gift. I need to coax it into something more. Something I can wield to get free.

I try for over an hour as the sky overhead darkens from the milky silver of twilight to the lush black spill of true night, all the while seeing the Blood Moons cross the heavens, taunting me. The entire time I watch the hut and pray more Accursed don't emerge. None do, and every once in a while I feel that spark, but more often I don't. And even when I do, it slips through my fingers, too rapid-moving and fluid to be caught, like the blood it is.

I take my eyes off the hut to glance up at the crimson moons again. They're a transient, celestial event that happens maybe three times each year. Old lore claims they were created by Amaka, the goddess of blood rites herself, and they give Amaka and those she favored power over the rest of all things that are Pantheon-blessed. If that's true, then the boost the Blood Moons are supposed to afford me should trump any magic of Onei's forest that might be dampening my power. But it's been hours, and I've yet to feel any uptick in the power I usually experience during Blood Moons. So it can't be the forest's magic that's the problem. That leaves me with the conclusion that the block *has* to be the result of my blood-gift healing my severe injuries, which started with the face-off with Caiman in my room. Fuck him to all the godsdamned hells that exist. I should've murdered him. If I get out of this, I *am* going to murder him. Slowly. Painfully. Excruciatingly.

No, actually, I'm going to keep him alive. I'm going to keep him alive and draw his torture out. This is his fault. All of it.

I'm angry and I'm scared and I'm desperate. Out of that desperation, I do something I've never done before. I pray to the goddess my gift flows from. I pray to Amaka with everything I'm worth. The words of prayer leave my lips in fervent, frenzied whispers. And even as I utter the prayer, I am absolutely sure the words won't matter. When the whole of Iludu turned its back on the gods and cast them off the planet, the gods vowed to forever turn their backs on us in return. Their vow included those who were their blessed flocks. Their ungrateful Chosen—like me—who didn't rally to their sides.

When time is running out, though, you might as well use it however you can. So I keep praying.

As I do, I narrow my gaze on the moons. I swear they turn a shade of red that makes their hue seem more sanguine—like the rocky satellites are drenched in blood and they threaten to dump a deluge of it onto Iludu. Then I blink, and the effect I think I saw vanishes. The moons are simply their ordinary red.

I am simply a chicken in a coop.

I wince. I'm gripping the bars of my pen so hard the wood digs into my palms. I flex my hands and bring them away from the bars to examine the ache in the center of my right palm. When I do, my blood coats the bar where I touched it and a cluster of splinters sticks out of my skin. My blood wells around the fragments in a larger amount than the slivers of wood should produce. My blood streams out of the microscopic wounds, down the side of my hand, and wets the dirt at my feet. Then my palm throbs with more than the ache from the splinters. The powerful electric jolt I've been struggling to call forth zings through it. The blood pouring from my palm shimmers the same deep red as the Blood Moons had when I'd prayed, and the thrumming power of my blood-gift spreads from my hand, up my arm, and over my entire body. It's so potent it knocks the breath from me, but that isn't why I gasp for air. I've experienced Blood Moons every year of my life. What I haven't experienced ever before is the surge in power seeming to be so immense that it's too much for my body to contain. The excess seems to pour out of me and swaths my entire form in the same red light that encases the forest.

I feel the power because I *am* the power.

The stave of my pen stained by my blood shatters. I don't have time to marvel at the occurrence or at what the red glow that bathes me means. I smear blood from my palm across multiple bars and will them to shatter like the first one did. My command is immediately obeyed, and the sound is deafening. I don't wait around for the Accursed to come out of their hut and investigate it. I snatch my pendant up from the dirt, because it's fucking mine and I'm not leaving it behind, and run.

9

ALTHOUGH I BROKE OUT OF their camp, I'm not done with the Accursed yet. My orders weren't to simply survive the forest for four days. I'm supposed to retrieve the head of one of those abominations. If my blood-gift is back, it should make becoming the hunter instead of the hunted possible while going at the task alone. It'll still be perilous and a fool's errand, but I'm already a fool for entering the trials in the first place. I'm not failing out though. I can't. This is for grandfather.

I'll kill as many Accursed as it takes to keep my place.

Shivering despite the moderate temperature, I retrace my steps until I pick up the stench of rotting flesh. I keep track of the Accursed who are still hunting me, and when the scent becomes so noxious my nostrils burn, I pick the tallest tree that's climbable and clamber high into its canopy. From my position in the tree's crown, I have a bird's-eye view of the forest below, and I see they have separated for the search. Down in the undergrowth, I see there is only the one with the narrow head, long nose, and overly round eyes. He tromps among the trees, alternating between snarls and grunts. I eyeball him as he squats in the dirt and sniffs the ground for my scent.

Please do not decide to stir at this moment, I beg of the wind. Thankfully, tonight is one for my prayers to be answered, and the air remains tranquil.

This far from Mareen, there's no need to worry about a tech-enhanced lodestone, so I scrape my thumbnail across the pinpricks of new scabs on my palm so I can bleed freely once more. I will it to stream off my hand in unstanched rivulets. Like I've practiced a dozen times within the safety of Grandfather's protective force shields, I command the river of blood to congeal into a lethal spike that possesses the hardness of steel. *You can't control what you don't understand*, Grandfather insisted. *And you can't hide what you can't control.*

I hope you're right, Grandfather.

No one has ever accused me of being a coward (at least, not without a black eye for the effort). Few things truly terrify me. But a fresh round of horror crashes into me as I peer down at the stooping Accursed. I gather strength, courage, and more of my power around me like sphere upon sphere of a protective shield. Then before I can talk myself out of it, I leap from the tree. I angle my body so it hurtles straight at my quarry, and I slam into the once-man. I stab and stab and stab at its head as we crash to the ground.

Onei didn't want her creations so easily killed, though, and the Accursed lashes its head back and forth, its thick skull doing its best to protect its brain. But it no longer snarls or growls. Rather, it screeches an eerie, chilling noise that makes it sound like it crawled up from the bowels of the deepest hellpit that exists in the After. I lash out again, and the blood spike sinks into the Accursed's left eye, but still misses the brain. It bucks me off and crouches down in a quadrupedal position that humans were never meant to assume. It gallops at me in a way that doesn't so much as whisper that the thing was once human. There's no trace of humanity left in its flat, black eyes either.

It's a monster, pure and simple. And I'm going to kill it.

I react with a preternatural speed of my own, faster than I've ever moved before. The three blood spikes I shoot unerringly stab it between those soulless eyes. The next round of three drive into the fucker's forehead. I know at least one of them pierces the brain beneath because its hideous eyes go vacant in midair. It doesn't so much as twitch when it hits the ground.

Still, I don't move an inch near the Accursed for a good long while. Instead, I take several steps backward and watch for signs that the undead creature isn't *dead*-dead—impossible tasks tend to have a way of becoming more impossible even when you think you're done. After enough time passes to calm my nerves and assure me I'm the only thing alive below this tree, I move close to the body and tap a shoulder with my boot. I jerk my foot back, half-afraid the action will prod the monster awake. It continues to lie motionless in the dirt.

Stop being ridiculous, Ikenna. You killed it.

I let that sink in.

I *killed* it.

Swallowing the traumatic memories of how it and its pack mates skinned and cooked two of my fellow aspirants, I kneel, form another hard-as-steel blood spike in my hand—this time edged like a blade—and hack off the head.

I wipe the back of my hand against my mouth to keep from vomiting. I wish I had a sack to put the head in to contain the smell.

I wish for a lot of things.

Holding my breath for long stretches of time, I tote my gruesome prize through the forest. With my Comm Unit gone, the only way out is to reach civilization. I find a clearing and search the sky for the constellation of Kissa. In a few minutes I find the six jade stars arranged in a dramatic curve that make up Kissa's Horn. When Kissa, twin to Krashna, claimed the kingdom as her dominion during the Pantheon Age and the kingdom's people claimed her back, she adorned the sky with her horn and assured Khanaians it would always light their way home.

I head toward Khanai. Once I get there, I can procure a new Comm and transport home.

I cross as much forest ground as I can while night and the constellation of the goddess of arts, riches, and wisdom persists. I won't have anything to guide my way come morning. When the ink-black sky lightens to dusky navy then ivory with splashes of blush and gold, I select a towering tree and climb into its crown. Passing the day in the canopy is better than on the ground where anything can get to me.

Onei didn't care for birds, so none of her creations possess wings.

On a particularly sturdy, wide branch, I finally rest. I place my back against the trunk and settle the Accursed's head in my lap, the worst plush toy in history. When this is all over and I get back to Mareen, I am standing under a scalding shower for days. Maybe weeks. I close my eyes and force myself to get some sleep. I need to keep my energy up. My blood-gift cannot fail me again while I'm here.

A voice with a familiar drawl shouts my name and drags me awake sooner than I'd like. I look down at the base of the tree to see Enzo, Bex, and an aspirant I haven't yet met, looking back up at me. I'm so relieved to see a friendly face I could cry. *Don't you dare*, I scold myself.

Securing the Accursed's head under my right arm, I climb out of the tree.

"You have no idea how happy I am to see you," I admit to Enzo when my feet touch the ground.

He wrinkles his nose, eyes bulging at my haul. "What the fuck, girl? How did you get that?"

"I'm glad you're happy to see me too." I shake my head. "It's a long story that starts with four jackasses walking into a forest."

He raises an eyebrow. "Come again?"

"Caiman, Greysen, Petre, and Brylin tossed me off a cliff."

Enzo's astonished stare turns from jealous at the head to flabbergasted to murderous. "They did *what?*"

"Your teammates tried to murder you?" says the third member of their crew in disbelief. His thick eyebrows furrow, trying to process what I just accused our fellow aspirants of doing. "Why would they do that?"

I give him a look. Is he serious? "Because they're bigoted fucks. But also, Chance ordered them to do it."

"He . . . they . . . *oh.*" He casts his blue eyes to the ground.

"*Did Dex help?*" Bex shakes her head vehemently. "No. He wouldn't."

"He didn't. He died while we fought a sabine," I answer her gently. I keenly feel the words as if he were someone I'd known all eleven years I spent at Krashen Academy and not for the few days since the start of the trials.

But my feelings are nothing compared to hers. At the news, she lets out a wail. Then she's sobbing without a care as to who witnesses it.

Shit. "I'm sorry," I tell her.

She lets loose a breath, wipes her eyes, and tries hard to pull herself together. "We knew these trials would be lethal going in. But Dex was . . . *Dex.* Big, strong, cocky, and sure he could wrestle the world and win. I knew if anyone could survive them, it would be him."

"He saved my life," I offer as some sort of comfort. "While fighting the sabine, he tried to divert its attention from striking a killing blow against me. I know it's little solace, but he died being a warrior."

"Our numbers got slashed too. We started with a team of six and lost three of our people trying to obtain a head," she says, nodding at my cargo. Every one of her words bleeds misery.

Her brother is dead, as are three of her companions, but I have to ask, "Was Selene or Zayne in your crew?"

Enzo answers, "No."

The second round of relief I feel at getting that answer is even shittier.

Please make it out alive, I beg them, wherever they are. Dex's screams being cut off by the crunch of his bones haunt me. Selene and Zayne cannot meet a similar fate.

"This trial is for shit. Why not just shoot us all in the head?" Enzo asks.

"And only two days down," Bex mutters. "I need the next two days to be over so we can be out of this hellhole."

"Two days we can do—if we look out for each other."

Enzo snorts.

"That's fine and good, but we still need to try for an Accursed."

Guilt—or insanity—drives me to help them out.

"Your team can have this head." I hold it out for Bex to take, though I know it's such an inadequate, insignificant consolation. "It's the least I can do for your brother sacrificing his life for me."

"But you'll fail out of the trials," she says.

"And that means they'll kill you anyway," Enzo adds.

"I'd love to see Chance try," I say. "My team left me for dead. I joined up with yours. We have a head. I don't think we violated any rule."

"He seems like the kind of prick who would think otherwise."

"Then he and I can have words; we already have a score to settle."

"Were you serious about him setting you up?" Bex asks.

I nod. "He instructed Caiman and the others to make sure I didn't make it back to the compound."

Enzo spits on the ground. "That's wolfshit!"

"Are you surprised? Look at me. I'm not full Mareenian."

"You're as Mareenian as me," Enzo says. "You were born here. You spent your childhood training to be a soldier for the Republic. Your grandfather spent his whole life in service to the Republic. Dual parentage doesn't make you Mareenian. Having the heart and courage of a soldier while upholding the Republic's creed makes you Mareenian."

It's all patriotic nonsense—and all things I've heard and robotically repeated since Indoc Year—but after the night I've had, it bolsters me to hear it.

"Your plan is good too—you stay with us. You're part of our crew now. We'll deal with shit from Chance about you changing groups when the time comes. If he wasn't playing strictly by the rules he set, you don't have to either."

"I'm with Enzo," Bex says. "My brother was an impeccable judge of character. He wouldn't have died for an asshat individual."

The third member of their team speaks up: "Honor is a part of the creed of a Mareenian soldier." More academy nonsense, and more solace I find in hearing it. "If what you say is true—and even if it isn't— the trial right now is survival. Survival as a *team*. If you're alive, then your own team abandoned you. But we found you, and so you are one of us . . . no matter what you look like," he says with a grin. "My home is Rykos in the east. We share a border with Darre. The people of my city do not share the bigotry of the rest of the Republic. We've long re- garded Khanaians as our neighbors. I have no quarrel with you joining this team and standing with you should Chance question your right to have defected."

"Thank you," I say, and mean it. "I'm Ikenna, by the way."

The Rykos aspirant answers that with a bashful smile. "I know who you are. It is my greatest privilege to meet and help an Amari. I'm Dasaun."

"Well, since you'll have me, will somebody *please* hold this foul- smelling, ugly thing for a while." I thrust it at Enzo.

He takes it, shudders when looking at it up close, and shoves it into a survival pack I'm just now noticing.

"Where did you get that?"

"You didn't get one? Reed gave them to us after he led us off the jet."

"I hate Chance."

The other three nod, and we start trekking through Onei's Expanse.

The remaining two days pass uneventfully, a thing I'm profoundly thankful for. Bex gives me one of her knives, but I can't use my blood-gift around anyone in the group, which makes me feel very vulnerable. After losing it and feeling utterly powerless while it was gone, I want to keep it right at my fingertips—and a blood spike in my hand.

We sleep in the trees at night, and my new team isn't made up of idiots who insist on a fire. We stay moving through the forest by daylight so we don't stall in one place for too long and allow something to sniff out our scents.

We act like we're trained Praetorians, and there's a sense of pride deep inside me, regardless of the true reason I joined the trials. Because before Grandfather died, I wanted to be a Praetorian for reasons other than vengeance and for reasons beyond the fact it was what he wanted for my future. I wanted to be a Praetorian for reasons that were all my own: camaraderie and the feeling of finally belonging. I wasn't naïve enough to think I'd find that anywhere other than Grandfather's old cohort, but I thought maybe if I pledged Gamma there'd be a chance. While I navigate the forest with Enzo, Bex, and Dasaun, I feel like I'm experiencing those things I'd always dreamed about, and it feels good.

It also comes with a keen hurt, and a bitterness, because joining up with their team shows me the way things could be, how I could exist if such hatred for people like me didn't run so deep in Mareen.

ON THE FIFTH day, everyone else's Comm Units beep as the sun rises with the coordinates of our pickup location.

As soon as I board the stealth jet, I make a beeline for Chance, who is trying his damnedest not to look stunned. That doesn't last long, because I punch him in his snake-ass face. "I'm going to kill you!"

Reed pries me off him. "Stand down, Amari! This isn't some bar. These are the trials. Respect them. You're in breach of deference."

"And he's in breach of honor!"

Everyone stares at me, my fury pulsating from my body. "Don't look shamefaced now, Caiman," I fire at my would-be murderer standing nearby. "Fuck your deference and let me go!" I holler at Reed. I struggle against his hold, but he has my arms pinned tight to my sides, and I can't slip his grip.

"Yes, let her go." Chance gets right into my face. "I don't know what hole you crawled out of to link up with another group, but you can scuttle back to it before you forfeit your life for being a failure. You clearly deserted your original team, which means you didn't pass the trial."

My hands itch for a knife. The bastard ordered my death. "The hell I didn't pass. I'm here, and I have a head. And *I* didn't desert anyone, as you well know."

I jerk my chin toward Greysen and Caiman. Both their faces are sheet-white. "Those are the deserters right there—the fuckers left me for dead. No, not just left me for dead. They *threw me over a fucking cliff* because you told them to make sure I didn't survive the trial." I don't see Petre and Brylin aboard the jet, which means they died in the forest. I can't muster any pity for that, but also don't find a ton of joy in it.

All I have is rage right now.

Chance doesn't bother denying the accusation. "So? Rules still apply."

"And I passed your test and all your fucking rules. My team abandoned *me*—so shouldn't they be the ones who fail?"

A snort. *Caiman.* Golden Boy has recovered from looking like he's seen a ghost. I'm going to gut him along with his lap dog. I should have killed him and Greysen when they attacked me in my room.

"You didn't survive," Caiman says. "The sabine killed you. We watched you bleed out on the forest floor. We merely did the forest a favor by taking out the trash the cat left behind so more wouldn't track us down from your blood."

"Clearly I did survive, asshat," I say, trying Dex's swear on for size.

"Then it's a miracle. Look, everyone—talking akulu garbage."

"*Motherfucker!*" Selene jumps up from her seat. Her eyes are red and swollen, like she's been crying for days. Zayne, who stands too, doesn't look any better.

Selene whirls on Caiman and throws a jab. He staggers back into Greysen. His right eye is going to have a nice shiner before the serum wipes it away.

Chance steps between Selene and an enraged Caiman. He blocks Caiman's punch meant for her. "Tribune Rhysien will have your ass, bro." He says it quietly, but with enough force to prove that while Chance has some sway during the trials, and Caiman has the clout of his war house, Selene is practically royalty as well.

Caiman shoots Selene a death glare over Chance's shoulder.

"Sit your asses back down," Chance barks at Selene and Zayne. His voice oozes menace when they don't move. "Are you hard of hearing? That's a direct order. *Fall in* unless you want to bow out of the trials."

"Sit," I urge them. "I can handle things."

Yet neither of them returns to their seat.

Enzo, Bex, and Dasaun stick tight to me too.

I love them all for it, but I don't need them to fight this for me—I *got* this. "Seriously—sit down. For me."

Reluctantly, they do, Selene glaring with an intensity I've only seen her reserve for lovers trying to ask her out on an actual date.

"The trial was to survive Onei's Expanse," I say to Chance. "I didn't abandon my team—Caiman just told you that. Instead, I'm standing right here, *alive*, which means I survived. The sabine didn't kill me. Neither did the forest. Neither did the shitheads you commissioned to do your dirty work."

Chance folds massive arms over an equally massive and heaving chest. He eyes me up and down. "How did you manage that?"

Iron control, I hear Grandfather's voice in my head when my temper threatens to slip its leash. *Anything less means discovery and death.*

"With skill," I answer, with an arrogance that rivals Caiman's.

"Did you sanction aspirants to kill her?" Reed asks Chance. His voice surprises me, even as his hold on me loosens.

Chance rolls his neck, glaring at Reed. "It's not your fucking place to question me. I'm the lead officer here. The trials are played by *my* rules. I have clearance to put the aspirants through whatever challenges I see fit."

"So you sanctioned *murder?* You couldn't just let the Expanse do its job, like it did to half the other aspirants? You're fucking swine." Dannica, our female officer, levels a death glare at Chance. She moves to stand beside Reed and me. I don't take her speaking up to mean that she actually gives a shit about me. Her support is about loyalty to her cohort brother and the Gamma symbol on her battledress uniform.

But I'll take the backup her words lend me all the same.

Reed releases me fully. "That isn't the way things are done. We have a code." The irony of him saying that isn't lost on me. But I can only deal with one bastard at a time, and I'm not above using Reed's pretenses of honor to help me win this round with Chance.

Chance scoffs. "The code doesn't apply to her. She's an akulu. The drop of Mareenian blood she possesses shouldn't mean shit. She shouldn't be taking part in these trials."

Several of the transition officers, including Nero, express agreement. A portion say nothing, neither siding with or against Chance.

"But she *is* part of these trials. As sanctioned by the Tribunal. So who are you to decide whether she should be here?"

Chance's eyes blaze with malice. "Careful, Reed. You keep speaking up on her behalf and I may start to think you have a thing for her."

"Fuck you and what you think. The former Legatus Commander was a part of Gamma. I don't know how Alpha does shit, but us Gammas look out for our own. Even after death. And the Legatus Commander . . . we *all owe him everything.* He—"

"Yes, we all know of his great deed." The contempt in Chance's voice is enough to take out the legs of the proudest woman. "Big shit.

He did what anybody else on that killing field with him could have done. Yet we're expected to all bow down at the mere mention of his name. Verne Amari was a godsdamn man, not a legend. Not a god. A man whose blood wasn't pure Mareenian. Herodus Chance was next in line for Legatus Commander. But he sacrificed himself in the war and that piece of shit akulu Amari exploited his sacrifice to get close to the Blood Emperor and earn himself a promotion."

"And yet he didn't. Get over it and your delusional view of your own grandfather's greatness. He wasn't a god either. He was a soldier, and did his job, same as Verne Amari . . . only he died." Chance seethes at this but does nothing. So Reed presses him a little harder.

"And while you're at it, get over the sting of Verne Amari's grand-daughter handing your man his ass in the bar."

Chance smashes his fist into Reed's jaw.

Reed spits blood. Then throws an uppercut-jab combo back. Chance takes brutal blows to his face and throat that he never has a hope of dodging. Compared to Reed, he's too slow. He only got that first hit in because it was a sucker punch. Chance wheezes for air.

Nero wedges himself between them. "Not here," he says, playing peacemaker. His eyes dart nervously back and forth between Reed and Chance. I can't make out whose wrath he's more afraid of. He nods to-ward the aspirants seated nearby. "We have a job that we need to work together to do."

The rest of us just stare.

So this is what it means to be a Praetorian?

Not exactly a ringing endorsement.

Reed shrugs Nero's hand off his chest and takes a step back. Chance stays rooted in place.

"You're out of control," a calmer Reed says to Chance.

"And you're out of protocol by challenging my choices as lead in front of aspirants. How is breaching the established chain of command in accordance with your fucking self-righteous integrity?"

"We keep saying the word 'breach' as if it's not some arbitrary nonsense at this moment. If she made it back aboard the jet, she passed the trial," Reed responds, terse. "Whatever your feelings about her are, these trials will be conducted with the integrity that is part of the Republic's creed. Me not speaking up for that is the larger breach."

"We can't break rank," Nero maintains again. "Not during the trials. They're too important. You said so yourself in the dome, Reed."

Dannica, who hasn't left Reed's side, speaks up. "Nero is right. But Chance is insane, and Reed is within his bounds as co-lead to balance that out or reel him in when he goes off the rails. That's the point of having a co-lead in the first place."

Chance's nostrils flare. I see whatever disgusting insult he's about to fling at her coming a kilometer away.

"Dude!" Nero says, jabbing his finger in Chance's chest. "Don't. Not with Dannica. You want to fuck with aspirants, that's on you. But you take on an actual Gamma, and Reed will lose his shit and you will for real brawl."

"And? I'm not scared to piss him off like the rest of you."

After what I just saw, I think we're all a bit afraid of taking on Reed, but no one says a word—barely anyone breathes. Nero steps closer to Chance. He whispers something too low for anybody else to hear.

"Whatever," Chance says to Reed when Nero steps back. "I'll let you have this one." He spins back to me, his anger a giant missile seeking an easier target. "Enjoy the reprieve. You will not make it through these trials alive. I bet my life on that."

"What odds will you give me?"

"Are you insane? I could kill you right now and be well within my rights."

"But you won't, and honestly, without someone else doing your dirty work, I don't think you could take me." I know this was the part where I'm supposed to take the threat seriously and my heart is supposed to race with fear. But that's not me—never has been, never will be. Chance is nobody. I arch one eyebrow to goad the snake and drawl, "So if you want to try, you're a dead man walking. Get your affairs in order."

"What did you say, bitch?"

I roll my eyes at the number of times he's spat that word.

"I'm still your superior. Remember that and show some deference."

I half laugh. Half growl. "You have higher rank, but you're in no way superior to me. But yeah, I'll remember that. Along with the fact that four assholes tossed me into a torrential river because you told them to. Just like I survived that, I will survive these trials. Come for me again and you won't. I bet *my* life on that, and obviously I'm hard to kill. By the way, I fetched you something while I was with my new team. Enzo?"

He tosses me the survival pack that has the Accursed's head inside. I thrust it at Chance. "Carrying its stench around the forest was more tolerable than standing here near yours."

I turn to Reed. "Can we go home so I can take a shower?"

10

"THOSE SONS OF WHORES!" SELENE empties a third clip into the man fifty yards away. Each UV bullet she fires off is an unerring head shot between the eyes. Selene with a blaster is like me with knives. She's freakishly good. She pops out the empty clip and jams a new one into her fifty-cal D-Phoenix. Twelve shots fired in rapid succession rip into her target's head with such force that the holograph enemy blurs. "They are dead. All of them." Selene slams her gun down on the loading table after running out of bullets again. "And Fuck! Shooting a holo isn't good enough! I need bullets to rip through flesh, preferably Caiman's, Greysen's, and Chance's."

"I'm right there with you," Zayne says as five rapid bullets penetrate his target's heart and explode into a spray of colorful fireworks on impact. He lays his blaster, a Centauri Starsploder, against the loading table and cracks his knuckles. "I'd like very much to break every bone in their bodies."

"Both sound like fantastic ideas." I halfheartedly fire kill shots at my target's head. I'd prefer to be in a sparring gym lobbing knives instead of the shooting room, but I'm glad to be here with my friends. My corpse could be back in the forest decaying.

Or in an Accursed's stomach.

Selene picks at her right temple. A long, slender gash mars the smooth, creamy skin. She was the one who hacked off the Accursed's head for her team, and she has a scar for her efforts. Instead of detracting from her beauty, it adds to it. It gives her a lethal bombshell air I'm a little jealous of. Misreading my stare, she sweeps her hair to the side so it covers the scar. Her beauty means everything to her, and she's vain enough for the mark to do a lot more than bother her.

"I can barely see it," I assure her. I'd tell her the truth, but she'd never believe me.

She frowns, sliding two fingers down the length of it self-consciously.

"Don't worry. It's already faded to pink in the three days we've been back. The bioserum will have it near invisible soon."

"Kenna's scars are already gone," Zayne adds his support.

Selene's wry smile ends in a grimace. "That doesn't help. Kenna is different." She slams her mouth shut as soon as she says it.

I laugh off the slip-up. "That's because all my major damage was internal."

"I'm still waiting on the full, *full* story," Zayne lets me know. He's been prodding me about it since we got back to the compound, and I've been dodging.

"It's what I already told you. My supposed crew threw me off a cliff after I got injured by the sabine. Accursed fished me out of a river and carried me to their camp. I got away, killed one of them, and took his head, then fortunately found Enzo, Bex, and Dasaun." Like every time he's asked before, I gloss over the specific details of my time in the camp and don't mention the Blood Moons being the sole reason I'm free.

Cannibalism and illegal magic don't seem like good conversation starters.

"That was remarkable to do all by yourself. Every team that went after Accursed lost people."

"Quite remarkable. I should get a statue on the compound's lawn. You don't believe that's something I'm capable of?" I make sure to sound annoyed when I ask. I'm an asshole for gaslighting him, but I don't have much of a choice.

"I didn't mean it like that."

"Then what did you mean?" My annoyance stops being all the way fake. "Why can't you drop it?"

He looks at me, wounded. "Fine. It's dropped."

Guilty, I mull over telling Zayne the truth. Selene already knows, and that's not how our trio works. We don't share secrets with one person and keep them from the other. The three of us are a unit. We have been for eleven years. He'll be hurt if he finds out later that I confided something in Selene while keeping it from him.

But trust isn't what dissuades me. I trust Zayne with my life. A lifetime of Grandfather impressing the importance of nobody discovering I'm Pantheon-blessed is what's hard to shake. Selene knows because there was no way to hide it from her. With Zayne . . . my years of hiding override my guilt. Grandfather and I once had the convo about my friends learning of my gift. Adolescent Ikenna didn't understand why she couldn't tell them. I'd told him Selene and Zayne would never turn me in to the Tribunal.

"I don't doubt they wouldn't," he'd said. "That isn't what you should fear. It's not for *you* that you hide, but for them. If your gift is discovered, those closest to you will fall under suspicion for knowing and be interrogated. Harboring such a secret is treason against the Republic."

Fear for Zayne's life is what keeps me from looping him in. Selene's father is a Tribune General, and she's the scion of a war house. She has protections that Zayne, the son of labourii fisherpeople, won't be afforded.

"I'm done with the shooting room," I say, shifting the subject. "How about we hit the mats?"

"Sure thing," Zayne mutters with dejection.

"HE'LL GET OUT of his feelings," Selene whispers as we enter the sparring gym.

Zayne trails far enough behind us that he can't hear her.

I'm about to respond, but beside me Selene growls. Zayne follows it up with a curse as he comes to stand on my free side. In the middle of the arena-style space, Caiman and Greysen grapple atop blue mats. They pause in their pathetic attempt at a Xzana dance to smirk our way.

Selene veers toward Caiman and Greysen. I reach out and grab her wrist, halting the hell she's about to unleash. "Don't. It's not worth it. At least not here. Come on." I lock arms with her and tug Selene to the opposite side of the room.

"Let's find another space?" Zayne suggests.

"No," Selene spits. "We aren't slinking away."

"We sure aren't." I give Caiman my back. The gesture is as much a silent *fuck-you* as it is an *I'm not afraid of you. Bring it.* "Just taking advantage of the big gym. Who's going to be my partner first?" I ask my friends.

Selene shakes her head. "I'm too pissed. I'm here because you two prefer the mats. My hands need to be holding a blaster still. He. Threw. You. Off. A. Cliff."

Yes, he did, and I want to murder him as bad as she does. But revenge needs to be a bit colder for now—I need to find out who all the traitors are first. In the meantime, his last name, his father's rank, and the resulting repercussions prevent me from hacking off his head.

Selene's homicidal gaze remains on Caiman. "My father's a Tribune

General too. I could likely get away with unloading a clip into his face. House Rhysien would have to pay restitution to House Rossi for the loss of its heir, but Caiman's father won't start an interhouse incident over him. These are the trials—death is expected, remember? Besides, the war houses are duty-bound to place the Republic before kin and self."

"I'm not here to murder anyone," I lie, "and neither are you. We're here for the Republic, remember?"

"I think the Republic would be better without Caiman's face attached to the rest of his body." I stifle a smile. I'd swear she was blood-gifted and reading my mind if I didn't know better. Or maybe great minds just think alike.

"Forget about Golden Boy. He'll get his." I glance over my shoulder to see Caiman has turned back to fighting Greysen. I laugh out loud. "They hate me so much because I'm part Khanaian, and yet they are practicing a style of fighting that originated in Khanai. The irony." The best part is that I know it grates on them to need to do so. But there isn't a more advanced or superior hand-to-hand combat style. Any soldier or warrior worth their salt across Iludu is well practiced in Xzana.

"Since Selene is spectating, that means it's me and you," I say to Zayne, hoping he accepts it as the raised peace flag I want it to be—discounting the fact that I always kick his ass, and he might not see this as a gift.

Sure enough, he says, "Works for me." But he looks across the room to Caiman and Greysen like he'd rather be fighting them.

"I'll go easy on you."

That easily, the friction between us dissolves and we're aligned to the same side again. He faces me, grinning. "You wish. You ready to get your ass kicked today, Amari? I was so close last time we sparred. With the serum, I might best you this time."

"Did you hit that pretty head of yours in the forest?"

"No. Well, actually, yes. But that's not the point. This is . . ." He sets his body into a flawless Xzana defensive stance. His legs are a fraction farther apart than his shoulders, his knees are bent at a ninety-degree angle for maximum balance and leverage, his neck is aligned with his stacked spine, and his fists are held out in front of his chin. High enough to quickly block a blow below or above the neck and high enough to jab out with power and speed just as fast.

"Your burial rites," I say, then set my body into an offensive stance. Weight balanced, feet scissored, and muscles coiled to strike. Falling into a dance Grandfather began teaching me at age four, I hurl a punch at Zayne's throat. He blocks it and counterattacks. I knock his fist aside and execute a kick that takes him off his feet. He springs back up off the mat before I fully reset my fighting stance. He launches a kick that I narrowly dodge with a backflip. His fist connects with my left shoulder as I'm straightening my body. We trade a flurry of punches and kicks and I'm loving every minute of it.

My skilled technique comes from years of practice. Zayne's comes from natural talent. He moves in a way that defies gravity. I'm finally slipping into a groove when Reed inserts himself between us, interrupting my fun. Or not.

I purposely pull a punch too late and connect with his chin. "Sorry," I say, stepping back. I'm not sorry at all. He might have stepped up to Chance on my behalf—twice—but his act is a sham *and* he participated in marching me onto the stealth jet and dropping me off in a deadly magical forest. There is also the matter of my knives.

And I like punching people. So there's that.

Reed stands in front of me unfazed by my hit. I'd feel much more gratified if he were rubbing his jaw or at least opening and closing it. It was a solid right hook, dammit. "What do you want?" I grumble.

He doesn't so much as blink or bristle at the blatant breach of protocol.

He ignores me, so I ignore him and look over toward the fight across the room. Greysen grunts as Caiman thrusts a side kick to his chest. Greysen's movements are too sluggish. And sloppy. He's an idiot, but he's clearly not stupid—he's intentionally letting Caiman maintain the upper hand. Reed looks their way. He clenches his jaw—maybe I did hurt him—then turns back to me. "I wanted to check on you. How are you faring?"

I motion down the length of myself. "I'm alive and whole." Again, he doesn't even blink. "How do you do it?" I ask because I really want to know.

"Do what?" he responds, confused. I'm talking about a lot of things, but I can only clarify one of them for him at the moment.

"Value human life so little. Value the life of your fellow Mareenians, fellow soldiers, fellow *Praetorians* so little. You participated in dropping us off in Onei's Expanse not caring if any of us made it through the four days alive." *You also killed your supposed mentor.* I don't care if he was acting under orders. He's a treacherous bastard.

"I cared."

"Not if you went along with things." I pick this fight because I can't pick the real one I want yet.

He squares his shoulders in a stubborn refusal to apologize. "Tradition is tradition."

I give him a look that lets him know how weak that sounds. "Are your words for me or yourself?" Did he tell himself some similar bullshit with Grandfather? When this is all over, I'm going to ask him. I want to know how he did it, why he did it. I want to know what made him not tell the guilty Tribunals to go fuck themselves and turn them in to Grandfather and Brock instead. They would've taken care of it. They would've addressed the threat, and Grandfather would still be alive.

His gaze hardens. He remains silent.

I shake my head and look in the direction of the entrance to the gym. "You can leave. There is nothing more for us to say to each other at the moment unless the discussion is about to turn to you offering me my knife back."

"You are like the Legatus Commander and nothing like him at all."

His observation knocks me back a step. He might as well have drop-kicked me in the chest.

No, he fucking didn't go there.

"What does that mean?" I practically snarl. There's no way I'm keeping my temper in check if he stays in my face much longer.

"He was deadly. Lethal. Fierce. He also adhered to decorum, and he wasn't hotheaded. He was disciplined and forward-thinking."

I go absolutely still. I sink into a dangerous place where my blood scorches *everything* from the inside out, a place where my gift itches to burst out of me, a place where it begs to be unleashed upon Reed. I imagine forming a blood spike in my palm and burying it into his jugular. Dimly, I remember where I am . . . that acting on the impulse will be disastrous. It's a hard fight, maybe the hardest of my life, but I rein in the bloodlust. I swap it out for a killing calm and try to be smart about the direction our conversation has turned. I can use it to get information Brock might not know about Reed's relationship with my grandfather.

"What would you know about him?" Despite my decision, I still tremble with fury when I ask. "You're barely a few years older than me. You wouldn't have served alongside him when he was a Praetorian in Gamma."

"The Legatus Commander was my mentor. He was also my Xzana hensei. I know *plenty*." He says it with an intimacy and unconcealed grief that makes me blink. It sounds so real. I'd believe it was real if Brock hadn't already outed him.

An irrational jealousy seizes me at the definite confirmation that Grandfather played Xzana master to Reed. Even if I know it was all faked on Reed's part, it wasn't on Grandfather's part, and that was something he and I shared. Something special that was solely between us. Something the rest of the Republic and all his duties and his position as Legatus couldn't muscle in on. That part of him was only for me. And to make it worse, Grandfather never mentioned serving as a master to and personally training anybody else. So not only did he do it, he didn't tell me about it. He hid it from me. How could he do that? And why would he train Reed at that level at all? Reed is full Mareenian. He doesn't have Khanaian lineage like us.

"I'd never heard about you before, so you and he couldn't have been that close," I say, chafed.

"Did you know everything about his endeavors?"

"Yes." *No.* Grandfather took me into his confidence about a lot of things, and other things he didn't. Clearly, this is one of those other things. However, Reed doesn't need to know that. I also don't think he believes me, so I want this conversation over with. At least for now. I know I should question him more, but my emotions threaten to resurge out of control. Grandfather was my kin. My mentor. My hensei. My *everything*. I hate that Reed stole a piece of him. I hate that he holds a piece of him that he doesn't even deserve. He can't have that piece. I want every part of Grandfather to myself. It's all I have left.

"If you don't mind, we were in the middle of sparring," I say, and try to keep the sharp hurt, the piercing grief, out of my voice. Reed doesn't get to glimpse that. I won't let him. Because if he does and he tries to commiserate with me, I will fucking lose it.

Reed watches me intently as I try to rein in my shit. I fail, and in doing so I'm an idiot because I show him a weakness.

When you engage in battle, the side that loses is always the one that betrays the greater weakness. If you want to win, Ikenna, be stronger than your opponent. In mind, in fortitude, in physicality, in all things.

It was one of Grandfather's teachings, and until now, it's one I never struggled with. But with Reed . . . I don't know entirely how to execute it. I feel like he's light-years ahead of me and I'm playing catch-up. He's standing in front of me cool and collected, and probably assessing me while I'm spinning out.

He looks like he's about to say something in response to whatever he sees, and I brace to have my thorough failure rubbed in my face. But then he doesn't say anything. He strides away, and I stand there looking after him, trying to cauterize my weaknesses and needing to start figuring out what the hell his are.

THAT EVENING, WHILE dinner is being served in the mess, I decide to make some more headway with my search for Grandfather's murderers. It's nice having a break from certain death to risk my life another way. I slip away from base and return to Terese Rhysien's vacated house.

The kind labourii woman answers the door again. She greets me with a puzzled but warm expression. I smile back in greeting and seize her hand. She gasps, startled. Before she can get out another sound, I push the guilt down and nick her arm with the small knife I grab off my waist.

You have to do this, I remind myself. *There's no other way.*

I don't just mean compelling her; I also mean inflicting the small wound. I don't have the level of power it takes to develop a bloodlink without direct contact with the target's blood. And in truth, I'm glad for the restriction. Being able to strip away a person's will by merely glancing their way leaps over the line of monstrous.

It's twice now that I've used compulsion—a thing I never would've dared do before. But this is too important and I don't see any other way to possibly start getting some answers about Grandfather's death, reasoning that if it went undetected once when I used it against Caiman, it should go undetected this one more time.

I hope.

I look Terese's housekeeper directly in her now-vacant eyes, wince, then make peace with the fact that even my brand of compulsion is heinous. The reparations I'm going to offer her will have to be enough to curb my guilt.

I hold up a hard currency chip I grabbed from a safe in Grandfather's office so the funds I give her can't be traced to me if anybody becomes suspicious about them. "The oddest thing happened to you this evening," I instruct the housekeeper, and she nods along. "You received a package addressed to you with no return address. It contained a currency chip worth five million credits and a note from a charitable stranger who wants to gift you retirement and remain anonymous. You're about to leave the house to think on it and celebrate. You've booked a penthouse suite under your first name at Chrysalis House in the inner sector. Order your favorite food, clothes from the hotel boutique because you didn't pack anything, you were so excited, and check out the spa. It's heavenly. Enjoy yourself and spend the night. You've already prepaid for an all-inclusive package in full so you don't have to use the currency chip when you get there. When you come back in the morning you can contact Terese or her husband from the house and tell them you quit if that's what you decide. Now, go get in the transport waiting for you that you've already called."

She reaches out and takes the chip, nodding. This way works better than simply bribing her to let me in, because she doesn't seem like the kind of woman who would take a bribe anyway and I can't risk her informing Terese or anybody else of anything. I want whoever orchestrated trying to kill me to continue to think that it was botched *and* that I'm none the wiser about it.

The labourii woman steps past me. I wait to make sure she gets into the transport and it pulls away. Then I step inside the house.

I find Terese's study on the third landing. It's located in a modest-sized room that's simplistic in its furnishings. A circular oak desk rests in the center of the floor. I go to it and turn on its slim personal computer. The passcode screen comes up. I take the mining chip from my pocket and slide it into the minuscule slot along the left edge of the screen. After the chip takes care of the password, I navigate to the storage drives. From among all the files, I filter out anything that isn't encrypted. There's no way the information I'm looking for isn't behind added security layers. The command I give the computer cuts what I've got to comb through down to about forty files. *That* I can get through in a night. Although it will take a good bit of time. I check my Comm

Unit. I've been away from the compound for about forty-five minutes. I'm still within the hour window we usually have for dinner, but it's almost up, and afterward our charming officers could decide to summon us at any moment. I grimace.

I hope to hell luck is on my side and they're done fucking with us for the night. If not . . . I'll deal with that craptastic predicament if it arises. For now, I concern myself with what I came out to the southern sector for.

The first documents I click on aren't anything useful. They consist of medical certifications, tax filings, and bank statements. I also find a copy of a patent for a metallic compound that's labeled confidential. Then I come upon a file that's behind a second encryption after the first one is circumvented, and things seem to have gotten interesting.

Very interesting, I think when the chip comes up against four additional stacked encryptions.

I lean forward, impatient, waiting for access to whatever they contain. I glance down at my Comm again to mark the time that's passed since my first check—twenty more minutes. Our time allotted for dinner is over with.

"Hurry up," I snarl at the mining chip. Not that it makes it work faster.

The securityware must be complex, because it takes a good hour before the chip clears it.

Finally the file opens and oddly familiar numbers pop up on the screen. It takes me a minute, but I realize that I'm seeing my height and weight. Below them is a chemical formula and numbers with a unit measurement behind them that indicate they're for a syringe administration of a liquid serum. It's exactly what I hoped to find. It has to be the formula and lethal dosage of what I was injected with.

I scroll down because there's more in the document. I read numbers that line up with Grandfather's approximate height and weight. Schematics on the biochip he received are also present that include its date of manufacture, batch number, and lot number. The same chemical formula that was present with my information is with his. The dosage accompanying it is a larger quantity. I type the chemical formula into a search engine and the hits it returns say the serum represents a mood stabilizer that carries the severe side effect of cardiac arrest with overdosing—and it's manufactured by Rhysien War House BioLabs.

My Comm Unit buzzes, and I jump. *Shit.* I check the message on the screen praying it's not reporting instructions. I let out a nervous breath when I see it's only a comm from Zayne.

I quickly read it, though, in case it's something about the trials.

Where the hell did you disappear to? Are you all right?

Yeah. I went to the apartments for a little while, I lie. *To clear my head after the run-in with Reed earlier. It's messing with me.* Which is the truth—it is fucking with me. But also, I feel like shit lying to Zayne in the manner that I am.

Understandable. But get back here. The urgency and admonishment in his words sound in my head with the same pitch his actual worried voice would carry.

I'll be back soon, I promise. Then I grip the edge of the computer screen, reading the open file on it once more.

I was right about how Grandfather was killed and about Sutton Rhysien being one of the Tribunes involved.

I sit back in the chair, and I should get moving with more expediency, but all I can do for a second is stare at the information on the screen. Even though I'd already come to the conclusion it shows, *seeing* it still feels like having the whole compound dropped on my head.

Tribunes tried to terminate us both.

It's no longer a theory or a guess. It's a confirmed fact.

In the moment, I don't have anger. I have something much worse for the Republic to reckon with. I have renewed purpose, direction, and validation of the agenda I entered the trials to make happen.

They won't get away with it.

I want from Sutton and whoever else is involved what they took from my grandfather and what they tried to take from me. I want their freedom and right to live. I don't care what it takes to make that happen, and even though it might require some time, they don't get to keep breathing while he isn't. One Tribune has now been indicted, tried, and judged in my mind.

Now I just need to figure out how wide the treachery spans.

That starts with Reed. He's the path to the others. If he's the one who used the serum on Grandfather, then he was given a kill order that directed him to do it. And if he was given one, then *all* the Tribunes involved signed it. If they were committing treason together, the constant power struggles and shifting of alliances means they'd all likely insist on mutually assured destruction. It's what I would do. I'd also want similar insurance if I were Reed so that self-serving Tribunes could never wipe their hands clean and place the blame solely on me. Any Praetorian worth their training would've kept copies of the kill order in triplicate. I just need to find one.

I copy the incriminating file to the data-mining chip and save a backup to my own drives on my Comm Unit. Then I force the shock to wear off, rise from the chair, and leave.

As I take a transport back to the compound and hope to get back before anybody other than Zayne asks questions about me missing, I mull over exactly how I might finally get to Reed's apartment to look for the kill order along with Grandfather's knife. *Knives.* It's a problem that doesn't have an easy solution. I can't do what I did tonight and simply turn up at his door and take another chance with compulsion. I'll need his blood to pull that off and that *definitely* won't be simple. As much as it itches my ass to admit Reed might be able to best me, there *is* a possibility I might not live through the attempt.

The best course, then, is to remove him from the equation and break into his apartment when he isn't around. But the only times I know for sure he isn't there and won't be returning for a while is when trial activities are being conducted, which I can't slip away from. Outside of the trials, when they aren't torturing us, I don't know what the fuck the senior Praetorians do with their time. I doubt they're pulling cohort duties while the trials are ongoing, so I don't think breaking back into the Tribunal's secure records for Gamma's duty schedule will be of any use.

In the middle of me trying to see a way to get at Reed, my Comm Unit buzzes—this time with trial orders, because of course.

I look at the location and time: the compound's entry hall in seventeen minutes.

At first, I think, What the fuck kind of time frame is that? But then the actual gravity of the situation sets in and all I think is *Fuck! Fuck! Fuck!*

I'm still out in the southern sector. It'll take at least twenty minutes to get back to base. There's no question that I'm going to be late. The officers will for sure shred me a new one—or opt to kill me for tardiness. If Chance has anything to say about it, it'll for sure be the latter.

I scream in frustration to an empty transport. "What the hell do they have planned for us tonight and why the fuck can't they give us more of a heads-up about these things?!"

I indulge in visions of telling the senior Praetorians to kiss my ass. Instead, I ask the transport, "Can we increase speed to shave any time off transit?"

It dings, registering it heard me. A second passes, then two, and I pray it's because the transport's calculations are about to give me the answer I want.

"Increasing speed to adjust transit time to eighteen minutes," it confirms.

I grimace, but it's better than nothing. I'll just have to dash like hell into the compound once I arrive, and pray I can appeal to Reed, ironically, and his sense of not looking like a sadistic jackass in front of people.

I just can't let them boot me out before I have a chance to kill him.

11

WHEN I SPRINT INTO THE entry hall a minute and fifteen seconds late, the officers aren't present yet.

Thank you, I say to the gods, or the cosmos, or good fortune, or whatever decided to look out for me tonight.

Selene and Zayne throw me a *What the hell?* look as I take my place in the line of assembled aspirants.

As we await the officers' arrival, the silver moonlight bearing down on our form from the skylight above turns red. I look up, startled that Blood Moons blaze in the sky again. Two occurrences so close together is bizarre. It's eerie, and it momentarily steals my attention from the impending proceedings. With no constellations in sight, it looks like thick, viscous oil sieged the sky and the red moons were the only things powerful enough to withstand the assault. They're also no longer the crescents of several days ago. They've morphed into imposing crimson orbs hanging low in the sky. I look at them impassively, but inside, my heart is bursting with the portent of the tableau.

I was born six weeks early during full-bodied Blood Moons. A neonatemedic cut me from my mother's womb after Grandfather found her dead in his apartments. The body was cold, and by all medical reasoning, I should have been dead too. Grandfather attributed my survival to being Pantheon-blessed with the blood-gift.

Of course, nobody else in the hall pays the Blood Moons heed. The thud of steps jars me out of my thoughts.

The transition officers descend a staircase at the back of the entry hall that leads to the upper levels of the compound.

"Survival," Chance says once he's standing in front of us. "Your sorry asses demonstrated you at least have that skill during your fun foray into Onei's Expanse. Tonight is about strength."

I finally see the pattern. *Combat. Survival. Strength. Strategy. Stealth.* The five pillars of a Praetorian. Those are the five gods—perched upon the Praetorian Creed—Mareenians worship in the Sovereign Age.

And they're not so different from the Pantheon. *We just use different terms.*

"Follow me." Chance pivots and leads us from the entry hall down a long, brightly lit corridor. We're shepherded into a large, windowless room with concrete walls, a cement floor, and steel cages hanging from the ceiling in a row. To the left of the cages, along the west-facing wall, is the Death Board. One hundred and forty-nine aspirants died in the forest; only six hundred and fifty-two came home. The latter names are arranged into tournament brackets, pairing off those of us who survived.

I look up at the cages, sick with seeing a cage of any kind after the forest. "Is this a trial or a spectacle?" I hiss to Reed, who happens to be standing right next to me.

He cuts me a look that says, *Shut up. You're in breach of decorum right now.* I want to tell him to take his phony preoccupation with decorum and shove it up his ass—

"ATTENTION!" Chance shouts.

We aspirants straighten into neat lines.

"You will fight in single elimination matches," he informs us. "Twelve pairs will face off at a time, and two transition officers will referee the rounds fought in each cage." He points to one of the massive contraptions swaying above our heads. "Once the cage is lowered around you, the only way out of it is victory or—"

"Submission," Reed cuts in.

Chance's jaw clenches. That isn't what he was about to say. He doesn't refute the terms of engagement Reed dictated though. I look from Reed to Chance and back to Reed. Something about their balance of power has shifted since they faced off on the stealth jet. Reed doesn't seem to be playing the position of Chance's second anymore. Are he and Chance more jointly sharing authority over the trials moving forward? Perhaps away from the aspirants, the officers decided that Chance needs more than a co-lead to keep his power trips in check.

I don't start awarding them points for deciding it now. They should've done it the first day of conditioning.

They should've done it before I was ordered to be murdered by Chance. Twice. If Caiman was acting on Chance's orders in the forest, I'm positive he was acting on them the night he broke into my room too.

And it's not like Reed has taken it easy on us.

And he's a murderer, so he has that going against him.

This whole thing is so fucked.

"You won't merely be judged by if you win or lose," Chance continues. "You will be judged by how greatly you win and how *badly* you make your opponent lose. That's what'll decide if you continue forward or not." The sick asshole is trying to get around Reed's boundaries and set us up to do more than beat the shit out of each other. He wants us to try to maim or kill each other.

Diminished authority or not, he is still a sadist.

The officers spread out across the line of cages and begin calling up aspirant pairs. Chance and Reed stand at the same cage to play referee for it, and I'm sure it's not a coincidence.

"Ignatius. Greysen. You're up first at mine." Chance nods to them in turn. Their names occupy two spaces near the top of the left-hand side of the bracket.

They step beneath the cage Chance calls them to. He presses a discreet button on the wall beside it. Ignatius and Greysen stand facing each other, already assessing each other's strengths and weaknesses as the cage slides into place around them.

Chance nods, relishing the power and position he holds, signaling the two to begin.

Ignatius attacks first. Greysen defends, moving with a great deal more speed and a lot more lethal grace and intent than he did when sparring with Caiman. He moves like a decent fighter when not kowtowing to his best friend. The match is over before it really begins. Greysen breaks Ignatius's right arm in three places and shatters his left knee in the first ten seconds. Ignatius tries to keep fighting, desperate not to yield, which is admirable if not a waste of time and energy. Greysen shatters his remaining good knee, and Ignatius collapses sideways, his jaw smacking into the cement floor. Greysen, not finished with him yet and trying to garner more favor with Chance, moves in on the fallen Ignatius.

"It's over," Reed yells before Greysen can do something heinous. "You won."

"It isn't over," Chance challenges. "Ignatius hasn't yielded."

Reed points to Ignatius, who is blacked out from the blow his face took to the floor. "An unconscious man can't yield."

Greysen looks to Chance for his orders. After a long, grudging beat, Chance pushes the button on the wall.

Most of the other first set of matches are ending as well.

"Take him to the med tower and come back," Reed instructs the two aspirants who've already won their fights standing closest to him. They go to Ignatius, haul his considerable bulk up, and carry him away. It's clear to everybody who was watching that if Reed wasn't present as a check and balance to Chance, they would be carrying away a corpse and not an unconscious man.

Several more vicious rounds later, Selene is in the cage that Dannica and Nero referee, facing a bruiser of a guy who is three times her size. *Selene is good. Selene can handle a bigger opponent*, I tell myself. I know how skilled she is. What she lacks in size and strength, she more than makes up for in agility, ferocity, and cunning. She can cut the guy she's fighting down with ease.

True to form, her fight is over in about sixty seconds. She hammers a side kick to his jaw, nearly taking his head off. He blocks the follow-up kick and flips her on her back. The crack against the cement makes pain shoot down *my* spine. But Selene rolls out of the way of the boot that tries to stomp down on her stomach. She grabs that foot and twists, breaking her opponent's ankle. He crashes to the ground. She hops to her feet then drops down beside him. She wrestles him into a submission hold that will snap his neck if he moves so much as an inch. "Yield," she demands, pissed about the attempted boot to her stomach. Spit flies as he shrieks the word.

When Nero takes his time pressing the button to lift the cage, Dannica does it herself. I think I might like her.

Selene takes her place back in our ranks while her opponent sprawls on the floor. It takes him some time to peel himself off the cement and limp back to the spot he just forfeited after tonight.

Zayne walks beneath Chance and Reed's cage two rounds after Selene. Caiman saunters beneath it too. Caiman doesn't wait for the steel cage to lower to launch the assault he's sure will result in a victory. For all of his posturing, Caiman is admittedly skilled, and strong as shit. The fight is brutal. Caiman is a head taller than Zayne and has more bulk, plus he's a hairsbreadth faster.

He also spends his time sparring with people who suck up to him.

Zayne spends the majority of the seven-minute fight pretending to favor his left side. When Caiman takes it for a tell he can use to his advantage, Zayne switches things up. He shifts his weight to the right, throwing Caiman off balance. Caiman's fist grazes Zayne's shoulder. Zayne's answering kick to Caiman's gut leaves him doubled over. He uprights himself in time to block another blow by Zayne. My breath catches in my throat when Caiman wrestles Zayne to the ground and into a full-body submission hold. I hear one bone then another snap. Zayne's grunts ring in my ears along with Caiman's gloating.

On instinct, I move toward the ring. Reed braces an arm across my chest. "Fall back in line, Amari." He has two seconds to move his damn arm or I'm breaking it.

My eyes jerk back to the ring at another grunt. This time it comes from Caiman. Zayne has reversed their positions. Sweat drips from Zayne's forehead. His face is a twisted mask of pain he's hellbent on pushing through to win. It's his left leg that's broken. He's bearing most of his weight on his right. Caiman throws his weight against Zayne and reverses the hold. They go back and forth, locked in a stalemate before Zayne gains the advantage.

"I'm bored," Chance drawls from beside the ring. "Draw."

"How is that a draw?" Enzo yells. "That call is wolfshit!"

Caiman releases Zayne with a heave. Zayne twists Caiman's arm, wrenching it out of the socket. "That's for Kenna," he says before disengaging all the way.

"What the fuck?" Caiman wails, clutching his arm. "Chance called a draw!" Of course he did. Caiman Rossi cannot *not* make it through these trials. Chance will have to answer to Daddy Rossi if Golden Boy fails out.

"Help Caiman to the med tower," Chance says to Greysen. "Drake, you can limp there on your own for the shit you pulled," he says to Zayne.

"Help Drake to the med tower too," Reed tells an aspirant, over-riding Chance.

Chance glares at Reed again, and I can't help but wonder what it would look like in a cage with those two in it.

Chance calls my name for his ring's last fight, because of course he does. I take Zayne's place under the steel cage. Reed calls up Wicker Caan to be my opponent. Wicker is a good foot taller than me, finished fifth in our cadet class, and is a scion of Caan War House. He's good at hand-to-hand, but I'm better.

Chance throws his arm against Wicker when he moves to step beneath the cage. "Change of plans. You get a free pass. Amari is going to face me."

"How is that fair?" Enzo shouts, once more calling out Chance. I can't say I disagree with him . . . but I also want this.

"What? Those aren't the rules!" Selene yells.

"You're both out of pocket. The rules are whatever the fuck I say they are!"

Reed steps in front of Chance when he moves to join me under the cage. "You're not fighting her." He jerks his chin at Wicker. "Get in the ring."

"It's okay," I say, arrogant, because there is no way in hell I'm passing up this opportunity. "If Chance wants our showdown to be tonight, we can go." I crack my neck on both sides and shake my limbs to loosen up. Ready for it. "I told him what I thought of his odds against me after the Survival Trial. I'm not going to be called a coward or a liar now."

"If she says she's good with the match, you've got no grounds to intervene. Unless there's something you want to tell me," Chance says smoothly. "Are you fucking her?"

"It's always about that with you. If I didn't know any better, I'd say you sound jealous, but there's nothing to be jealous about," Reed responds, shaking his head. "Don't be a bastard."

"I'm loath to even fight her, because that means I have to touch her,"

Chance sneers. "But she needs to learn her place." He shoulder-checks Reed and swaggers to the center of the ring.

All the melodrama aside, I'm about to fight a fully trained Praetorian, and I'm guessing he's not going to let me yield if it comes to that.

So I guess it can't come to that. And I roll my neck as if to say, *Bring it.*

Whatever matches were about to start alongside mine have paused. Everyone, aspirants and officers, watches the impending face-off between Chance and me. I'd rather not do this with an audience, but I'm pissed enough after the forest to not particularly care either. If Chance is going to give me a free pass to bash his face in without having to wait until after the trials when I can't get kicked out, I'm not about to pass it up. I already lack restraint on the best of days, and there isn't that much discipline in the universe.

Chance calls for Reed to lower the cage.

Reed stands beside it, tense, looking from me to Chance. There's a dressing-down all over his face that's comical—especially since it's not directed at Chance. *He's reproaching me?*

As I thought earlier, these whole trials are fucked.

Then Reed swallows whatever he's feeling, smooths out the expression, and slaps the button on the wall.

Adrenaline surges as the steel bars drop. I can attack first or wait. I can let Chance come to me and use it to gauge how he fights, his strengths, and his weaknesses. I choose what Grandfather would counsel and sink my weight into the back of my heels, assuming a defensive stance.

Chance no longer smirks or sneers. His face is predatory, and he stalks toward me with deadly intent in every step. I take his measure. He isn't telegraphing by favoring a side. There's a blaster at his waist and two knives strapped to his hip. I don't put it past him to draw a weapon at some point. Fair fight to fair fight, hand to hand, I'm positive I have him beat. Chance won't fight fair, though, especially once he realizes he orchestrated a fight he won't win.

But I'm not an idiot—I forgot about fair days ago.

There are two knives tucked into each of my boots if I need them.

For now, Chance keeps his weapons sheathed, confident that he can take me out in hand-to-hand.

One of us is about to be shown up as overconfident.

He stalks close enough, and once he does, I switch tactics and throw a punch he doesn't anticipate. I catch his chin, and his head rocks back. His answering cross-jab smashes into my jaw. My teeth tear into the side of my mouth. I spit out blood. Habit makes my eyes snap to the red on the ground. It's minuscule enough not to matter, and I immediately refocus on Chance. I block the roundhouse kick flying at my head and drop to my knees, landing an upper cut to Chance's ribs. He knees me in the chest before I can jump up and get solid footing. It knocks the wind out of me. I stagger off balance. Chance seizes the opportunity to hammer punch after punch at my stomach. For every step I stagger backward, he takes a victorious one forward. I can't make this look easy like I foolishly did in the bar. My back bumps against the bars. I whip my head to the left in time to avoid Chance's fist from shattering my left eye socket.

Time to attack.

I curse and throw out two jabs that land beneath his right eye. The skin splits open and blood trickles down his cheek. I keep punching, fighting my way out of the corner he's boxed me into. I feel the skin on my knuckles rip and the open tears sting as air and blood and sweat infect the wounds. My next punch doesn't land—Chance dips below it. He doesn't barrel an uppercut into my stomach like I anticipate. Rather, he stays low and jabs my right knee. Pain shoots through it. The tendons tear as bone shatters. Chance is biochipped, he's strong as shit, and his Xzana form is decent. All of that combines to make this precarious dance—the one where I need to beat Chance in the end but make it look like I struggled to do it—difficult to master. I stagger to the left, then fall.

He pounces on me while I'm down, grappling me into a full-body sub hold, similar to the one Caiman used on Zayne.

"Throw him off you, Kenna!" Selene shouts from the sidelines.

I try to maneuver out of the hold. But Chance is too big, and I'm outmuscled. He laughs. I headbutt him and smile at the grunt it elicits. Easing the sub hold, his fingers dig into my left arm and tear my shoulder from its socket. White-hot pain shoots down the length of my arm as my eyes water. I bite the inside of my lip to keep from giving him the satisfaction of hearing me cry out. Still holding my arm, he twists it hard in a way that would have made it break at my elbow if I didn't turn into the hold to alleviate some of the tension.

Using the spin, I knee him in the chest and hear the satisfying crack of broken ribs. I'm done playing games. I refuse to let Chance pound me anymore.

Perhaps sensing this, he draws the pair of knives. Shouts come from outside the cage, but I don't have time to discern what's being said. I'm pretty sure I can guess anyway.

I dodge the first blade. The second sinks into my stomach. I hiss and snatch it out as I buck him off me, roll to the side, and jump to my feet. This time I'm able to get myself set, and I lob the knife at his chest with my good arm while I snatch one of my own from my left boot. The weight of the knife in my grip centers me. It sings through the air, sailing toward Chance. It sinks into his shoulder joint. The one I grab from my right boot sinks into his gut.

Now he draws the blaster, and things start to get interesting.

Reed hollers his name. My friends yell mine. Their yelling isn't bulletproof, though, so I dodge two projectiles on my own. The next three rip into my torso. Selene screams louder. Reed curses at Chance. I drop to my knees. Chance's foot connects with the center of my chest, and he kicks me flat on my back. He rests the same foot on my ribs then presses down, returning the favor of breaking three of them. Chance drops to a knee beside me and gathers a fistful of my hair. He yanks me back to my knees. The cool steel of a knife kisses my throat. His lips find their way to my ear. "I'm not going to slit your throat. That would end this way too soon. You forfeited the option of a quick, clean death by remaining where you don't belong. In this cage, you die slow. Like your grandfather. It's a pity that couldn't've been messy. He was where he didn't belong either. Then he got terminated."

It isn't an explicit admission of guilt, but how could he possibly know what Grandfather's death was like unless he'd been there? And what he says, about it being slow, matches what I found out about the lethal bioserum. Fury douses me. It isn't made of the white-hot, electric thing in my blood that sets it spoiling to burst loose every time I'm pissed off. It's cold, quiet, and simmering. It's pure, destructive rage blind with grief. Wounds split open that make my physical ones feel like scratches. I have bullets in me, but these verbal injuries are made of the worst kind of hurt that runs bone deep. Soul deep. Blood deep. My grandfather is gone, and Chance could've been involved in ripping him from me.

He should have just slit my throat.

I wrap my hand around the one Chance uses to hold the hilt of the knife. His muscles bunch as he throws his weight into pushing back against me. I struggle for every inch the knife scoots away from my throat. When it's far enough, I pry it from his grip. He tackles me, but he doesn't know the extent of my zeal. I am pure adrenaline at this point, and I end up straddling his torso holding the knife against his carotid. If I slice it open, a hundred biochips can't fix the damage fast enough. His death will be sloppy, and he will get what he deserves. I need to hurt somebody. I need to make somebody pay. Not later. Now. And while Reed isn't within my reach at the moment, Chance is.

A red haze overlays my vision. The power in my blood ignites into a raging firestorm. It tangles with the fury and produces something new and utterly chilling. Ikenna fades while a thing that's alien and primitive yawns awake. I want to obliterate Chance. I want to obliterate the room. I want to obliterate the entire world for the offense of stealing my grandfather away from me. And yet it is exactly this need for vengeance that is the only thing that keeps me slightly tethered. I latch on to that need and focus on it. I use the leash it dangles to pull Ikenna, to pull *me*, to the forefront. I lean in close to Chance and speak low so what I say is strictly between the two of us. "Are you saying that *you* terminated him? You're a Praetorian, which means you would've been acting out a kill order. Who gave it? How did you do it? Who aided you? You're not skilled enough or smart enough to have taken him out all by yourself." If I didn't have an audience, I'd rip the answers from him with compulsion.

Chance glances down at the knife and smiles back up at me. "I have no idea what you're talking about."

I can't kill him. If I kill him, I lose this new lead. But he's not going unpunished. I remove the knife from his jugular and drive it into the pressure point beneath his right ear. "Yield, fucker."

Yield so you can live and I can extract the info I want out of you later. And hurry the fuck up.

Because as much as I want him to submit so this fight is over, I *need* Chance to submit before my weakened state forces me to give up the advantage. The rapid blood loss, multiple wounds, and my gift expending copious energy fixing the extensive damage is sapping my strength. Poised above him, I sway, praying to whoever will listen for Chance to yield.

At the tell, his blue eyes flash with resistance and elation at the impending win. "No. I think I'll wait you out." He spits blood in my face.

"*Yield.*"

I press the knife deeper into the pressure point and this time thread a sliver of my blood-gift into the directive because I've become desperate. I don't look anywhere else except straight into Chance's blue eyes, and I hope nothing about the demand that would ordinarily be made in a fight to submission sounds strange. I'm taking a risk, but there is no other way this fight can end. Chance cannot die, and I cannot pass out before he yields first.

"I yield." He whispers the words. Surprise that he's uttered them flits across his face, but the cage is already rising, incoherent shouts of surprise and alarm getting closer.

He's said the only words that matter. They come right on time. I slump to the side. Chance pushes me the rest of the way off him with ease. He stands over me and I know I can do nothing to defend myself against the pure hatred he stares down at me with. Nothing to stop him from doing what Zayne did to Caiman.

Nothing aside from Reed, who appears beside us, inserting himself between me and Chance. He stoops down and hauls me up. "You need to get to a medic."

He and Chance must've been working together. It makes so much sense. One man couldn't have taken Grandfather out alone. No matter how duplicitous or adept. I throw my head back and laugh, wild, the red haze threatening to return and make me attack him right there. I likely would if I wasn't so injured.

Selene pushes him out of the way. "I have her." She slides an arm underneath me. I step away. Well, I try to. The attempt is feeble, and Selene's arm stays where it is.

"I'm not going to the med tower," I say between one ragged exhale and a fucking torturous inhale. It's bad enough I'm bleeding all over the fight space. I don't want to be bleeding all across the base and all over the med tower too. Plus I'm not trusting any medic after my lethal bioserum injection. Because the more I think about the injection, the more I realize *all* the medics that day were likely slipped some variation of the order to dose me with something different. Reed might've nudged me toward Terese Rhysien's shorter line since she was fully knowledge-able about things, but what if a viable excuse to maneuver me with-out raising suspicions hadn't arisen? He—or whoever—would've had a contingency plan if I didn't end up in the preferred line. It would be the smart, prudent thing to do. Moreover, as soldiers of the Republic, we're trained to have several plans during an op. Which means similar orders to kill me could be delivered to the medic who ends up treating me at the tower.

Reed regards me like I'm an idiot when I protest. "The UVs need to be extracted. Otherwise you'll die." He says it slowly, as if speaking to someone who's dense.

"I know that," I snap. If the UVs aren't removed in time, they'll explode inside me. Mareenian weaponry loves a good failsafe. My blood-gift will not repair that level of havoc, and it leaves me between a damn boulder and a hard place. I can't dig out the bullets myself, and I can't ask Selene to do it because we don't get that level of training as cadets. Maybe all the rapid blood loss affects my brain or maybe it's sheer stupidity that makes me say what I do next to Reed. "You can dig them out." He is the last person whose hands I should place my life in. But I don't have any other alternatives. So, I take the gamble that for whatever reason, even if he wants me dead alongside my grandfather, he doesn't want to do it in any conspicuous way, and me bleeding out in his care in the compound would definitely be conspicuous.

"That's insane. Get to the med tower. It's an order. Take her," he instructs Selene.

Selene's arm tightens around my torso, and I shove against her. "No. I said I'm not going anywhere."

The pitch of my voice makes Selene's hold loosen. She stares at me bewildered, then pales with understanding.

The hard set of Reed's jaw says he doesn't give a shit about my wishes. He's about to have me dragged to the med tower whether I like it or not.

Dammit. In my weakened state, I can't put up much of a fight if he decides that course. I have to tell him something that will make him listen to me. So very loudly where everybody else can hear it, I play on his supposed honor and the ruse he's trying to keep up that he gives a shit about me. "I can't go to the med tower because there are people other than Chance who don't want me to get through these trials alive. Attempts on my life have already been made. Mareen didn't want to see an akulu man hold the rank of Praetorian. Do you think it wishes to see an akulu woman? How many times have I been put in a position where the rules didn't apply to me? I'm not trusting a medic or anyone else I'm not sure isn't a bigoted asshole with my life. You're a Praetorian with combat casualty training. That's good enough. You can do the extraction job here."

Reed gapes at me.

"Yes, yes, I know. I'm insane," I respond, heading off him informing me of that point a second time. "You can say yes or you can let me die. Those are your two options. Which one is it?" Now I've backed *him* into a corner. If he says no, it might seem like he wants me to die.

"Just do it here," Selene begs. "*Please.*"

"Can you grab an emergency trauma kit and bring it to the common room above the mess?" he tightly asks Dannica, who's hovering near.

She faces me instead of him. "You sure about this, Amari?" It's the first time she's addressed me directly.

Instead of answering with words, I set my face into an immovable, absolute stare.

She laughs, and it's the last thing I expect her to do. "You've got balls. I'm on it," she says to Reed, and sprints off.

Reed emits a long-suffering sigh. He steps up to my right side and hooks an arm around my waist. "I've got your insufferable friend," he tells Selene.

I do my best to not pass out.

12

DIGGING UV BULLETS OUT OF a person is messy, bloody work. It's also damn painful. Thank the cosmos there's only three of them embedded in me, because after Reed roots around my insides to fish out the first one I am done. I bite down on a wad of gauze to keep from howling when he yanks the bullet free of the tissue its lodged in below my left breastbone. I'm not successful at staying silent when his surgical tweezers delve into the tender center of my upper abdomen to grab the second bullet. It feels like he's thrust a hot poker into my midsection instead of a sliver of cool metal. The scream that tears from me leaves me hoarse and drenched in sweat.

Maybe he is trying to kill me after all.

"Why the hell did that one hurt so bad?" I rasp as Reed drops the bullet onto the wooden table beside my head. I'm lying on my back on a couch that's at least covered in a sterile tarp from the trauma kit.

I expect a wisecrack from Reed at my display of pain—an academy instructor would've torn me a new one. He only grimaces. "It was lodged in deep tissue, and I grazed your spleen coming out. I couldn't avoid it." He wears a pair of mag-res glasses from the kit that allow him to view my internal anatomy as high-resolution magnetic images, but he's still not a surgeon in a fully equipped med suite.

I draw in a steadying breath and grip the tarp while I wait for him to extract the third bullet. "What is it?" I ask when he hesitates.

He looks at me for several moments, then shakes his head. "Nothing." Then he sets to work. As he probes my lower belly for the exact place of the final bullet he mutters, "I know veteran Praetorians who wouldn't willingly do this outside of a med tower unless it was life or death. A medic has general anesthesia that trauma kits don't."

"The choice *was* life or death. Believe me, if it wasn't, I wouldn't be here with you." The glib chuckle costs me. Fire ripples through my midsection.

"I didn't know there'd been attempts on your life other than the bullshit with Chance. How many were there?"

I automatically go on high alert. I'd be a fool not to consider if there's a hidden agenda.

"Too many," I say ambiguously, undecided about the intent behind it. He could be keeping to the image he projects, or he could be probing me for how much I know.

He looks at me hard. "That's not a number."

I continue to evade. "Why do you care?"

"Amari, how many?" His tone is inflexible, damn near commanding. It hits the perfect note of concern and pisses me all the way off.

"Don't act like you give a shit." *Don't act like you're not responsible for one of them,* I want to spit. But if I do that, I could tip him off that he's under suspicion, and there's no way to explain the enhanced durability, stamina, and strength I've displayed thus far. Exceptional combat-arts training or not, nobody without a biochip or its equivalent could do what he saw me do against Chance.

"I do care."

Oh, I want to laugh so bad at that, but I have no desire to repeat the anguish spurred by my earlier chuckle.

Instead, I opt to seize an opportunity I might not get again. Chance shooting me in the ring was good for one thing: I'm alone with Reed and close enough in proximity to him to wield a compulsion. I can find out exactly what he knows about Grandfather's death. I can force all the conspirators' names out of him, and I can force him to turn over the kill-order file. Yes, I need his blood, but that might be not so challenging to maneuver since he already has a sharp object in hand.

Do you have the strength to hijack it though? A rational voice says.

I tell it to shut up, stubborn, and reach for my blood-gift—and the attempt entirely saps what little strength I'd regained. I reach for it again. All I get for my second effort are shallow breaths as the room spins. I curse all the Pantheon, and Amaka especially. If the gods are so high and mighty, why the fuck can the blessings they gave be depleted? I probe for my gift again. It should be present. Yes, it exerted copious efforts to keep me alive in the ring and is expending more energy afterward to heal me, but there are Blood Moons in the sky. They should already be countering the drain. The forest was different. Another god's nullifying magic was at play. Right now, it isn't, and Grandfather and I tested the bounds of my blood-gift under Amaka's moons countless times. The amplifying effect is normally instant. I grip my legacy pendant, wondering what the hell is going on.

I curse the gods a million more times in my head. What's the use of this gift if it keeps fluctuating during the times I need it the most? It faltered in the ring with Chance too. His eyes didn't turn immediately vacant like they should have, his response to the compulsion was delayed, and it did not strip him entirely of consciousness when he yielded. The effect on Chance was more like a diluted persuasion than a true compulsion. Which was why he was so immediately surprised about yielding.

I cry out when Reed's fingers graze a particularly sore spot on my lower belly. The pain brings me back to the room and what's happening inside it.

"Sorry," Reed says, low. "Removal of this third one is going to hurt more than the last."

I clench my teeth around the gauze. Of course it is. "I'm going to murder Chance," I vow to the cosmos. "And after I do, I'm going to find a way to reanimate his corpse so I can murder him all over again. I—"

I wail at the sharp bite of pain that erupts in my lower stomach. Reed drops the last UV bullet onto the wooden table.

I glare at him. "*You fucking shithead.*"

He reaches into the trauma kit that's atop the table. "That's an interesting way of saying *thanks for pulling bullets out of me. I owe you gratitude.*"

I owe you a blood spike to the chest. Several, in fact.

"A warning would've been nice so I could've braced for it."

"I did give you one. Then you went off the deep end like you always do, so I figured while you were distracted, it was as good a time as any to yank it out."

I fish the gauze out my mouth so I look and sound more dignified. "I do not go off the deep end. When I'm angry, it's always justified."

His mouth twitches.

"What is so funny?"

"The Legatus didn't have your temper," he responds as he cleans, cauterizes, and applies medgauze to my wounds. "He could remain calm under the grossest affront. I mean, he was always calculating how to cut the knees out from under his enemies, too, but he fought his battles with finesse and a lot more subtlety. You, on the other hand, are brash in everything you do."

I should go ballistic after he dares to talk like he was actually, genuinely close with Grandfather. But when I open my mouth, all I can do is snap it shut again. I don't know how to respond to what he so plainly stated, because while it should be infuriating, I can't even deny or argue against the accusation. It's wholly true. It was a thing Grandfather berated me for all the time. Still, I'm not giving Reed the satisfaction of thinking he's rendered me speechless or embarrassed.

Though I definitely pay for it in stars, I snort, irreverent. "My grandfather believed in détente. He also believed the best way to strike down an enemy was for them to never see you coming when you launched your assault. I don't believe in either. I want my enemies to see me coming, and I want them to tremble when they do. I want them to shit themselves while I cut them down, gut them, then carve them apart. Grandfather tried to minimize the spill of blood wherever he could. He tried to curtail the amount of violence he had to unleash. I relish both. Any past, present, or future enemies I have would do well to remember that." I let that threat hang between us, a promise, a vow, a fucking oath that I'm going to fulfill with his life, Chance's, and everybody else's I go after.

He doesn't say anything in response to my oratory. By the time Reed finishes patching me up, I realize my blood-gift must have kicked into overdrive to help heal me because fatigue is about to do me in. Soon I'm going to be comatose, and I don't wish to sink into that deep a slumber in a common room where I'm exposed to attacks. I rise to a sitting position on the couch, then stand up. "I'll chuck this in an incinerator on the way to my room," I say, bending down to collect the blood-smeared tarp before I go. A wave of dizziness makes me brace a hand on the couch instead. Shit. I really need to hurry up and get away from him. Having him fish bullets out of me is one thing; being unconscious around him is a completely different thing.

"You need to lie back down." Reed grabs my elbow and tries to prod me into following his directive.

I resist. "I need to get to my room." I don't care if my logic that he won't kill me at the moment was basically proven true when he dug bullets out of me without any shady play. He could've easily found a way to end me then. A trembling hand or a "slip" with the surgical tweezers would've done the job well. It dawns on me only now what I failed to consider before when I had this brilliant idea: My insisting he treat me was a slip-up. It could've been spun as entirely my fault. He ordered me to the med tower in full view of everybody and I refused to go.

I just don't understand why he *didn't* use this opportunity.

I'm too foggy to figure that out right now. I'm also weak enough that when he picks me up and lays me back on the couch, the fight I put up is pathetic. I threaten to gut him. It's the only defense I have left.

It's his turn to snort. "You're in no shape to go anywhere, ass-kicker. And until you can physically fight me on that, you stay here. Besides, you don't have any knives at the moment."

I reach down and realize he's right—there's nothing in my boots, and whatever I was holding against Chance must have been dropped. I curse.

"You suffered serious trauma, Amari." Reed's tone shifts from exasperated to a soft rumble as he says it. "Relax and let the bioserum do its job or that round two you're spoiling for with Chance won't happen because you'll be dead from round one."

"I'm exhausted." Heavy, near delirious fatigue drags the admission out of me, along with other truths I should be keeping concealed. "I feel myself falling into a coma. I don't want to fall asleep in this damn common room. People want to kill me. You might want to kill me. I'll be an easy target."

Did I just say that out loud?

His expression is completely stupefied. He blinks several times. The bewilderment on his face is so intense and seemingly real that *I* have to blink to make sure I'm reading him right. I'd swear it was real. I shake my head, trying to clear the fog. The bone-deep tiredness is making me sloppy, and it's making me imagine things that aren't there—those are extremely dangerous things to do around Reed. I've seen firsthand how convincing he can be. How much he can make people want to believe him. Want to follow him. It was almost as if he cast a spell over the lecture dome, or had the abilities of the old war-gifted Mareenian generals.

Okay, now I've definitely slipped into the insane side of sleepy. None of that is remotely possible.

"Kill you? I've tried to have your back as much as I could from the start. The Legatus—" Reed shakes his head, a stoic, inscrutable expression slams over his face. Then he drops back into the chair he was sitting in while playing medic. "You need to rest before expending the energy of relocating," he says firmly. "It's not a request; it's an order. But to help you feel better about it because I understand your concerns, I'll give you two promises: I'm not after your life, and I won't leave your side while you're out. You have my word that nobody will attack you. They'll have to get through me first to do it." He speaks with a soft rumble again. This time it has a fierce edge to it. Like the entire world will go down in a blaze if it crosses him.

Gods, it would be nice if that were true. If I had somebody capable of backing me up to the extent Grandfather did. It'd be nice not to have to shoulder my burdens all alone. Not to have to take on the whole world without a strong ally who would help me cull the threats. But that person isn't Darius Reed. Which is why I gather my bearings, as much as I can, to march from the room. I take a step toward the door. A wave of dizziness crashes into me. I manage a second step before I pass out.

I BOLT AWAKE. The first thing I look for is Reed. He remains in the chair beside the couch that I'm lying on again. He's hunched over, with fingers steepled under his chin. He isn't turned toward me and staring. That would be creepy. He watches the door to the common space, unblinking. When I push up to a sitting position and stand this time, I don't nearly collapse like some green cadet after a bad training exercise during their first years of the academy.

"You might be the most stubborn person I've ever met," he says. Reed angles his body so he can see the door and me. He scrutinizes me head to toe. "You're upright on your own. That's a good sign. How do you feel?"

Good enough to kick his ass for making me sleep here. "Decent," I say.

He smirks.

I brush past him. I spin around when I clear the door and he's on my heels. "Can I help you with something?"

He dangles my legacy pendant, which should be on my neck, in front of my face. "I figure you want this back. It was blood-splattered and a breeding ground for an infection with your open wounds, so I took it off you while you were out."

As I take it from him, I notice there's no trace of blood on it. I arch an eyebrow. "You cleaned it?"

"Yeah."

"Umm. Okay."

His mouth twitches as I slide it into my pocket.

"What?"

"You really have an aversion to the words 'thank you.'"

"I do. But I adore the words 'fuck you,' 'kiss my ass,' and 'go to hell.'"

He jerks his chin in the direction of the hall I was headed for. "I'll escort you to your room."

"No thanks. I can get there myself. I feel fantastic," I add, when he attempts to protest.

"Walk, Amari," is what he responds with. "You can either go with an escort or remain in this room with one." A wiseass, he parrots the lilt of how I sounded earlier when I demanded he patch me up.

I scowl, not in the mood to fight with him. I'm ready to shower the blood and gunk off me and then be alone. It's too unnerving to be around him at the moment. He kept his promise. He stood guard over me while I was vulnerable, and I have no idea what to make of that. I pivot and continue on my way while pretending he isn't skulking behind me. We get to my room, but he's not done being a pain in my ass. Selene isn't there, and he insists on waiting around until she appears.

I ping Selene to get her ass to the room so I'm not stuck with Reed for longer than I have to be and stalk to the shower, adding one more tick mark to all the reasons why I despise him. He snatched my knife; he almost kicked my ass; he's one of the officers putting me through hell; he likely killed my grandfather; he tried to kill me—I think. I was so sure of that last one before he played surgeon and then bodyguard. But those actions combined with the way he truly looked baffled when I accused him of being one of the people angling to see me dead goes beyond being an impeccable liar or being in possession of extraordinary skills of subterfuge. He's either a sociopath or he's innocent, and if he's not guilty of attempting to kill me—if I've been misreading his actions all along, steered by my own grief and my own fury—then I have to consider what else he might be innocent of.

I go back to why he was a suspect in the first place: my conversation with Brock. Yet Brock never specifically said Reed killed Grandfather. He never even said he was the only suspect. He merely said he was the *chief* suspect, and Chance all but admitted last night he himself was present for Grandfather's death. One thing isn't fake: the heavy animosity between Chance and Reed. No matter which way I turn it over, now that I'm thinking clearly outside the haze of bloodlust in the ring, I can't see them working together in something so critical and something that would come with catastrophic consequences if they fucked up. Maybe Brock thinks Reed is the chief suspect because that's exactly what the people who killed Grandfather want him to think. The mentee Grandfather met with hours before he died is the perfect scapegoat. Anybody with suspicions would focus their intentions on Reed. And if they did, they'd be following the wrong trail, never uncovering answers or getting any closer to the truth.

The possibility makes my head spin—not just that I might be wrong but that I may have been wasting time finding the truth—and I scrub my hands down my face once I close the door to the bathroom. I lean against the wall, and I don't move for some time. I try to pull the truth from the tangle of things that I know. However, it's impossible. There are too many gaps in the info I have, leaving too many possibilities of what actually happened with Grandfather. The only thing I know for sure is that he was killed with a formulation of a mood-stabilizer serum in toxic doses. I'm still positive the answers lie at the end of the path that leads from that bit of intel. But I might need to switch up the direction I'm looking in. I'll have to deal with Reed and figure him out soon enough, but Chance is my new priority, given his admission.

Round two is definitely coming.

STANDING IN THE narrow stall of the shower, I probe for my blood-gift, seeing if the stretch of sleep helped restore it. I hate that I'm my most powerless without the full magnitude of it. I tilt my head back and look at the spray of water shooting from jets in the ceiling. I'm underground and there are no skylights or windows in the bathroom, but I see tonight's Blood Moons as clear as if there is a window to view them. They are the reason I didn't have to limp back to my room and I'm able to remain upright in the shower. My already accelerated healing is at hyperspeed. I feel the benefit they afford me, yet nothing else.

The triplet moons glow red in my mind's eye, and I try to push my gift further. I try to snatch power from the Blood Moons to buttress my gift through sheer force of will. I sigh in relief when the familiar influx of power hits me. But then behind it, I shiver violently even though it isn't cold in the room. Goosebumps break out along my arms and the back of my neck. I rub my forehead with a suddenly clammy hand. My skin is burning up. I was freezing a second ago. The air inside the bathroom turns humid and sticky, slick and viscous. Sweat drenches my body alongside the deluge of water. An inferno blazes beneath my skin. I reach for the control panel mounted on the wall, change the water to a cooler temp, and sag against the glass door when the frigid spray pelts me. It takes close to half an hour for my body temp to feel normal again.

After the raging fire is doused, I blindly press a selection on the control panel and a cube of lavender-scented soap juts out from the slit below it. I bathe the day's sweat and blood and grime away, shut off the water, and step out of the shower. I grab the fresh towel hanging on the rail outside the door and wrap myself in the plush, white cotton.

I step out of the bathroom and freeze. With all the weirdness of the shower, I forgot about Reed lingering in my room. He's standing in the strip of space between the foot of my bed and the dresser, staring at the one picture I bothered to stick on the wall. It's a small print of Grandfather in his Legatus Commander regalia on the day he was sworn in to office. I was six and awed at being important enough to earn admittance inside the Pinnacle Tower's Ceremonial Hall. I'd sat in the first row in front of the dais, wedged in the center of a line of intimidating Tribune Generals. Grandfather had stood on the dais. I'd watched giddy and anxious, barely able to keep still in my seat, as Grandfather—*my* grandfather—was confirmed to the highest office and rank in Mareen. After his predecessor had affixed shiny Legatus Commander medals to Grandfather's maroon-and-black ceremonial coat, he had taken the oath of his new office:

"*I serve the Republic. I honor the Republic. I protect the Republic. My duty is first to the Republic,*" he'd vowed.

I'd mouthed the words back at him, seated on the edge of my chair and gripping the rim. I'd been wide-eyed with wonder. People who looked like us didn't occupy the highest rank in the Republic. Grandfather was the first—and he died for it.

Reed looks away from the picture and stares at me.

I feel raw and exposed, and sink malevolence into my voice as a defense. "You really don't need to still be here."

He remains rigidly still for a moment. His eyes sweep down the length of me in the towel, lingering in spots where they shouldn't. "I . . ." He stops and clears his throat. "No, I shouldn't remain here."

"Glad to hear it," I say, tightening the knot that holds my towel closed. "Good night." He needs to leave. For some ludicrous reason, my being naked beneath the towel makes me flustered. The very same fact also causes strange stirrings that have no place between us. Except now my eyes complete a perusal of *his* body, like his did to mine. They take in his broad shoulders and muscled chest, and the defined, toned arms his fitted black tactical shirt shows off. The low neck of the shirt leaves the inktat on the right side of his neck of the four-pointed star of the Republic in full view. Blue eyes aren't my thing—I prefer brown—but inktats are. I scrunch my face up in a way that I'm positive isn't flattering, not knowing where the hell my ludicrous musing comes from.

For his part, Reed is looking at me quizzically, too, like I'm some puzzle he can't figure out.

My eyes roam from the inktat on his neck down the length of his fit form, and they catch the bulge straining against his black tactical pants. I blink at that last bit of detail I glean, and my mind races in directions I *really* don't want it to.

I should outright tell him to leave. Or I should just shove him out. Instead, his presence and my near nudity and that bulge in his pants causes a warped desire to flare. The fire the shower quelled reignites under my skin. It returns with a vengeance so savage it knocks the air from my lungs. I feel like it's singeing my insides to ash. I'd claw my skin off and let it rage free if it'd give me relief. I lean against the bathroom's doorframe to steady myself.

Reed flashes to my side. "Are you dizzy again?"

Instead of answering, I appraise him again. I remember our fight during the combat trial. When he wrestled me to the ground and his body ended up wedged between my legs, pinning me down, I'd fit against him in a way that allowed me to feel all the right hardness in all the right places. I'd ignored it before.

Or, obviously, I hadn't ignored it at all.

The raging fire twines with the sudden lust, each intensifying the other. I itch to rip open his shirt, run my hands across the hard planes of his chest, down his smooth, rigid stomach, and then run them farther.

My eyes venture down the path my hands want to explore. When I raise them, Reed's gaze is electric blue instead of a plain cobalt. My tongue darts between my lips, wetting them, and Reed's searing gaze follows the motion. His own lips part.

Whatever is making me react this way also causes my feet to close the distance between us and my arms to snake around him. My palms flatten against the flexing muscles of his back as I press our bodies together.

My breathing is erratic. My pulse thuds in my ears. My chest heaves up and down, drawing Reed's stare to the swell of my breasts peeking out from the top of the towel. Every inch of me feels hypersensitive and on fire and like extraordinary senses beyond what I knew I had are thrumming to life after lying dormant. I feel like I'm shedding a skin meant to be temporary and preparing to don a new one. The sensation is inexplicable, terrifying, and delirium-inducing. I have no idea what is happening to me. The part of my brain that manages to retain a small fraction of rationality reasons that whatever is happening is the result of the Blood Moons amplifying my blood-gift in some bizarre way I've never experienced before. I stand pressed against Reed, heady and buzzed and completely out of control.

"Wh—"

I press my lips against Reed's, silencing whatever he was about to say. When I kiss him, he kisses me back, wild and barely leashed—exactly how I feel. He gives as good as he gets, and our tongues clash and tangle then engage in a violent, demanding dance. His hands finally touch me, and it's everything I need. They circle around my waist, then make their way to the top of my towel. A quick, deft tug has the knot coming undone and the towel falling to the floor at my bare feet. I grab his shirt and rip it down the middle. He shrugs his muscled arms, allowing the torn halves to fall to the floor. He has more inktats other than the star emblazoned on his neck. Three thick, black bands encircle both biceps. They're Xzana bands, traditional warrior tats that started among Khanaian fight artists. Similarly, emblematic black swirls dance across his pectorals and down his abs. The numerous ornate, powerful markings are a peculiarity. Tribal ink is a Khanaian thing. Mareenians get inked with more representational images, like the Republic's star on his neck. The star and the tribal ink together form an incongruous combo on a singular person. Grandfather had a pair of Xzana bands to honor his Khanaian heritage. He did not have the Republic's star. I should be furious that Reed has the former, but our lips and teeth and tongues clash again and my thoughts scatter.

I banish all comparisons between Reed and my grandfather.

I wrestle with Reed's pants. I pop the top button loose and drag down the zipper. I shove at the offending material that's in the way. I feel the right corner of his mouth tilt up into a smile as his hands cover mine and help me slide his pants down muscular thighs. He steps out of the pants and then we're both completely nude. There is nothing left between us but skin. Skin I want to lick and slide my hands along every inch of. Skin I want him to lick and slide his hands along every inch of.

This isn't the time for exploration, though. My back slams against the wall beside my bed. Reed's hands shoot up to cradle the back of my head so that it doesn't smack into the wall too. His mouth crushes down on mine once more, and his arms lock me against him. His hard nude body presses into mine, and every spot we are molded together at, every rigid, sculpted point, sends wave after wave of anticipation through me. His hands cup my ass and he hoists me up, wrapping my legs around his waist. I think he's going to drive into me at that exact moment, and I brace for the delicious onslaught while begging for it to begin. He doesn't, and I'm almost ready to kill him. He affords me a sly, knowing, smile that's all finesse and male arrogance I've never seen him possess then dips his head down, kissing a wet trail from my neck to my collar bone to the swell of my right breast. He catches the nipple between his teeth and bites down hard enough for it to sting. I moan. The sound escalates when his tongue darts out between his lips and soothes the small hurt his teeth caused.

My head lolls against the wall when he pays my left breast the same homage. My legs tighten around his hips when one hand slides around to the front of me and his fingers delve between my folds, immediately becoming slick with my wetness. I bite down on my bottom lip but can't stop the breathy, pleading sound that escapes. I writhe against him, needing his fingers to be replaced with something else. Or to touch something else. Or both. Or everything.

I reach between us and circle my hand around the thick width of that something else. He shudders when I run the pad of my thumb across the bead of moisture collecting at its head. He goes still, then makes a low sound deep in his throat that reverberates around the room. Then his fingers are leaving me, he's lifting me more securely around him, and he's finally, gloriously, driving into me.

My body quakes as he buries himself to the hilt.

Tremor after tremor of sensation wracks me as I adjust to the fullness of him. We stay like that, both absolutely motionless for a minute. I love how it feels, but I don't want nothing right now. I want everything. I dig my nails into the flesh of his shoulders, slick with a fresh sheen of sweat, and he starts moving again. Like our kisses, there is nothing tender or controlled about it. He moves in and out of me furiously, with movements that have barreled way past barely leashed. They're wild and erratic, and I relish his loss of control. Reed snarls. His arms around my waist tighten. My own hands travel from his shoulders to his corded back—I have to settle for that since I can't reach the tight globes of his ass—and I pull him closer, deeper, urging him to move faster. More furiously. Harder. Deeper.

I cry out, and a guttural sound erupts from Reed a split second later. He moves inside me, once, twice, then a third hard, upward thrust before he stills. His forehead drops against mine and we both stay like that, breathing heavily and spent, and unable to do anything else.

I'm not a virgin. I've had sex before.

This wasn't sex. I've never had what just transpired.

The haze lifts from my mind. I regain a modicum of sense.

"Shit. Fuck." Reed says. We disentangle—my legs about as wobbly as they were after my fight in the cage. Reed pulls on his pants, then boots. There's no hope for his shredded shirt.

I rummage around the top two drawers of my dresser and find underwear, a sports bra, and a pair of sweats. I quickly pull on the clothing.

"That wasn't supposed to happen. That shouldn't have happened," he murmurs more to himself than to me. "How did I let that happen?"

His words echo my thoughts.

I plop down onto the bed. Whatever that irrational, overriding desire was that came over me, it's gone. We stare at each other dumbly, me on the bed and him standing stiff a few feet away. I keep getting flashes of what we did, and the sensations from the memory make my body tingle with need and with . . . not shame. But with wanting to kick myself for the recklessness of it all. He hasn't been cleared of Grandfather's death, even if I have my doubts now, and he's my transition officer, which makes what happened grossly inappropriate any way you cut it.

Not to mention Reed was the one always going on about decorum.

Things in this room are seriously fucked.

I giggle at the thought, and Reed glares at me.

The sound of the door sliding open breaks our silent stare-off. Selene gapes in the doorway. Her eyes dart from a shirtless Reed to me. Her mouth then upturns in a devious smile.

"Is this some new emergency medical technique?"

Reed leaves without a word. I stare after him, still unable to form speech, but definitely noticing how his back muscles bunch and remembering the feel of them flexing the same way under my hands as he drove into me. More tribal ink ornaments the smooth skin of his back.

I face Selene after he disappears from view. I open my mouth to explain, but no sound comes out. What can I say?

"You . . ." It's the first time ever I've seen Selene rendered speechless. "You banged one of our transition officers? And the *hottest one?*"

I rub my forehead. "It wasn't like that." I realize how comical the response sounds, because it was exactly like that.

Selene hooks her left foot over her right ankle and leans against the wall with folded arms. She's not ready to let me off the hook. "Really? Because what it looked like was you and *Darius Reed* just got it on. It definitely smells like it," she says, grinning. "Majorly." Her gaze sweeps over my messy, damp curls that Reed's hands were tangled in not that long ago and my kiss-punished lips. I bite the bottom one, trying in vain to push Reed out of my mind. I screwed him and he might still be on my kill list.

Selene pushes off the wall. Her nosy, gleeful gaze turns serious. "Does that romp mean you're all the way healed? I know the bioserum is supposed to speed things up, but did—" She glances over her shoulder at the open door. "*You know . . .* did *that* aid too?"

"Yes," I assure her. "I'm good."

Very, very good.

The worry doesn't flee her. "Are you sure? You were messed up really bad. Chance shot and stabbed you. You were . . . I thought . . . Fuck, Kenna, there was a minute there I thought I'd lost you for the third time during these hellpit trials." The words rush out of Selene, and the same sheen of wetness I saw glisten in her eyes when I was in the ring glistens now. She grabs my shoulders and pulls me into a hug. "I can't

believe I'm saying this, but I'm thankful you have that thing if it's helping keep you alive while people keep trying to kill you."

"*I'm fine,*" I stress again, hugging her back.

She nods, satisfied. She plops onto the bed and pulls me down with
her. She grins the devious smile from before. I groan because I know
where the convo is headed. "Since you're all good, I don't feel bad about
grilling you then. Tell me about Mr. Hotness. How was the sex? Was it
scorching? Was it dirty? Was it— Ouch."

She rubs the shoulder I punched. "Oh—so it was kinky. I can see
that—"

I punch her again. "We're not discussing it. Ever."

"What? Why not? I tell you about all my debauchery."

"Without me asking."

"That's not the point. I haven't slept with a Praetorian yet—though
I plan to be a winning Donya and collect a slew. Give me details of what
to look forward to. Is Reed as savage in bed as he was when he kicked
your butt and punched Chance? What was it like to have all that lethal,
ruthless skill focused entirely on sexing you? I've always wanted to know."

I hop off the bed. "One, he didn't kick my butt. I held my own during the combat trial. Two, I'm not having this conversation." Indulging
Selene will be counterproductive to what I need to do. Push Reed far,
far, far away from my mind. I slip on a tank top I pull from the dresser
before wrestling my hair into a knot and shoving my feet into boots.

"Where are you going?" She is way too amused, but also a touch
concerned.

"For a run." I need to get out of the room and clear my head. I need
to stop envisioning Reed having me pinned against the wall and thrust-
ing into me.

"You can't go for a run!" Selene says grabbing my hand. "You got
stabbed and shot tonight. You need to rest and recover."

"I'm recovered. Remember that thing you're thankful for? There's
no way I can rest right now."

"Yeah, but what about everyone else? How are you going to explain your recovery to them?"

"I'll tell them they can kiss my ass, and they'll be healed too."

"Cute." Selene stands up. "I'll come too, then, since you're going to be stubborn." She goes to the dresser to change into running gear. "Even if you are fine, you're not going out alone with people trying to murder you." That truth packs a vicious recoil in the aftermath of my recent idiocy.

"You can only come if you keep any and all further quips about Reed to yourself." I know her. She'll pester me with it the entire run if I don't extract the promise.

I'm pretty sure she'll pester me anyway, but maybe we can at least start before the grilling continues.

"You suck," she grumbles. "My best friend finally enjoys a little debauchery of her own and she won't allow me the fun of gabbing about it."

"You'll get over it."

Selene clutches her heart, grinning cheekily. "You are cold and cruel, Ikenna Amari."

Then she looks at me quizzically. She cocks her head and plants her hands on her hips. "Before we leave and I'm barred against speaking on it, I have one more question."

"Will it get you punched?"

"Absolutely, and I'm asking anyway. *Prince or Praetorian?* Slutty minds want to know."

I remind myself you shouldn't decapitate your friends.

"I get it. It's a hard choice. Personally, I'd choose them both. Preferably at the same time."

I smile sweetly. "You'd actually choose Enzo, *rulebreaker.*"

That shuts her up.

Great.

I do not have the bandwidth for Enoch Gyidi to be a topic of discussion tonight.

AS WE RUN, keeping stride with each other, I glance at the Blood Moons in the sky for the hundredth time. It's nearly dawn and the moons persist despite the ivory and gold strokes of rising sunlight. Slowing to a walk, I stare at them, probing myself for that unleashed wildness that gripped me along with the phantom fire beneath my skin. Both phenomena have disappeared.

Selene gasps and reaches toward me. "Kenna, your eyes." She grabs my shoulders, forcing me to a halt.

"What about them?"

"They're red."

I rub my eyes. "I'm sure they are. I'm tired, and I'm ready to crash for a few hours."

"No, I mean your irises. They aren't brown anymore."

I look down at my reflection in my Comm Unit to see what she's talking about. "Shit. What is happening with them? What is happening to me? Nobody else can see me like this!"

Her hold on my shoulders tightens. "Why did they change colors?"

I'm as bewildered as she looks. "I don't know. It's never happened before." But it must be related to the Blood Moons. What are they doing to me this time around? What is making this night different from all the other times they've presented? My heart races when I think about whether a night like tonight will happen again. If this becomes my new normal when they appear, how in the hell am I supposed to keep the sort of uptick in power I experienced tonight a secret? Especially if it makes me spin out of control like I did back in my room? Such massive power surges could leave a potent enough signature that could finally be detected by the Tribunal Council. And then there's the fact that I bled all over everywhere tonight: the fight ring, the common room, the halls between. There wasn't shit I could do about it then, and there isn't shit I can do about it now. *Gods, I might already be damned anyway.*

"Selene, I'm scared," I admit. I tell her about the significance of the Blood Moons and what happened in the steel cage and in our room.

"Okay," she says when I'm done, "let's deal with one crisis at a time. The most pressing worry is your eyes. We'll get you back to the room and avoid literally everybody on the way. I can get brown eyefilms delivered from the inner sector in a few hours when boutiques open up. They will cover up the red—oh." She clutches my face. She leans in close to me. "Your eyes are all brown again. Look." She holds her Comm Unit up to show me. I sigh in relief.

I look back at the sky. The sun has risen over the horizon and the damning red moons are gone.

The full moons have set and things should return to normal. Except I can't shake the same feeling I had earlier in the night when first sighting them—the feeling that they're some kind of foretoken. Dread constricts my chest that there's no way anything will ever be normal again.

13

A KNOCK JOLTS ME AWAKE. I stumble out of bed foggy-minded, trip over my boots, and stub my toe on Selene's bed. She grumbles in her sleep at my yelp. Between the late night, the early morning, and the drama with my eyes, she's as dead to the world as I was before the knock.

Irritated, I stalk across the room and press the control panel to open the door. "Why aren't you taking advantage of a rest day and sleeping it away?" I groan at Zayne through the door. Despite my bitching, relief sweeps through me that he's healed enough to have been released from the med tower.

When the door slides open, it doesn't reveal Zayne, though. It reveals the last person I want to be standing in front of while half clothed in a sleep tank and underwear.

Reed's tense posture mirrors mine.

His eyes dip to below my waist, then jerk back up. I complete my own skim of him. He's in the casual Praetorian uniform. Its sleeves are long enough that they cover the Xzana bands high on his biceps. The only tat exposed is the Republic's star at his neck. Though the tribal ink adorning his chest, abs, and back is hidden by his shirt, I can see the strong slashes and swirls of solid black, deep and robust as if carved into a masterpiece of art, in vivid clarity. The material is unable to cover my memory.

Neither of us say anything. I stand on my side of the door, and he stands on his side. The silence drags out, turning ridiculous.

"Your inktats," I say, the oddness of him having the tribal ink prodding me into breaking the awkward silence. "Why do you have them?" I don't need to elaborate which ones I mean.

"I like ink and they look cool." That's all he offers, and it isn't enough. I want to hear the reason he bears them. Like the Xzana bands, the tribal markings are Khanaian in origin and they are rendered on his skin too precisely and too perfectly not to have been placed there by a Khanaian hand. Whoever did them wouldn't have permitted Reed, an outsider, to have them unless the artist found him worthy of bearing them. I'm positive who the artist is.

"My grandfather inked you." I figured it the moment I saw him shirtless, even as I did my best to not think of my grandfather last night. Reed claims Grandfather was his mentor and hensei. Henseis ink their pupils once they deem there is nothing more they can teach them. The markings covering Reed signify he's achieved a master status of his own.

The same resentment and jealousy from the sparring gym returns. Reed has another piece of Grandfather, and this time it is a piece of him that I don't have. Grandfather died before he could ink me. It was supposed to be a Commencement Day honor.

I do not make the same mistake from the gym. I keep my face as blank as stone, my mood calm, my voice flat and betraying nothing. "You don't have Khanaian blood. Why did he give them to you?" Grandfather's Xzana pupil or not, it's a thing that isn't done. It goes against custom and tradition. Grandfather held strict to both. And Grandfather was a good enough judge of character and a shrewd enough bastard when he needed to be that he wouldn't have given the markings to even a concealed snake. *Something* should've given him pause. There's no way Reed's deception could've been that flawless. Which adds to the possibility that Brock was wrong about Reed and I'm right about Chance. *Or I'm just trying to make myself feel better about fucking him.*

Reed's face goes as blank as mine. His tone as flat. "I'm not subjecting myself to an interrogation over my ink."

"They aren't yours to have."

"They also aren't up for discussion." His coolness slips.

I'm getting nowhere, so I try another tack. "Are you checking up on me again when I don't need you to, or did you want something else this time?"

"Something else," he says, curt. "We need to talk."

I arch a nonchalant eyebrow while my stomach turns an anxious flip. We are *not* having a convo about last night.

He clears his throat. He glances up and down the hall. His measured gaze flicks past me to Selene's sleeping form. He returns his focus to me and steps forward, putting our bodies in way too close of a proximity. The heat emanating from him isn't something I need to feel.

"What words passed between you and Chance in the cage? I intended to ask yesterday." His question isn't at all where I assumed things were headed. It takes me a minute to process it and respond.

When I do, I make sure it's as flippant as he'd expect. "Did you really need to come here to ask me that? I'm sure you can guess. It's nothing different than the shit he's been giving me since conditioning. If that's all, goodbye."

I tap the control panel, directing the door to slide closed.

Reed sticks his hand between it and the frame, making it slide back open.

I move to close the door again.

He grabs my wrist. "What did Chance say to you when he had the knife pressed to your throat? You looked utterly wounded and then like you wanted to tear him apart with your bare hands. The exchange was not quite like all your others before. What exactly went down? I want the specifics."

"Why do you care?"

"Because I do, and I'm your officer and that's all that matters."

Oh, that response is *wolfshit* after—the thing I'm trying not to give more mental space to with him in front of me.

He holds on firm when I wrench away. "Tell me what happened. I know what I saw, and it wasn't the usual." *Damn him for discerning too much.*

I level an unamused look at his hand. "Let me go or you won't have a hand to keep grabbing me with."

His gaze lightens. I frown at the ghost of a smile playing about his lips. He leans a fraction closer and breathes, "That's right. You do have a penchant for knives."

"Yeah. I do." My tone is frigid and threatening like I intend it to be, but the searing look darkening his cobalt gaze makes my knees want to buckle. It takes everything in me to pry my gaze away. I fix my stare pointedly on the hand still clutching my wrist. "Last warning. There will not be a third. If you don't let my wrist go, I'll show you how much of a penchant I have."

"That . . . I think . . . might be fun." The abrupt shift in his demeanor startles me into looking back at him. His eyes dance with mischief. "Especially considering I'd be very interested in seeing where you have a knife hidden right now."

"We're addressing *that* now?" I force the scowl on my face to stay in place.

He takes another step closer, bringing our bodies so close my bare toes touch the tips of his boots. If either of us leans closer a fraction more, our lips will touch. Other parts of our bodies will touch too. At the knowledge, my body thrums alive in a way that is entirely uninvited.

"*That*," he murmurs, looking at my lips in a manner that makes me scowl harder and shiver simultaneously. "Is that what we're calling it?"

My snicker escapes embarrassingly breathy. "*That* sounds better than *it*."

He rasps a laugh, then quickly sobers.

What was *that* or *it*? I almost forget myself and ask.

Before I can say anything, Reed's Comm Unit vibrates. He drops my wrist and takes several steps back, reading whatever is on the screen. "I have to go. We aren't done discussing Chance. I also came here to warn you that whatever exchange you two had in the cage has him hellbent on your death."

"Hellbent-er."

"What?"

I check my response so that it's irreverent and not the same savage, murderous look he glimpsed in the cage. "You could've saved yourself a trip. That's nothing new. He had me thrown off a cliff. Duh, he wants me dead. I'm the akulu bitch that shouldn't be taking part in the trials."

"No," Reed says. "That was his normal idiotic bigotry. This is different. It's personal for him now. Be smart and watch your back."

Yeah, well, then Chance and I finally have something in common, because it is personal for me now too.

In this cage, you die slow. Like your grandfather. He was where he didn't belong either. Then he got terminated.

I will find out what Chance meant by that. After I do, it won't be my death that is slow and messy. It will be his and everybody else's who was involved. I just need to find a way to get Chance alone so I can compel the truth from him.

"Where is he at right now?" I feign that it's a question born out of vigilance.

"You should be clear for the day," Reed answers. "Biochips have the same disadvantage as bioserums. They can heal injuries at staggering speeds, but when the injuries are plentiful, the healing process is taxing on the body. You did a number on Chance. It should take him a full day to recover."

Good. Let's hope that means he's recuperating, alone, in his quarters.

I expect Reed to leave then. He stays rooted to the floor and gives me an assessing look. "It should've taken you a full day too." A bizarre self-recrimination colors his face. He clears his throat. "Last night—I should've exercised better judgment."

It takes everything in me not to reel back or betray any panic at the statement. I fucked up yesterday in more ways than one.

I give him my best wiseass grin. "I'm uber special and fucking spectacular in everything I do, including having crazy sex." I arch a brow and lean against the doorframe, arrogant, hoping it will clear me of any suspicions.

He shakes his head. "You are certainly one of a kind, Amari. Still, don't overdo it today. Rest. You won't get any trial orders. All the officers have a Tribunal forum to attend."

After Reed leaves, there isn't any way in hell that I'll heed his command with that information he gave me. I won't get a better opportunity to go after Chance than today, when he's not operating in top shape and the rest of the Praetorians who would be walking around the upper levels are at the Pinnacle. That also means I can get into Reed's room, too, while I'm up there.

I STAND OUTSIDE Chance's door and punch in Grandfather's all-access code to override the required biolock scans.

The security panel accepts it, and I slip into Chance's apartments and shut the door. It's pitch-dark, without a sliver of artificial or natural light. I give my eyes a moment to adjust. My blood-gift means the total darkness doesn't render me blind. I move through a spacious living room with sparse furnishing. An L-shaped sofa, two end tables, and a holovid panel are the few items in the room. I clear the living room and hasten down a hallway with the same plush carpeting that makes it easy to move without a sound. The first door off the living room is a guest bathroom suite. I surmise that the door at the end of the hall on the right is Chance's bedroom. I grab a knife from my boot and the blaster that's secured beside it. I press the Open command on the door's control panel. It doesn't have a biolock like the front door did. I train the blaster on the door as it slides open. If Chance is sleeping inside and my entry stirs him, I need to be ready to act.

The bedroom is as scant with furnishings as the living room. Only a four-poster bed and cherrywood armoire are inside. I never would've pegged Chance for a minimalist. The fucker seems more the flashy, garish type. His sleeping form is positioned in the middle of the large bed. I put my blaster away, prick my palm with the knife, then stalk over to the bastard and snatch him up by the front of his cotton shirt. He startles awake, muscles bunching instantly to meet the unknown threat.

"Don't fucking move," I snarl. I dig the point of my knife into his jugular. It breaks the fragile skin and a trickle of blood drips down the front of his neck.

"You're dead, bitch."

"Nah, you keep failing at that."

"I'm a Praetorian, and this is treason," he says. "When the Tribunal finds out about this, I won't need to kill you myself. They'll fry you. Standing back and watching alongside the rest of the Republic will bring me much more satisfaction than doing it myself."

"See, that's where you and I differ," I say, leaning in close like he did to me in the ring. "I prefer dirtying my hands when I have a vendetta to settle." I dig the knife deeper into his throat. The fearless act slips. I see the exact moment he's sure I'm about to slice his jugular. His eyes detonate with the denial and terror any person would have when staring down their imminent death. I ease pressure against his throat and give him my psycho smile from the bar that I gifted his buddy. "Don't worry, I'm not here to kill you—yet. I need something more important from you first."

I remove the knife entirely from his throat and grip his neck with my bleeding hand. I briefly think about squeezing harder than I must to restrain him—I think about crushing his fucking windpipe. But I'm the new Ikenna, the one filled with restraint.

"You will answer every question I ask you truthfully. Then you will go back to sleep, forget the exchange, and forget that I was here."

The spark of consciousness behind his murderous stare winks out. His eyes turn vacant. This time, I don't flinch at wielding this aspect of my gift over another like I did when I had to with Caiman. Chance fucking deserves it. Actually, Caiman fucking deserved it too.

"Did you kill my grandfather?"

He answers with an automatic, quick "No."

Don't lie to me, I almost snap, then remember that he can't.

"Do you know who did?"

"No."

"Do you know how he was killed?"

"No."

"Do you know the Tribune Generals behind his death?"

"No."

"Do you know who received the actual kill order and carried it out?"

"No."

"Dammit! What do you know?" I shout. "Was he killed with a lethal bioserum?"

He denies any knowledge of that too.

His eyes bulge and blue veins pop out around their lower lids. I realize I've cut off his supply of oxygen. At this point I should keep squeezing and strangle him. But what kind of monster would it make me to do it while he's under compulsion and stripped of free will? He can't fight back and he isn't remotely conscious of what is happening to him. I curse at the inconvenient prick of my conscience and relax my hold. I remove my hand from his neck. I don't need to be touching him to maintain the bloodlink.

Also, it wouldn't be hard to trace his death back to me.

"You ordered Caiman to make sure I didn't survive Onei's Expanse, correct?"

Chance gulps down breaths of air. "Yes."

"And did you tell Caiman to attack me in my room?"

That gets another denial. It is another thing that throws me off-kilter because I was sure he did. But it's also logical that Caiman and Greysen acted on their own the first time. The two of them definitely hate me enough.

"What about Terese Rhysien, the medic? Did you know she would inject me with a toxic serum? Do you know who sent her into the compound to do it?" Even if he didn't orchestrate it himself, whoever did perhaps told him something, since he was acting as lead in the trials.

"I don't know about any medics," he says.

"The two times you tried to kill me, you weren't acting under orders from the Tribunal?" I ask to be sure. I want direct confirmation.

He says no, meaning his motives were his own. Meaning this has gotten me nowhere further in my investigation.

I remind him of the second part of my command. "Go back to sleep. Forget I was here."

I leave his apartments, confused. What the hell did he mean by what he said in the cage if he knows nothing about Grandfather's death? Was it really only a taunt that struck too close? I don't want to believe that. I want it to have been more. I want to be making continued headway with Grandfather's murder.

I'm frustrated that Chance is a dead end, but he isn't my only path to the evidence I need.

I pull up the compound's floorplans on my Comm Unit and navigate to Reed's apartment.

When I get there, I punch Grandfather's access code into the control panel.

It lights up red with a DENIED ENTRY. COMPLETE BIOLOCK SCANS message.

I punch it in again.

The same message pops up.

I don't try the code a third time in case there's an alarm trigger after multiple failed attempts. The cosmos has to be fucking with me, because otherwise why isn't Grandfather's code working when it just worked for Chance's apartment? I step across the hall to the apartment facing Reed's. I check its biolock with the access code. It opens immediately.

Which means Reed doesn't have the programming in his lock that everyone else does, and I don't need to wonder how he made that happen. I didn't have a standard lock in the academy, and I wouldn't have one if I moved into the compound while Grandfather was the seated Legatus either. For added protection, because he was never without threats the length of his term, he had my lock reprogrammed to the same setting that's on the lock at his apartments so an all-access code couldn't override it. I turn back to Reed's door and glare at it. This is Grandfather's doing. Reed's Xzana bands signify a relationship as deep as any that would run between him and kin, which would explain a lot—and invite so many other questions. But the key is that if Grandfather felt like that toward Reed, then it makes sense he'd afford his mentee the same protections he gave me. That fact stands double if Grandfather took him into his confidence about the policy initiatives they were working on, because the sweeping changes he wanted in the Republic were so controversial. He would've preemptively shielded Reed from being targeted and from being under surveillance by those who opposed him.

It's more evidence that points to Reed being more than a mentee. Like the Xzana bands, it points to Reed being a protégé.

Being a *confidant*.

Why? I ask again. If Reed was that important, why keep him from me? It's a question I don't have an answer to. It makes Reed a massive mystery, and it makes me once again question if Reed *is* the one who killed him.

It's something I'm having a harder time accepting.

However, either way the answer makes me want to punch the door in frustration. If he didn't assassinate Grandfather and neither did Chance, I am so, so far away from unraveling the web. And if Reed is the killer, I'm still possibly light-years away because then I still need to figure out how to bleed him to compel him *and* make sure the attempt is successful.

Dammit.

Getting into his apartment was supposed to give me for-certain answers about him. It was supposed to give me answers about a lot of things.

I give in to the urge to punch something and ram my fist into his door. It's steel, so it fucking hurts, but I also do it again because, gods, I thought I was finally getting somewhere.

The success at Terese's house should have placed me significantly closer to my end goal, but it really hasn't. The data I copied off her computer is only enough to prove that *she* tried to murder me and was involved with Grandfather's death. It isn't enough to stick any charges to Sutton Rhysien, and it tells me nothing of the other Tribunals who might be involved. I was so sure that between Chance and Reed I had all the conspiring fuckers. But Chance knows nothing, and Reed is a fucking pain-in-my-ass question mark when he was supposed to be the target.

I trudge down a staircase that'll return me to the subterranean level, floundering for answers I don't have. What rubs me wrong the most is that I won't even know where to look next if Reed does turn up innocent. I should know. I should have various contingency plans. Any capable soldier worth their training would. That goes double for a Praetorian. That goes triple for my grandfather's kin.

But I don't, and I'm furious at myself for my inadequacy. I fling open the door that spits me out on the floor my room is on. Maybe I am in over my head. Maybe Brock was right about his reservations. All of my attempts to uncover intel have either been blunders or amounted to dead ends. If Grandfather were in my position, he wouldn't be botching things so badly. He was a strategic prodigy from the time he entered the academy as a cadet. He would automatically know what to do next and then five moves down the line after that. But strategy has never been my strength. Fighting. Combat. Attacks. That's what I can do. And in this instance, those strengths aren't fucking enough. I can't fight my way to the answers I seek. I can't fight my way to exposing Grandfather's murderers. Proving my self-loathing comically right, I become so angry I want to punch one of the concrete walls boxing me in. My laugh has a type of acrimony to it that's projected inward. I suck.

I turn the corner, and Zayne stands outside my door a ways down the hall.

He turns my way and waves.

I'm too miserable to wave back.

"Did you just get released?" I ask when I approach him. He's back in the compound and whole. At least that's a positive to my shitty day.

"I've been back for about an hour. I pinged you and Selene both to give you an update and to check up on you two. Neither one of you answered." Gah. My Comm Unit isn't on my wrist. I left it behind in my room.

"I'm sure Selene's still catching up on her beauty rest. How do you feel?" I look him over for visual confirmation that his injury from Caiman's bitch-boy stunt is healed.

"Between the bioserum and a medic resetting my bones, wonderful," he marvels. "With the same injuries in the academy, I would've been out of commission for weeks." He sobers, leans over, and pulls me into a hug. "I'm glad you're okay too. Enzo told me what happened."

My upswing in mood plunges again.

Zayne catches it. "What's the matter? You looked terrible when you approached me. Where were you coming from?"

"I feel worse," I admit. "But I don't want to talk about it." That isn't true. I need to unload. I *can't* talk about it with him, however, which makes me feel worse still, and so I'm now in a cycle of feeling shitty.

I step around Zayne and open the door to my room. He follows me inside.

"You seem like you need to talk about it. You can't do what you did with your grandfather's passing and keep things pent up until they explode in a reckless stunt. I thought you were ready to get beyond that version of Ikenna."

I whirl on him. "Did you not hear me? I said I don't want to. So drop it. You don't get to judge me. Not for this."

"Who's judging you?" he asks, genuinely confused.

"What's going on?" A groggy Selene sits up in bed. "What are you two fighting about?"

"We aren't fighting about anything," I say.

"Where were you coming from?" Zayne asks me again, not letting things go. "You weren't in the mess at dinner with the rest of our class. It's why I came to check on you."

"A sparring gym," I say lamely.

"You don't look like you've broken a sweat."

"Leave me the hell alone!"

"Why are you being so testy?"

I open my mouth to respond. I snap it shut because I've got no legitimate reply.

Selene tosses a smirk my way. "I know where she was. You didn't break the same sweat this time? That's a pity."

"Selene, shut up."

My immature friend wiggles her eyebrows, making things worse.

Zayne scrutinizes the two of us. "What did I miss?"

I shoot Selene a death glare. "Nothing." He's already called me reckless once tonight. I'm not about to give him ammunition to back up the charge.

Zayne frowns. "Another secret, like with the forest?"

Fantastic. He chooses this moment to still be annoyed. "I thought that was dropped."

"You *want* it to be dropped. But you're acting weird, and I'm supposed to be your friend, and I want to help but you're not letting me because you are hiding behind secrets. Remember: the three of us get through this together? Well, it doesn't feel like I'm part of 'together' anymore."

From Zayne, this hurts like nothing I've felt in a while. Yet I school my face into an expression that doesn't reek of guilt. "It isn't another secret. Selene is being an ass."

"I am. That's all it is," she assures him.

"You two are terrible liars, and you're sharing a lot of secrets lately that I'm not a part of."

"Don't leave," I call after him when he turns for the door.

"No, I think I should before I say something I'll regret." He takes another step for the door. Stops. Then spins back toward me. "You know what, you're right: maybe I should say this. I've *always* been there for you, Kenna. I've always had your back. I've never shut you out of my stuff. I don't appreciate you shutting me out of yours. That's not what we do. Is it me? Did I do something to change things? Did I do something to make you believe you can't trust me? Gods, Kenna, tell me what it is so I can fix whatever you're pissy about."

"I . . . No. It's not you. I swear. Nothing is wrong." It's a weak response that makes me an asshole for continuing to lie to my friend.

"Then what is it?"

"I . . . I can't—"

Where he'd been open with his feelings before, indifference now slams over his face. "Forget it."

"So that's been festering since the forest," Selene says after he departs. "Don't worry. He'll get over it."

I flop down on the bed. "He's right to be upset with me." She and Zayne are usually the ones who butt heads. He and I are always good. The fact that there's a rift between us gnaws at me.

"I should go after him," I mutter.

"I'll come with you," she offers. "Maybe I can help. Him getting mad is partly my fault."

"It's all your fault," I say, though it's unfair. No, not unfair. *Untrue.* Her riding me about Reed is what set him off this time, but the strain between Zayne and me is my own making.

I've already failed too much today. I've failed *people I love* too much today. I need to do something that's the opposite of that. Something that reminds me what accomplishment feels like instead of feeling fucking deficient.

I go to find Zayne.

14

ZAYNE'S IN A GYM THAT'S empty except for him and the dummy practice bots. He dips gracefully into a Xzana defensive stance then springs out of it and delivers a flat-footed kick to a dummy bot's torso. His execution is flawless, lethal, and envy-inducing. The pressure point he connects with lights up red.

"Can we talk?" I ask.

He delivers a second kick to the bot. The pressure point between its eyes lights up. "It depends. Are you going to continue being weird, or are you actually going to tell me what's going on?"

"No. I mean, yes. I mean . . . clearly I'm going to be weird."

He laughs at that, and I let my mind race to figure out the best way to not be as bad about this as I have been. I have to tell Zayne something to smooth things over, so I decide on the one thing that's even a possible option.

"This is something I haven't told you either," I say to Selene, prepping her for the flamespitter I'm about to drop. I still can't tell Zayne that I'm Pantheon-blessed for his own good, so what I say now had better be good. "The night before Commencement, Brock told me Grandfather was murdered. It's why I got my shit together and declared Praetorian."

Selene's stunned stare accuses me of not telling her sooner.

Zayne gapes like the compound has toppled.

Great—now both my best friends are upset with me.

"That's impossible," Zayne finally says. "The Legatus Commander was matchless. He defeated a man in battle who has evolved into something close to a god. How could someone kill him? How could *anyone* kill him? *Who* could kill him?"

Those are all questions I have too. "Brock thinks Tribune Generals conspired to assassinate him and they gave orders to a Praetorian to execute it." I don't name Reed because I'm no longer sure he's involved. I was wrong about Chance. I could be wrong about him too. Plus, I maintain that Grandfather *would've* discerned something was off about Reed if he were a plant instead of a true mentee. Grandfather wasn't stupid. In fact, he was brilliant. He wouldn't have given Xzana bands and markings to a kiss-ass or a snake.

Disbelief, then anger, then pity washes over Zayne's face. "Republic's sake, Kenna, why didn't you tell us sooner?"

I shift my weight from one foot to the other. "Brock insisted I didn't tell you at all. I only changed my mind about the trials to find out who among the Praetorian ranks carried out those orders, get close to them, and find proof that incriminates them and the Tribunes."

"And you don't think we could have helped?"

"I—didn't think, okay? He's *my* grandfather. I had to do something."

"I get that. But are you sure that's the right course?" I know from Zayne's measured voice he's aware he's about to piss me off.

"What other course do I have?" I yell, trying not to fully flip out. "What else should I do?"

"Let someone else do this, for starters? Brock is a Tribune General.

He's the spymaster! He has the power to handle this without you. You should let him. Don't make yourself a glaring target. This is serious, dangerous shit, Kenna. You could get yourself killed. Oh, wait—you almost did. Multiple times already."

His caution is an echo of my earlier self-doubt, and it stings. "Glad you have faith in me. It feels great to have your support. Guess you don't actually always have my back in everything, huh? You pester me into telling you what I've been keeping from you, and this is what I get? Fuck you, Zayne. I don't need your confidence in me."

"You know that's not how I meant it."

"Well, that's what you said."

"That's how you wanted to hear it," he says, but he does so quietly. He's not angry. He's just trying to show me that maybe my anger isn't actually directed at him, and that I'm the one being an ass.

This is not a mirror I like looking into.

I take a breath and once again realize I should have pulled Zayne into this right away. He's not just a good friend, he's a rock you can actually rely on. My earlier accusation tastes like ash in my mouth.

"Which Tribune Generals does Brock suspect?" Selene inserts the question very neutrally.

I can tell her I don't know or simply not mention her father. But I'm tired of lying more than I have to. Besides, we will have to deal with that nanogrenade eventually—we might as well detonate it now. "All of them have the capacity, and as far as Brock is—and I am—concerned, they're all suspects. Which is why Brock specifically asked me not to discuss his suspicions with you."

She discerns what that means as quick as I did when speaking to Brock.

"No," she says without consideration. "He can be a bastard at times, but he wouldn't do that. My father wouldn't commit treason against the Republic. It would throw Rhysien War House into disrepute. He wouldn't bring ruin upon our name."

"Would the disrepute really be that grave if the man he killed was the Republic's akulu Legatus Commander? We've been at the trials for a little under two weeks. Does it seem like he was held in universally high regard? Half of Mareen would praise those involved." As I speak, my words turn from careful to bitter once more.

"How do we know the Tribunal Council is for sure behind the assassination?" Selene asks. "Accacia's Blood Emperor sent assassins several times over to strike at the Legatus Commander. Including the night—"

"I don't talk about that."

"Yes, but you don't talk about a lot of stuff, and that's not really working, is it? It *did* happen, and we both know the Blood Emperor has held a grudge since the battle. In the wake of the Legatus Commander's death, he's already started to instigate hostilities in our westernmost cities. It would stand to reason that he sent operatives that were finally successful in killing your grandfather so he can renew his Divine Campaign unimpe—" She mashes her lips together. I see the moment she realizes she's spoken too much. She's said stuff that we had zero knowledge of. Zayne and I stare at her, urging her on. I'm especially happy to know I'm not the only one with secrets.

"I . . ." she backtracks. She sighs. "Listen, the western cities are the province of Rhysien War House. My father asked me not to divulge such struggles. He and my brothers are handling things, and our house will look weak if it gets out that Accacia thinks the cities we guard to be the easiest attack points."

"Gods," I say. "And you've been keeping that to yourself?"

"*You're* talking about secrets?"

Right—I was hoping she forgot about that.

She hasn't, though, and presses, as defensive as I had been with Zayne. "It's rich, considering your indiscretions last night."

"I thought you weren't judging me for that?"

"I'm not judging. I'm just saying this hasn't exactly been the sharing circle, has it?"

"Judging you for what?" Zayne asks.

"Nothing," I say too calm and Selene says too quick.

He grinds his teeth. "More secrets?"

"No." Yes. Shit. Gah! What the fuck is happening to me and my friends? This isn't how me going after Zayne was supposed to turn out. I was supposed to be patching things over. Not ripping a jagged hole in not only my friendship with him but my friendship with Selene.

"Kenna got down and dirty with Darius Reed last night," Selene supplies. "That's the secret."

I'm going to murder her. "You have a big-ass mouth."

Zayne stares at me.

At first I think he's jealous, but that's not Zayne. That's never been our relationship, and so I'm confused. Clearly so is he.

"Wait—hold on. Kenna, you've known since Commencement Eve that Brock thinks Tribunes had your grandfather assassinated, and you lost your mind and slept with one of our transition officers? And Selene, you've known for how long that freaking Accacia has started up skirmishes in the wake of the Legatus's death? Barring the breach in decorum of sleeping with a transition officer, this is all huge, important shit. Shit we should have confided in each other. The type of shit we don't keep from one another. We're a unit. We have been for the last eleven years. Did that change?"

"Screwing Reed was a mistake," I mutter. "A temporary moment of Selene-level insanity that won't happen again."

Selene sniggers. "Sure it won't. And the sun won't rise on Iludu tomorrow morning."

"What the hell is that supposed to mean?"

She raises her hands, all innocence. "Nothing."

"Can we please focus?" Zayne says.

"I'm trying, but I don't know if I can do this right now."

"So things have changed."

The accusation hurts. Partly because it's true. I'm not ready to fully accept that, though, so I bite my lip so I don't do something I'll regret.

Something *else*.

The three of us stand in the center of the gym full of dummy bots, silent.

"We all need to take a minute and cool down," Zayne says at last. "Which, if you remember, is why I had come here in the first place. I'll catch you two later."

He leaves me and Selene alone with the apology that needs to be issued hanging thick between us. I hate how this all played out, but I'm also not convinced that I've done anything wrong where she's concerned. And I refuse to be the one to say sorry first. Not after she tried to shift the blame from her father without so much as considering that the hateful fucker might be guilty. I fuck a guy, and she thinks that's as bad as her father possibly being part of a coup?

It burns worse than the UV bullets that ripped into me when I fought Chance.

"Are you planning to leave?" I ask. "Because I need to pummel a dummy bot in the worst way, and I really don't want to use your face in its place."

She blinks. Without a word or the apology she owes me, she marches away.

I HAMMER A kick into the chest of a bot. I spin out of the kick at the sound of approaching steps and the deep timbre of the voice that calls my name. Maintaining the momentum, I lift my leg a few inches higher and aim a follow-up kick at Reed's head, testing his reflexes and letting my anger loose on an actual person. He grins while dodging the kick and sweeps his foot out in a move I never see coming. My legs fly out from under me, and I land on my ass.

I curse, tensing muscles to surge to my feet, but Reed is on top of me and pinning me to the ground before I can. He collects my hands above my head in a steel grip.

"That's twice now," he points out.

In response, I jerk my head forward. My forehead slams into his. I was aiming for his nose. It would've felt good to break it.

"You should find a different move. That one is growing boring."

I fully realize I'm spiraling into the reckless, hotheaded Ikenna that does dumb shit out of spite that I vowed to Brock I'd leave behind after being confirmed—a vow I've broken a few times already. It doesn't help that the fight with Selene and Zayne has me wound tight. They are all I have left after Grandfather. I lost him, and it feels like I'm losing them too.

"Good advice."

I tear an arm free, wedge it between us, and jab my fist into his solar plexus.

Stop thinking the worst, I tell myself. *It's nothing that can't be repaired.* For some reason, it doesn't seem like that's true.

Reed grunts and his full weight collapses on top of me. The heat from his body is searing. Parts of me that shouldn't react to our bodies melded together do. Reed's eyes drink in my face. They trace my lips, the top one first then the fuller bottom one. My lips tingle with heart-racing memories of kissing him. A particular part of Reed's body presses against me harder than the rest, making other places on my body tingle with memory too. I don't have boosters available; my body yearns to indulge in something else that will take the edge off my problems.

Something shifts in Reed's gaze. It loses its combative edge that's driven by adrenaline and becomes a thing that's darker, driven by a baser emotion. My body quivers and tenses in anticipation, denial, and the abject wrongness of it all, because he still *could* be treacherous. The conflicting urges to shove him off me and haul him closer wage war inside me.

The open lust in his gaze disappears, replaced by iron control and absolute discipline. He leaps off me. I spring to my feet. My stare snags on the smooth, inked skin of his bare chest and his delicious ab muscles. *What the hell is wrong with me? I'm thinking like Selene.*

"What do you want?" I ask.

"The same thing I wanted before. What did Chance say to you in the cage when he held the knife to your throat?"

I tense. Why is he so adamant about knowing? Why is everyone so keen on *my* secrets?

"You already asked me that and I told you the answer."

"Not the entire answer. Whatever he said made you snap."

"I have no idea what you're talking about. Did I butt you in that pretty head of yours too hard? Are you delirious?"

He steps a fraction closer to me. "I'm a Praetorian. Death, war, and combat is what I live and breathe. I saw the way you looked at Chance in the cage after he took his lips away from your ear. It's the way a person looks at another person when they're envisioning tearing them apart with their bare hands."

"Is this an interrogation?"

"Not unless you make it one."

I bristle. I hold on to the anger and hurl it at Reed like blood spikes. It's the preferable emotion to any other twisted thing I'm feeling. "Don't threaten me."

"Then don't evade me and answer the question. I won't relent. I want to know."

"Why?"

"Because I think it was something fucked-up, and as one of your leads, I will make sure the remainder of these trials are conducted with integrity."

So that's what this is about. I almost laugh; it's such a mundane answer.

I pass him a droll smirk. "You all are making sure we drop like gnats. Our lives have no significance for you since we aren't lauded

Praetorians yet. These trials never started with integrity. They've been complete elitist shit from the beginning. Why start now?"

His jaw spasms. "I explained the necessity for their stringency in the dome. We are making sure you are fit for war."

"If that's what you need to help yourself not feel like an asshole, go with it."

I step around him.

He grabs my arm to prevent me from leaving.

I jab my free elbow into his throat. "Don't take liberties with touching me."

"Chance—" he starts up again, tightening his hold on my upper arm.

"Forget Chance! What happened in the cage doesn't matter, and your preoccupation with it and him is a joke. You and Chance are two sides of the same blade. You might not be as bad as he is outwardly, but you're a callous, superior jerk all the same. Your insides are conditioned the same." He and all the transition officers are awful. Even if it ends up that he didn't betray Grandfather, I'm still disgusted with myself for having slept with him. "I swear I am going to kill you if you do not let me go." I sink enough ice into my voice to freeze over the entire gym.

His hand falls away from my arm.

I summon calm. Instead of attempting to maim him and soothe over the mistake of screwing him, I retreat from the gym.

Need to work on those interpersonal skills, Ikenna, I hear Grandfather say.

I take my first stab at it by not telling him to shut the fuck up.

15

I WALK INTO THE MESS the next morning and search for Selene and Zayne. It's an act that's instinctual, and I don't become conscious of doing it until I spy them sitting at a glass table near the back of the room. They aren't sitting as a huddled duo alone like we usually do. Instead, they're seated at a table with Enzo, Bex, Dasaun, and a handful of other aspirants. Selene sits at one end across from Enzo. Zayne sits at the opposite end beside Bex. I grab food from the serving line, but then I have to make the decision where I will sit. I can find another table or go be awkward along with them. Either action is going to be telling for anybody who knows us. Not wanting the extra attention, I go to the table my friends occupy and sit in the empty seat beside Selene. She offers me a small hello. I offer the same back. It's the first time we've spoken to each other since our fight. We spent the night in our room pretending the other didn't exist.

Zayne glances our way from his end of the table. Hurt flashes in his blue gaze a moment before he looks away. Instead of feeling bad, I'm irked at the unfair accusation. I literally sat in the only empty seat and he's found a way to give me shit for that too.

"GOOD MORNING, LOSERS!"

I grip my tray at the sound of Chance's voice behind me. I consider picking up my fork and severing his carotid. For the hundredth time, I rethink the decision to let him live when I had the opportunity to be rid of him for good.

He's standing with Nero and three other officers at the entrance to the hall. They are all in battledress.

"If you're healed enough to be chatting like Donya ladies over breakfast, we can resume the trials, stat, and get back to business!" Chance thunders.

"I don't recall seeing them address us with a salute," one of the officers, Liim, another Alpha prick, drawls. He stands with arms folded over his chest. He's taller than Chance, six-foot-four by my estimation, and has sun-blond hair and brown eyes. Built like a bruiser, he cracks his knuckles, trying to further intimidate us. I roll my eyes.

"I don't either," Nero says. "Why are you all at ease? Get your asses up and snap to attention. Your lead has a message to deliver."

Chance's trademark sadistic grin pops onto his face as we follow the order. He points to an aspirant to his right. "You, come here."

The aspirant takes a few wary steps in Chance's direction.

"Take a swing at me," Chance says coolly.

"Wh-What?" The aspirant sputters.

"You aren't hard of hearing. I said take a swing."

"Respectfully, I'd prefer to decline."

"Why?"

Oh, we've played this game in the academy, too, with our instructors.

"Because during the trials, you're my superior officer. Violence against a commanding officer is a violation of Conduct Code RoM.54.L1."

"Repeat that very smart response louder."

The aspirant shouts a repeat of what he said.

"I'm glad you know how to operate under proper protocol." Chance hops onto a table at the front of the hall, addressing the whole of the mess. "But not all of your peers have your intelligence. My fight with Amari the other night was a test, and she failed it dismally. I pulled punches in the cage to see how far she'd breach protocol."

"I wasn't aware he knew such big words," Enzo mumbles under his breath.

It takes all of the discipline I have not to shoot forward and call out his lie for what it is: an attempt to save face. Because that's what he wants—even more "breaches."

"And you're all about to pay for her inability to display deference to her betters. Her actions have changed the nature of your coming Strategy Trial. What you get next will be something extra special. It will make Onei's Expanse seem like a vacation. Thank her for that." It isn't a turn of phrase. He makes the whole mess pivot toward me and shout, "Thank you!"

I don't bow, as I'm sure that wouldn't go over well.

Chance hops off the table, and the officers stride out of the mess.

"The senior Praetorians are assholes," Enzo groans after we sit back down. "Assholes who are going to give us a strategy trial that puts us in the ground."

"Sorry," I mutter, though it isn't my fault. Chance, the fucker, just set me up for everybody to hate when he was the one who was trying to murder me in the cage. Hate me more, that is.

"You have nothing to apologize for," Enzo says, letting his voice carry over the mess. Not that it helps—most folks are aiming furious stares my way. "I saw that fight, and Chance is full of wolfshit. He was trying to slaughter you. He was pulling punches . . . with his knives? With his gun? Please. What were you supposed to do? Stand down and let him? I wouldn't have done anything different than you did."

"Do you think any of the other aspirants care about that right now? Especially if they're killed because of it?"

Enzo doesn't give an answer, because we all know the truth of it.

"What could they possibly come up with that is worse than the forest?" Dasaun asks with no small amount of trepidation.

Bex shudders. "I really don't want to know."

After the hellpit of the Expanse, neither do I.

I definitely should have killed that fucker.

16

THE TRANSITION OFFICERS TOY WITH us and let days pass that stretch into a week between the Strength Trial and the impending Strategy Trial. They keep us on edge and bracing for the next round of torment, which they hint at with a sense of glee that verges on manic sadism. The week off is the opposite of a peaceful break. The speculations about what's coming next grow wilder and wilder. Every day, different and more terrifying horrors are spun, making us all tense, anxious, and nervous. I am sure it is the mission of the senior Praetorians for us to do exactly what we are doing. We're playing into their mindfuck, and it's a game they're winning.

During the lull, we are called to lecture each day. It's at the same time—before dawn—and under the same conditions. I've started going to bed in sweats and a long-sleeve top. I might as well be comfortable during these interrogations—the transition officers aren't subjecting me to the misery of sitting for three hours in a dome that's as cold as the Ice Wastes while we wait for them to show up.

But the break isn't all bad. It gives me the time to really start digging into Grandfather's murder and trying to recover the ground I lost with Chance and Reed. Outside of lectures, I keep to my room to do exactly that, and Selene always finds somewhere else to be. I don't attempt to mend our row. Aside from me still being angry, her intentional efforts to keep out of my face give me the space to do what I need to do without her hovering and asking a bunch of questions it may not be smart to answer if her father is involved.

With a plate of biscuits and fruit I grabbed for sustenance from the mess, I hunker down in my room after our latest lecture and pull up the encrypted file I created on my Comm Unit for the fifth day in a row. The web of Mareen's fourteen Tribune Generals, plus Haymus Rossi—our new Legatus Commander—pops up. Since I'm alone, I project a holograph of it into the space between my bed and the bathroom. I stare at the names and faces of the Republic's leaders. Rossi, Zephyr Caan, Sutton Rhysien, and Rudyard Brock are clustered together on the left side of the web. They are the four most powerful men in the Republic. Nothing as momentous as the assassination of a Legatus Commander would happen without the knowledge, order, or sanction of at least one of them.

There is an X over Brock's face, because even if he did have the capacity to betray Grandfather, him as a guilty party doesn't make sense. Brock has been by Grandfather's side since before they were cadets at Krashen. They've been friends since my great-grandfather worked for Brock's father while they were young boys in western Mareen. Why wait fifty-plus years to flip loyalties when you've had clear and unrestricted access to that person for decades?

Rhysien and Rossi, on the other hand, I'm near positive are coconspirators. They're twin heads of the same bigoted snake. Caan has a question mark above his head. I can't decide about him. The dark-haired man has a reputation of being a wild card. Like his Tribune father before him, the newest member of the Tribunal Council is a master of deception. *The young heir to the Caan War House is ambitious, and he isn't nearly as tame or as relaxed as he likes to appear.* Grandfather imparted this more than once while schooling me about war house politics. *If Rossi and Rhysien are the vipers looming over you, fangs dripping venom and ready to strike, Caan is the snake that lies in wait. He's the one you don't expect to bite until you feel its poison coursing up from your heel, shutting down your system.* Caan's crotchety old father made no secret of despising an akulu man as the Republic's Legatus Commander. When the younger Caan took his seat on the Tribunal, he was never vocal about his hate, but he was never amicable to Grandfather either. On some policy initiatives, he supported him out of practicality, and on others he opposed him simply to be difficult.

Rossi, Rhysien, and Caan all wear superiority like a battle suit in their photos. While Rossi's brand is brash, Caan's is understated and Rhysien's is smug. My biggest hope is that all three aren't in cahoots. United, they're too strong, and Brock would find it impossible to take them all on. They have the largest numbers in their war houses, the highest concentrations of wealth, and they've collected or coerced the best bioscientists and engineers onto their payroll. When Grandfather was pissed at Caan for blocking some initiative, he would accuse him of being a slippery, cocky bastard who didn't care to play nice with others. I hope those charges prove true, and he hasn't aligned with Rossi and Rhysien. One thing fostering that hope is that Caan's war house and Rhysien's have been at odds since the civil war that allowed Accacia to invade Mareen. Their feud has grown so vicious that the impending implosion of Iludu likely wouldn't squash it. So for now, I discount Caan as a co-conspirator, since I can't fathom what might make him suddenly play nice with Sutton Rhysien, whose involvement is proved by his connection to the lethal bioserum. I activate the mindlink feature on my Comm Unit. I picture an X over Caan's face and the marking appears on his holograph photo.

A separate cluster of Tribune Generals consists of Geels Lennon, Yarric Bjorr, and Lydya Denton. Denton is the lone woman who sits on the Tribunal. The trio leads mid-status war houses that have long competed for footing with the big four. They're essentially a coalition to make sure they're not bullied from above, and they've all been strong allies since before the civil war. If one of them is involved in Grandfather's murder, then all of them are, and if one of them is innocent, all of them are. Like the younger Caan, none of them voiced opposition to Grandfather's Legatus appointment or supported any hate propaganda toward him. Yet they didn't vocally support him either. Brock was alone in that. Their stance was to remain neutral and silent in service to what was best for the Republic. For the time being, an X covers their faces, too, because supporting an assassination would be detrimental to Mareen *and* their own war houses, given that Grandfather was a continued buffer against Accacia. The information about the skirmishes out west that Selene let slip proves how much Grandfather shielded us from aggressions. Rhysien and Rossi might be arrogant enough to dismiss Grandfather's importance, with Mareen having long fortified the cracks our civil war left exposed, but the mid-houses would be more hesitant. Their smaller numbers would mean they'd feel the effects of any renewed conflict the hardest.

The remaining eight Tribune Generals preside over less notable war houses than any of the other six. I place question marks above all their heads. While they don't have the influence or power to commit such treason, they could have easily been persuaded to assist. They aren't without their network of spies, too, like any shrewd war house. Power is relative, and being a war house is worth more than *not* being a war house, no matter where you stand in the pecking order. All the Tribune Generals make it their business to know the maneuverings of their peers. Which makes it farfetched to think Rossi and Rhysien staged an assassination without at least one or more of the lower war houses knowing and potentially helping to cover it up, either for favor or for blackmail against the two men to use later.

I study the web, trying to solve the puzzle I've been mulling over for the past six days. But that's hard to do when I'm missing critical pieces: witnesses and unassailable evidence. The files I lifted off the medic's computer aren't good enough. How do I prove a solid link between Rhysien, Rossi, and Grandfather's murder with Terese unreachable and Reed being relatively inaccessible for the moment too? And you don't become a Tribune General simply because of your family—these men and women are intelligent bastards. The greatest strategy, assault, and war minds in Mareen. There's unlikely to be any glaring trail they've left behind. I only stumbled upon the lethal bioserum because their attack on me with it failed.

So I need to look for trails that don't glare quite so bright. I start by refocusing on Sutton Rhysien, and I finally acknowledge a truth I've been trying to avoid. Terese isn't my only link to him. I'm roommates with his daughter. I'm supposed to be *best friends* with his daughter. I have unimpeded access to Selene, and she was super quick to defend her father when I named him as a suspect. What if that is because she already knew of his guilt? The Selene I know would've at least taken the time to ponder it.

Which would mean playing nice and getting close to her again.

And then you can compel the truth from her.

The insidious thought blindsides me, and I balk at contemplating something so atrocious. It's one thing to compel Caiman or Chance—or even Terese's housekeeper, who is a stranger. But Selene is my friend. My best friend. My sister in every way that counts. *She's kept the secret of my blood-gift,* I remind myself. Selene might have defended her father, but she didn't have prior knowledge of his actions. I'm sure of that. We've been friends for eleven years, and Sutton has attempted everything he could to sever our bond—including threats, bribery, and disavowal—but Selene has stuck by me. She's never betrayed me before, and she wouldn't betray me now on such a level. She *would have* warned me about the threat to Grandfather.

I shut off the holograph as the door to my room opens.

"I'm sorry about our fight," I say to Selene when she strides inside. An apology is the least I owe her after the terrible thing I considered.

"I'm sorry too," she says after a second. "I reacted to the news badly. Instead of being there for you, I jumped to Sutton's defense when I know how despicable he can sometimes be. You have every right to suspect him. It wasn't the time or the place to voice my opinion on that."

It isn't an absolute condemnation of the asshole like I'd prefer, but it's her father, so I think maybe my expectations are perhaps a bit high. At least she acknowledges she was shitty in the way she reacted. "Thank you for saying that," I say, instead of voicing my feelings. It would only keep more bad blood between us. "I don't want to fight with you anymore. I don't want to fight with Zayne anymore, either, but . . ."

"But that will be complicated to fix."

"Very complicated." I sigh. "I'll have to tell him so much for him to accept my apology and stop being hurt. But if I tell him everything, I'm endangering his life. Knowing about my blood-gift and not turning me in is treason. You're the scion of a war house. You're protected. He isn't."

"Maybe you don't get to make that decision for him," Selene says gently. "How would you want him to handle things if your situations were reversed? Would you care about being protected or would you want to know what's going on with your friend?

"As mad as he is," Selene continues when I don't answer, "you'll lose him all the way if you keep hiding things from him. So you gotta decide which is more important: filling him in on everything and mending your relationship or keeping him ignorant and safe. Which outcome could you live with?"

"You're not supposed to be the wise one in our group."

"Well, Zayne is off somewhere sulking and we all know the rational, level-headed choice is never your first one."

I throw her a look, and her white cheeks flush pink. "That was probably too soon and we probably aren't back to that place yet. I didn't mean anything by it."

I smile at her because I want us back in that place. I want my best friend back. "You *might* have a point."

"So . . . Zayne . . ." she hazards. "Are we telling him about your thing?"

I shake my head. "I don't know." She's right though. I have to make a decision about what's more important: protecting him or keeping his friendship.

17

THE SIREN BLARES THAT CALLS us to the lecture dome every morning. I'm out of bed and snatching on my boots before Selene reaches the door. We expect the drones at this point, though the officers like to switch up the nasty surprises they drop. A day ago, they shot a spray of old-school crescent stars around our room. One of the throwing knives nicked my cheek and another sliced off an inch of my damn hair. Another particularly fun time, the drones dropped pinless nanogrenades inside the rooms and the halls. Aspirants had fifty-nine seconds to clear the subterranean level before the grenades detonated. This time the drone that whizzes inside our room hovers near the ceiling suspiciously inert. Only an idiot would wait around and see what it does.

So we run.

It darts out of the room behind us. When it catches up to us, it keeps with our pace.

"I bet you a hundred credits that fucker is about to spew acid that eats through skin," Selene says, glancing up. "We've been bombed, blazed, shot up with UV bullets, and sliced up with throwing stars. Acid is about the only unique thing left."

"There's always gassing us," I say as I pull ahead a fraction in front of the drone. There's no way I want that thing above my head.

Selene speeds up her stride too. "They did that during the first trial. Our officers don't like to be predictable."

"They gassed us with toxic, *nonlethal* fumes. Gassing us with something that stops our hearts on inhalation would be novel."

She groans. "Yes, it would. Fuck them and fuck these trials."

The drone catches up to us. I brace for whatever it's going to do. It swings between me and Selene as if it were sentient, giving the impression that it has eyes and is watching us. Then a deep laugh pours from it and the others flying above aspirants sprinting down the hall, confirming my hunch. "You should see the lot of you," Chance chuckles. "Stop acting like scared little bitches. I'm not training up skittish fucks. You're embarrassing me. You know where to go. You got two minutes to get there. HUSTLE."

The drones follow us to the lecture dome, but they don't deliver any nasty gifts other than rousing us *before* the ass crack of dawn again. I swear to the gods if the transition officers make us wait in an icy dome for three hours, I might murder somebody today.

We file inside the dome, all dressed in warm gear, having learned from the previous times. We sit on the observer benches near the presenter's pit and wait. After about twenty minutes, the iciness of the dome eases. After forty minutes, the air turns mild. An hour into waiting for the officers, the temp shoots from mild to the uncomfortable side of warm. Ten minutes later, it is Silver Desert sweltering. Sweat slicks my skin. My long-sleeved top and sweats stick to my body, retaining too much heat. They've switched from trying to give us hypothermia to trying to induce a heat stroke.

Because of course they're not fools.

They're worse. "Our officers are real shitheads!" Enzo makes sure he yells loud enough for all of them to hear if they are listening. But they aren't. They're getting a few more hours of rest while they try to kill us from heat stroke.

"Motherfucker!" I yell. "That's why they were watching us via the drones. They think they're funny." I'm not the only one who wised up and started dressing appropriately for the freezing dome. "Everyone has on warm gear. The transition officers saw that beforehand and decided to turn our preparedness around on us."

"I swear when this is all over, I am going to punch a good number of them in the face," Bex promises.

At this point, the lot of us grumble agreement without a care as to who hears. We've come a long way from that first lecture.

By the two-hour mark, we've all stripped down to our underwear. Even the minimal clothing of my sports bra and bodymold shorts remains offending in the sauna they've created.

"I . . . I can't stand it in here much longer," Dasaun wheezes. His skin has a pallid sheen. He leans forward and pukes.

"Eww!" Caiman, who is sitting in front of him, jumps forward. "Keep your damn body fluids to yourself."

"Sor . . . sorry," Dasaun says, shuddering.

"Don't be an ass," I tell Caiman. "Chill."

He cuts me a glare. "You're pathetic," he says to Dasaun. But he isn't as unaffected as he's pretending to be. He's stripped out of his clothes like the rest of us. His ivory skin is lit up with angry red splotches. He shudders slightly, though he quickly squashes the tell.

An aspirant whose name I don't recall lumbers to his feet. "I'm done. I can take anything except this heat. I am done!" He shouts down at the presenter's pit. "Let me out of this inferno!"

When silence answers him, he ambles to the door and starts banging on the biolock. He shouts a flurry of curses until what strength he has is sapped. Then he slides to the floor, mumbling to himself.

"Delirium is a symptom of heat shock," Bex says sympathetically.

"So is an eventual coma," Selene snarls. "Stop the fucking games!" she yells down into the presenter's pit.

"Pipe down, Rhysien," Caiman says. "We were injected with the bioserum. They could keep us locked in here for days and the heat won't kill us. It'll only make us wish we were dead."

"Fantastic." Enzo punches the air. Then he says to Selene, dead serious, "If we are still in here at the end of this day, find a way to put me out of my misery."

"Stop being dramatic. Soldier up."

Enzo spins Caiman's way. "Nobody was fucking talking to you, Golden Boy."

Surprisingly, it is Greysen who wedges himself between them. He prods Enzo a few steps back. "Why don't we all settle down? Fighting inside this hotbox won't get us anywhere."

"Yeah, whatever. Tell your buddy that. Maybe he'll stop being a dick for once."

The heat has everyone's tempers running hot. Four more verbal spats break out, and two aspirants exchange punches.

Breathe, Kenna, I tell myself, drowning out the drama. The room is wobbling, I'm panting, and my heart thuds in my chest. It's crazy, but I swear I *feel* my blood scorching my veins. Nausea rolls through my stomach in waves. The room shudders black. I drag in several breaths, refusing to embarrass myself and vomit like Dasaun or faint.

Selene touches my elbow. "You okay?"

It takes me a minute to gather my bearings and respond. "Yes."

"You don't look it."

"Do any of us?"

"True."

And although I said it, the other aspirants don't quite look how I feel. I'm roasting alive, but my discomforts are more than that. My blood no longer feels like it's scorching. It feels like it's boiling. I wipe a hand across the back of my sweaty neck. Every inch of my skin prickles with hypersensitivity. A current, not unlike what my blood-gift sparks in my veins when my temper gets the better of me, shoots into my palm and fingers. The current morphs into a buzz of power that reverberates up my arm and floods the rest of my body. I bite my tongue so I don't yelp at the shock of sensation. My senses sharpen, my body blazes heat, and I slip into near delirium. An itch ignites beneath my skin; I scratch at my arms, furiously and futilely. I want to rip my scratchy, offending underwear off I'm so hot.

I heave myself from the bench. I pace in front of it. I can't sit still. I can't summon calm. I'm spinning out of control like the night of the Blood Moons. I think about my eyes. My hands fly to my face. If they turn red like they did that night, I am fucked. Then I remember I'm wearing eyefilms. I silently thank Selene for the save. My vision blurs. My head pounds. My blood and bones thrum with the crackling power. I drink it in, becoming heady and drunk. I'm too hot. I'm too constricted. I'm too everything. I suck in gulps of air, trying to calm the fuck down and make whatever is happening in front of my whole aspirant class stop. It's broad daylight. There aren't even any damn Blood Moons in the fucking sky. I shiver, feverish.

"Kenna?"

"Kenna!"

Selene's and Zayne's distorted voices blur together. Selene was sitting right next me. I don't know how Zayne is beside me now when he was sitting several rows behind me before.

"Kenna!" Selene grips my shoulders and halts my pacing. "Focus through it. Focus beyond it. We got this."

"Don't let those bastards' game get the best of you," Zayne adds.

I shake my head because my problem isn't that at all.

"I think the heat is making things weird. Everything including my blood feels hot," I say, and hope Selene reads everything that I pour into the careful admission.

Thankfully, understanding dawns on her face. She regards me with the outright terror I am mustering all the bravado I've got to hide.

She grabs my hand and tugs me to the bench. "Sit down. Breathe."

She wraps an arm around my shoulders. I sag against her. A second ago, I was crawling out of my skin with energy. Now I'm depleted. "I feel weak." It's worse than in Onei's Expanse when I struggled to stay upright and awake.

It's the last thing I'm conscious of saying.

I slip into sleep and experience a bizarre dream. I'm standing in an unfamiliar field beneath Blood Moons.

"How old are we?" A girl who looks identical to me asks. "Have we not reached the age of maturity?"

"Nineteen." I answer numbly.

She clasps her hands behind her back, assuming the air of a wise old woman rather than a girl of nineteen. "Ah. So we have crossed the threshold this year. It's time for our gift to evolve." She studies me approvingly, then her face scrunches up. Her eyes flash with reproach. "Why haven't we fully begun yet? What's delaying it?" She leans forward, dark brown eyes narrowing and peering at me as if she can glimpse the core of what comprises me. "I see that it wants to evolve. I see that it has already started attempting to do so. Why do we block it?" Her words are sharp. Like a rap against the temple for misbehaving. "Answer me? Why do we block it?"

"I . . . I don't know what you're talking about. Who are you? Where am I? What is this?"

You're dreaming, Ikenna, I remind myself so I can calm down. I'm not anywhere, and the replica of me is nobody. I am having a heat-induced delusion.

Replica Me clucks her tongue. "You are foolish. Does this feel like you aren't really present?" She holds out her palm and a blood spike shoots from it. Faster than I can track, it flies at me and buries itself in my chest. In my heart. I cry out at the pain I expect, though there is none. At least, not in the agonizing sense. Instead, a jolt of power strikes my chest where the blood spike impales me. It burrows inside my skin and detonates like a sundisk. My body becomes too small a vessel to hold the enormity of it. It fills up my insides then begins pouring out of me in waves of crimson.

"You are blessed with Amaka's gift," Replica Me says. "You must cease blocking it. You must accept it and your evolution fully. If you do not, it will consume and destroy you instead of empowering you." The feminine voice that pours out of her mouth no longer has the same pitch as mine. It's foreign. It has a cadence and timbre I've never spoken with before.

I stare down at the bright crimson light—no, *power* (that is the only term that wholly fits)—pouring out of me. It silhouettes my frame. A lifetime of hiding my blood-gift kicks in, and I'm horrified by the visual manifestation. I want it to go away. I want to stuff it back inside me where the rest of the world can never see it. If it's glimpsed, I'm dead. Then, I have another chilling thought. What if the same thing I'm experiencing in my dream is happening back in the lecture dome? What if crimson energy is pouring out of me there too? "Stop!" I yell at it. "Stop!"

But the crimson power continues pouring out in waves and waves and waves that give no indication of ebbing. I stand in the center of Onei's Expanse under the Blood Moons paralyzed with terror.

"Please make it stop?" I beg of Replica Me.

Her face is pitiless. She does not deign to listen. Then, as abruptly as the power surge began, it ceases. The pain I initially braced for rips me apart from the inside out, dousing the crimson light pouring from me and the power surging through my veins.

I double over panting. "Thank you," I say.

Replica Me's face twists with disgust. "We did not do that." As she speaks, cracks appear in her form. They appear in the field and the Blood Moons above too. There are only a few slivers at first. Then they proliferate into dozens and dozens and dozens of cracks. My fractured surroundings shimmer like a holograph and shatter apart like glass. Instinct makes me throw up my arms to shield my face and eyes. The shards I brace for somehow don't burrow into my skin.

I come awake shivering, my head propped on Selene's shoulder and my body tucked tight into her side back in the dome. Her arms are protectively curled around me. Zayne sits on my other side with a worried expression.

I lift my head from Selene's shoulder. The dome is no longer a furnace. The temp is back to moderate and rapidly falling.

The podium rises out of the floor of the presenter's pit, carrying our transition officers atop it. "Don't try to outsmart us," Chance says. "You freeze in the dome or you burn. Pick one. You don't get to be comfortable."

The grill session passes in a blur. Reed lobs a question at me. Selene has to elbow me in the side for me to snap to attention as she repeats it. I squeeze out a sufficient answer, then try and fail to cling to some semblance of lucidity. My heat-induced hallucination has me shook. I know it wasn't real. But I keep checking my hands and arms and torso for a condemning red glow.

The whole time, I worry that as the transition officers were observing us someone saw something that gave me away. And as has been the case during these trials, it is only my gift that has me this scared.

18

WHEN WE'RE CALLED TOGETHER IN the dome on the seventh day, the transition officers are present when we arrive. They aren't in the usual battledress they don for lectures. They've shed the black shirts with maroon stripes for the microprene suits we aspirants wear. Ours are nondescript, while their cohort insignias shimmer gold high on their left biceps.

They aren't domineering and pompous either today. They are giddy and restless and buzzing with energy. Their change in demeanor puts us aspirants more on edge.

Nero calls us to attention. It's Reed, not Chance, who then takes over the proceedings. "Combat, Survival, and Strength. Those of you standing passed the first three trials. You have one left: Strategy." He ascends the steps of the presenter's pit and walks among us in the observer gallery as he speaks. Though his raised voice resonates with authority, he doesn't bark the words like Chance would, and he looks each aspirant in the eye as he walks by them instead of regarding us as if we are nothing. We are considerably lower in number than when the trials first started. Our class has been sliced to less than half. There are roughly three hundred of us left who see our names unmarred on the Death Board that stretches along one wall of the dome.

When Reed reaches me, he pauses. I tense at the jolt of whatever is between us. He stiffens, too, at the same pull. He cuts his eyes away from me and continues down my line. "Sometimes, we go into an op blind. We don't realize the danger until we're chest-deep in quicksand and sinking fast. Those are the easy ops. Those are the conditions we tossed you into with Onei's Expanse. You can't lose your nerve when you have limited intel going in. Other times, we take on an op that we know is shit and the chances of not coming home are pretty high. Those are the hard ones. They're the ones that really test if you have what it takes to be a Praetorian. Can you march into a mission that most of your team won't return from? Can you say 'fuck you' to the nerves and the self-doubt and do your job to the best of your ability? Can your team count on you not to freeze? That's what this next trial is about."

"The Strategy Trial is the reason I volunteered to transition newbies," Chance crows. He smacks the gold Alpha symbol on his suit. "For those of us who've already earned our letters, we get to have a shit-ton of fun. We get to play Defend the Fortress and do our level best to beat, break, and murder your lousy asses while you play the *pitiful* and *outmatched* advancing team."

"What does SSEE stand for?" yells Nero.

"*Stealth, Subterfuge, Evasion, and Escape,*" we respond back as a unit.

Dannica appraises us. "You're in sync. Good. I suggest you stay that way. Teamwork and all those things you named are components of good strategy. They *may* help you survive this."

"My third is right," Reed says, throwing a nod to his Gamma comrade-in-arms and apparently Gamma's third-in-command. *Interesting.* "SSEE is not about the individual. Like the real ops when you're out in the field, it is not the place for pride, petty squabbles, or arrogance." I swear he looks my way, and I smart. "SSEE simulates the sort of life-or-death ops you will encounter. If you fuck up, it isn't only your ass that gets dead. You get your comrades-in-arms dead too. Having to live with yourself being the reason your comrades died is not a position any of us wants to be in." There's a haunted look on his face when he says this, and as I look around at the rest of our officers, I see similar cracks, even in Chance. *How many of your friends have died?* I wonder.

Reed continues. "You get the aid of three warnings going in. Warning one: you *shouldn't* have suffered heavy losses in the forest. Despite Chance's taunts, we didn't set you up to all die. We told you to survive the Expanse and we told you to retrieve an Accursed's head. We did not tell you to go after them during daylight, which many of you did for fear of marching through the forest at night. But the thing that takes the most nerve, the most risk, is usually the path to assured victory. War is never easy, and if it is, you should be suspicious of the circumstances." He pauses and lets what he's revealed sink in. He watches as we visibly try to fit the pieces together and discern what we did wrong in the forest. We try to discern how more than a hundred of us didn't need to die—how we might have saved those who did.

I think about Dex and the guy in the Accursed's camp whose name I never got. I'm sick with knowing I could've saved them. But how? I'm more sick that it's a question I can't answer still—there was some aspect of that trial that I failed, and I have no freaking idea what it is. All I know is that I came up short somewhere, and according to Reed, people died because of it.

Reed starts speaking again, and when he does, he hands me and the rest of my class an explanation of how we failed: "For whatever reason, the Accursed operate at peak strength under the sun. At dusk, their preternatural strength diminishes—it's when they're closest to the human men they used to be. From there and throughout the night, they should've been relatively easy kills for individuals equipped with bioen-hancements. During years one through four as cadets, you learned the geography and history of Iludu. Your instruction didn't delve deep into the parts relating to the Pantheon, but you got basic knowledge. You learned about Onei's Expanse and the Accursed that prowl it in year three. You had the information you needed to go into the forest and survive. The rest of Mareen dismisses most Pantheon Age history as myth, or simply chooses to ignore it. But you, as Praetorians, don't get the luxury of being ignorant of the gods, or forgetting aspects of their existence and their creations' existence, because enemies like the Acca-cians possess power from the Pantheon in abundance."

The room is quiet and grim, not just because what Reed is saying could technically be considered heresy, but because he is right. We did have the tools for many more of us to survive the forest, and it was our fuck-up for forgetting crucial intel. I recall those year-three lessons in full now, whereas I only remembered bits of them while in the forest. I want to blame my forgetting on the perilous circumstances, but it's not an excuse. The mettle of a soldier lies in excelling under pressure—you don't go to shit when it matters. So it's my fault, in part, Dex got killed. We never would've been in that glen for the sabine attack if we had been out hunting Accursed.

"Feel it. Digest it. Then get over it, because that's the only way to move on from a huge fuck-up," Reed says. "But also remember that as Praetorians you don't get to have another one because when you do, people die." He gives us a moment longer to sit with it, to lick our wounds, and regroup. Then he says, back to business, "Warning two: this trial is the most brutal. Once we drop you in the field, you become the enemy of your transition officers. We will treat you as we would any other threat. We will come at you with everything we've got. Treat us as your enemy in turn. Breach of deference no longer applies. And warn-ing three: None of you will survive SSEE if you fail to work as a team. *Do not split apart when you get on the mountain.*"

Chance, the bastard, chuckles at the apprehension that ripples through us. "You all look nervous at the mention of a mountain. You should be. Rossi, you're running point for the advancing team. Aspirants, he's your lead in this exercise."

Enzo grumbles at the officers naming Caiman our lead. "That's such nepotism wolfshit." Selene, Dasaun, and a few others grumble too.

"What was that?" Chance shouts from the presenter's pit. "Who has a problem they'd like to voice with my decision-making? Don't be yellowshit. Speak it with your chest!"

"Why does Caiman get to be lead?" I shout before I can help myself. "His leadership skills are abysmal. He'll only look out for himself and his friends." I keep on because I've already breached deference anyway. "And if his decisions in the Expanse are anything to go by, we'll all end up dead if we have to follow his command. He didn't listen to a thing I advised and it drew a pack of sabines upon us. A pack of sabines that killed a man." Dex might be partially on me, but his death is also on Caiman.

Caiman, who sits in the row in front of me, spins around. "Dex Dulsiner was fighting alongside *you*. It wasn't me who got him killed."

I do not let him see how much that rubs.

"I told you and your obtuse friends that blasters wouldn't take down one of those creatures. I told you to use steel. I told you not to start a fire in the first place. You didn't listen. So you all were useless." I was, too, but we're talking about his shortcomings right now.

"Your way isn't always *the* way, Amari. Verne suffered the same hubris."

Is he serious? Is he really accusing me of being arrogant again when his ego is inflated enough to span the whole planet?

"Keep my grandfather's name out of your disgusting mouth or I promise you'll be missing teeth."

"That's enough!" Chance says.

I bite my tongue, fuming. "With all respect," Enzo says—with not that much respect, I'd wager, "why *was* Rossi named lead? If we have to follow someone on this op simulation that could end in our deaths—again—and we shouldn't split apart, I think it's fair to ask that my class be allowed to select the lead for ourselves instead of being handed one because of his war house's stature."

By now, the rest of our class aside from Selene watches the proceedings with shock. They look between me, Caiman, and Enzo and down at Chance in the pit for his reaction. He remains uncharacteristically cool.

"Rossi is lead because he's first in your class," Reed says as a buffer.

"Based on what?" Enzo asks.

"Based on our evaluations," Reed says. He's not angry, but he's not happy at being questioned about this either. I may hate him like I hate the rest of the transition officers, but he wouldn't lie about something like that. He's been trying to at least keep the trials balanced and fair. Him taking up for me twice with Chance makes that apparent. Caiman must be doing something better than the rest of us.

Chance wastes no time reminding us of exactly that. "If someone else wants to be lead, you should've worked harder at not being a fucking loser. If you aren't first, you're nothing. Remember that."

Enzo pushes his shoulders farther back. "I still say it isn't right."

"And you mistake that I give a shit what you think. This is war, asshole. Not a fucking social club. Opinions aren't necessary."

"It's good to be number one. Don't be bitter because you guys suck," Caiman says with an obnoxious wink before turning around to give the officers his full attention.

"And it's good to not be a prick, so that those you lead actually follow you," Reed says coolly. Caiman flushes, and it's the best I've felt in the last few days.

"Regardless of how anyone may feel about the choice," Reed continues in a tone meant to sweep over the hall and quell dissent, "it was your senior officers' choice, it upholds the tradition of how the lead for

SSEE is chosen, and more importantly—as Chance said—you all are soldiers. Soldiers follow commands. They don't dissect them." He absolutely projects that last bit of censure at me, even though it was Enzo arguing more. I imagine landing the kick I hurled at his head in the gym. Damn, it would've felt good to connect.

"Enough whining. Show them the locale," Chance says to Nero.

Nero punches a command into his Comm Unit. A vast stretch of ice, wind, and subzero temps appears on the rounded ceiling.

Damn them all to a hellpit. We are completing SSEE in the Ice Wastes. We were right to be nervous when Reed mentioned this trial would take place on a mountain.

He didn't say it was *the* mountain.

Chance doesn't give us long to swallow the fact that they are dropping us in the middle of a place that is ice and snow and dead bodies beneath it for hundreds and hundreds of miles. "You'll be executing standard HALO night jumps at this drop point." A red laser points to the base of a craggy, hulking mountain range called Hasani's Wrath. Atop its peak is where Hasani, the god of death, committed an unspeakable atrocity. Several united nations once sprawled across the fertile lands that predated the Ice Wastes. Hasani froze the lands over, raised the massive mountain range, and called forth an avalanche that snuffed out the lives of the millions who are buried under the Ice Wastes. It was his vengeance against the people who betrayed him when they banded with the rest of the planet to cast the gods off of Iludu.

We all know the history. But it's a good reminder of why the Republic exists in the first place, and why the final test is here. We're being sent to sacred land, and we'd better well be prepared for it.

"The bioserum's enhancements to your physiology isn't enough to withstand the extreme oxygen-deficient conditions of the mountain for an extended period," Chance says. "You're going to need rebreathers to make it all the way up, but you won't be dropped with any. What would the fun in *giving* them to you be? You're going to have to earn the lifeline."

"What does that mean?" an aspirant calls down to the presenter's pit.

"It means to figure it out, you stupid son of a bitch. I'm briefing you, not handing you the Praetorian rank."

"The rebreathers are positioned where you'll need them to be on the mountain," Reed says, more forthcoming, but still damn cryptic. "You need to find their location."

So on top of throwing us into a frozen wasteland, they're further fucking with us by making us go on a scavenger hunt in it for gear? Lovely.

Chance's laser points to the mountain's summit. "This is your target. You'll be completing an ascent to the fortress we've set up. Rhysien is playing hostage."

Selene explodes. "Like hell I am."

"Did you miss hearing I don't give a shit how you feel? If you don't like it, *you*, *Donya*, have always had the option to walk away *and* keep a cushy life, since your friends want to call out nepotism," Chance says, pitiless. "You can go sit pretty in Rhysien Manor and play Lady of your war house if you don't like your assignment."

The blow hits exactly as hard as Chance intends. Selene clenches her hands into fists and drops back into her seat.

"The precious Donya," Chance says, picking at Selene by repeatedly using the title she loathes, "flies with us. We'll be holding her under guard in the fortress. As a team, you'll have to mount an extraction mission from the low-ground position. Move up the mountain without being detected or captured, get your man out, get off the mountain, and get home, *if you can*. You've got forty-eight hours to pull it off. This is it, you sons of whores. Complete SSEE and you're one of us." He says it slick because he knows they've given us an impossible task. We ran defend-the-fortress drills in the academy. However, the advancing team and the defending team were always equally matched, and deadly force wasn't allowed. We're about to go head-to-head with seasoned, biochipped Praetorians. The transition officers are going to slaughter whomever the savage Ice Wastes don't kill.

There must be a way to survive this. So close to the end, it would be too much of a waste to let three hundred highly trained soldiers simply die because we didn't quite live up to the standards of the Praetorians—and not even all the Praetorians, but these select few. What's more, Reed just told us the forest *seemed* impossible but wasn't. He could've revealed that earlier, yet he didn't. That means he purposely waited until this exact moment to tell us. His whole lecture was that they wanted us to learn from it and apply the lesson to the mountain.

But I have to admit: I have no idea what that lesson was, and what the path to survival is that we're supposed to discern.

I look over at Caiman, his face casually smug.

Then I notice his eyes seem just as frantic as mine.

We're fucked.

19

I'VE NEVER BEEN AFRAID OF heights. I've run through drop-zone drills as a cadet dozens of times. But jumping out of a stealth jet forty thousand feet in the air in a virtual sim and jumping out of one in real life prove to be two different things. I grip the straps of my jet pack. *You can do this, Ikenna. Don't bitch up.* My sudden terror of heights reminds me that if my jet pack is faulty, I'm splattering all over the ground.

"I cannot believe we're about to do this," Caiman exclaims to Greysen. They're four bodies behind me in the jump line. As leader, Caiman will jump last, making sure the rest of his team lands in the drop zone first.

I adjust the straps of my pack, making sure they're snug. After Enzo jumps, I'm next.

"Dex would've loved this," Bex says to me. "Drop drills were his favorite." She's in the line next to mine, waiting in the same first queue position that I am.

"Yeah, it seems like his thing," I offer back.

We fall into a moment of silence for her brother.

"Is it really Caiman's fault he died?"

Even though I threw that accusation at Caiman in front of everybody in the dome, the question rattles me. Also the way she focuses intently on a single spot on the cabin wall so her grief doesn't come spilling out makes everything that happened with the sabines surge back. *Yes*, I want to say. *He failed in his position of leadership.* But I can't get the words out. "Partially," I say instead, and that truth isn't only because I forgot about the Accursed's weakness. "Like I told you, he died fighting beside me. I led him in that fight. Which means his death isn't ultimately on Caiman. It's on me." He died because I couldn't keep myself *and* someone else alive. I couldn't do it with the sabines, and I couldn't do it with the Accursed either. I do not let the images form in my mind of the aspirant's body roasting above a spit after I promised him we'd both get free. Dex's mauled body haunts me enough.

Zayne stands behind Bex. We haven't interacted much outside of my episode in the dome. I'm going to have to be the one who makes the first move to repair the strain between us. But I still haven't decided if I want to. It might be better and easier to let our relationship remain strained so he stays at a distance. He reaches forward and squeezes Bex's shoulder. "Don't jump with a messed-up head," he says gently. "Take a moment if you need to. We can change queue positions if you want." His offer is precisely why I should leave things as they are. Why I can't tell him the whole truth. He won't care about the danger to himself. He'll only be concerned about supporting me. It's who he is. It's what he does.

Bex vigorously shakes her head. "No. I have it together."

The aspirant in front of her launches himself off the jet. Enzo does the same a ten-second count later. The darkness of the night swallows them. I step up to the open cargo door and stare over the edge. It's like peering into an unforgiving black hole. This far up, I can see nothing below me. My blood-gift yields zero aid. I activate the night-vision mode on my tactical goggles, and the blackness looming below me turns to shades of green. Whips of icy wind batter me. I plant my feet farther apart to retain my balance.

"Are you sure you're ready?" I ask Bex. I'm also asking myself. Yes, I've turned yellowshit.

"Rip the medgauze off, Amari. Let's move!"

That's all the warning I get before Caiman shoves me. It's twice now that bastard has sent me careening toward the ground at guts-splattering speed. Terror paralyzes me for a perilous moment, then my training kicks in and I'm shaking it off and pressing the trigger button on the right strap of my jet pack. I can't hear the rumble of its dual rockets flare to life over the roaring wind. But the heat at my back assures me they have, and I relax slightly at the activated pack. I angle my body downward, hurtling to the ground at terminal velocity for a few necessary moments. I count to ten thrice, perhaps a little brisker than I'm supposed to; then I press the button on my left strap that cuts the rockets' engines and erects a vector force around my body that counters the effect of gravity. It slows my descent to nonlethal speeds without the risk of entanglement in a parachute. Once I'm near the base of the mountain, the force field readjusts my net velocity so my feet plant on the rock smoothly.

Beside me, Enzo hoots. "That might've been better than sex!"

On the ground, I tap the side of my goggles and the thermal cam activates. "I'll be sure to let Selene know that," I say as Bex lands.

"Please don't. She'll shoot my balls off."

Zayne and the last few remaining aspirants who were behind me land. When Caiman touches down, I play nice and don't go for his throat.

Caiman lays out strategy to the group, and of course he solicits minimal feedback. I don't speak a word of dissent. The officers appointed him lead so Golden Boy can have all the glory and all the responsibility that comes with it. If the op goes to hell and people die, it won't be on my head in any way this time. Once he's done with his spiel, he doles out specific jobs. Enzo and I are told to complete a thermal scan of the area for friends lurking nearby.

"What the fuck is taking so long?" Caiman barks in the middle of our task.

I am falling back and letting him be op lead, so I ask him evenly and earnestly, "Do you want a thorough scan?"

"I want you to not suck and perform a swift job."

"It's almost done," I growl.

"If I break his legs, we'll need a new op lead," Enzo says to me quietly. "You wanna volunteer for the role?"

I sure don't.

"Keep joking around, Enzo. But either swallow me being op lead or fuck off," Caiman retorts. "Nobody wants to hear you groaning about it anymore. It's a distraction, and one we can't afford."

Enzo pushes his goggles up on his head, spoiling for a fight.

"Don't," I tell him.

He doesn't listen. "Fucking off sounds like a fantastic idea. I don't need you to lead me up the mountain."

"Caiman is right." I regret my words as soon as the stupid, snide smirk pops onto his face. I can't believe the admission flies out of my mouth. Either the Ice Wastes are melting or the hellpit Caiman belongs in is freezing over. But I'm not here for either his or Enzo's pride. I'm here to survive, and I'm here to find out who killed my grandfather. And surviving SSEE is the only way that's going to happen.

I put my hand on Enzo's arm and take off my goggles, looking him in the eye. "We can't do this now," I whisper. Louder, I say to them both, "Reed warned us that we need to get through this as a team and not split up. Let's just work together to get up the mountain, extract Selene, and get back down."

A cold droplet splashes onto my forehead.

I assume it's melted snow from a tree that's stuck to my hair.

Then more of it pelts me.

Sheets of white flurries fall rapidly around us.

Enzo curses. "Snow is exactly what we need."

"The weather data the officers transmitted with the land-nav maps projected no precipitation," Caiman says, blinking up at the falling snow dumbstruck.

"Did you cross-check that for yourself?" I ask.

The way he stiffens means no.

I just played the diplomat, and now Caiman has thrown all my goodwill into the incinerator. "Great job, Golden Boy. If you hadn't spent the majority of these trials being favored, you'd be aware that our transition officers are assholes and Chance is a madman. He fed us faulty intel." Reed warned us that all the odds would be stacked against us. They are making good on that. "Anyone have new weather updates?"

"A system is moving through the area that will turn the snow to sleet and plunge the temp to negative 95 in a little under an hour," Greysen says grimly. His eyes are glued to his Comm Unit. He stares at it like he can maybe unsee what he's seeing. "An ice storm will move in behind the sleet thirty minutes later. It will plummet the temp to negative 103. If the officers knew about this, they set us all up to freeze to death."

The grimness in his statement settles over the group.

"Chance would pull that stunt," I say, refusing to resign myself to dying on the mountain, "but it doesn't make sense that Reed, who is now acting as lead alongside him, would send us into a situation we have no possibility of coming out of alive. Reed is the one who forced Chance to change the cage fights to submission matches instead of death matches. Why do that to turn around and slaughter us all?"

"They sent us into the Expanse knowing we could all die," Enzo counters.

"That's my point exactly. *Could die* is not the same as *will die*. We're here now, aren't we? In the dome, Reed said we didn't need to lose as many people as we did in the forest. They might've sent us into a situation where we all *could've* died, but none of us *needed* to die. Not if we'd used all the resources at our disposal—all the knowledge we should have collected and retained throughout our basic then advanced training years in the academy. They made the forest into a puzzle we needed to solve, but we didn't. That's why the Accursed hunts were a disaster. I think the mountain is the same setup. There's a trick to us all getting through it, to us all surviving this, even with Caiman's blunder."

"What the fuck do you know?" Caiman's challenge drips disdain. "You're the reason SSEE is happening on this deathtrap of a mountain. Chance said so in the mess. You are such a dumb, thoughtless, entitled bitch, Amari. First, you get us in this mess, and now you want us all to take your word that there's a way out of it solely because you and Darius Reed have some gross fling going on. Don't deny it," he says when I go to do exactly that. "Greysen saw him leaving her room half-dressed after the fight matches," he informs everyone, and I flinch. "Fucking Reed during the trials seems sloppy, even for you. It's a move I'd expect more from Rhysien. But I guess with your grandfather dead, you have to ensure you stay relevant and retain the life and status you've been accustomed to some sort of way. Fucking your way through these trials and into Gamma cohort will certainly ensure that."

I want to reply to all of that. To note that he keeps believing Chance when clearly that asshole has lied to us. To note that if I'm so entitled, why did he—Caiman—try to kill me in the Expanse (not to mention in my room). And if he thinks fucking a transition officer is the worst sin an aspirant can commit, I should point out that the amount of Rossi shit Chance eats is the real affront to nature.

Instead I slam an open palm into his Adam's apple, making him choke on his ugly words.

He rushes me.

I lose my footing on the snow-slick ground, but I take him down with me. On top of me, he drives a punch into my stomach. I rock his head back with an uppercut to the chin. He jumps up. I do too.

Greysen grabs Caiman. Enzo grabs me.

"Quash it!" Greysen shouts. He steps around Caiman and inserts himself between us. Caiman starts for me while Enzo restrains me. Greysen plants his hands on Caiman's chest, shoving him back. "I'm serious. Quash it. This isn't the time. I don't give a shit about the animosity between you two or what or who the fuck Amari did at the moment. Did you not hear what I said about the incoming storm? We don't have time for fights."

"I, for one, am more concerned about not freezing to death," an aspirant says. "The two of you can go jump off the mountain for all I care." The rest of our class agrees.

"Amari is making sense," Greysen insists to Caiman. Under different circumstances, I'd have a good laugh at the fact that Caiman Rossi's lap dog readily agrees with me over him about anything. "Land-nav maps. Can somebody pull them up?" Greysen calls to the group. "We need them. There isn't one mountain range on Iludu without caves. We had to memorize all seven of the major ones and their cave systems the year after we studied all the forest areas."

Calmer, I wiggle out of Enzo's hold and finish Greysen's line of reasoning. "If our officers didn't send us on a suicide mission, that means they dropped us in a zone with shelter we can find before the weather turns lethal." I start pulling the maps up on my Comm Unit immediately. "The nearest cave is exactly an hour and a half climb up the east side of the mountain. We won't get to shelter before the sleet, but we can make it before the worst of the ice hits. From there, we can make the rest of the ascent in spurts by daylight when it will be several degrees warmer. We can identify a string of caves as rest stops to warm up in along the way."

Enzo spits in the snow. "Our transition officers are devious pricks, but it's good to know they aren't soulless."

"Hold on," Dasaun says. "Reed also told us that the thing which takes the most nerve and risk is usually the path to victory. He said we should be suspicious if things are easy. What if the officers are testing us on that too? Using the caves for shelter makes the op a lot simpler. It also gives us a pretty *easy* route to the summit. What if an ambush is waiting for us in one of the caves?"

"It doesn't matter," Bex says. "We need the caves to survive the storm. And if we're supposed to be making use of them, I'd also bet credits that the rebreathers we'll need are stashed in one of them. Likely the cave closest to the base, since we won't get too far into the climb without them. If this is a setup, we can't avoid it, and we deal with that. We just have to go into this expecting the ambush, prepared for it, and if it comes, we show those asshats that we aren't easy marks when we go up against them this time. There's three hundred of us and twenty-four of them—and we have bioserum injections, which we didn't have when they kicked our asses in the combat trial."

Bex is my type of girl. I jerk my chin toward her. "I agree about the rebreathers, and I like her thinking."

"So we're letting two women strategize for us?" some asshole calls out.

"Couldn't've said it better myself." Caiman rakes me and Bex with a condescending, irritated glower.

I fold my arms over my chest and smile at them both. "If anybody's got another idea, I'd love to hear it. If not, shut the fuck up with your sexist bullshit."

"I'm behind Ikenna's and Bex's plans," says Enzo.

"They're good ones," Zayne adds.

"It's the best strategy we've got," Greysen tells the group, to my infinite amazement.

It's lousy that it takes three males to back us to get them to start considering it seriously, but chauvinism births the best fools.

Golden Boy, of course, has an objection to give. He has to wrestle control back somehow. He's looking at land-nav maps that he's pulled up for himself. If he'd done that with the weather maps, we wouldn't be in this catastrophe, but we're already past that point. "The east face of the mountain Amari wants to climb is steeper. That route is more hazardous. We're climbing the north face instead. It has the gentler terrain. And if we're working from the assumption that the officers primed us to choose the more difficult route, then we can maybe avoid an ambush altogether. As for the rebreathers, if my aim was to truly make this a challenging but passable test, I'd place them along both paths so they'd be accessible regardless of which way we ascend."

"Then we're back to the same problem," Dasaun says. "Given our predicament, Reed's advice is contradictory. The more difficult climb could be what they expect us to choose and an ambush could still be waiting there too, or the less challenging climb could be the one we *aren't* supposed to choose and if we do, there's some peril we'll run into as well."

"That doesn't change anything," I say. "Not when *time* is our greatest threat. If we choose Caiman's course then the ascent will take longer. My east route will get us to the summit quickest and reduce the time we have to endure hypothermic conditions."

Greysen hitches a thumb toward the part of the mountain that begins to slope upward. "We need to get moving instead of standing around for round two of an argument. The subzero insulation of the suits will start to falter as soon as the air drops to anything below negative 90. We want to be exposed to the life-threatening temps the sleet will bring for the least amount of time."

"Which is why we need to climb east. Convince your friend of that so we can move out."

"This decision involves all of our lives. We should put it to a vote," Zayne says.

"A vote would be fairest," Enzo says.

"A vote is fine with me if we make it fast," says Greysen.

The eastern route with the quicker climb time gets the majority support. Yes, I'm petty enough to pitch one of the gloating sneers Caiman loves so much his way. I am mature enough, however, to refrain from verbally ribbing him like he would have done me.

I end up leading the climb, since it's my route we're following. It isn't until we've moved out and I have my entire aspirant class trailing me that I realize Caiman might be op lead, but I'm the one who is marching everyone up the mountain. Now if people die, it's on me. I've placed myself in a position with this trial that I said I didn't want to be in.

Great job, Kenna.

That's what Amaris do. We lead.

I grimace at Grandfather's voice and that particular expectation he drilled into me lesson after lesson.

Not this Amari, I tell him. *I suck at it.*

Then, I pray to the entire godsdamned Pantheon to help me not fuck up.

20

"**THE STORIES ABOUT THIS PLACE,** you've heard them, right?" Enzo says to Bex. He hoists the survival pack we were all afforded higher up on his shoulders. He's fidgeting. Enzo doesn't fidget.

"Of course I've heard the stories. I'm from Cara," Bex says, clutching the straps of hers.

Dasaun shivers in a way that doesn't seem like it has anything to do with the cold. "We hear them in the east too."

Caiman—Krashen City–born and Krashen Academy–trained—rolls his eyes. "Those myths are drivel."

"Reed said—"

"That we need to remember the basic stuff. The lore about this mountain goes beyond the basics. It leaps into the absurd."

"I haven't heard many stories," Greysen, northern-born, too, says nervously. "Care to humor me and share the drivel so I know the full extent of the fun we might encounter? Wish I'd known a detailed story or two about Onei's Expanse."

"Pull yourself together. You're embarrassing me," Caiman hisses.

"Drivel or not, we could probably all use a story that instills a healthy dose of fear," Zayne says. "Trepidation is good. It keeps you alive."

"Agreed," Enzo responds. "Give us a good one, Bex."

"You're all stains on the Republic and what it stands for," Caiman mutters. Yet he doesn't turn his ear away from Bex.

They're all marching with me at the front of our tight formation. We trudge through the snow that comes up to my knees. It slows my steps like I'm running in sand.

"We all learned in the academies that the mountain range is named Hasani's Wrath after the judgment he leveled at the civilizations he pampered as his flock who revolted against him. But the stories not told in our history units over the Pantheon Age say that Hasani's Wrath became more than a mass grave. The millions of lives snuffed out at once caused such a disruption in the cosmos that it created a tear in the fabric of Iludu itself at the site of the calamity. It created a rip that traveled straight to the hellpits Hasani condemned millions of innocents to suffer in beyond death. Some in Cara still pass down stories of the gods to their children. My grandparents are some of those people," she says without shame. "My gran told me that because of that rip, Hasani's Wrath is a site where the living can access the hellpits in the After without dying and the dead can access Iludu if they're able to slip past the watchful gaze of Hasani himself and the hellpits' guardian serpents."

Caiman emits a derisive snort. "That entire tale was a waste of oxygen, Dulsiner."

Greysen, who'd prodded her for lore, follows it up with a dismissive laugh. "I thought you'd relay something useful. Not a kid's bedtime story you heard from your *gran*."

"The dead don't ascend from the After and the living can't access the dead," says another northern-born aspirant who graduated from Krashen.

Bex flushes with embarrassment. "That part might have been embellished. But this mountain range *is* supposed to be drenched in Pantheon magic like the Expanse was." That puts an end to Greysen's chuckles. Even condescending Caiman stiffens. Neither is quite able to hide his alarm at the stories most Mareenians consider rubbish these days.

"I'd take heed of what Bex shared with us," I say. "This mountain has a living, sentient feeling exactly how Onei's forest did." I'd been sensing it since we touched down at the mountain's base, and it's been worrying me for the last hour that we've been marching. The range gives off an air that leaves little doubt that it's a Wonder created by none of the natural means that forge a mountain. The air around us, the falling flakes, and the shin-deep snow we slog through look and smell and taste and feel preternatural. Like it's all something greater, and more powerful, and superior to us mere humans trekking through it.

I decide to let the cold *and* the fear drive me faster.

Once we'd started up the mountain, our night vision goggles were no longer needed. The darkness we should've remained submerged in thinned. The fluffy layers of snow blanketing the ground began to shine with a whitish-blue light that the rest of my class chalked up to some type of chemiluminescent effect. But that doesn't explain the freshly falling snow radiating the same hue, and it doesn't explain the fact that I can see the crystal lattice structure of each individual snowflake when it should be impossible to glimpse with the naked eye. Plus, there are the odd physical properties of the snow itself. It never snows in Mareen, so my peers don't discern that something isn't right about it. But Khanai has a three-month period I've experienced every year of my life during the Winter Solstice holiday. The snow on Hasani's Wrath isn't the same snow that dusts Khanai every year. Despite its cloud-soft appearance, it's thicker, denser, and downright more contrary. It's a recalcitrant force we have to finesse to gain any ground. The same whitish blue of the snow silhouettes the craggy peaks on the horizon, the juts of exposed mountainous rock towering around us, and the huge body-size boulders of ice scattered about. And for all the ethereal, terrible, harsh, glowing beauty around us, above us swirls a mass of gray clouds that block out the sky, moons, and stars like a death shroud. They churn in the sky as one congealed, angry amalgamation, an ever-present reminder that we're trapped on a mountain that is the physical manifestation of a death god's rage, heading toward Praetorians who want to kill us.

"Heads-up! We're about a hundred yards away from what the land-nav map has labeled as the death zone," Caiman alerts the group. "Keep your wits about yourself. Drink water when you need it to stay hydrated, but remember to ration what you have."

We all had to endure a semester of geography studies in the academy. We all know what a death zone on a mountain is. But while all high-altitude mountains have death zones, on Hasani's Wrath, the zone doesn't occur near the summit like with a regular range. It occurs closer to the base, and it is vicious. Despite the amount of reading we did in a textbook and the simulation drills of high-altitude ops, like with the jet pack jumps, a virtual sim and reality prove to be two different things. The toll on the body from entering the zone hits us quick.

Feeling like I haven't drunk water in days despite marching in the snow for a mere hour, I pop a hydration pellet in my mouth. Two of them were in the survival pack, and I want to preserve the canteen of water for more dire times. I go to wipe away the cold sweat drenching my forehead. But the droplets freeze into hard beads before I can. The extreme cold from the temperature plunge when crossing into the death zone is blistering, numbing, torturous, even with the heat-retention and homeostasis tech of my suit. I inhale and panic that I'm suffocating; the amount of oxygen saturating the air has plunged too. Human bodies weren't meant to linger in a mountain's death zone for even short stints of time. Human bodies weren't meant to linger in the death zone of Hasani's Wrath for *any* length of time. The bioserum will lend my peers little aid. My blood-gift isn't doing much to assist me either. The blood-gifted evolved in desert and grassland climates at mild altitudes. There was never a need for the gift to provide its bearers resilience at thousands of feet above sea level.

After a couple more sluggish steps, my lungs scream for oxygen and I'm shivering; the body suit's tech is no match for the frozen Ice Wastes. My mouth is dry like I've swallowed dirt instead of my two hydration pellets. I want to guzzle the entire contents of my canteen. I flex my fingers, which are supposed to be protected beneath microprene gloves, and my toes in my boots. My digits are numb. They tingle with the nip of frostbite already, and the last stretch of our trek to the first cave spans the death zone.

"We've definitely entered the part of the climb where rebreathers are needed," Greysen says. His breathing is ragged. "If they aren't in the first cave, I'm not sure if we'll reach a subsequent one."

"They'll be there," I say. They have to be, because Greysen is right: if they're not, we're dead.

"How far out are we?"

I check the land-nav map on my Comm Unit. "Twenty minutes."

"Are the temps plunging faster than predicted?" Bex asks, shuddering. "I swear my suit isn't functioning."

Greysen checks the weather data he's keeping track of. "No. They're on par with what we projected."

"Then why does it feel like they are a good thirty degrees lower?" Her teeth chatter.

"It's a function of the death zone," Dasaun wheezes in reminder. "Your body starts dying minute by minute, cell by cell, the moment you cross into one. The oxygen dips severely, the altitude surges, and your body struggles to make adjustments quick enough to prevent hypoxia. Our brains and lungs are starved for oxygen. Our judgment is impaired by now. Our brains could have begun swelling already. We're surviving on one-quarter of the oxygen we'd need at sea level. It was dangerous to have to mount a rushed push to the first cave. We didn't take the time to acclimatize before taxing ourselves."

"Shut it!" Caiman says to Dasaun. "The officers didn't give us time. An op might not give you time. You're losing your shit like you did in the dome, and this time it's affecting the group. We don't need to hear any of those useless facts. We need to push forward and get to our destination."

"We can do this," Enzo wheezes. "We can do this. We're almost there."

"We can get there," I tack on. "We've got eighteen short minutes to go."

"I hope you're right about that, Kenna," Zayne says without much faith.

"Don't do that," I say. "If you think you're already dead, then you are. You will collapse and die before we get to the cave because you will give up. And then your body will give up. You physically won't have the strength to continue on if you mentally resign." *And I can't lose you, so pull it together,* I don't add because of the strain that I need to leave between us.

He nods in affirmation, but the belief and determination I need to see isn't there.

His and Dasaun's grimness is like a malefic infection. A virus that spreads among us, proliferating fast. I find myself agreeing with Caiman. Dasaun should have shut up from the start. "Fifteen minutes," I say. "That's nothing in time. Don't give up now."

We cover about five hundred more meters in five minutes' time. "Only ten minutes left," I tell everyone. "Almost there."

A rumble akin to thunder sounds in the distance. It's low in pitch at first, but it becomes louder as it booms closer and closer to where we stand.

Enzo curses. "Please tell me I do not hear that. Somebody assure me that noise is a symptom of my brain shutting down."

A mammoth cloud of snow becomes visible as it plummets down from an eastern peak. I get all of five seconds to look at it, to take it in, to try to think of a way out of this shitstorm when there is none, because it is impossible to outrun an avalanche, and then hundreds of thousands of cubic meters of snow hurtle into us. I'm knocked off my feet, gasping for breath, upon the bone-shattering impact. Snow and ice and debris howl around me, trapping me in a vicious vortex that's like the destructive front of a storm or the epicenter of an explosion. I hear yells and screams from aspirants, but I can't see anyone else in the group. All I glimpse is the calamitous storm of white, white, and more white. I sprawl on the ground frozen with dread.

Swim. The one-word order is delivered in the stern timbre of an academy instructor's voice. I've been through training for mountain ops before. I've experienced avalanche simulations before. *Swim.* The second order to do it when I don't immediately move comes in Grandfather's firm tone. *Swim.* The third more persistent and harrowed order comes in Grandfather's voice too. *Swim.* That's how I survive. I have to stay on top of the avalanche. I have to not get buried in a grave of snow. I move my arms and legs like I would if swimming in water. I move with the current so I don't sink. The avalanche drags on, and it drags me along with it. My hand scrapes something hard along the ground. I grab whatever it is and hold on to it, straining against the force of the rapid snow that wants to carry me down the mountain with it.

When the avalanche has moved on and thankfully left me behind, I can clearly see the boulder my body is curled around. I'm not alone where I've landed. It's a heavily forested area we trekked through on the climb up. Several members of my aspirant class took advantage of the trees and boulders around and used them as anchors. But there's a good number of aspirants I don't spot. I let my boulder go and lumber to my feet. I can't raise my left arm without feeling like someone is ripping it out of the socket, so I'm pretty sure it's broken. My blood stains the boulder and the snow around it. More of it seeps from my side. I spot

Zayne lying on his back beside the trunk of a tree. A puddle of blood drenches the snow around him. He isn't moving.

Refusing to believe he is anything other than alive, I limp over to him. I drop down beside him and press two fingers to the side of his neck. His pulse is present, but faint. I sling my survival kit off my back and root around inside for a trauma kit. "Hold on," I say, needing my good arm to stop trembling so I can find and clasp the damn kit. "You're going to be all right." He has to be all right. He can't die on this mountain.

"Ikenna," says a voice. "You can't help him if you're injured too. You need to have someone tending to you while someone tends to him."

"I'm fine enough. I don't need any help," I snap at Enzo.

"Yes, you do." The last person I want to deal with right now kneels beside me. "Take care of her," Caiman directs Enzo. "I'll deal with Drake."

I shove him away from Zayne. "You don't even like him! I'm not putting his life in your hands. Besides, I'm okay. I just said that." My blood-gift will deal with my injuries. It's already started to. I won't die. But a bioserum might not be enough to keep Zayne alive, depending on what is damaged.

"I'm lead. You have an order," Caiman says, getting too close to Zayne again.

"Fuck your order and fuck you being lead."

"Enzo," Caiman says, tense. "Help me out here with your friend."

"I don't trust him with Zayne," I say to Enzo. "You shouldn't either."

He curses because he knows I have a point. But he also doesn't tell Caiman to back off.

"You help him then," I tell Enzo, since they're both being morons. "And Caiman, you patch me up."

Enzo looks between me, Caiman, and Zayne, torn. "He tried to kill you in the forest."

"That's exactly why I don't want him touching Zayne. You can fight me on this, and he will die while we debate it, or you can do what I ask and help our friend. I can handle myself with Caiman."

Enzo sighs and nods. "If anything shady happens to her, Rossi, I will put a bullet in you. I don't care who your daddy is or what execution sentence I'll face behind it. You got that?"

"Oh, I've got—"

A tremor breaks out on the mountain.

Enzo looks at the shuddering ground. "What the bloody fuck is going on now?"

The mountain beneath us roils with destructive, quake-like force. A chasm rips open too close to the four of us.

Enzo, the dumb, stupid idiot that he is, doesn't fling himself out the way. He wastes precious moments trying to hurl me with him. Caiman tries to do the same for Zayne. Then the four of us are falling into the hole in the ground. I scream at the top of my lungs. Caiman's and Enzo's screams tangle with mine. We fall. Fall. Fall. Twenty feet. Forty feet. Sixty. Eighty.

Too, too far.

21

I SLAM INTO SOMETHING HARD enough that I'm sure I break my back. Then darkness slams into me.

I don't expect to ever resume consciousness. At least, not among the living. My eyes blink open to total darkness, and I accept I'm in the After. All the darkness probably means I'm in a hellpit for getting Dex killed. For letting a young man be cooked alive by the Accursed. For being a shitty friend to Zayne. For being an even shittier granddaughter and fumbling my attempt to expose my grandfather's murderers. For leading my entire aspirant class up a mountain route that likely got half of us killed. All of these are reasons I deserve to pay penance in a hellpit. All of these are reasons I should never ascend to the Light Fields.

"Ikenna." My name is uttered low. On a wheeze. I blink rapidly in the darkness, willing my eyes to adjust in the absence of light. I squint and see Enzo leaning against the side of the crevasse.

"I'm not dead," I say, dazed. "You're not dead!" Giddy, delirious relief bubbles up in me. I laugh. Then I pay for it and hiss in a breath from all the pain that explodes everywhere.

"Caiman?" Enzo calls out. "You with us too, Rossi?"

Silence answers him. I tell myself I will not feel bad about Caiman perishing. I deserve to have woken up in a hellpit for many things, but Caiman Rossi meeting his demise is not one of them.

"I'm here." Caiman rasps.

The voice I want to hear—the voice I need to hear—is Zayne's. *He was out before the fall*, I tell myself. *He wouldn't be conscious to voice his survival regardless.* I try to calm my worst fear with that fact.

I scramble to my knees. A beam of light projected from Caiman's Comm Unit makes me squint. A beam from Enzo's Comm Unit joins it, more fully illuminating our surroundings. They both aim their lights at Zayne. He's deathly still. His lips bear a purple tint, and his tanned skin is paler than a northern-born's. I crawl to him. I cover the chest wound that needed to be triaged back on the mountain with my hands. "A trauma kit now!" I shout as I apply pressure and begin to stanch the blood loss. "He isn't dead." My chest tightens with dread when I say it. "*He can't be dead.* There's a chance he's still alive. He could be in shock. Or unconscious. *He doesn't have to be dead.*" I look around, wild-eyed, for Enzo. "Help me!"

"Live!" I cry, my hands sticky with Zayne's blood. "Live! Live! Live!" There's no hope for a trauma kit now, and I'm too far gone to think about one. I don't care who's around. I don't care who witnesses what I do next. "Live!" I shout at Zayne again. My hands got scraped and scratched in the fall. There's a dozen open cuts on my palms. I force my blood to flow out from the scratches and into his chest wound my hand covers. "*Live!*" I force every drop of my will into the command. I'm blood-gifted. The blood-gifted can snatch the mortally wounded back from death. It's something I know of in theory. Something I've read about. Something Grandfather had me study. But it's something I never fucking learned to do. Something we never attempted in our training before. The magic signature would've been too large. I hate that we played it safe. It's a skill I need to know how to properly execute. "FUCK!" I shout when Zayne doesn't stir. Color doesn't warm his face. His wound doesn't knit closed. His chest doesn't start to rise and fall. "Breathe! Live!"

"Ikenna, he's dead."

The words slice into me. They rip me apart. It feels like they stab straight for my heart and carve it out. I try to speak. I try to refute the obvious. My throat closes up.

I flinch when Enzo tries to pull me away from Zayne. I find speech that wouldn't come before. "You're wrong. I can fix him. I can help him."

"There's nothing you can do," says Caiman. "We have to move off of this bridge and get climbing. It might not hold after our impact. It's all ice."

He sweeps the light from his Comm Unit across our surroundings so I can see the fragile ice bridge we landed on below us. It's wide enough to hold us all, but it's so sliver-thin in depth that I can peer straight through it. Below us stretches more darkness. More of a distance to fall.

And in the moment, I laugh and think about the bridge shattering and me tumbling down into the chasm. Careening down, on an endless, bottomless, agonizing, permanent fall. That's what it feels like losing Zayne. First, I lost Grandfather, and now him. I've never had many constants in my life to begin with, or many kin—people whose bonds run thicker than blood, down to the heart and core of who you are. But Zayne was one of them and now he's gone. I rub my chest, desperately trying to massage an interior ache that I know I'll never reach. It's another jagged tear that won't heal. The people I love, the few people I have who I can call *my kin*, keep dying.

"We've gotta start climbing."

I shake my head. I hear Enzo, and the self-preserving part of me insists I need to listen. But all I can do is stare at Zayne's broken body.

Get up! I shout in my head. *Get up! Get up! Get up! You can't die on me too!* Then I stare at my hands, and anger with my gift, with myself, with my fucking inadequacy, washes over me so heavily that I tremble. I lost him. I lost Zayne. I lost my best friend. I lost him, and I can't do a fucking thing about it when I should have the ability to snatch him out of the After. It's that fact, my utter powerlessness over the situation, that makes the hurt feel like it's slashing my insides apart.

"We have to go," Enzo says more urgently. "Zayne wouldn't want you to die down here with him. He'd tell you to get your ass up. He'd tell you the best way you can honor him is to make it out of this crevasse. He'd be pissed at you if you didn't."

Enzo finally gets through to me, because Zayne *would* say that and he would be furious if I did anything else.

I stand, sway at the rush of dizziness, then stoop down to heave Zayne onto my back once I'm steady. There's no way I'm leaving him behind. Zayne and his pragmatism can shove it about that.

"You can't carry him in your condition."

"Then you do it," I beg Enzo.

His features contort like I've jabbed a knife in his gut. "I can't carry him in my condition either. I can barely keep myself upright." His stinted breaths punctuate that point. Blood drips from his right temple. There's a gouge down the length of his left thigh. He's placing most of his weight on his right leg.

"We can't leave him here!" Yet Caiman is no better off than the two of us, so I can't plead with him to carry Zayne either.

Enzo lays a hand against my shoulder. "He wouldn't want us to die for his corpse." As much as I want to shrug his damn hand off, I don't. There is no way to get Zayne's body out of the crevasse with us.

There's no way to tell him what I kept hidden.

I never told you, Zayne. Never told you my secrets. Never trusted you enough to let you make a choice. Never healed the breach between us. I couldn't even save you with my so-called gift. I'm sorry. I'm so, so sorry.

I want to cry. I want to scream. I want to lie there next to my best friend and let the cold take me too.

But something inside me won't let that happen. Something pushes me forward.

I jerk two collapsible ice axes off the belt on my hip that we hadn't expected to need until further into the climb. The pair that looks like a set of slim knives elongate when I press the buttons along their sides. I drive the axes into the vertical wall of ice stretching above us. Enzo and Caiman do the same. We start the long free climb upward.

It's the hardest battle of my life. Not because of the vertical sheet of ice but because I have to desert Zayne at the bottom of it.

22

THE ICE STORM BATTERS THE mountain when we emerge from the crevasse. The avalanche swept us back about a mile from where we were when it descended upon us. In the midst of the storm, the insulating tech of our microprene suits fails quickly. My blood-gift is stretched to its limits and so is the bioserum pumping through Caiman's and Enzo's systems.

Dasaun sees the three of us amble into the first cave along the eastern climb route. He murmurs a prayer to the Pantheon that we're okay. Normally, he would be derided as a Mareenian praying to the gods, but under the circumstances nobody says a word.

Greysen rushes over to us with a backpack. "You and Bex were right," he says as he reaches inside and pulls out rebreathers. They're compact models that look like nose plugs. "Put them on, then warm up." He points to the blazing fire in the center of the cave. "It helped us thaw out quicker to peel off the suits. They'll dry faster that way too."

"Where the hell did a fire come from?" I ask, gaping at it and so relieved to see it that I could cry.

"The pit and the flames were present when we got here—another lifeline we earned from the officers, I guess. There also wasn't an ambush, clearly, *thank the Republic.*"

Caiman, who looks around at our diminished numbers, nods. Out of the three hundred of us who marched into SSEE, there are only two hundred left. Bex is absent. All those deaths—every last one of them, including hers—are my fault. Caiman wanted to take the gentler route. I chose this eastern climb. The northern face wouldn't have had an avalanche at all. *I killed Zayne. I killed my best friend. And I killed Bex.*

I couldn't keep her brother alive . . . or her. I wonder if her family will ever learn that and call in a blood debt.

At this point, I wouldn't blame them.

Caiman strips out of his suit, mute. I do the same. So does Enzo.

"Drake, he fell with you . . ." Dasaun says hesitantly.

"He didn't survive the fall." Enzo beats me to having to say the words. It's one small mercy I'm grateful for, though I don't deserve any favors.

I plop down on the ground in front of the fire. My teeth chatter. I'm no longer in danger of freezing to death within the next ten seconds, but frostbite still gnaws at my numb fingers, nose, and toes. I should scoot closer to the heat. I don't. I invite the lingering coldness to continue pervading my extremities. It's at least some semblance of the punishment I'm due. I bury my head between my knees. I don't care who is around me or who marks me weak. I sob and embrace the fatigue that the adrenaline and peril of needing to reach the cave had kept at a distance. It spirits away my strength. I wait for it to take my consciousness. It doesn't do what I want, and I internally rage at that bitter irony. When I want to be dropped off a ledge into a deep slumber, I don't get the respite. I surmise that the time I spent knocked out in the crevasse is the reason. Or Hasani could be toying with me. Maybe the god of death is the one keeping me awake this time around, making me live in the waking hell that I deserve to be in, alert for every knifelike second.

I twist around at a scratching noise. An aspirant stands in front of the wall behind me, carving names into the stone. There's dozens of them.

"Those are all the people who died on the mountain so far," I say, scanning them. He's created a memorial stone of the casualties among our aspirant class on the wall of the cave.

He squeezes the handle of the knife he's doing the work with. "They are. I have a lot more to go."

I drag myself to my feet. I walk to the wall. "I can help."

"Don't bother if you're going to do it like that," he says as I'm pulling up our class roster on my Comm Unit. His tone is tinged with disgust. "You should know their names without using a roster."

"There's so many. A lot I didn't know."

"Exactly—and that's the problem," he says icily. "I can carve their names on the wall without needing a roster because I took the time to know them. To give a shit about them. You didn't know their names, and they were your peers. Your class members. You've endured three trials with them, and you never bothered to get to know them or at least learn their names. You don't know most of the names of those of us left either. You Krashen elites are all the same. You have your closed-off circles, and you can't expend the energy to care about anyone outside of them. The rest of us don't exist. Those of us from the east don't do things that way."

"That isn't true for me," I protest. "I got to know Bex, her brother, and Dasaun. I'm not like the others."

"You named three, and you think that makes you different? What's *my* name?"

I'm not equipped to deal with more muck being flung my way. "Never mind," I say, and go back to sit at the fire. As I stare into it and wish I could fall into the oblivion of sleep, the scratching noises and the accusations haunt me as the aspirant continues his rudimentary memorial stone. I don't know a lot of the names of the people who died. Who I killed. I stare at the roster that remains on my Comm Unit, hollow. I learn the names. Each and every one of them. I learn the names, what academy they trained at, and if they are eastern-born, northern-born, western-born, or Southern Isles–born.

The cold was my penance before. This is my penance now.

"We have a plan to get up the mountain, but how are we going to break into the fortress, fend off the officers, and extract Rhysien once we reach it?" an aspirant, Wintin Favvs from the western academy, asks. He leans into the fire, rubbing his hands together.

"We accomplish it by being strategic," Caiman answers, like it'll be simple.

"How do we complete an extraction job in broad daylight since we have to make the rest of the climb by sunlight?" Biorn Navarre, an aspirant that graduated with me from Krashen, asks. His face sets into deep, heavy lines. "The officers will see us coming a mile away and pick us off from the high ground."

Greysen scrubs a hand across his jaw. "I'm sick of these trials. I should've never declared Praetorian. I did it because of my father. He's a legacy, and I couldn't break the line. I wanted to serve as a craftsartisan, maybe a weaponsmith for a war house or the Tribunal itself, but that would've broken tradition."

Enzo scowls. "Tradition is overrated."

Up on the mountain, too many of my class agree. After the heavy losses, our spirits are shattered.

Caiman's response isn't the ridicule I expect. "I knew the trials would be hell," he says low. "I didn't know they would be this much hell and involve so much death. I get the preparedness reasoning, but from a resources standpoint and a strategy standpoint, it's a waste of manpower. Especially with a possible impending war. The Republic is sacrificing competent soldiers. Numbers can sway wars." I look at him like he looked up at the sky dropping snow on our heads. I'm rendered dumbstruck.

"What?" he says to my gaping at him.

I'm so stunned, the truth is out of my mouth before I can curb it. "That is the first time I've heard you utter something that isn't riddled with snark, superiority, or condescension."

"Maybe hypothermia has set in and we're sharing one big delirious hallucination," Enzo cracks. "The three of us may still be down in the crevasse and we didn't make it out."

"Very funny," Caiman drawls. "Neither of you know me."

Just like you don't know me, even though you think you do because of my skin color and gender. But I do know you—at least, I know enough. I know you're a pretentious jerk.

I think we're done with things when Caiman says earnestly, "I lost longtime friends in the forest. Their deaths are on me, but they're also on the structure of these trials."

I blink. I refuse to sit around a fire and develop any sort of camaraderie with Caiman Rossi. He threw me over a cliff in the forest he's suddenly all woeful about.

I steer the conversation back onto non-awkward ground. "It doesn't matter if we approach the summit during night or day," I answer Biorn's concern. "The officers are going to slaughter us anyway." The inevitability turns over in my mind. "We maybe could've taken them on, like Bex said, before so many losses, but with the numbers we have left—combined with their experience—it won't even be a fight."

"You're probably right," Caiman says, pensively. "But maybe we can use that and the element of surprise to our advantage. They appointed me op lead so they'll be expecting our siege strategy to be something I'd come up with. Which means we need to switch it up on them. We need a strategy that I'd never come up with."

"What are you thinking?" Enzo asks.

Caiman flicks a glance at me, and I stiffen. *Please don't pull me into the planning. I don't want to be part of it. I don't want to have input in another decision that results in casualties.* Caiman shoots me a wiseass salute. "For once, Amari isn't going to be useless. I'm thinking we come up with a plan that's so brazen and reckless, so *Amari*-like, that it blind-sides them and throws them off their game long enough for us to grab Selene and retreat like hell."

Enzo turns the suggestion over. "Something like that could work if we finesse it right."

"It could," Greysen says. "What do you have?"

Caiman projects a holograph above the fire of the land-nav map I used to get us to the cave. "We stick to Amari's plan. We move out as soon as the sun is up and make a swift vertical ascent up the east face before it gets dark and the temps plunge again. The sleet we've got to move through will obscure the transition officers' visibility down the mountain once we get close as much as it will obscure ours up the mountain. Plus, even without the heavy precipitation, nobody would be able to see anything from the defense or attack position in the terrain the map shows. Twenty miles out from the summit, stalagmites as big as trees stretch up from the ground. They are crowded together enough to provide us cover. We climb, get the fortress in sight, and storm it straight on and draw them to us. While we're creating the diversion, one person steals into the fortress and gets Selene. Once they have her, we retreat. We don't have to beat the senior Praetorians in a fight. We can't, and they know we can't. What we're supposed to do is outsmart them. We don't need biochips to do that, or numbers on our side."

Enzo slaps his knee. "That could work! They won't expect us to have the gusto. I wouldn't expect us to if I were in their place. I'd have the defense team watching the sides and flank of the fortress, and I'd be expecting us to ascend via a circuitous route around the mountain to further evade detection." Despite his brawn, Enzo's strong suit is strategy too.

"Exactly," Caiman says. "Any objections?" I'm surprised he solicits the opinion of the group instead of loftily deciding for the whole of us.

He specifically looks at me.

I shrug. "You're op lead. Your call."

"Don't shit me, Amari. You always have an opinion about *everything*."

"Well, in this, I don't."

"You had one when we started up the mountain."

I can't take his gloating about the disastrous turn of events. I will snap. So I beat him to the punch to lessen the sting. "You won't get any dissent from me. I'm falling back and shutting up like I intended to do from the start. I fucked up the climb. I chose a route with an avalanche and mountain tremors." I sweep a hand at our cleaved numbers. "I'm the reason a third of us didn't make it to the cave."

I wait for him to rub the screw-up in my face. Instead he murmurs, "You chose the route, and I didn't catch the bad-weather intel that forced a desperate decision. And this time we do things differently because I'm damn sick of tradition. It's not a majority vote. If everybody on the team doesn't agree, we come up with a different plan. So how do you feel about things Amari? Are you good with the plan? You don't get to opt out."

"Yeah," I mutter. "I don't care."

He holds my gaze a moment longer like he wants to say something else, but he doesn't.

THE PLAN GOES well for the entire miserable, wet march up the rest of the mountain. We don't lose a single additional person. Fifty yards away from the summit, we crouch between gargantuan stalagmites to conduct reconnaissance.

The fortress we sight has an outer wall of wooden spikes driven into the unforgiving ice with barbed wire running across the top and middle of the spikes. They are positioned far enough apart that we have a clear view of what's behind them. About two meters inside the wall sits an empty lookout nest. Twenty meters from the nest is one large cell that can fit a group and three smaller cells wide enough to squeeze about two bodies inside. A sizable, sturdy—and I bet insulated—corrugated steel hut is located about five yards away from the cells. I'm sure that's where the transition officers are hunkering down. A small shack sits beside the hut. We guess that the shack is where they have Selene.

"The perimeter is probably trapped with nasty surprises before you reach the wire," Greysen says.

"They'd have to drill into the ice to hide foot bombs, and that'd be grueling work," Enzo responds. "My credits are on us tripping an invisible beam that sends drones swooping in to drop fun stuff on our heads. We're well acquainted with how much they love those."

"Amari, complete a sweep alongside me," Caiman says.

He could have given the task to anyone else. What part of me falling back for the rest of this trial doesn't he get? But I do as I'm told and I jab the side of my goggles to activate their thermal scanner. My daylight surroundings turn dark blue with the silhouettes of aspirants showing up in red, yellow, and green. However, when I focus on the hut and shack, I get nothing.

"I don't see any bodies inside either structure," Caiman says.

"Me either," I confirm.

"I bet my left nut they have a shielding field up," says Enzo.

Caiman curses. So do I. "We have to extract Rhysien blind then."

I deactivate my therm vision, not liking the prospect.

"I got a bad vibe about this." Enzo scratches at his hand. "My right hand is itching. Whenever I'm gambling that's always a sign that the hand I'm playing is foul. This is where I'd fold."

"This isn't a damn card game." Caiman thrusts his goggles up on his head. "This is real shit."

"What's our move?" Greysen asks.

"We stick to the Amari plan." I really wish he wouldn't call it that. "Any volunteers to be the man who does the grab? Rhysien has to be in the shack. It's an interrogation cell if it's separate from but near the main building."

I do not allow myself to think about what they could be doing to her in there if she's playing hostage. I haven't veered down that path the entire trial.

"I'll go get her." Enzo slides a D-Phoenix off his hip. His finger is tense on the trigger.

"No," Caiman responds quickly. "You're too close to her for the job if they have been treating her like an enemy hostage. You aren't extracting her, either, Amari, for the same reason," he says before I can demand to be the one.

"I can get in and get Rhysien out," Greysen tells Caiman. "Let's get this over with."

Caiman gives him a curt nod. "Get as close to the east side of the gate as you can. Wait for us to draw them out, then make a go for it. Stay alive."

Greysen takes off and Caiman turns to Enzo. "What you can do is light the whole grounds up with explosives."

Enzo's stare is fixed on the shack with Selene inside. "My pleasure." He holsters the D-Phoenix and brandishes a Centauri Starsploder. It features a setting that turns it into a hand cannon. The starsploder elongates and triples in size after Enzo activates the setting. He kneels, hoists the cannon onto his left shoulder, and steadies it. An eye scope slides out of the top. Enzo leans forward, closing his right eye and looking through it with his left. He adjusts the scope's view.

Before he can squeeze off a round, however, controlled micro blasts detonate all around us. They explode out of the ice, blasting it apart, popping off like endless pyroworks hurling deadly circles of ice around instead of pretty lights. Enzo was wrong.

The officers *did* put in the grunt work of drilling into the ice to give us a welcome gift.

Things are about to go to hell—again.

23

I DANCE AROUND THE EXPLOSIONS, trying to keep from being blasted to bits. They are going off too close together for me to dodge them all. I'm hurled four meters away by one I'm not quick enough to evade. I sail through the air on a trajectory toward the lethal point of a stalagmite. I manage to twist my body enough to the side that it grazes my bicep instead of stabbing a hole in the center of my torso. I slam into an adjacent stalagmite instead. My brain rattles inside my skull and all I see is pulsing black before the mountain comes back into blurry focus. Shrill ringing in my ears drowns out any other sounds around me. My back slams into the ground. The force knocks the wind out of me. Bright agony blooms down to my bones. My entire body throbs. I hurt everywhere. I'm sick of this. I'm done with being thrashed by the trials. For a moment, I stay lying down. The frigid ground has become inviting. Blissful. It's a refuge from the additional pain that will come when I try to stand.

Pain is good, the academy instructors would tell us whenever we got our asses handed to us in a training exercise. *Pain means you aren't dead. Pain means you've got some fight left. So get the fuck up and start fighting.*

The academy instructors can kiss my ass. I'm not moving.

Ikenna. The stern voice is Grandfather's. The only time he places the *I* in front of my name is when he needs to be deadly serious. I don't think I can tell him to kiss my ass.

I taught you better. Amaris do not give up. Amaris fight until we have nothing left, and then we continue to fight anyways. Amaris are resilient. We don't break. We don't bend. We don't yield.

Get.

Up.

It is Grandfather's voice I listen to. It is his voice that heaves me off the ground and to my feet. It's always been his voice that's moved me. I can't disappoint him. I can't have him being ashamed of me. I can't let him down.

I stand, swaying, and a sack is thrown over my head. I struggle against my assailant. They win, pulling the cord affixed to the sack tight around my throat.

"Walk," a voice chimes in my ear. It's high-pitched and feminine. It belongs to Dannica. She jams the round snub nose of a D-Phoenix against my spine.

"If I weren't so banged-up and half frozen already, I could take you regardless of the blaster," I growl. I'm better than her.

Her laugh is throaty. "Perhaps. However, I'm the one with the gun *and* I'm completely healthy *and* quite warm, so get moving. My trigger finger gets itchy when enemy combatants don't obey the orders I give the first time. But please resist and give me a good reason to shoot you. With as much animosity as you've built up amongst my peers, I'm pretty sure I'd get a promotion."

She's probably not wrong, and the fact that Dannica doesn't just automatically drop me gives me some sort of hope as she marches me up to the summit. She tugs the hood off my head once we're inside the fort. She deposits me into a line that fills up with the rest of my captured class in front of the sizeable cell.

My hope diminishes.

"Get on the ground!" Reed yells.

"Now, you fucks!" a Delta transition officer hollers when we don't drop to our knees fast enough. He, Dannica, Reed, and the other Alpha officer, Liim, walk down the length of our line kicking the backs of our knees so we drop to the ice.

Dannica grabs a fist full of my braid and shoves my face to the ground hard enough to bruise my cheekbone. A grunt is all I allow. I clamp my teeth so I don't howl in pain. I refuse to give her the satisfaction.

"Who is your lead here?" Reed barks, playing the role of the enemy. "Give them up!"

Nobody speaks.

He drags Enzo off the ground. He places a knife to his throat. "Spill it." The steel edge of the blade digs into Enzo's neck. Reed is pitiless about drawing blood. He's been participating in these trials as a transition officer all along, but during SSEE he reveals a side he hasn't yet shown. He's stepped into a shell that is every bit as ruthless, brutal, and merciless as the rest of our officers have been all along. He's no longer playing the good guy to Chance's bad guy. On this mountain, *everyone* is the bad guy.

"Every second you don't tell me something, my knife digs deeper into your neck."

"Go to hell," Enzo rasps.

Reed makes good on his word. More blood coats the knife. It trickles down Enzo's neck. My heart races.

"That makes you a liar," Enzo spits. "I told you something."

Reed pushes the knife in deeper. Another fraction more and it will nick Enzo's jugular. He'll bleed out.

"Stop!" I yell. "Are you really going to kill him?" I shriek in disbelief.

He isn't insane like Chance. I thought he'd stop his game before it went that far.

Reed's eyes flash with a brutality that might make the Blood Emperor himself falter. "Do you want to take his place?"

"Yes," I say immediately. "Let him go." My palms itch to return the favor Reed is paying Enzo with a blood spike. It sucks I can't give into the impulse.

Reed keeps that savage expression locked on me. "Your efforts are admirable, Amari, but not well thought out." He removes the knife from Enzo's throat and pushes him toward the Delta officer. "Take him for interrogation." To me, he says, "You just made your man more of a person of interest. You've marked him as special."

My gut twists when I think about what might happen to Enzo in their hands. But I don't let the worry show. One, I'm not giving Reed the satisfaction, and two, the dress-down he meant his words to be is partially wrong.

"You're right about me intending a different outcome," I return. "I should've thought about the alternative. But I also wouldn't have made a different choice if I had. For now, my man is alive and will stay that way for as long as you believe he might be important. If this was true war, I'd rather keep a comrade breathing and have to mount a rescue attempt than have them die—and I know Enzo enough to be sure he'd prefer that option too."

I expect a counter response, but instead, Reed nods. "Same, Amari. But if you make that decision in real combat," he says, momentarily slipping into the role of instructor, "be prepared to live with the weight of it—even if it's what your comrade would want—because sometimes being trapped behind enemy lines ends up worse than death."

Then he goes right back to being an asshole.

"Lock the rest of them up," he tells his team.

Chance and Nero are both missing from among the officers at his back. Where the hell are those two? This is Chance's type of party. He's too sadistic to miss out on the fun. Unless he and Nero are with Selene. I ball my hands into fists, pinning my arms tight to my sides to keep from doing something stupid. If Chance and Nero got watch of her, they are torturing her—of that I'm sure.

We're yanked from our knees and tossed into the large cell.

Reed places his hand to his brow and salutes us. "You failed the extraction. You got caught. There are no more caves up here. No way to make a fire, and a cozy one will *not* be provided for you this time. If you want out of the cell before you freeze, find a way free."

He and the other officers execute a turnabout and disappear inside the hut.

"We're going to freeze to death," Wintin says, his voice cracking. "I'm going to die on this mountain. We're all going to be frozen corpses. Shit. Shit. Oh shit. Oh shit. Oh shit."

Caiman slaps him across the cheek. "Pull it together, or that *is* what your fate will be."

"It's what your fate's going to be too!" Wintin says.

"Not if we think. Amari is still right—they want us to go one way, but there is almost certainly another way. We just need to think of it."

Wintin straightens, accepting Caiman's pep talk, and mostly calms down.

"Let's move into a huddle," Caiman instructs. "The sooner we use what shared body heat we can to stay warm, the better chance we have of staving off hypothermia for at least some of us." He doesn't give the false impression that we will all make it out of the cell alive. We won't. A good number of us will die if we do not find a way out, his faith in me notwithstanding.

Once we're crowded together, I laugh, rubbing my hands together for friction. "I detest the fucking cold," I say to nobody in particular. "And look where I am. In the Ice Wastes, trapped outside in a downpour of sleet. I swear these trials better be worth it in the end."

"If we make it through as Praetorians, they will be." It's Caiman who says this, with enough conviction that it bolsters the morale of our meager group, though I meant something different.

"You said it to Wintin—they must have some belief in us as candidates, right? If we are still working under the premise that they don't intend for all of us to die, there has to be a way out of here, correct?" As I say it, I'm already scanning the bars, the biolock, and the ground for a clue.

"The bars rise too high to climb, they're too close together to wedge through, and biolocks can't be picked," Wintin says, unraveling again. He slumps to the ground, and I see the fight go out of him.

"Get up!" Caiman and I shout at near the same time.

I grab Wintin's right arm, Caiman grabs his left, and we haul him to his feet.

"You don't get to die on my watch," Caiman says, getting into his face. "Not yet. Not if we can find a way free." He looks to me. "You really think there has to be a way? You still think the officers don't intend to leave our corpses behind when they depart the mountain?"

Reed's new demeanor stalls me from immediately answering with the sureness I insisted on back at the start of all this. "Reed *is* acting different, I'll give you that," I say, thinking aloud through it. "But underneath the bolstered ruthlessness, he showed the unbreakable moral core he's been projecting all along when he had Enzo. He could've killed him. He would've been within bounds to kill him, since we failed the op and got captured. But he took him as a prisoner instead . . . which I think means that this last test is still going on—because if we'd truly failed, Enzo should be dead. We should all actually be dead. That was the price of failure in the forest, and they did not intervene then. They left us to our own devices to either persist or perish. I think the same thing is happening here. In fact, I'm sure of it," I say, making a final decision.

I just have to hope I'm right.

Caiman's nod is curt. "You don't get to die either in this cell, Amari, just so you know." The assertion is completely bizarre coming from him. "I need you. You've helped me get our class this far and keep us alive. Let's get them the rest of the way through and back home."

His grim proposal makes me realize that with Zayne, Selene, Enzo, and Greysen gone, we've both lost the people closest to us we'd otherwise lean on. If we weren't in such a fucked-up predicament, I'd laugh at the irony of teaming up with the same asshole who tried to stab me in my room then threw me off a cliff when we were on the same team before.

"Let's get them home," I say, because that doesn't matter now. What matters is that we don't end this trial with another slew of casualties.

I grind my fist into my hand. "They didn't take our weapons." It took me too long to notice this.

"Why would they need to?" Wintin says with despair. "They subdued us with them in hand. They have us beat regardless."

"I'd still strip my enemy of weapons," Caiman says. "It's an arrogant rookie mistake and Praetorians are no rookies."

"Which means they left us with them for a reason," I say.

The door of the shack is thrown open. The Delta officer emerges, dragging a barely conscious Enzo. His limp body leaves a trail of blood in the snow. Nero walks Selene out next in cuffs. Chance follows behind them with the captured Greysen.

"We brought the rest of your team to freeze to death alongside you." The Delta officer slings Enzo against the bars. He groans and rolls to his back.

Nero drags Selene in front of us. "Is this what you came to get?" A gouge runs across her forehead that gushes blood. Her left eye is swollen shut. The right one is bruised. She holds her center hunched inward like it's tender. I go ballistic. "What the fuck did you do to her?"

Nero yanks Selene's head back by her hair. The creamy skin of her neck has rope burns. "You didn't think the Donya would get to sit up in the fort nice, warm, and pampered with us, did you? She's still got to go through her trial, too, right? Got to be fair," he says, grinning.

My hands grip the bars. In the moment, I seriously think about saying fuck it to hiding my gift. It was one thing when I was trying to save Zayne—there was no way Enzo or Caiman could have known what I was doing. Here, though, I could do some damage. I wrestle with the urge to smear my blood across the bars and shatter them to get to Selene. "I don't care about fair. I am going to smash a flamespitter into your face as soon as I get out of here."

"I'll worry about that *if* you get out of there," Nero taunts, the tone of his voice evidence he doesn't think we have a chance.

"I'll find a way out," I promise him.

"The Republic will throw a parade for you when you do," he quips.

Chance brings Greysen to stand beside Selene. His hands and feet are bound, and he looks as worked over as she does.

"Your man botched the extraction," he says directly to Caiman. "Your class failed the op and you failed as op lead." Chance grinds the heel of his boot into the side of Greysen's knee. "Kneel, worm." There's a loud snap and Greysen drops. Chance stoops and wrenches Greysen's head back. He jabs him in an already bleeding temple. "Have any of you ever seen a man take a UV blast to the head at close range? The splatter pattern is fascinating to watch when it's made by the right type of gun." He points a Starsploder at Greysen's head.

"No!" Caiman bangs on the bars. "What the fuck are you doing?"

"Teaching you a lesson about the penalty of failure," Chance answers coldly.

"If you harm him," Caiman snarls, "I will bring all the hell down on your head that's in my power to do." It's the first time during these trials Caiman has tried to pull rank like he did all the time in the academy. It's true that the transition officers are our superiors when strictly speaking of Praetorians. But Caiman is the scion of a war house and its heir who will eventually ascend to Tribune General when his father relinquishes the rank. That means something within the Republic. It means that, technically, Caiman outranks Chance when you start getting into political intricacies.

A republic with an aristocracy always is a lot more intricate than one might think.

Chance's answer is to brandish a knife and thrust it into Greysen's side. "Go ahead and try," he drawls over Greysen's moan. "My orders come from the *sitting Tribune General* of your war house. Take your whining about the price of failing *repeatedly* to get a specific task done up with dear Dad, not me."

An understanding about whatever Chance is referring to dawns on Caiman's face, "Don't kill him." It isn't an order this time. It's rasped out as a plea. "He doesn't need to die because my father's a bastard."

Chance digs the barrel of his blaster into the back of Greysen's head. His index finger curls around the trigger. I should let him do it. Greysen helped Caiman throw me off the cliff. But during this op, we are supposed to be acting as a team—a team I've assumed partial responsibility for. I offered up the plan to make a brazen, vertical ascent. And Greysen backed me. He's my teammate right now, more than anything our past might have made us. I vowed alongside Caiman to get what we could of our team out of the cell and home. Greysen, Selene, Enzo, and everybody else needs me to do something.

"You're a piece of shit!" I shout at Chance. "Greysen is defenseless, so of course you're happy to murder him. But when it was just you and me, it wasn't quite so easy, was it? I should've killed you in the cage when I had the opportunity."

That gets his attention. His focus and the gun snaps to me. I take the blast he'd originally meant for Greysen. It takes a chunk out of my chest and I fly back, hitting the back bars of our cell. The shot also blasted a hole into the front bars. Caiman and I share a look, and I don't need to yell at him to make use of the opening. He charges out of the cell and rushes Chance. The rest of our class follows his lead.

I lie on the ground, hoping the fight is capturing everyone's undivided attention as a massive amount of blood that shimmers redder than I've ever seen before rushes to the site of my chest wound. As my gift ratchets up in intensity and works overtime to repair the damage, I swear I see slivers of gold amidst the red again. Or maybe I'm delirious and near death again. Maybe this is the trial where I do die. My chest is a shredded mess. Worse than with the sabine. And I'm hemorrhaging blood. So much blood. I'm not sure my blood-gift can set things right this time. My surroundings become colder. Dimmer. I don't tumble into blackness. I simply shudder, close my eyes, and then . . . there is nothing.

I WAKE UP on a jet. Selene, Enzo, and Caiman stand over the seat I'm slumped in. That third person is all wrong. I groan. "Fuck. I died this time and of course my eternal torment involves Caiman." But why Selene and Enzo? They're good guys.

Hell-Caiman's lips twitch. "You aren't dead, Amari. You're on the stealth jet we took into the Ice Wastes."

I blink. I look around and see the battered aspirants of my class. The exact two hundred and one of us who were locked in the cell are all on the jet. I loose a breath because, miraculously, we don't have any further losses. Pain lances through my chest after the small exertion. "Ouch." I clutch the spot in the center of my sternum where it hurts the most.

My microprene suit has been cut away from the waist up. I'm wearing an oversize fatigue shirt. A huge swath of medgauze covers the hole Chance blasted into me beneath it.

"You took a critical hit," Selene says, gripping my hand "I thought it was lethal. I'm so glad I was wrong." Her eyes are wide, and it's all she can do to not say more. I appreciate that.

Caiman scrutinizes me as she says it. His brow furrows as he stares at the center of my chest. "Either you have the cosmos looking after you, or you're near immortal, Amari." I shift in my seat uncomfortably at the assessment. It strikes a little too close to the truth.

"Greysen," I say to pull his attention to something else. "How is he?"

His gold gaze turns stormy. "Sleeping near the front of the jet."

I sit up straighter in my seat, hissing through the pain. "How did you get everyone down the mountain alive?"

His dry laugh is self-deprecating. "My actions only resulted in faulty weather intel and my friend almost getting killed. *I* didn't do anything to get us off the mountain. You did. Your hunch about Darius Reed was right. The aim wasn't to make sure we all died. Reed and the others emerged from the hut after the blast you took for Greysen set us free. He reeled Chance in and let us leave the fort with all our people." Caiman looks at me, puzzled. "You . . . why did you divert the blast from Greysen, given—" He clears his throat. "Given our past history."

"You mean the cliff and my room?" I say sharply while holding his stare and making him face up to the reprehensible actions.

He clears his throat again, and . . . *Does he look apologetic? No gods-damned way!*

I shrug and simply say, "They had Selene. I wasn't leaving her life in the hands of Chance when Reed was nowhere in sight to curb that asshole from being a maniac. I wasn't letting her die on that summit, so I took a gamble and goaded Chance into shooting at me instead of your man." I use that as my excuse for saving Greysen's life when I should have let Chance splatter his brains in the snow; I've got too much pride to admit to Caiman that I actually gave a shit about Greysen in the moment, despite his not giving a fuck about me.

Caiman shakes his head. "But they wouldn't have killed her. She's a scion of a war house. She and I have had different rules from the start."

I crack a laugh and it's another abrupt movement I pay for. A fresh stab of pain explodes in my chest. "So you're admitting that finally?"

There is no irreverent or smug reaction. "Greysen was supposed to be protected too. I didn't care about anybody else, but Greysen could not die. My father assured me he would get my same protection and he would come out of the trials intact." His expression turns thunderous, but the ire isn't projected at me. "Anyway, whatever your reason for it, thanks for the assist with him."

I brace for our jet to fall out of the sky because Caiman Rossi condescended to tell me thank you. "You *did* throw me off a cliff," I remind him, because I can't entirely give up being petty and I won't let everything go between us just yet. Caiman is a snake that I don't like. I crack it as a joke though, instead of spitting with venom. "Don't go all mushy because of SSEE."

He looks slightly contrite, the way he did when I first climbed aboard the stealth jet with Enzo's crew after the forest. "I was acting under orders. We may not be official Praetorians yet, but in this Republic, you become a soldier the moment you are born. Soldiers . . ."

He purses his lips. That trademark sneer is back. However, I get the distinct impression that like the thunderous look from earlier, it isn't directed at me.

"Soldiers follow orders. We don't question them," I finish for him.

The sneer stretches. "The Republic could do with some change."

If I could feel more shock, I don't think my blood-gift would be able to revive me.

The Republic is *long* past due for change. Grandfather knew that. And I perceived it from the time I was eight and starting at the prestigious Krashen Academy as an akulu girl who dared think she could train alongside the Republic's most promising. However, I never expected to hear such a thing come from the mouth of Haymus Rossi's son.

"It sure could," I finally say. Then I ask, "What did you do for your father to give Greysen a death sentence? What did you fail at a bunch of times?" It didn't seem like it had anything to do with the trials.

Caiman's expression twists with further consternation. He takes his time with what he says next. "You saved my friend's life. You saved me and our entire class. I owe you one, so I'll give you the truth. The order for you not to make it out of the forest alive came from Chance, but he isn't the only one who doesn't want you completing the trials. My father wants you dead before they end. I'm supposed to see to that without it looking like an intentional hit from above against Verne Amari's granddaughter. When I didn't succeed in your room because you kicked my ass, the Expanse was the next perfect opportunity. I did what Chance asked me to do because I was under orders for it anyway and it presented a good cover—and perhaps an easier way to get at you. I was supposed to try a third time during SSEE, but I needed you."

"I'm so glad pragmatism kept me alive this time. No matter how many attempts you make," I promise Caiman, bitterly, "I won't die. I refuse to."

"I've learned that about you." Silence stretches in the renewed tension between us. Right when I am about to turn away and be done with Caiman, he says, "I've known Greysen since before the martial academy. Our fathers served in Alpha cohort. After my father took his place as a Tribune General, he elevated Greysen's father to Guard Captain of our private war house contingent. They bled for each other a dozen times over during the war. That should mean something. It apparently doesn't to him, and I know the reason is because Greysen and his father are beneath us in his eyes. Technically speaking, as the granddaughter of a late Legatus Commander, Greysen is beneath your rank too. Today, you bled and almost died for the same Mareenian whose life my father considers insignificant simply because of his station." He extends his forearm to me. "You've earned my respect, Amari, and I owe you a life debt for Greysen. You don't have to worry about any more threats coming from me."

I eye his extended arm. I don't need his approval or acceptance. However, I say fuck it, and extend my arm back, because I have too many other people to fight with the trials concluding. We clasp each other's forearms in the way of respect between Praetorians.

"What will you do the next time Daddy orders you to kill me?" I hedge.

Caiman arranges his features into a cool expression. "He and I have a battle to fight that's bigger than you. I'm done taking orders from a man who went back on his word and who would spit in the face of his brother-in-arms. But first I have to finish these trials."

You and me both.

With that, Caiman releases me, goes to a seat beside Greysen, and sinks into it.

"The Ice Wastes just melted," Selene quips about the display of a truce between Caiman and me. She eases into a seat next me. Enzo sits beside her, clearly hovering. She shoots him a scowl. "You don't need to stay fused to my side."

He settles deeper into his seat. "You can threaten to shoot my balls off all you want. I'm not moving from this spot, Rhysien."

Selene glowers at him. It's a look that would slice a lesser man to ribbons. Enzo returns a lazy smile like he has all the time in the world to sit back and relax at her side. She huffs and turns away from him to face me. It's all I can do not to howl in laughter at the exchange. One, Selene will murder me, and two, I am in no shape to be laughing so hard.

As Selene looks at me, I notice her gray eyes aren't as bright. I see the grief she's trying to cover up because it's the same grief that I'm trying to hide while on the jet. A bright pain rattles in my chest that has nothing to do with the heavy breath I suck in.

"We should be the ones to fly out and tell his parents," I say thickly. "When they hear it in person, it should be from us." Nobody else sent to deliver the news will really give a shit. It'll just be a job the Tribunal hands them, and Zayne will just be some southern labourii boy who had ambitions above his station that got him killed. I won't let his parents be informed that their son is dead like that. I owe them so much more—I owe them their son being alive and flying home on the jet with us—but I can't give them that. What I can give them is the respect they and Zayne deserve when they're informed of his death.

"It should. And we will," Selene says vehemently.

We sit quietly for a long time.

A WHILE LATER, Selene nudges my shoulder with hers. "Reed broke Chance's jaw atop the mountain after he saw what he did to you. Reed is who patched you up and got you stable before we climbed down. I thought you might want to know that. In case it's important to you."

I sit there still mute—and dazed—because Reed keeps doing a lot of things I don't understand. He's saved my life multiple times now. Which makes me sure his objective can't be to discern a way to kill me. And I'm sure he couldn't have been working with the medics to dose me with a lethal serum. It doesn't make sense for him to do either of those things just to turn around and ensure I live—twice. Especially when both times he could've let me die without raising any suspicions. Neither instance had anything to do with him. Chance and Haymus Rossi, according to Caiman, have been the two forces trying to kill me the whole time.

And then I get to thinking . . . if Chance didn't have anything to do with the medic—which, after my interrogation with my blood-gift, I have to believe is the truth—that leaves Caiman's father as the culprit there. Which ties Haymus and Sutton together as co-conspirators with something more substantial than me knowing they're both bigots. When the injection failed, that's when Haymus must have instructed his son to kill me. Caiman's first attack came after the shot, and Caiman had much better, and more consistent, access to me. He is also someone Haymus could be confident he had the absolute loyalty of . . . except he clearly doesn't. At least for the time being. If Caiman's feelings of betrayal and anger hold when we get back to Mareen, I could possibly exploit it—actually make nice with Golden Boy. If he and his father were close before SSEE and he's Haymus's precious heir, Haymus might have confided in his son something about his schemes. Or if he didn't, Caiman may at least know a piece of information that could tie his father and Sutton concretely to Grandfather's assassination, the same way Selene knew about things happening in the west that none of us were privy to.

I have the possibility of a hint of a new clue.

It's as close to figuring this out as I've been in a while, and even if it means working with Caiman, I'm going to take it.

"Aircraft has lost function," a computerized voice cuts into the plans I'm designing. "Crash is imminent in four minutes." Orange warning lights flash around the cabin. Alarms ring behind them.

Of course this isn't over. *Of course.*

I jump up despite the pain I'm in and rush to the storage lockers at the tail of the jet alongside the rest of my class. We snatch jet packs out of the lockers, fit them on, and make quick, blind jumps from the jet into the middle of who-knows-where.

24

OUR JET HADN'T CLEARED THE Ice Wastes when it started to go down. The rushed jump we make is into a portion of the wretched place that's crowded with jagged, sword-sharp icicles jutting up out of slippery ice and compacted snow. The icicles rise three feet off the ground, and we have to carefully maneuver our landings around them so we don't impale ourselves on their points.

We safely touch down and enjoy all of a second of relief. Then movement disturbs the impenetrable darkness that blankets the outer edges of the Ice Wastes. More Praetorians than our twenty-four transition officers pour out of the night. They swarm our group from all sides. Caiman engages the person who attacks from his left. I engage the Praetorian who comes at me from the right. I'm sluggish and off-kilter because I'm nursing an injury. Otherwise, my opponent wouldn't be keeping pace with my every move. I fake a right punch then jab with my left fist. They counter before I throw my weight behind the hit.

They block the blow and nail me in my right temple. Pain pricks the side of my neck. My attacker jerks out a syringe. Consciousness rapidly flees me. I sway on my feet. The fight I put up is futile against whatever serum was in the syringe. My knees buckling is the last thing I register.

I'm getting tired of going unconscious.

I REGAIN CONSCIOUSNESS to somebody slapping me hard across the face.

"Wake up, Amari," says a high-pitched voice I'm getting sick of.

I pry open my eyes. Dannica stands in front of me. My eyes flutter closed. The serum she dosed me with leaves me drowsy.

Sleep.

I just want to sleep.

Another slap rings across my right cheek. My bottom molars shred my lower lip, and I swallow blood. Dannica's slender frame stoops over me. Her small hands grip my shoulders. "Focus, Amari. I could keep slapping you—it's kind of fun—but I don't think either of us want that. You're at the finish. You survived SSEE, but you've got to Cross."

"Where is everyone else?" I look around for my team as much as being restrained allows me to. Selene isn't around. None of the other aspirants or officers are present either. I follow my first question up with a second, more important one. "Where am I?" There was *nothing* around in the Ice Wastes. I'm chained to a metal chair in a tiny, windowless space of steel walls. I could be in the subterranean level of the compound. They could've knocked us out and carried us back to Mareen. I could also be somewhere else. I could be in a Tribunal holding cell, several feet below-ground. Zayne's lifeless body appears in the small space. It becomes too cramped. The walls morph from the silver of steel to the crystal white of ice. I close my eyes and count to ten, first forward then backward, when I start hyperventilating. Now isn't the time to lose my shit in some post-traumatic episode. I open my eyes when I'm done counting and sigh in relief that the walls are back to silver and Zayne's body is gone.

Dannica straddles the metal chair in front of the one I'm bound to by my hands, feet, and waist. "Your peers are in Pinnacle interrogation holes like this one."

So I *am* in a Tribunal cell.

I pull against my restraints, testing how secure they are. "What exactly does Crossing me consist of? Judging by the chair, the room, and the slaps, I'm guessing some form of torture? I thought we were done with the torments."

"Oh, we aren't done yet." She smiles sweetly at my snarl. "Congrats on making it this far. Many don't." The fake, too-sweet smile turns eager and vicious. "Remember when I could have just shot you in the back on the mountain? Remember what I said? A lot of the others don't like you. You should thank me for volunteering to Cross you. Can you imagine what they'd do?" She leans in close to me and whispers like we're close girlfriends, "Reed couldn't do it. I know my cohort brother, so I know he has a conflict of interest when it comes to you."

I don't bat an eye at that. It's a barb that's meant to unnerve me. "Do what you've got to do," I say. "But I'm warning you, I got through the other trials and I am going to get through this. When your fun is over, remember that I'll be free of restraints *and I know I can kick your ass.* I will break your pretty face along with every other bone in your body if whatever you do pisses me off too much." I am done with the senior Praetorians and their hazing.

She snorts. "That was a cute speech. But don't underestimate me—I passed these fucking trials too." She stands from the chair. The too-sweet smile reappears, but this time it's venomously sweet. "Tell me a secret, Amari. Your deepest, darkest one. It's okay if it's about Reed," she croons. "Spill your guts and you Cross."

"I thought SSEE was the last trial?" I tug against my restraints again, but there's no slack in the chains binding me.

Her violet eyes glint with amusement. "It was. But you forgot the Praetorian Creed. You've shown strength. Survival. Strategy . . ." She holds up a hand and curls down a finger every time she rattles off part of the creed. "Resilience got displayed in all of the trials." A fourth finger shoots down. The bitch skips her middle finger and leaves it as the lone one standing in this riot act. "What are you missing?"

"Nerve," I growl.

"Exactly. Frankly, I don't think you have it, but we have to try anyway, seeing how you made it to this point. This is your *Crossing*, Ikenna. We covered that already. I thought you were smart. Keep up. Your secret," she prompts. "Make it a good one. I'm growing bored."

When I don't immediately answer, she cocks her fist back and nails me in the stomach. "Next, I aim for *your* pretty face. I wonder if Darius will be so smitten with you then."

"Go to hell," I snap.

She barrels an uppercut into my chin. The back of my head smashes into the chair. Blood stings a cut in my scalp. It trickles down my neck and wets the collar of my maroons. I panic. I'm in the Pinnacle Building, bleeding. The threat it poses would be enough to make me tell her anything she wants to hear if the actual truth wouldn't damn me as much as bleeding so near the lodestone might.

"Tell me your deepest, darkest secret," Dannica repeats.

The point of this exercise is clear. It's meant to see how well we'll hold up under torture. Praetorians are privy to the Republic's secrets. To the Tribunal Council's secrets. To the secret secrets, if you get what I'm saying. Dannica is testing if I'd die to protect it all. The answer is hell no. The Tribunal is polluted with bigoted fucks.

But I *would* die to become a Praetorian and avenge Grandfather.

I stare at her, mute.

She reaches forward and lifts my legacy pendant from where it hangs a few inches below my neck. "This is shiny," she says, fingering it. "Though for you types who engage in the tradition, I never understood why these are given *before* you get through the trials. It seems to me like they don't mean shit until then. And yours doesn't mean shit either until you Cross."

She drops the pendant and slides a knife from a sheath on her wrist. She presses it to my throat. "Reed might prefer you alive, but I don't. A secret. Tell me something good and juicy unless you want blood drenching your absurd trinket."

I press my lips into a line.

The knife breaks the skin at my throat. Though I'm acutely aware of the blood that coats the blade, I force myself not to freak out. I stare into her eyes unblinking and calm. If the point is to test if I'll spill, she won't kill me if I stay quiet. She might beat me to within an inch of my life while I'm chained to the chair, but she won't kill me.

Dannica smiles the sly smile of a sabine. "Ah, you've caught on to the game. Good little Amari. Let's really play, then. Are you as tough as the great Legatus Commander? Us women are so few in the upper ranks that we have to be. It's the only way you'll earn respect or survive."

She smashes her fist into my jaw. The knife follows behind it, sinking into my left shoulder. I hiss, straining against the chains.

"This keeps up until I get a secret."

I spit blood onto the floor. "This keeps up either way. It's a test. The only way to pass it is to endure your little torture game." A game that needs to end sooner rather than later. If I leak much more blood in the Pinnacle, I won't have to spill anything to Dannica. My blood will do it for me.

Her saccharine sweet smile never falters. "You are so right. This is the last time I ask nicely. Tell me your secrets or the next thing I do to you will leave you howling in pain."

I clench my jaw and stare at a spot on the wall above her head.

Her smile widens, delighted. "You gave me the response I was hoping for."

She pulls a syringe out of her pocket and godsdamn I don't want to see another one of those fucking things. I struggle against my chains as it nears my neck. The minute she jabs the needle into my skin, fire roasts me alive from the inside out. I start screaming, howling in pain as she promised, writhing and frothing. My blood-gift answers my distress. It ignites, power sparking in my veins. This is the worst time and the worst place it could flare. I shove the escape it offers me down deep. My jerky movements tip the chair over and my injured shoulder slams into the floor.

"It's *gravier* venom," Dannica says. "You have six hours to divulge your secrets before it kills you. I'll be back in one. Maybe you'll be ready to talk then. In the meantime, enjoy the effects. They're a blast."

The bitch skips out of the room and slams the door, leaving me in total darkness.

The fever induced by the venom from the gravier, a water scorpion native to the Southern Isles, hits minutes after she leaves. I break out in hives and a sweat.

Weirdly, the hallucinations are pleasant when they first start. I imagine snatches of my childhood with Grandfather. His private beach villa in the Southern Isles was our home away from home. Our sanctum outside of Krashen City, where the ugliness of Mareen felt far away. I didn't have to worry about not fitting in or being made fun of or having to fight every day to prove my right to exist. The air is balmy, and I can taste the saltiness of the sea on a soft breeze. Overhead, the sun is visible and so are the triplet moons.

"Again!" Grandfather shouts. "You keep missing. Try again." His voice is wrong. Garbled. It's more guttural than his usual stern yet patient cadence. It holds all of the frigidness of the Ice Wastes and none of Grandfather's warmth.

I turn in the direction the distortion of Grandfather's voice comes from. Nobody is there.

"Again!" he bellows, as gnarled as before. "Focus on your target."

Confused, I turn to the dummy bot we always practiced with. Beside it, Grandfather is tied to a pike. He looks the exact way he did the day of his funeral. He's dressed in his black Legatus Commander uniform and a full accompaniment of medals. His eyes are closed like they were in the casket. Unlike in the casket, his skin is the right shade of dark brown. It isn't chalky. It's glowing with the vibrancy and warmth of life flowing beneath it. I race to Grandfather, horrified, struggling to pull him free. His eyes fly open, and they're the wrong color. They're the pitiless black of the Accursed's eyes instead of mahogany brown. His brown skin turns bloodless, then pale, then ash-white. It dries and cracks and chunks of it slough away from his face, neck, and hands. He transforms into an Accursed. I scream. I jump back.

"Do it!" Grandfather snarls. "You need to kill me. Hack off the head."

A gash appears across my palm. A blood spike forms in my hand. I'm crying and sputtering my refusal, pleading with him to tell me what's wrong with him.

"Do it!" he growls.

"No!" I yell back. "I'd never hurt you." Not even in the terrifying state he is in. But a force takes control of my body and compels movement. My hand tightens around the blood spike on its own. My feet shuffle toward Grandfather. My arm rises and the blood spike rams into his neck. I hack and hack and hack until his head pitches forward. It lands on top of my feet. The blood that oozes from his mutilated neck is the same hue of pitiless black as the wrong eyes that stare up at me. I scream his name. Over and over again.

His features stretch and contort in the most horrendous, grotesque ways. His severed head is replaced by Zayne's.

"You didn't die like that!" I shout. "Neither of you did! This isn't real. This isn't real. This isn't real."

Good girl.

The head vanishes.

A rendering of Amaka, the goddess of blood rites, with her head secure on her shoulders, replaces Grandfather's body on the pike. She wears a crown of blood rubies and robes of the same crimson hue. Smiling down at me like a doting mother would, she easily disentangles herself from the pike in a way Grandfather couldn't. She holds out her hand. "It is time, Ikenna, to finish evolving and become what I birthed you to be."

"You're not real either," I whisper. "This is all some feverish, venom-induced hallucination." Remembering that, I drop to my knees from the sudden agony ripping apart my body. Every muscle, every bone, and every cell writhes in pain. A blistering inferno consumes my insides. The fire shifts rapidly, and now I'm plunged into the dark, icy hole of the crevasse. Then the darkness recedes, and I'm no longer on Grandfather's private beach. I'm no longer a little girl either. I'm the current Ikenna, and I stand facing the goddess of blood rites in the same field beneath Blood Moons from my dream in the lecture dome.

It's all a hallucination . . . and it all feels so incredibly real.

Amaka still wears the majestic red robe. I wear an identical one. Something weighs heavy on my head. I reach up and remove a crown of blood rubies that is the twin to the crown worn by the goddess. My fingers tingle from touching it. I throw it across the field. As far away from me as I can launch it. The red jewels in Amaka's crown . . . Accacia's Blood Emperor has a crown of blood rubies too . . . His entire palace is one massive blood ruby. It had been Amaka's home once long ago, and the Blood Emperor added a wing when he claimed it as his dwelling. The sheer number of people who needed to die, who were slaughtered, the massive amount of blood that had to be spilled to create such an abominable structure . . . I tremble. The thought chills me down to my marrow.

I open my mouth to speak. I'm not sure if it's to curse Amaka or tell her to go away or implore why she has appeared to me or to do all three. Regardless, I don't get the chance to do any of those things. No sound comes out.

A good foot taller, Amaka smiles a regal smile down at me. She appears every bit the goddess-queen that her blood-gifted flock once worshipped her as. "You may not speak. I allowed you speech the last time. Your voice was . . . piercing. My ears are too delicate to deal with it now. This time, you will listen and listen only."

I thrash about, my tongue and mouth moving to and fro, and yet nothing emerges. She stares at me with patience until I finally settle, gazing at her with hate and wonder.

"Better," she says. "Now you can hear my words. You are my daughter. A blessed child of Amaka. One of my Chosen. I am threaded into your DNA and your blood. You will not continue to dishonor me by dampening my gift and blocking your access to me."

I try to shout once again. None of what she says makes any sense. I'm not dampening or blocking anything. But when I reach for the words, they stick in my throat as they did before.

The goddess's regal, motherly skin peels away. The tender glint to her eyes turns merciless. She lets her immense power slip its leash. It seeps from her pores and silhouettes her entire frame in a blood-red glow flecked with gold. Her power is blistering. It batters my senses and physical form, threatening to shatter my mind and flay the skin from my bones. "Submit," she demands. "Evolve. Accept what you are. It is time, Blood Daughter. You cannot escape who you are. You cannot deny who you are. Submit to me and take your place as one of my Chosen."

Her power forces me to my knees. Any earlier submission I might have exhibited is gone. With every cell of my being, I fight against the compulsion she wields to force me to do as she commands.

"Don't resist me," she says, tender again.

The harder I fight, the more her power thrashes me. It jars my own power free, and my gift floods out of me. My power and the goddess's churn together in a terrifying tangle of red with gold specks. Joined together, they incinerate me down to every tiny part of my being. When they're finished with that, they begin eating away at my soul until the forest field fades and I'm plunged into an alien coldness and darkness more terrifying than the crevasse. Some innate, primordial place in me that remembers my soul being birthed in the cosmos. I am in the vast emptiness, in the place where time and space and planets and gods and new souls are birthed. I am at the origin site, the womb, of everything that exists. Formless and weightless, I float like a fetus inside its mother. A sliver of light pierces that cold, alien, dark place, and suddenly I have a form again. I have mass again. I shiver, then groan, feeling the ache of metal digging into my back. Remnants of the interrogation hole I was thrown in flood me, along with a consciousness that's in tatters. Awareness fully slams into me when Dannica steps into view.

The harrowing dream that the venom incited refuses to leave me, even though I'm lucid again. Its lingering presence makes it feel more like a daunting vision or an Old World communing. Whatever it was, Dannica seems much less important to me now.

Dannica shuffles toward me. When she nears, she stands over me and holds a glass vial filled with a green, opaque liquid in her hand. "The antidote," she says. "You can have it if you tell me what I want to hear."

I gnash my teeth. The effects of the toxin combined with my head spinning from the events of the dream make me feral. Why did my dream version of Amaka keep calling me her Chosen and Blood Daughter? Replica Me from my dream in the dome called me those things as well. They're not empty words. They are terms the real goddess bestowed on the elect among her flock. What does it mean that my subconscious keeps applying them to me? Most blood-gifted are under the dominion of the Blood Emperor. Is it my deepest, darkest secret (which I haven't admitted even to myself) that I yearn to be among those who share my Pantheon blessing? Those who are like me? But it can't be. I will have nothing to do with the Blood Emperor. I'd endure a hellpit before becoming one of that butcher's subjects.

All this time, Dannica is still standing there, and I can't quite grasp what she's doing here—why her presence has any meaning for me anymore. She glances at her Comm Unit. "I was gone longer than I intended. Five hours and fifty-nine minutes to be exact. You have sixty more seconds to live. Come on, mini Amari. Tell me what the gravier venom made you see."

I lay shuddering on the floor. My jaws clamp together as I fully recall the importance of where I'm at and Dannica's appearance. A "fuck-you" becomes etched into every inch of my tensed body. This was never a game that Dannica or anybody else would win. My secrets are too precious. They are literally life and death. Perhaps if that weren't the case, I would've broken a long time ago. However, it is, and Hasani himself could threaten me with an endless hellish After and I wouldn't give them up.

"Fine." Dannica sighs dramatically.

Her violet eyes dance with respect as she kneels, uncorks the glass vial, and holds it to my lips. I swallow when she tips my head back, and the cold liquid fills my mouth. She reaches into the pocket of her tactical pants and produces a key. "You Crossed!" she gushes as she inserts it into the lock of the chains around my wrist and yanks them away. She does the same to the set securing my ankles to the legs of the chair. She frees my waist last. I roll onto my back and stare up at the ceiling. I breathe heavily. It takes a few minutes for the antidote to work its way into my system and take effect. When it finally does, my breathing evens out and I stand.

Dannica yanks me into a hug. "Yay!"

I look at her like she's lost her mind.

I'm surprised at how easily I got to my feet. I'm also surprised by how normal I feel, all things considered. "Shouldn't I be incapacitated or at least severely weak after being a few seconds away from dead?"

Dannica waves off my worry. "You should if I actually injected you with venom. I didn't. What I gave you was a neuroserum that binds to receptors in your brain and simulates the effects of the poison. The antidote was a neutralizer to the neuroserum." Her full mouth twitches.

She beams. "You aren't going to tell me I'm pretty this time?"

I try to remember when I said that. "I told you I was going to punch you in your pretty face."

"Exactly—you called my face 'pretty.' Not anymore?" She shakes her head. "That's a pity. I thought you were favoring me earlier in lieu of Reed. Speaking of Darius . . ." She clasps my uninjured shoulder. "Be glad for him and his principles. During our Crossing, we actually *were* shot up with gravier venom." I'm not sure I believe that, but it doesn't matter. She takes her hand from my shoulder and clasps my forearm. "This is where you clasp my arm back. You've proven worthy. Congratulations, you're a full-fledged Praetorian, Ikenna Amari."

I am . . . and I'm not sure how I feel about any of it.

This started as a means to an end. As a way to bring down Grandfather's murderers. I now have the rank to do that in full—to investigate, accuse, and challenge them so it can be my kill—but I'm so, so far away from that goal. So far from any solid proof. I don't even know all the parties involved yet. The progress I've made has been minimal. So many of my friends—and it's not like I had a lot to begin with—are dead, and I have to wonder: even with the rank, will it change anything when the people I'm going up against are Tribunes?

Yes, it will, I decide.

I don't leave room for any other outcome.

I cut away the doubt. I cut away the insecurities. I cut away my past failures and inadequacies. I've endured *hell*. I've endured numerous attempts on my life. I've weathered the forest and sabines and the Accursed and a crevasse and being stabbed and being fucking shot, repeatedly. And I *survived*. I'm still standing. I'm still alive. *I didn't break.*

We are forged by adversity. We are tempered in perseverance. We are Amaris. We are as strong as Khanaian steel. We do not bend. We do not break. We do not bow. We do not yield.

It's not Grandfather's voice that sweeps into my mind to remind me of it this time. It's my own voice, staunch, vehement, fierce, and assured. I did not break during the trials and I will not break or fail in what comes next.

I am proud to have made it. Proud of who I am. I grasp Dannica's arm tightly and start thinking about my future.

25

"I'VE DECIDED TO PLEDGE EPSILON, not Gamma."

I'm in mid-chew when Selene says it. I swallow the tasteless scalloped potatoes and place my fork on the table. "Okay."

"Are you mad?"

"No."

The word comes out of me, and I try not to sound disappointed or accusing. I try to sound like I really mean it. But it's just a word, and I must be communicating so much more.

Of course Selene immediately picks up on my too-pleasant tone. "Yes, you are."

"Okay. Fine. I am," I admit. "Well, I'm actually more disappointed than mad, but I'll get over it. I've lost one best friend and I don't want to hurl myself into a fight over something I can't change with the one I have left. You'll always be a scion of Rhysien war house, you'll always be Sutton's daughter, and he'll always have sway over you given both of those things even if he's a bastard." I don't add *who I'm positive murdered my grandfather* because that would be counterproductive to the effort I'm making not to argue with her.

"This is a give and take for us," she says in a low tone. "If I'm getting something I want by not having to fulfill the responsibilities of a Donya right away, and hopefully not ever, he has to get something he wants in return to help make that permanent. If I break with tradition too much, he'll fight more fiercely to iron-fist one of my cousins into the Praetorian rank so he can oust me—and then lock me up."

I give her a supportive smile, and I strangely mean it. I could fill this conversation with condescension, but what would it accomplish? This is her choice, but it's also really not. "I really do get it," I say. "War house scions must submit to duties and pressures that the rest of us don't, and on top of that, the dance you're doing as a woman for the freedom you want is a delicate one. You gotta do what you've gotta do, and that's the only Selene I want to know."

"I was so scared to tell you." I'm about to say that she should always feel like she can come to me, but then she says, "I don't want to lose you either. Losing Zayne is enough."

The lunch I've eaten so far threatens to come back up. *It's my fault. It's my fault. It's my fault. It's my fault Zayne is dead. It's my fault he isn't at this table in the mess with us right now.*

Selene's focus shifts to something over my shoulder, and it allows me to spit my food into my napkin so I don't throw it up in front of everyone. When I look back at her, a devious grin spreads on her face. I turn around, curious about what she has spotted that's caused the abrupt change of mood.

When I see the target, I scowl. The furious spark that's lit when I spy Reed in the mess is the perfect thing for me to focus on that will shove aside the added grief, guilt, and pain that I don't want to feel. I've been waiting to approach him until I was in decent enough shape to kick his ass if I need to. Today, I am in well enough shape—physically, at least. Mentally, emotionally, I'm even *more* ready. "Excuse me," I tell Selene. "There's something I need to do." I plant my hands on the table and push to my feet. "He has something I need."

"Mmhmm. I bet there is something you need." Selene's drawl is loaded with wickedness.

I roll my eyes and shake my head but don't bother telling her I'm talking about my knife. He may not be the person who took Grandfather's, but he for damn sure still has mine.

I ignore her and stroll over to Reed. I corner him in the serving line. "I'm glad you turned up here."

He reaches around me and grabs a bowl of chowder from a droid. He places it on the tray he carries.

"I want my knife back."

He picks up a plate of vegetables and a saucer of seared fish. "I was wondering when you'd insist on that again. I took it as contraband. It's still contraband. So who said you were getting it back?" At the end of the serving line, he grabs a beer. He carries his tray to a nearby table and takes a seat. I follow him, and I consider seizing the fork he unravels out of a napkin and stabbing him in the neck with it.

I'm starting to realize I have a thing for stabbing people in the neck. I might want to work on that.

Or I might want to just grab the fork.

I try the approach of détente to get better results. "If it's contraband, then no one should have it. But you used it in the Ice Wastes, and it wasn't yours to use. It isn't an ordinary knife. My grandfather gave it to me. I would like it back. Please."

An eyebrow raises as he looks at me.

"Did you just say 'please'?"

"Yes," I say through clenched teeth.

He gives a faint smile as he pinches off a bite of fish. "Saying it isn't ordinary is an understatement. It's blue steel. There's, what, maybe a dozen of those blades circulating outside of Khanai? The precious metal is one thing our neighbors do not trade. It's a magnificent weapon, and the weight was perfectly balanced for me." He takes another bite of fish, and then has a sip of beer. "You know, I think I'll keep it for my own collection."

"I swear to the Republic that I will murder you in your sleep if you don't give my knife back." I'm done playing nice. It didn't work.

Reed stares back at me, his face completely serious. "You can try."

I see red, and I have to dig down deep to summon calm. There's a slew of senior Praetorians in the mess. Members of every cohort have started arriving for the pledging ceremony. I don't imagine Reed's peers will accept me maiming him. "The trials are over. I Crossed. I'm a Praetorian. My shit is no longer contraband. Give it back."

"You're not a Praetorian until you've pledged a cohort. Technically, your special knife is still prohibited."

Dannica plops down next to him. A Praetorian who didn't act as one of our transition officers slides into the seat across from him. Like Dannica and Reed, he is in the battledress Praetorian uniform with a gold Gamma insignia shining against the maroon and black. His brown eyes glint wickedly, his dark hair is longish and tousled, his jawline is handsomely pronounced, and then there are the ripped muscles that stand at attention down the length of his body.

My knife is temporarily forgotten as I take him in.

"Is this the Amari girl?" he asks Dannica. His accent marks him as being from western Mareen. The question marks him as a wiseass. Clearly, I'm *the Amari girl*. I'm the only one in the mess hall with dark skin.

"Who else would I be?" I say hotly, already pissed about Reed and my knife and no longer bedazzled by this newcomer.

He raises his hands in a placating manner. "It was a joke. Obviously, you're one of a kind." He dons a roguish grin that would give Zayne and Dex both a run for their money. Not that either one would ever get that chance again . . .

Twinges of grief accost me. I set them aside to unpack later. Or never.

Dannica swipes up Reed's pint glass of beer and takes a long swig.

He swipes it back. "Get your own."

"Why would I do that when yours is right here?"

Reed's nostrils flare. The exchange makes it apparent that they are awfully close.

Dannica looks between me and Reed with a slick smile. "What did we barge in on between you two?"

"He stole my knife during the Combat Trial," I say, because I am not letting it go. "I want it back," I assert to Reed. "Right now."

"The blue one?" she asks. So the bastard has been showing it off.

"Yes," I say. "It's special."

"It's Khanaian steel. Duh, it's special. Give it back, Darius."

"Stay out of this, KaDiya."

"Lovers' spat?" she asks sweetly.

"Stay. Out. Of. This."

He looks like he wants to strangle her, and I can't help the cackle that slips free.

"The way you aggravate him would make me like you if I didn't owe you an ass-kicking," I say to Dannica.

She huffs a laugh. "That's fair. I punched the Praetorian who Crossed me in the face as soon as I got the chance. I'll give you one freebie. Do you wanna take your swing here?"

I consider it. "Later." I have more pressing business. I turn back to Reed. "Why are you still sitting here? Stop being an ass and get my knife."

The Gamma member I don't know slaps the table. "She told him to go fetch *and* called him an ass. You're right, KaDiya. I like her too. She will fit in well with Gamma." He affords me a formal salute but tacks an audacious wink on to the end of it. "I'm Haynes. Welcome to the team—unofficially of course. We need another person around who doesn't automatically worship Reed's perfectness. It'll be a thrill getting to know you better." There's no small amount of innuendo in that.

"She didn't know that yet," Reed says curtly. "And Gamma has a non-fraternizing policy."

Haynes claps Reed on the shoulder. "You're our *ass* of a leader. I play by the rules you set. She's off limits. Got it."

Dannica coughs, and I remember what she said about me and Reed during my Crossing. Whatever she believes is between us isn't. He made that glass clear in the sparring gym, and I want to stab him, so yeah, she has it all wrong. I don't care that I'll never be able to fuck him again, because I'm not here to have sex with Praetorians in the first place. I'm here to find my grandfather's murderer, and I doubt I'm going to find too many clues in the beds of my comrades.

In response to the tidbit Haynes let slip, I list off all the insults to Reed that he's slugged at me over the course of the trials. "You think I'm undisciplined, hotheaded, lack deference, can't adhere to decorum, and that I'm brash. So why would you extend me a pledge invitation into your cohort? More important, who says I would accept one?" I add to be ornery.

"What the hell else would you pledge?" Dannica cuts off whatever Reed's response was going to be. "You're Verne Amari's granddaughter. It's your birthright to be in Gamma. Plus, you're a badass fighter, you stand for something, and I need a girlfriend in the cohort. All the testosterone gets exhausting. I Crossed you because Gamma takes care of its own, which means we Cross our own, and Reed couldn't do it himself because, well, you know.

"Also—and no offense," she says, "but I doubt any other cohort takes you."

I turn away from her. This chat has gotten so off track. "Why are you being difficult?" I demand an answer from Reed.

"Because he is difficult about everything in life," Dannica cracks, once again talking for him. "Oh, and it is also his way of flirting. Perfect Reed is a stickler for rules and he can't handle that he broke his own code by sleeping with you during the trials when he was your superior.

He also wants to do it again, which is still against his rules if you're pledging Gamma. So there you have it. That's why he's being cantankerous. He's turning beet red because he's got a case of blue balls."

Haynes chokes on the swig of beer he took. Dannica grinds her fist into his back. He clears his throat and looks at Reed with a shit-eating grin. "How the mighty and righteous have fallen!"

"Just remember who sets the duty roster." And with that, Reed collects his tray and leaves the table.

Haynes hoots after him as he does. "I am never letting him live this down after all the flak he gives me." Whistling, he leans back on the hind legs of his chair, lacing his hands behind his head. "So that's why he bashed Chance's face in. I was wondering what made him lose his cool. I've gone from liking you to being in love with you, Amari, for ruffling his uptight feathers."

I blow him a kiss and then leave the absurdity of Dannica and Haynes behind and go after Reed. I catch up to him outside the mess. "I'm serious about my knife."

"Oh—I hadn't noticed based on the eight-thousand times you've demanded it of me. One of those might've been swapped out for a *thank-you.*"

"For fucking what?" I say, keeping pace with him when he speeds up his walk.

His steps get more clipped. "For the mountain. For making sure you got home."

I laugh. "Are you serious? Is that what your pissy attitude is about right now? That I didn't offer the great and honorable and noble *you* an expression of fucking gratitude for making sure I lived through the crap you and the other shithead officers orchestrated? Fuck you, Reed. And don't pretend your actions were even about me in the first place. They were about my grandfather and your allegiance to him and Gamma. Hasn't that been the reason you've been giving all along when you pitch me an assist?"

He draws himself up rigid. "If it will get you out of my face, Amari, follow me." He pivots and marches toward the elevator nearby. I glare a hole in the back of his head and envision kicking him in his skull as I walk behind him. Yeah, Gamma was the goal, initially, to get close to him. With that being no longer necessary, I consider if I actually wish to pledge Gamma. It *was* Grandfather's cohort—the thing he rebuilt from the ground up. He made it what the Republic should be instead of the cesspool which it is. If I put my personal tensions with Reed aside, I can't deny that he, Dannica, and Haynes make Gamma seem like it's still what Grandfather made it. It's still a slice of the Republic that has all the virtues that he envisioned pushing through the whole of Mareen one day, which makes Gamma of more importance to me than it basically being my birthright like Dannica said. It's a place where I can be me, fit in, enjoy true camaraderie, and not have to fight for respect and my basic right to exist just because of the complexion of my skin. And I want that. After learning that Tribunes killed Grandfather and after all the attempts on my life during the trials, I *need* that if I'm going to continue to live and exist in the Republic. Especially with the conclusion I came to about Brock. I don't know if he's guilty, but if he is . . . with Zayne dead and Selene joining Epsilon, that leaves me with nobody. Selene and I will always be close, but being in different cohorts will change things, and I refuse to serve in Epsilon, which is full of her father's handpicked people, even if they'd have me, which—as Dannica pointed out—they won't.

I also think back to how I felt in the forest when moving as a unit with Enzo, Bex, and Dasaun. I think about the pride I experienced in it. I felt like I was doing the thing I was always meant to be doing. Being the person I was always meant to be—and that went beyond Grandfather training me to be that person or anybody else's expectations of me. It was a sense of fulfillment and purpose that *I* felt about *me*. I felt it again after Crossing. But with all that said, even though I want to pledge Gamma for reasons that are all my own and I don't see myself pledging any other cohort, I don't know how Reed and I will ever work together. Even if he's no longer my enemy target, we clash too much.

"Wait here," he says, gruff, when we get into his apartment.

He steps around me and stalks out of the living room. The apartment suite has the same plush cream carpet and maroon-and-gold walls as the hallway. It's lavish and spacious, with an open kitchen that looks like it's never been used. A wet bar chiseled from black marble sits to my right. The living room's wraparound sofa, foot table, and holovid wall are as luxurious as the wet bar. A grand fireplace is nestled adjacent to the sofa. Behind the fireplace is a gold stained-glass window that overlooks the lawn in front of the compound. The opulence of Reed's apartment is an ironic contrast to the plain state of Chance's that I never would've expected. If I saw the two apartments blind of their owners, I would ascribe Reed's to Chance and Chance's to Reed. *Huh.* Apparently there are still a million things about Reed that are confounding.

He reappears holding Grandfather's knife. "Take it and go."

I snatch it from him. "What is your problem?" It can't be what Dannica said. That is ridiculous.

"You seem to be the one with the problem, Amari. *You* have the attitude and *you're* demanding and *you* don't seem to care about anything but *yourself.* Yet you're a Praetorian now, and you have skills we can use, and I don't just dismiss that because of some bad traits. So here's the thing: *I* don't have a problem. You got what you wanted. There's no reason for you to linger."

"Whatever," I mutter, and head for the door. "I really don't care why you have such a stick up your ass."

I've almost cleared the living room when I see it. It's brazenly on a display shelf built into the bottom of the wet bar. I make a beeline for the match to the knife I just got back.

I grab it out of the simple black stand it rests in and spin to face Reed. "How the hell do you have this blade?" My tone is shrill, accusing, and violent. Everything I felt when Brock first came to me rushes back.

He *was* involved in Grandfather's murder. He *did* carry out the kill order.

He holds out his hand like it's a perfectly reasonable thing to do. "You were leaving. I'll take that back, and you can proceed as you were."

I plant my feet several inches apart, repositioning my weight for a fight. "I am leaving, and I'm leaving with this as well. There is no way in hell I'm handing this blade over that you stole."

"I did not steal anything."

"You're a liar."

"No, I'm not."

"Then how did you get this? Where did you get it from?" I'm not actually interested in any answer he'll give—at least, not of his own volition. But I do want to keep him talking . . . and distracted.

"That's none of your business." He steps closer to pluck the knife from my grip.

"It's exactly my business. This was my grandfather's." I rear back and out of his reach. "You need to be very careful around sharp knives, Reed. Because they have a habit of cutting of their own accord."

"Again, I'd like to see you try."

"You're not getting this knife unless you pry it from *my* dead hands."

"That is tempting," he says, "if only because then maybe you'll finally shut up for once." He takes another step forward, quiet fury threaded into the movement. What the fuck does *he* have to be angry about?

I hold the blade out before me, ready to slit his throat. I want to do it so bad. I *itch* to do it. Bloodlust roars at me to do it. I will, but first I'm extracting a confession that includes every name that was a part of the coup. Then I'm making him hand over the kill-order file. After that, he can die. As messy and as bloody as I can make it.

Grandfather's knife is in my left hand. Mine is in my right, hanging by my side. I discreetly shift my hold on mine so I grasp it by the blade end, letting it nick my palm so I have the advantage of added weapons if I need them. My blood wells around the knife, and with it my gift flares, eager to be used. *Not yet*, I tell it and myself. *But soon.*

See, I've learned some restraint.

Reed's gaze darkens. Then, he curses.

"I swear, Amari, you are insufferable. I told you the Legatus Commander was my mentor. I would never steal anything from him.

"He gifted the knife to me."

I scoff, and I can't help letting him know how profoundly stupid that sounds. "No, he didn't. Mentorship aside, you are full Mareenian. He would not have given you a Khanaian blade no matter how deserving he thought you were. Which clearly"—I rake a disgusted glower down the length of him—"he was wrong about. The precious metal is sacred to Khanaians. Inking you is one irksome thing. Placing blue steel in your treacherous possession is quite another. He upheld the customs and traditions of his Khanaian heritage the same as he did for his Mareenian half. Giving you that knife would have been a blasphemy. Not to mention gifting something of this value to a subordinate violates protocol on so many levels. So try again. Or don't. It doesn't matter—I know you killed him."

"I did—"

I lunge forward with both knives while he's busy protesting.

One catches the sleeve of his shirt, slicing through it. The other never gets near him.

He leans out of range of the second attempt. "I didn't kill Verne!"

I don't respond. I'm past words. I step forward as he steps back and hurtle both knives toward his left bicep. From his little rant a moment ago, he thinks he knows me, so he'll be expecting me to attack with successive killing blows. But I don't need to land a mortal wound to draw the blood I need for a compulsion.

He dodges me again, and this time instead of stepping back, he steps forward. He catches both my wrists and my knives stop an inch from his chest. "Stop and listen."

"Let me the fuck go." He doesn't get a warning about his hands this time. He's *going* to be missing them.

"You're right," he says, tightening his grip when I try to jerk out of his hold. "Your Grandfather was an honorable man, and he would never betray his own heritage. He *did* give me the knife, and in doing so, he was not committing blasphemy. He was honoring tradition. Yes, it violated protocol, but we all do that from time to time . . . or did you forget about our tryst?" I can't help the flush that goes through my skin, and it disturbs me how much being reminded of that from him bothers me, even as he keeps talking. "And I didn't steal anything. The one you're holding isn't the same one from his office."

"What you're saying makes no sense." I can't get my hands free, so I knee him in the groin. I tear away when his grip relaxes as he sucks in a breath and get ready to finish him off.

He rasps out, "*It does if you know that I am half-Khanaian.*"

Astonishment stops me from springing toward him. My response is a roar of laughter. "You are so full of shit."

"Fuck you, Amari." His face twists with affront. "I'm from Rykos. My mother was Khanaian."

"And where is this supposed mother now?" I challenge.

"Where's *your* mother?"

It's a brutal retort, and it does its job—it shuts me up. He continues, "She's dead, along with my Mareenian father. They were killed in one of the postwar skirmishes the Blood Emperor continues to provoke."

"When?"

"I was eight," he says with a hard edge. "It was the day after I left for Krashen Academy. Are there more wounds in my past you want to reopen? Are you done with your ludicrous accusations and interrogation?"

"No." But I'm not sure what I'm saying no to. Is it to opening more wounds, or asking him more questions?

I study his features, really study them, because when he speaks of his parents his voice rings with a grief that resonates as earnest—a grief I know well. Also, no Mareenian would sully themselves by claiming partial Khanaian heritage. My scrutiny turns up signs of the Khanaian lineage he claims, but the traits are so faint they're easily masked by the light hair, fair skin, and blue eyes he inherited from his father. "I'm guessing you don't flaunt your other half?" It comes out exactly as sharp and disparaging as I intend. "And by flaunt, I mean have mentioned to anyone at all. Because I've yet to observe the hostility I've dealt with my whole life directed toward you." Though I make the accusation, I don't expect him to look ashamed. He does. Good. He should be.

Yet his response isn't what I was expecting, either. "People know. The Republic is too obsessed with lineage for that not to have been included in my academy files. I got the same shit you do when I first arrived at Krashen. However, me wearing the markings of privilege help people overlook what they've been conditioned to believe. But I am not embarrassed by who I am. I loved both my parents. I'm honored to be a product of their union, and I never try to hide it."

"Is that why my grandfather became your mentor? Because you were orphaned and you were like him?" I probe, wanting to know the full story. Needing to know the full story. He is so much like Grandfather. So much like me. And I never would've known if I hadn't seen the knife—the one still in my hand.

"I guess so," Reed says. "He took an interest in me as soon as I arrived at Krashen. He is the reason I am a Praetorian and the reason I am in Gamma cohort." He nods at the dagger. "I don't know what happened to his, but that isn't it. Verne gifted me the Khanaian blade at my Pledging Ceremony. He said it was to remind me that people like us could rise above the bigotry of the Republic."

Right up until the moment that bigotry murders them.

But that's not what's really on my mind at the moment. Instead, I look down at the dagger in my hand—the one I thought was Grandfather's, and realize it *is* different. It's subtle, but the handle is a slightly lighter color of leather, and the patterns etched into the steel are not the same as my knife.

So I consider Reed in a new light. If he was really as close to Grandfather as he claims—and I trust he wasn't part of the assassination himself—he could be a potential and advantageous ally to help reveal Grandfather's murderers. The fact that I was thinking the same thing about Caiman on the plane shows just how crazy my life has become since I entered the trials.

With Reed, though, I'm realizing all the animosity was coming from me. So he might have *always* been an ally, and I was just too blind to see it. And while I'm still going to want to use Caiman if I can, Reed has been a Praetorian for long enough to already have forged links with a good number of his comrades to do some poking around. And for some reason, he thinks I'm right for his cohort.

Well, let's see how deep that goes.

I'm still nowhere. I need help, especially among the Praetorian ranks. So I take the gamble and pitch him a test of his own. "You seem to hold a deep regard for my grandfather," I say carefully. "What would you say if I told you I had solid intel that he, your mentor, did not die of a failed biochip. He was assassinated, and one or more Tribune Generals hatched the plot."

Reed does not inform me how farfetched that sounds. Instead, he considers me in the same fashion I was considering him moments ago, taking my measure and calculating how much he can trust me. *Which means he knows something.* "I would say that I have suspected the same thing, and I would ask where the confirmed intel came from."

"Brock," I say, giving it all up. There's no point in doing this half-assed; that's why I add, "Though I'm not sure he isn't guilty himself."

"That makes two of us suspicious about a second thing." He shakes his head. "They killed him."

Again, there's that edge of grief in his voice, the sharply honed kind that cuts with a serrated edge. Then, understanding dawns on his face. "You're not just in these trials to achieve the rank. You are in them to discern who is behind the assassination."

I don't deny any of it. I give him a she-wolf smile. "To be honest, I couldn't give a shit about being a Praetorian in terms of duty to the Republic. So you're right—I'm here to find a killer. But I also declared Praetorian so when I *do* find out, I have the rank to charge the bastards with treason and see that they're executed. I want the truth and blood."

"I want that too."

"So you're in?"

"I'm in all the way," Reed says. "It is a dishonor that needs to be righted." As he speaks those words, the savage, vicious Reed from SSEE peeks through. "I owe your grandfather too much to let this go unchecked."

My response is to finally hold the Khanaian knife out to him. Grandfather gave me one out of his set, kept one for himself, and procured a third, nearly identical dagger for Reed. I don't think that's a coincidence. I think—as much as it chafes me—that we're meant to be working together. We are both connected to him, which means we're connected to each other. He taught both of us how to live and thrive in a Republic that would not be kind to us, and trained us to fight that same Republic if it came to it.

Reed takes the knife, and we regard each other in silent acknowledgment of what the passing of it means. It is a peace offering that I extend and he accepts. It is also a pact.

"You pledging Gamma will make this all easier," he says.

Yes, it will. I hope that it will also get things moving along faster. "You extending an invitation makes sense now, but you didn't know about Grandfather before. Why were you already intending to do so?" I'm legitimately curious about his motives.

"All the very true things you listed in the mess aside, you are Verne Amari's granddaughter through and through. You have his principles. His integrity. His honor. His ferocity. You are the type of Praetorian he fought to mold all individuals of the rank into once he became Legatus. I don't believe in legacy—I think it's bullshit that keeps people like Caiman in his place of privilege. But I believe in ability. In character. Maybe that's corny as shit . . ."

It is.

"But it's important to me. You don't belong anywhere else besides Gamma."

I could be pithy here. Could be my normal, snarky self.

But instead I decide to bask in the pride oozing from me at being compared to Grandfather in such a manner, and pray I don't let him down.

26

THE 201 OF US LEFT out of the initial 1,007 stand at attention on the compound's front lawn a week later. We're dressed in the formal Praetorian uniform we decided was worth bleeding and dying and being tortured for. We've assembled in alphabetical order instead of academy rank. I'm at the start of the line and Selene is near the end. Zayne should be standing five bodies down from me. My throat closes up at his absence. At the loss of all the aspirants—the scores of names I memorized in the cave. They died because of a broken system. I have a bigger priority—finding my grandfather's killers—but their memory gives me a sense of purpose too. It makes me begin to think about how as a Praetorian, an Amari, and a member of Gamma, I can effect change.

Our transition officers comprise the front lines of senior Praetorians, with Reed and Chance at the center. Dannica stands to Reed's left and Chance's Alpha brother, Liim, stands to his right. In a cluster separate from the senior Praetorians stands Mareen's Tribune Generals and its Legatus Commander. Speaking chummily with Rossi are Sutton Rhysien and Zephyr Caan. Rhysien I expect to see at his side. My gaze snags on Caan's presence. It's atypical, and I don't like it. If Caan, Rhysien, and Rossi are all in cahoots, it will be near impossible for Reed and me to bring treason charges against them. Law or not, the might of their war houses is too powerful combined.

Brock, who stands among Geels Lennon, Lydya Denton, and Yarric Bjorr, watches them too, then turns my way with a nod of congratulations. This is the first time I've seen him since Commencement Eve, and my gut twists because I hope he really didn't play a part in Grandfather's murder. I've lost so many people as it is. I don't want to lose him too.

Reed steps forward and affords us neo-Praetorians a salute. We salute him back. I surmise that he was selected to give the formal address on the lawn because Chance could never be the orator Reed proved himself to be during our dome sessions.

"You have passed your trials," he declares. "You have shown that you possess skills of combat, survival, strength, strategy, stealth, resilience, and nerve far beyond that of what a common soldier is expected to possess. You are the elite of elite soldiers. The most deadly, the most cunning, the most skilled." His voice rings out across the lawn, ardent, eloquent, and resounding, proving my assumption true. "The Republic was built on military strength. The Republic has thrived, survived, and evolved because of its military strength. We are one of the most formidable powers in the world because of our military strength. Every Mareenian fulfills a duty in service to our Republic. Your duty is and will forever be to serve as one of its decorated, revered Praetorians. I challenge you to serve with prowess. With purpose. With strength." He stops and scans us new Praetorians that he speaks directly to. His speech has cast a visible spell over the whole of our group. The senior Praetorians and the Republic's leaders seem to be held in stasis as he talks too. "I also challenge your class to serve with integrity, valor, and honor." He recites the additional principles Grandfather upheld. The entire lawn hangs on his every word. Silent and enthralled. The effect is staggering and fascinating to witness. Reed pivots and gives a nod to his fellow transition officers. They disband their tight line and spread out. They move to join the Praetorians, gathered by cohort group, that assembled to watch the pledging ceremony.

Haymus Rossi steps from Rhysien's and Caan's side. He strides front and center. "As your Legatus Commander," the bastard says, "it is my honor to congratulate and acknowledge you as Praetorians. The officers that led your transition have sorted you into cohorts. I give the proceedings back over to them to extend pledge invitations."

Haymus takes his place back among his Tribunal Council. Chance steps into the space he vacated. He names Caiman and Greysen to Alpha cohort. Caiman and Chance might be at odds now, but the Republic's Golden Boy heir to its most powerful war house wouldn't end up in any cohort other than the one founded by his kin.

The leader of Beta cohort, a blond-haired man who looks about a decade older than Reed, welcomes three neo-Praetorians to his squad. Nero occupies the space to the man's right, taking up the formal position of his second. As he calls out the names, I wonder who would've called Dex's name, Bex's name, Zayne's name, and the names of the rest of the aspirants we lost. The original five cohorts are highly selective, but the rest will be more generous with their invitations.

Reed calls out his selections next, with Haynes occupying the spot on his right. Dannica remains standing to Reed's left. Reed calls Enzo's name and my name. I walk to stand among the Gamma cohort Praetorians.

Once I'm there, fresh grief cracks wide open inside me. I'm a Gamma Praetorian as Grandfather was. I look at the Tribunal Council standing stoically off to the side, twenty yards away. Brock passes me a salute of praise and approval. Grandfather should be standing beside him doing the same. He should be among the Republic's leaders to witness this day, and he's not because some of them took him from me. My temper sparks. My blood heats. My gift flares alert with my growing bloodlust. I could easily put blood spikes through each of their hearts where they stand. With all the Praetorians and the whole Tribunal gathered, I wouldn't make it off the lawn, of course. But I could do it, and I'd feel just as good doing it as I would welcoming my execution.

I resist the reckless urge, though. This isn't just about vengeance—not completely. Grandfather had the wrong hair texture and complexion. It provoked resentment from the time he spoke his oath of office. I don't want to kill Republican bigots. I'm going to make Mareen *eat* its bigotry. I am a Praetorian now. I'm going to have children I pass down the Amari name and Khanaian traits to who'll become venerable Praetorians themselves. The blood Grandfather and I share will evolve into a legacy line and a war house. I will give him the honor of a long-held dream being actualized instead of deferred.

And then I'll help destroy the rot.

Selene is named to Epsilon, the cohort that all Praetorians in her war house belong to. At the conclusion of the ceremony, Brock breaks from his council and comes over to me. He embraces me in a fatherly fashion, pressing a kiss to my cheek. "You did it. Verne would be proud. I am proud." I smile at the pronouncement and agree, because it's better to keep him believing I'm the Ikenna he spoke with on Commencement Eve who didn't have a clue—about a lot of things. But Brock is wrong; this isn't everything Grandfather wanted.

He'll be proud after I accomplish everything that comes *next*.

27

WE CLEAR OUT OF THE subterranean level the same day and relocate to the upper floors of the compound—stopping long enough in the mess, where medics are to administer our full-suite bioserum. I'm definitely nervous about an attempt on my life again, but Reed is there to personally hand the medic my vial. If the medic finds this strange, she doesn't say anything, and I don't feel any aftereffects like I did the last time.

My new residence is on the fortieth floor among the rest of the Gamma Praetorians' apartments. I sit on the chocolate-hued leather sofa that comes with the apartment along with some other pre-furnishings. Restless, I study the connection web I made of the Tribunal Council. It's projected on the living room's holovid panel. I remove the question mark from above Caan's head and place his image with Rossi's and Rhysien's for now. A buzzer rings. The screen of my Comm Unit switches to a video feed of the hallway. Reed, Dannica, and Haynes stand outside my door. I punch commands into my Comm Unit that shut off the projection of the web and direct the door to open.

Dannica breezes into the apartment ahead of the guys. "Hiya!" She crosses the living room and plops onto the sofa next to me.

Yes, please make yourself comfy.

Reed remains standing beside the door. Haynes leans against the wall with folded arms.

"Why are the three of you here?" Reed I was expecting at some point. His second and third showing up like we're old friends is peculiar.

Dannica kicks her boots up on the glass table in front of the sofa. "You're Gamma now. We don't need a reason to stop by to hang. We barge in on each other all the time when in-residence. Get used to it, Kenna."

"My name is *Ikenna*."

"I've heard Rhysien call you Kenna."

"Selene is different. She's like family."

"Well, Gamma is a family, which means I can call you Kenna." Dannica declares it like the matter is settled and there's no further need to discuss it.

I wonder if I should get my punch to her face out of the way now.

Haynes chuckles at my scowl. "You'll get used to her."

My scowl deepens.

Dannica grins my way like a fiend—and like she's reading my mind. "You want your fight today, Amari?"

"Dannica," Reed says. "That's not what we're here for."

She flicks the glossy black braid hanging over her shoulder behind her back. "You're no fun. I was only trying to lighten the mood before things turn serious."

"Serious about what?"

Reed walks farther into the living room. He stops a few feet away from me. "I looped them in. They're here to help."

I'm not sure what to say to that. It's discomfiting, and I wish I'd gotten a heads-up. I don't verify that he trusts them. That much is evident. Moreover, if accepting their assistance gets me the answers I seek sooner versus later, I won't turn it down. Two additional seasoned Praetorians could be useful. But having been on my own for so long—hiding so much, isolated by my appearance and heritage and gift—means that it's hard to just let go of the paranoia.

"You can trust them," Reed says quietly. "The Legatus trusted them enough to support me when I wanted them as Gamma's second and third. Their allegiance is to him." That and the look in his eye are enough for me to take a deep breath and nod.

I re-project the connection web I'd made vanish when I answered the door. "If you're offering your aid, there you go. This is what I'm working on." I also fill them in about my lethal bioserum injection, Terese Rhysien, and Caiman's admission on the jet.

Haynes pushes off the wall. He turns to the web of faces of the Tribunal Council. "Are we assuming the Legatus Commander was killed because of hatred or because half the Tribunal wants a renewed war with Accacia?"

"I didn't know there was a second option. Since when do half the Tribunes want a war with Accacia?" It's something Grandfather would've never supported. He gave the Republic peace and made it his life's work to see that it held.

"Since about six months prior to Legatus Amari being killed," Haynes answers.

"But it isn't yet knowledge anyone beyond the four of us in this room is privy to," Reed says. "Your grandfather placed me, Dannica, and Haynes onto a special intelligence assignment before he died that he wanted to keep hush from all the war house heads. He had a suspicion he asked us to confirm. Half our Tribunal wants to avoid war, but to be prepared when it blows our way again, and half the Tribunal has been courting taking a war to Accacia's doorstep and invading the empire like it did to us for the better part of a year."

"Can you activate the touch feature on your holovid panel?" Haynes asks.

I do as he requests.

He moves Lydya Denton, Geels Lennon, Yarric Bjorr, Brock, and Uther Hale—a lower war house Tribune General—to the side of the panel where Cann's, Rhysien's, and Rossi's images are. Then he moves Haymus Rossi out of the group. "Those are the seven Tribunes who are both arrogant and stupid enough to want to instigate a war with the Blood Emperor. They reason that we will see a renewed conflict with Accacia regardless. It's just a matter of who will strike at whom first. They believe it will give Mareen the advantage to start a war on the offensive instead of the defensive."

I frown. I did say if Brock betrayed Grandfather, it would have to be for something other than bigotry *and* it would have to be over something pretty extreme. But him being a part of the coup for this new motive doesn't make sense either. "Are we sure about Brock? He has always been against a war. He and Grandfather both worked to maintain peace." And if that changed, it's another thing Grandfather didn't tell me and should have. Yet . . . he mentioned nothing of being at odds with Brock over anything. Before his death, they behaved as the brothers-in-arms they'd always been. Which is another thing that seems incongruous with Brock aligning against Grandfather. Their disagreement on the matter wouldn't have simply been some difference in policy they could put aside outside of Tribunal chambers. It would've created a fissure between them.

And it leaves me more confused about Brock than ever.

"I ran the intelligence on Brock myself," says Reed. "It's solid, and your grandfather accepted it as solid."

Why didn't Grandfather tell me about any of this?

No, I wasn't privy to everything—he obviously hadn't told me he mentored a boy with Khanaian ties named Reed, and it *still* rankles— but this is about more than me sulking over being kept in the dark.

If war was remotely a possibility, Grandfather should have told me due to the enormity of how it might affect me—because of my mother, because I'm blood-gifted myself, and because my nation would be fighting against and remembering their extreme hatred for an enemy identical to me. It cuts, deep, that Reed and the others know so much, while I knew nothing.

Reed must read the betrayal on my face. "You were in your last year at the academy. You were preparing for exit tests. I imagine he didn't want to drag you into Tribunal politics and split your focus worrying about things you couldn't really help with."

Although he doesn't know what that serves as an answer to, his reasoning *is* sound. It's precisely the sort of thing Grandfather would do. I wish he'd told me though. My own hurt feelings aside, I should have known about the new potential threat to him. If I had, I wouldn't have wasted three months after his death believing there wasn't foul play involved. I would've discerned he was murdered sooner and done . . . what?

What you're doing now.

Pantheon, this whole patience thing was going to kill me.

"Okay," I say, digesting it all and focusing back on the web because Brock isn't the only person I have questions about. "How are we sure Rossi is out?" Haymus is *not* innocent—of this I'm certain. "He was Grandfather's most vocal opponent. He despised having an akulu man in the Legatus seat. If there was a conspiracy to murder my grandfather, Rossi would jump at the chance to aid it."

Dannica shakes her head. "You're erring by assuming Rossi's guilt simply because of his disdain for Legatus Amari. They hated each other, but they hated the idea of war more. The two of them agreed on wanting to avoid a second conflict with Accacia for as long as Mareen can. Rossi is many reprehensible things, but he is dedicated to the preservation of the Republic. And he's smart. His efforts to block a war alongside the efforts of Legatus Amari are the reason why the opposing faction haven't gotten their way."

It still doesn't sit right with me to discount Rossi. However, if we're assuming the motive to be the courting of a war and not bigotry—and if their intel on Rossi is solid—then I have to accept that I could be wrong about his role in Grandfather's death. Rossi might've simply wanted me dead to prevent another akulu from polluting Mareen's upper ranks.

He might have just wanted me dead because he wants me dead, and politics have nothing to do with it.

It was a weird blow to my pride.

Dannica points to Sutton Rhysien. "Sutton is who we found to sit at the head of the cell that wants war. He talked Caan and everyone else in this group into supporting his agenda."

"How did he convince *six* Tribunes of such a thing after the catastrophe of the last war?"

"That's what we were in the middle of discerning when Legatus Amari died," Reed responds.

"And you just stopped?" I try not to sound too accusatory.

Reed stiffens. "We're Praetorians. We aren't leaders of the Republic. We had orders, then Verne's death voided those orders. Standard protocol no longer gave us the authority to investigate war house heads without Verne—the only person who knew about the assignment he handed us—alive. If we were caught still doing it, we would've been court-martialed. Soldiers don't undermine their command." He catches my defiant look and says, "Good soldiers, that is."

"Do you ever get tired of being chained to your protocol and your rules?"

"You see chains. I see justice. The difference is that I care about doing this right, and throwing out everything because you're scared or angry isn't a strategy—it's petulance. It's how you get yourself—and others—hurt. There's a system for a reason."

"The system is what's so messed up! How do you not see that?" I stand up, but Haynes gets between me and Reed before I show him how petulant I can be. "Fighting amongst ourselves won't get us anywhere," he says.

I try very hard to internalize that. I turn my anger toward a different target so I don't blow up at Reed. "My grandfather died because of Sutton Rhysien's agenda *and* because of his heritage. Rhysien is ruthless and unscrupulous in getting what he wants." That much I know from Selene. "He might have seen Haymus Rossi as too powerful and too untouchable to remove as an obstacle by treasonous means, but he wouldn't have had those same reservations about an akulu Legatus. He would've surmised Grandfather the easier mark, whose untimely death would be quickly forgotten by a Republic elated to have its status quo returned."

"On that we both agree," Reed says darkly. "A faction of the Tribunal Council may have orchestrated this, but none of them are the hand that carried out the hit. A Praetorian or a team of Praetorians carried out the orders. The Tribunal Council doesn't lift a finger to do things they have us at their beck and call to do."

"Which means we need to figure out who did it," Dannica says.

Without specific orders to do so, I think. *So now* you're *all in to investigate things without proper protocol?*

I'm getting what I want, so I keep the jeer to myself.

"Lykas Chance has been gunning for Kenna hard during the trials. I've never liked him. He's grimy, and he would have no qualms performing the hit," Dannica says.

"My name is *Ikenna*, and it wasn't him. I've confirmed it," I say. "I snuck into his apartment and interrogated him with a truth serum I swiped from Grandfather's study," I lie.

"That was both stupid and at least takes one name off the list," Reed says. "So if not Chance, it's someone else in a cohort that's heavily connected to either Rhysien or Caan. If Brock is involved, he was connected to Gamma, and my people sure as fuck did not kill Verne."

"Or it could've been the medic that vanished from the city?" I say. "It makes sense if she fled west. It'll be hard to get to her if she's sequestered away in Sutton's Hyacinth home. She could have had access to Grandfather during a standard med tower visit."

"The Legatus had his own handpicked team of medics," says Reed. "He wouldn't have let anyone unverified touch him. He rotated the team out so it didn't seem that way, but everyone who ever performed an exam or treated him for something was triple-checked for their loyalty and paid handsomely to remain that way. Verne was a kind and just man, but he was as shrewd and paranoid as any Tribune General." On that point, Reed is correct. "It was a Praetorian."

"We don't exactly have a narrow Praetorian pool here," Haynes says. "What's the game plan? It's not like we can go snatching up a slew of the Republic's best and interrogating every one of them with truth serums. Eventually, someone will wise up, and we want this kept under wraps until we have proof of the Tribunes' guilt."

"We need to focus on Rhysien," I insist. "If Terese isn't involved, someone else close to Sutton that he trusts and who had the capacity to get close to Grandfather is the person that dosed him with the bioserum that mimicked a heart attack . . ."

The horrifying thought crashes into me that someone like that might have been literally staring me in the face for years.

Selene would be the perfect sort of person for Sutton to use.

She's my best friend, she's been close to me and Grandfather for eleven years, and my grandfather wouldn't have had any reason to have his guard up around her. Further, I wouldn't put it past Sutton to do something as vile as assigning his own daughter such a task. Selene is someone that nobody would think to suspect. She might have had qualms with it, but she is also a war house scion. Her duty is to her father and war house first, which would dictate that she wouldn't have had a choice if her father ordered her to do something heinous. Refusing would be outright rebellion from her family—and that's something I would have noticed.

The thought now consumes me, and I'm sick at the fact that Selene is who I need to interrogate. I can easily find out the truth if I compel her, but it's a nauseating concept. I'm also furious at myself for so quickly dismissing the idea that she might know anything. I immediately considered Reed because he was a stranger, but it never dawned on me to think of Selene, despite having her father in the conspirator column. Yes, I was wary around her for a bit, but not because I thought she was the actual killer.

It was because I didn't *want* to think of it.

And that burns me. I could have had answers about Grandfather's death weeks ago. His murderers could already be dead. An instinctive aversion to my task percolates from somewhere deep down. I gnash my teeth at its existence, disgusted with myself for feeling it.

I could have killed Selene by now. But also . . . *will* I be able to kill her if she is guilty? The fact that it's even a question makes disgust swirl inside me even more. Gods, I thought my world couldn't go to shit any worse than it already has. Guess I was wrong.

"You don't look well."

I'm pulled out of the pit of churning anger and grief and revulsion by Dannica's high voice. She, Reed, and Haynes stare at me, concerned, and I can guess that my face and body language reveal the sweeping sickness that has me sitting stiff on the sofa with my hands clenched into fists.

"Yes," I respond. I inhale a slow, controlled breath. I count up to ten and backward from ten in my head. I have to calm down in front of them. I'm not yet ready to name Selene as the potential culprit to the group. The pain of it is too personal to share with people I barely know, and I want to be certain. I've already lost too much, and even just the thought has put me in a kind of tailspin.

"All right," Dannica says, still watching me in a manner that makes me wish she would look away. Her boots are kicked off and her feet are curled beneath her butt on my sofa. "This is going to take some time to figure out. I think we should call it a night. It's a lot for you to process, Kenna. It's a lot for us all to process."

"It's a lot to process, but what isn't is using my name wrong—*stop* calling me that," I hiss, needing an outlet for the unbridled rage and raw grief that didn't dissipate all the way.

Reed's Comm Unit buzzes before anyone can react to my anger, and Haynes groans. "Don't tell me it's an op. I thought I'd get to enjoy a few more days of relaxation in-residence." Haynes cuts off his griping when Reed's face goes bloodless. "What's the transmission?"

For a long stretch, Reed doesn't respond. He stares down at his Comm Unit, gripping the rim of its screen. He swallows, and lifts his head in a slow, grim fashion. "Rykos in the east and Hyacinth in the west are under siege by Accacia. Both cities burn."

"And Khanai?" I ask, horrified. It lies right across the border from Rykos.

"The transmission doesn't say. It only relays details of Mareen."

"Where are we headed?" Dannica asks. "West or east?" I may want to solve Grandfather's murder, but I need to know the answer, too, because this is real, and I'm really—at least technically—a Praetorian, and that means we need to focus.

Praetorians are trained to remain calm under duress, but Dannica hops up, pulls her boots back on, and starts to pace in front of the sofa. She shoves a hand through her hair. It tangles in her braid. She yanks a blaster off her hip, checks its rounds, and re-holsters it. For all Dannica's frantic fidgeting, Haynes has been death-still since hearing the news. He stands and stares at Reed and does nothing else.

"I don't have orders for Gamma yet," Reed answers. "We need to gather and inform the rest of the team." I'm pretty sure I nod. At least, I think I nod. My nerves are shot to shit. If Accacia is on our shores, that means the Blood Emperor is about to revisit the atrocities he committed against us the last time. And in addition, there's my own personal horror that I've kept locked in since Reed dropped the news.

If blood-gifted armies swarm Mareen, the Tribunal could start closely monitoring the lodestone again to keep track of the Accacians.

I've come this far and now I'm in danger of losing everything.

28

"RYKOS AND THE BELOVED HYACINTH are lost. The Blood Emperor's attacks break the treaty. We are at war."

At Haymus Rossi's announcement, a timorous silence slinks through the Pinnacle hall we've gathered in for the war briefing. All twelve of the Praetorian cohorts are present. We stand at attention and give Mareen's Tribunal Council—its commanders in chief during wartime—our full, petrified focus. It is odd to see Praetorians, the Republic's best and fiercest, so frightened. But the truth is, the situation we're being thrust into is new for every Praetorian present. None of us are old enough to have fought in the last war. The maroon-and-white flags that flew in front of the compound and on the walls of the hall this morning when we woke up have flown across Mareen our entire lives for many of us, or a good bulk of them for the rest. The former group has never seen the maroon-and-gold wartime flags that have replaced the peacetime ones in the hall, on the flag post on the lawn of the compound, and throughout

Mareen. We've all braced for it to happen eventually perhaps—that is, we've trained for the inevitability—but I don't think any of us imagined such a thing would happen this soon. Or maybe at all. A decade plus of friendship has me almost breaking form to turn around and risk a glance at Selene, who stands two rows behind me among Epsilon cohort with her brothers and the rest of the Praetorian scions out of Rhysien War House. Hyacinth is her mother's and father's ancestral home.

I wonder how she feels.

I wonder if she's complicit.

"The Blood Emperor's legions have moved on to Vinitri in the east and Cairstock in the west," Haymus continues from behind a podium. His words are grave. His disposition staid. "Intelligence efforts have told us that Accacia means to sack the major port cities of our western shores and the important mining towns along our eastern border. The strategy will effectively cut off the bulk of our trade routes—imports and exports. It will be a crippling blow to Mareen at the start of this war if successful." Haymus's tone turns from grave to inflexible. "We obviously cannot allow that to occur. By this great Republic's fortune, all of you are young enough to have not served in the last war and experienced its horrors firsthand. However, history reminds us that it was long, arduous, and bloody. *I'm* here to remind you"—his eyes are slightly haunted, so subtle you'd really need to be paying attention to see it before his mask is back on—"Mareen suffered great losses to country, resources, and kin. That will not happen again. This time, Accacia will find that Mareen is not as vulnerable as it believes us to be and as we once were."

Sutton Rhysien stands from his seat. He walks to the podium with sure, confident strides, and Haymus Rossi steps away. Disgusting elation the rest of his Tribune peers don't have wafts off him. It is evident he wants this war badly, and I don't have to wait long to find out the reason.

"Rhysien War House recently engineered a bioweapon that can be used against the Accacian legions," he declares once he's standing behind the podium. "We've been conducting tests of its efficacy. Those tests are near complete, and the bioweapon has proved to be effective in neutralizing the blood-gift. The scientists in my war house's employ have discovered that the metal iridium releases vapors much the way liquid mercury does. Iridium's vapors are poisonous to the blood-gifted. It pollutes their blood and dampens their Pantheon-linked abilities by blocking a blood-gifted individual's connection to the goddess of blood rites they worship." He explains how Mareen is confident of victory in this second war with Accacia, and the unmasked revulsion for the Accacians, their blood-gift, and the fact that they still worship one of the Pantheon saturates his tone. His glee is contagious to the others on the podium. To the Praetorians in the hall. They *want* this. To end the blood-gift. To destroy Accacia and what it represents.

I try not to cringe, even internally. I try not to think too hard on what it means about me, even though it's hard not to. *You're an akulu. They'd despise you regardless,* I remind myself. *And that isn't why you stand among them anyway. You don't want their acceptance or need it. You want justice, you want vengeance, and everything else you have a right to take.*

But now there's this bioweapon to consider. This chance to win the war . . . and destroy me. He doesn't actually care about me—or, really, the blood-gifted at all. No, he cares about something much more powerful: money.

Because in Sutton Rhysien's boastful briefing, I mark another reason for my grandfather's assassination: greed. We are at war with Accacia. All of its legions are blood-gifted. Every last one of its soldiers, its army's commanders, and its emperor are blessed by Amaka. They fight with that gift. They can defeat whole enemy contingents with that gift in a matter of minutes. They've destroyed whole cities before with that gift. Mareen will need to mass-produce iridium if it has any hope of winning this new war, and it will need to do so with expediency if Accacian forces are already sacking our cities and mines. When Rhysien's War House mass manufactures iridium, it will demand a handsome sum from the Republic, and the Republic will rush to pay it. Countries outside the Republic might even try to buy it.

Rhysien could end up being richer than the Republic itself after this war if Mareen comes out victorious.

And that is almost certainly why my grandfather is dead. So a rich man can get richer, and bloody hands can get bloodier.

Rossi stands at the podium again and Rhysien retakes his seat. "The information shared with you here is classified," Rossi says. "It will not be disseminated to the larger public. Our aim is to swiftly and quietly deal with the Accacians and to do so before their intelligence agents learn of the iridium we can use against them. Your specific orders will be dispatched to you through your cohort leads. Some units will be headed west or east alongside corps of common soldiers to fight the Accacian legions. And there will be a few cohorts that remain in Krashen, as the protection and guard of our seat of power is critical. As long as Krashen stands, Mareen stands. A war summit with our allies will also take place immediately. It will be held in Khanai. Select members of the Tribunal will journey there to participate. Two cohorts will accompany them as their Praetorian Guard."

He looks out at us, stern and unyielding.

"You have trained for this. Mareen has prepared for this. We *will* prevail. The maroon-and-white flags will fly once again.

"And this time they'll fly over the capital of Accacia. We won't just win a war. We'll topple an empire. We will *take* an empire."

The Praetorians in the hall snap to attention. There is no cheering— that isn't our way—but you can feel the pride pouring off the cohorts.

Pouring off everyone but the one person whose blood will become poisoned because of Rhysien's greed.

29

ALONG WITH ALPHA, GAMMA ESCORTS Haymus Rossi, Zephyr Caan, and Brock to the summit.

We disembark *Omicron Majoris Castor*, one of the two official stealth jets outfitted for travel by the Tribunal Council. Gamma is first to step into the hangar. A Khanaian delegation greets us. We complete a visual security sweep of the surroundings and the receiving party. It's comprised of persons wearing royal guard uniforms of violet and cerulean blue, Khanai's national colors. The kingdom's national flower, a mist-white snowglory, sits high on the left shoulder of their uniforms. Its six petals are wide, veinous blooms. Khanai's military doesn't have a retirement reserve. As long as you are able to and wish to serve, you can. The collection of royal guards range in age from individuals who look about my nineteen years to servicepeople who appear upward of fifty. One proud face among the twenty is familiar. Keenly so. The second snowglory on the young man's right shoulder sets him apart from the rest as special. Brown locs with gold filigree fall loose around his face. They sweep his shoulders in a mane that's about four inches longer than when I last saw him: Enoch Gyidi. The length and styling adds veracity to the moniker he assumes these days: "The Lion of Khanai." A fitting title he's earned since stepping into the dual role of Khanai's adored Crown Prince and Emrir, the leader of his nation's vast armies. My childhood friend slides me a miffed look. I deserve it for ignoring all his attempts to reach out to me these last four and a half months, but I pretend I don't see it.

We'll see how long he lets that continue now that I can't ignore him when he's right in my face.

Mareen's leaders deplane the jet once Reed communicates the all-clear. Alpha exits behind them.

Enoch steps forward from among the line of Khanaians. He folds his left arm behind his back and touches his right fist to his opposite shoulder. "Welcome to Khanai," he says to the brasses.

Brock returns the formal greeting. Rossi and Caan don't bother to mimic the Khanaian custom. They do things as Mareenians would and snap terse salutes to the Emrir. Rossi doesn't curtail his sneer that says he is superior in every way to the Khanaian he deigns to salute, and Caan returns Enoch's amicable smile with a bland visage.

Years of rigid training is the only thing that doesn't make me gape at them both. To be on Khanaian soil, needing the kingdom as an ally, the two men are being incredibly rude. Their bigotry cannot be making them this stupid. The Tribunes are many things, but they *aren't* verified idiots. So I can only conclude that they'll be more courteous toward the Grand Monarch and Queen, and they simply deem Enoch's estimation of them as irrelevant since he doesn't truly helm Khanai. They remain reprehensible for their behavior, but I am given some comfort—and hope—that the war summit won't be a disaster of our making. It's only a very tiny measure of comfort, because regardless of what the Tribunes think, Enoch's opinion of them *will* be heavily valued by his father and mother.

I look to the Crown Prince, internally wincing at his likely response. He can sometimes be as hotheaded as me.

"Follow us to your transports," Enoch says. If they want disdain, he
can dish it out as easily as he receives it. He gives the Mareenians his
back and strides away. He holds himself as kingly and as stately as ever.
The only tell that he's aggrieved is how his left hand curls around the
pommel—a gold lion's head in mid-roar—of the blue steel ceremonial
sword that rests inside a jeweled sheath at his side. But he just as quickly
relaxes his grip, making it clear it's merely a place for his hand, not that
he wants to whip it out and see how many Tribunal jugulars he can cut
through in one swipe.

Outside the open doors of the hangar, a line of luxury transports are
hovering. They're a glossy dark violet with black tinted glass and small
white snowglories painted on the doors that signify they are transports
of the royal house. As the Khanaians escort us to the vehicles, the contempt is clear on Rossi's and Caan's faces. Mareen's military elite only
ever travels in a fleet of armored transports.

As Rossi, Caan, and Brock are shown to the first luxury transport
in the line, Enoch catches the looks. "Trust us—we know what we're
doing," he informs them. "The jets you pay a fortune for aren't the only
things we engineer well." I swallow a smile at the subtle dig; mirroring
his smug grin would be *indecorous*, I suppose. But inside I cheer him on
as he and two of his guards duck inside the transport with the Republic's ruffled leadership.

Alpha is divided between the next two vehicles. I climb inside the
fourth one with Reed, Dannica, Haynes, Enzo, and three more Gamma
members. The other half of our cohort fills the one behind us, and the
last two are occupied by the remaining Khanaians.

The ride from the hangar on the outskirts of Natarra, Khanai's
capital city, to the Jade Palace at its center is quiet. The opaque tint on
the windows is a one-way thing. A vibrant, colorful view of Natarra
is clear from inside the transport. In the silence, I turn to the window

and look out at the glittering municipality I know as well as Krashen City. Grandfather had a home on Cara in the Southern Isles, where his parents lived, and he owned a home in Natarra, the place of his father's birth and childhood too. We didn't visit it often, since we mostly traveled to Khanai only in an official delegate capacity and as such stayed with the royal family as friends of the kingdom so Grandfather could remain in close proximity to Mustaph Gyidi, Khanai's Grand Monarch. It facilitated ease for whatever round of treaty or trade talks he was visiting to hammer out. But he did show that home to me on a few occasions because he wanted me to know our roots. It was modest and beautiful and nestled among a cozy neighborhood of similar elegant flats and terraced homes. We pass a neighborhood like that now. Though the one Grandfather's father grew up in is located on the opposite side of the city, I imagine it and its ivy-green shutters and ivory roof among the residences we pass. Technically, the deed to that home belongs to me now, as does the villa in the Southern Isles and the apartments at the Tribune General tower on base. The three residences also come with a considerable fortune, something the lawyers explained was placed in an accessible trust, but I honestly don't care about it. I don't want any of it. *I want Grandfather back.* I dig my nails into my palms, using the sting of pain to chase away the fresh misery that blindsides me.

We leave the residential quarter behind and glide through the streets of the Spice Quarter, one of Natarra's sprawling open-air markets. It isn't as high-class as the Silk Quarter on the east side of the city, where Grandfather's flat is. Spice Quarter merchants don't deal in fine wares, opulent clothing, and custom jewels.

No, this market is better.

Because the Spice Quarter on the west side features the best food and entertainment you can find in Natarra. It serves every delectable dish and fanciful dessert Khanai has to offer. Diners can gorge and enjoy a day in the company of world-famous musicians.

The tangle of spices whirling through the market are so potent they suffuse the transport. I inhale, leaning closer to the window. The honeyed sweetness of rudda, the peppery tanginess of rii, the citrus fruitiness of ilin, the sharp zestiness of cyree—all of them are bliss. They tug me into a happy place where a four-year-old Ikenna meanders through the Spice Quarter with her grandfather and samples all these things for the first time while he watches her gobble up everything with utter delight and amusement. My senses are especially teased by the sugary syrupiness of becel, which Khanaians like to drizzle over most desserts and a variety of fruits. I mark the fuchsia stall that sells baked blushing apples. Their juiciness splashes into your mouth as soon as you take the first bite and their hard candied exterior tastes like spun sugar and pinkberries. Two vendors down is a charcoal smoker pit, where you can get the best blackened redfish slathered in rii sauce.

I went through the trials, and this seems like the worst torture I've had to endure in months.

"All these aromas have my stomach growling," Haynes rumbles, stirring me out of my memories. "We should make a pit stop, Reed," he jokes.

Dannica is turned to the window too. "I wish we could. I hope the food they provide us in the palace smells the same. We don't get dishes like this in Mareen."

Reed peers out the window like the rest of us.

"Or Reed could also stop being a jerk and cook things for us," Dannica snarks.

"Not in a million years," Reed returns. "You can feed yourself."

"Yeah, but not the sort of food you can whip up," Haynes, a grown bruiser of a man, whines.

Reed stares at them unmoved.

"You're a bastard," Dannica grumbles.

"You cook?" I ask Reed, both shocked and curious enough to want more details. Most Mareenians don't. They eat synthesized food or droid-prepared food. "Khanaian dishes?"

"Of course I do," he answers like he's insulted. "If you're going to eat for pleasure instead of simple nourishment, the only food to eat is Khanaian food."

I gape at him dumbstruck, yet again, by something else new that I've learned about him. The revelation is the only thing that could've pried my attention away from the market and the vibrant scenery of Natarra. "Where did you learn?" I don't know how to cook Khanaian food or any food for that matter. Grandfather didn't cook a thing either.

He shrugs like it's no big deal. "My mother. She refused to bear a son who didn't know how to cook for himself. Said it would be a disgrace to her parenting skills."

I laugh. It is something a Khanaian mother would say. Enoch's mother, Queen Akasha, used to drag him by the ear into the kitchens when we were younger and make him watch while she shooed the staff away and prepared a meal for her son to learn. He'd whine that he was a prince and didn't need to. She'd then leave and come back when he was so hungry that he was clutching his belly from the pain. Then she'd tell him that royals weren't above needing to know how to feed themselves and not embarrassing their mothers.

Khanaian women did not produce sons who were useless in a kitchen.

I find myself chuckling harder at the memory and the lingering amazement of finding out Reed can *cook*. I collect myself and smother the laughs. "Sorry," I say. "Learning that just made me think of something."

"Think of what?" Reed asks. But we've come to a stop inside the gates of the Jade Palace, the royal family's primary residence and the seat of government for Khanai. The sheer size and breathtaking beauty of the palace made entirely of jade steals everyone's attention. Its roof is a mixture of domes, spires, and Old World turrets.

It's also full of shadows, so we stay on alert as we exit the transports and march behind the Tribunal Council up to the entry courtyard. A statue of Kissa, the goddess of arts, riches, and wisdom, is its centermost adornment. It's made of rare amethi rulizi, a dark-purple precious stone found among the northern mines of Khanai. The goddess's coils are braided into a crown. Her lips are stunningly full and her nose is elegantly wide. Her cheekbones sit high. Her beauty is captivating and worship-worthy. It takes me a moment to pry my eyes away from the statue that has always enthralled me. Kissa's ethereal loveliness comes second only to Amaka's, the older sister with whom she shares so many features. Except renderings of Amaka depict that Amaka's looks congeal into a force of intense attractiveness that are alluring and fierce, as opposed to Kissa's vestal, delicate prettiness.

We're not here for statuaries, though. Nor the fern-green topiaries of geometrical shapes and the animal life native to Khanai that also decorate the courtyard.

This is a council of war, and we are soldiers. We take in the beauty, but unlike the last time I was here, I am observing the palace for potential threats, not its aesthetic wonder.

For the first time, I actually feel like a Praetorian, and I'm not sure if I like it.

Enoch breaks away from the royal guard and stands among his family—the Grand Monarch, King Mustaph, his wife, Queen Akasha, and their young daughter, Princess Nishia. They are assembled on the far side of the courtyard right outside the open doors of the palace. King Mustaph, a man with skin of the darkest ebony so beautiful and breathtaking and brilliant it gleams nearly obsidian black under the sun, stands in the center of his family. His dark hair hangs in thick dreaded ropes down his back. His locs belie how much longer he's had them than his son has. A gold crown inlaid with amethi rulizi, black diamonds, and jade rests on his head. A plush fur made from the pelt of a sabine lies across his shoulders. Thick gold herringbone chains crisscross over his chest, denoting his status as Grand Monarch. Beneath the adornments, he wears a navy, waist-length kaff, the linen dress shirts in fashion in Khanai, and cream pants. His shoes are suede chocolate loafers. He's sixty-eight turns of the sun. The same as

Grandfather was. He and Grandfather held political and social ideologies that were so similar, it was easy for them to enter into a friendship based on mutual respect.

A true equal to her mate, Queen Akasha stands to her husband's left and at his side instead of a step behind him. Mustaph may be the Grand Monarch of Khanai, but Akasha is the glue that holds the royal family and the country together. The Queen's medium-brown complexion is the color of honeywine. Her eyes are the green that follows the wet season. There are already songs and poems and stories about the two of them, and I have no doubt the love between the Queen and Grand Monarch will be immortalized in history. It is so solid, unbreakable, and uplifting that I'm positive monuments across Khanai will be erected in remembrance when the sun sets on the Grand Monarch and his wife.

Enoch stands to his father's right, in the place of Khanai's heir. Beside Enoch is thirteen-year-old Nishia. She has her father's darkest-of-ebony coloring, her mother's green eyes, and her brother's height. She's growing into a young woman who might rival Kissa in beauty in the years to come and doesn't look at all like the baby-faced little girl she was when I last saw her.

None of this should really matter, but Khanaians pride themselves on impeccable manners and irreproachable hospitality. So their appearance matters. Their bearing here matters. How they show themselves to the world—to Caan and Rossi and Brock—matters. All of it is why the royal family greets our Mareenian leaders as well as each one of us Praetorians when a different sort of noble might address only the Tribunes and ignore their guard.

Rossi and Caan keep up the superior air they carried in the hangar. When the other royal family members offer them the same formal greeting and show of friendship that Enoch did, they don't return it with the Grand Monarch, Queen, or Princess either. I'm so stunned, a stupefied expression steals onto my face before I have a chance to quickly wipe it away.

This second time around, Enoch merely regards the Mareenians with a chilly incline of his head. At least Brock maintains his same geniality. I want to choke some sense into his counterparts. Caan and Rossi are the *Tribune Generals of a nation at war, for Republic's sake.* They should be placing their personal prejudices aside right now and strengthening ties with Khanai.

What the hell is wrong *with them?*

If they're not going to at least feign civility toward any of Khanai's royals, why did we even travel to Natarra at all?

When I near the Gyidi family in the receiving line, shame warms the back of my neck for serving as guard to the generals as well as for another reason: Enoch isn't the only one whose messages I deleted unread and whose calls I silenced the past few months. Each of the individuals before me reached out to offer sympathies and support after Grandfather's death. My behavior in turn was atrocious.

Not that they'd say anything of it to me. "It is nice to see you, dear," Queen Akasha says, proving as much. She kisses my brow, a Khanaian custom that elders bestow upon children they are close with.

"Your grandfather was a king among men that the world didn't know it had, child," Mustaph says when I step in front of him. The Grand Monarch speaks the highest honors of Grandfather, paying me the condolences for his passing that I wouldn't permit myself to previously hear. "When you have a break in your duties, visit in your free time. Verne's open invitation extends to you. I hope you've known that." My chest tightens at the assertion.

"I have," I say. Except I wasn't actually sure it was true. Part of the reason that I've ignored the Gyidi family is because I wasn't sure that the affection they held for Grandfather extended to me in his absence. It was a closeness to people who looked like me, loved me, and accepted me unconditionally that I'd treasured. I hadn't wanted to lose it, so I'd put up a wall first before I could be hurt.

Nishia throws any semblance of a greeting becoming of a princess to the wind. When I'm in front of her, she flings herself at me and wraps me up in a hug. I can't help my wide smile. Khanai's Honored Princess is the best kind of exuberant, energetic, and impulsive. I hope she never loses that about herself. I hug her back, tighter than I intended. "You suck for staying away and not speaking to anyone," she pouts. "I called you. The whole family did to check on you. We were worried." She's wiggled out of my embrace and her hand is on her hip as she glares at me, putting me well in my place.

"*Nishia.*" The Queen throws her daughter a stern look. The princess ignores it. Her hand remains on her hip as she looks at me expectantly, waiting for the apology she's owed. I laugh again because she's going to make a marvelous woman when she is grown.

"I'm sorry," I say. "Things were hard."

Her hand falls away from her hip. She hugs me once more. "Promise not to do it again. Ever."

I give her my word, and she allows me to move past her and for the receiving line to continue.

And not just move along the line. To maybe, actually, continue living.

Thank the gods for bratty teenagers.

"IT'S COMMON KNOWLEDGE that Legatus Amari and the Grand Monarch had a genial relationship. However, I want your account of how it evolved. That isn't such common knowledge," Dannica says. She's been harping on the topic since Gamma gathered inside Reed's suite. We're supposed to be going over Gamma's duties during the summit. It's a fact Reed reminds her of after her third interruption. Being Dannica, she waves him off. "We can talk about the boring bits later. I want to hear the interesting stuff that historical accounts from Mareen's perspective don't relay. This part always gets glossed over, and we have Kenna here to give us the details."

Reed scowls in consternation, but Dannica is like an immovable force once she locks her mind on something. Hence, the *I* that I can't convince—or threaten—her to tack onto the beginning of my name. Reed sighs and gives in. "If Amari wants to indulge you, let's make it quick so we can focus on our job."

"So, Kenna." Dannica grins. "Tell us everything."

It makes me a little anxious being put on the spot and asked to talk about Grandfather. But I actually adore the story she's asking for. "When Grandfather and the Grand Monarch first met, they were young men and it was during a leave Grandfather chose to pass in Khanai," I say. "They met at one of the salons Khanaian intellectuals throw. At first they clashed because Grandfather was part Khanaian, which to Khanaians means he is full Khanaian, because any amount of their blood makes you one of them, and Grandfather was serving Mareen. We weren't allies then, as you know. We weren't at war, but hostilities and mistrusts ran deep between our nations. Mustaph couldn't understand why Grandfather chose to live in Mareen amidst its bigotry instead of relocating here, where he'd enjoy an easier life. Somehow, their natural curiosity was greater than their disdain, and their difference in views led them to keep in touch and further argue their sides. Over time, they realized that despite that one difference of opinion, they held similar views on politics, trade, commerce, war, and humanitarian issues. Those commonalities burgeoned into a mutual respect and admiration for each other. They eventually became good friends."

"That's why when Accacia marched on the Minor Continent, it was Legatus Amari who convinced Mustaph, Khanai's new young king, to ally with Mareen against the common threat of the Blood Emperor." Haynes inserts the part that Mareenian history books do relay.

"Yes," I say. "Grandfather is the reason Mustaph so readily put his personal hostilities and resentments toward Mareen aside. He didn't trust the Tribunal Council or the rest of the Republic, but he trusted Grandfather and he listened when Grandfather impressed that an alliance was the only way that both nations wouldn't fall to the Blood

Empire. After the war, Grandfather and Mustaph remained close. Grandfather was the entire Minor Continent's war hero by then, and the man who ensured that the treaty between the Ally States and the Blood Emperor was drafted and signed in good faith. He hadn't been elevated to the Legatus rank yet, but he had been functioning as Mareen's envoy with Khanai since the war started. He continued in that role after it ended and continued working with Mustaph to make sure the treaty forced on the Blood Emperor held and to better relations between us and Khanai for the good of everybody."

"Do you think the alliance will hold with him gone?" Haynes asks the question I'm not too sure of myself.

"It's only been a few months. I can't see things disintegrating that quickly," I hedge, and hope like hell it's true.

"A few months is a lifetime in politics," Reed says.

"Then I don't know, especially considering the way Rossi and Caan acted today. Their behavior won't exactly inspire confidence or broker goodwill during the summit."

"Their attitudes were terrible," Dannica says.

"They were an embarrassment," Haynes says.

Reed steers us back to going over our duties during the four-day summit. As he speaks, I only partially listen. The bulk of my focus is consumed with further worry over Haynes's question. We *need* this alliance. And yet . . . I'd swear the Tribunes were trying to *keep* Khanai at arm's length—or sever our ties with them altogether. But that's ludicrous if we're at war. Plus, if we're in the Jade Palace, leadership must recognize the importance of Khanai as our ally on some level.

So, again, I ask myself, *What the hell is going on with them?*

WHEN I LEAVE Reed's suite, I intend to make my way to my rooms and settle in. However, that isn't where I end up. I aimlessly roam the palace halls instead, still mulling over the infuriating, nonsensical actions of Rossi and Caan.

A tall, curvy woman steps into my path when I turn a corner. "You are not permitted in this area," she says, sharp. Beside her is a shorter man. He wears a scowl as severe as hers. They're dressed in the royal guard uniform and each has a hand on the blaster at their side.

I blink, stepping back while looking around, then understand why they look like they're about to place a bullet in my head. I'm a Mareenian guard. A Praetorian. And I've wandered into the royal family's private residence wing. The breach isn't intentional. Ending up here is from muscle memory. It's the wing Grandfather and I would stay in during our visits. That's how affectionate with each other he and Mustaph became. I should've realized where I stumbled. There's no excuse for me not recognizing where I am. This part of the palace has turquoise and citrine tones instead of the jade-green, violet, and cerulean that adorns the rest of the halls. It's warmer. Cozier. More intimate. It feels like a home instead of an enormous state building that's also praised as a Wonder of Iludu.

"Please excuse the error," I ask the guards. "I intended no harm or insult. I got lost."

"No, you didn't," says an amused voice. Enoch strides to stand beside me. "Stand down," he tells the man and woman. "Her presence here is fine. She can come and go from this wing as she likes."

I stare at him as dismayed as the guards. Except they can't say to their Crown Prince and Emrir what I do. "Are you an idiot? You can't give me that sort of clearance. It's a gross breach in security. I'm part of the Mareenian team.

"And speaking of your idiocy, you also don't have a sufficient number of people posted at this entrance. There should be more than two with so many foreign visitors in-residence for the summit. I hope your individual security details are functioning better than this. Where is *your* personal detail? What?" I say when his mouth twitches. "Don't laugh at me. This is serious."

The female guard coughs several times. The male guard looks mortified, like he'd rather be anywhere else.

"One, I don't need a security detail. I'm my kingdom's chief warrior and commander," Enoch says haughtily. "I can defend myself against any threat that comes my way." I roll my eyes but let him continue. "Two, you've always been able to come and go from this wing. You've stayed here in a room across from my own and next door to Nishia's how many times? I trust you. The family trusts you. In Khanai, we don't give trust lightly, so why would we snatch it away so lightly? Three . . ." His eyes rove over my formal Praetorian uniform. He breaks into a full-out laugh. Dimples stab into the mahogany brown of his cheeks when he does. "You sound like a Mareenian and like Verne."

I give a chuckle too. "I do, don't I?"

His laugh softens. "You do. He'd be proud."

My heart squeezes. "I hope so," I respond.

"Come. Walk with me, please. Let's finally talk away from a horde of guards and heads of state."

It's an easy thing to fall in step beside him. I've walked this part of the palace with him dozens of times. I've *run* through it with him, getting into all types of trouble.

"How are you doing? Really?" Enoch asks. We end up in Akasha's garden of starwatcher flowers. The wide, pink blooms that are speckled coral give off a fruity, fragrant scent that makes them smell as nice as they look. Enoch plucks one off a high-hedged bush and holds it out to me. "You always thought these were pretty. Have one."

I don't dare touch it. "Your mother is going to have your ass for that." He will not make me complicit in his crime. The immaculate garden is Akasha's pride and joy that she tends to and prunes herself. She will know if the smallest of blooms is disturbed or missing. I know because I used to try to sneak and pick a few and she'd always find me out when I was little.

"I've grown too big and too important to the kingdom for Mother to kill me for my misdeeds now," Enoch jokes. "Khanai can't be robbed of its Emrir *and* Crown Prince. Nishia would make a terrible Grand Monarch. It'd be like placing you on a throne."

I push the starwatcher away and slug him in the arm. Hard.

"Ouch!"

"I thought the great warrior could protect himself."

"Touché."

"Now, why don't you tell me what you mean about me being on the throne, princeling?"

"That you're the type of person who will assault a royal in his own palace when you're supposed to be a part of the delegation seeking to reaffirm an allyship with his kingdom," he teases. "You and my sister have no détente. A Grand Monarch needs détente."

"Neither did you the last time I saw you," I shoot back. "You were as hotheaded as us."

He shrugs. The purple coat of his Emrir uniform pulls across broad, strong shoulders. "That was three years ago, and the responsibilities of both my new official stations forces one to change."

I eye him. I suppose he has changed. As he stands tall and proud in front of me, I see very little of the boy I grew up knowing. In the last three years he's matured into a formidable man. The Lion of Khanai is stamped into every inch of his bearing. He exudes a warrior's ferocity that he doesn't bother to temper. And while the kind, merry demeanor he's always possessed remains alongside it, there's a seriousness and a wisdom about him that he never embodied before. Well, at least one of us actually grew up and matured. I'm a massive mess, barely holding things together for appearances' sake on my best of days. On my worst of days . . . well, on my worst of days I'm either the reckless, dumbass

Ikenna from my last three months in the academy or I'm the idiotic Ikenna who got one of her best friends killed for her poor decision-making and ineffectualness.

"I don't like the disposition of your face," Enoch says, frowning.

I shake off what he sees in my expression. I paint on an uplifted smile. "I'm fine. It's nothing."

"You're *not* fine." He takes my hand and tugs me down onto a stone bench. He has the grace not to tear into me like his sister did, but he does say, "I wish you would've allowed us to be there for you in your time of need. You have no family in the Republic, and we could've been your support."

"It was too painful," I say to him in the privacy of the garden. I couldn't do this by Comm, but here, something opens up inside me. "I was a mess. I'm still a mess."

His hold on my hand tightens. He settles it into his lap. "You have a right to be that way. You deserve to unravel a little after losing the only parent you've known. I'd unravel too if I lost either of my parents. Give yourself a little, actually a *ton* of grace. I understand if you need to keep your distance for a while if that helps you cope. But if there is anything I can do, will you please let me know? And try to give the family a call once in a while to let us know you're all right."

I extricate my hand from his hold. "I appreciate your words, and I made a promise to Nishia that I will stay in touch." Although I'm already discomfited by it, I intend to keep my word. "As for everything else, I am working on making it better. There isn't anything you can do to help."

Enoch nods and graciously leaves things at that. He leans forward and kisses my cheek. It's feather-light and chaste. When he pulls back, he says, "Mareen, which treats people who look like you as filth, isn't the sole home you have. Your Grandfather was Khanaian. *You* are Khanaian. You're one of my people as much as anyone else in the king-dom is. You have a place in Khanai if you want it, and you can make a home among my court. Soldiering is in your blood and you won't give it up. I know that. I can always use another capable general or guard captain for my father. I extended the offer in each of the messages I left. Did you read any of them?"

"No," I admit. And regret crashes down around me as I flounder for a more adequate response to the gesture. Because his generous, kind invitation might have made a difference back then.

But it certainly doesn't with what I know now.

30

THE NEXT MORNING, THE HONORED Princess turns up at my suite and drags me into the same garden. The Grand Monarch, Queen, and Crown Prince are seated at a square oak table sagging with dishes of pastries, breads, jams, fried fish, fruits, sweet wines, and tea carafes. The Queen looks flawless, as always. Her hair is immaculate—it is an unbound waterfall of constructed corkscrew coils today—and her day gown is a lilac sheath cut at a slant right above her knees. Opals twinkle at her neck, wrists, and ears. Nishia wears a gauzy canary-yellow dress. Enoch is dressed in his Emrir's uniform again, and Mustaph wears a silver kaff under his black sabine pelt.

Queen Akasha rises from the table when Nishia and I near it. "I'm glad you could join us, dear." Without anyone else around, she ditches formality and hugs me. Mustaph and Enoch do too.

We're halfway through the early morning breakfast when the Grand Monarch informs me, "I would like you to be present during the alliance talks that start today. I'd value your input and assessment of Mareenian intentions if you have anything to offer. I'm not asking you to compromise your duty or allegiance to your country. I would never ask such a thing of you. I am asking that when and where you can, you give me your honest assessment of the proceedings. I knew Verne. I trusted Verne. I trust you."

"But you don't know or trust the Mareenian leaders that are here," I finish for him. "I'm not surprised you feel that way after their atrocious behavior toward you and your people yesterday. Haymus Rossi showed he's a bigoted idiot, and the young Zephyr Caan isn't proving to be any better."

Annoyance flashes across Enoch's face at the reminder. Queen Akasha presses her mauve lips into an insulted line. Mustaph dips his head in confirmation. "Yes, that was observed. But I don't care much about their manners at the moment—I care about how they will act as allies . . . or not. Which is why I'd feel better if you were a party in the room."

"I don't have the rank to be present unless I'm on guard duty inside the room, and I wasn't assigned to it. I'm sorry. There's nothing I can do."

The Grand Monarch smiles. "I requested your presence as a condition of beginning the necessary talks. The Mareenians had no choice except to assent. Of course, I'd never place you in a position that you aren't comfortable with, which is why I wanted to inform you of my wishes and ask if you would do me the honor of acting as my trusted Mareenian envoy as your grandfather did."

The request is a punch to the gut. It is an honor. An honor I could never live up to. But I will not deal the Grand Monarch and the royal family an insult by declining. Instead, I admit the truth and hope they take heed. "I'm not my grandfather. I'm nowhere near as wise or cunning or formidable as he was. More, I have almost no stature amongst the Praetorians—they won't like that I'm given such treatment. I just don't know if I will be much use."

"All of what you say about stature is true, and yet none of it matters to me," Mustaph says in a warm tone. "And as for the first string of nonsense, I understand why you may believe that. You are young and untested and for some, it takes time to gain confidence in who we are.

"Let me start by giving you some of my own confidence in you. Hopefully it will blossom inside you."

SEVERAL NATIONS FROM across the Minor Continent amass in the palace's forum hall for the opening of the war summit. It's been more than thirty years since so many of the continent's powers have assembled together in one place. As I stand beside the quickly filling table where talks will occur, I drink it all in, captivated and horrified by the scene at the same time. It's both a staggering thing to behold, and something I never wanted to witness.

Mareen's leadership has already taken their seats at one of the long ends of the table where their name placards rest. Rossi, Caan, and even Brock are sitting with spines stiffened by condescension as the rest of the summit's participants take their seats.

The Federation of Lythe's six Hearth Mothers settle at the table after us Mareenians. Their reserved space is near the head of the table that faces the hall's entrance. The leaders of matriarchal Lythe, the third large nation that occupies the Minor Continent, are marked by the silver diadems that crown their heads. The diadems are identical except for the tribe affiliations etched into the teardrop emeralds that stand center. The Hearth Mothers' accompanying entourages that entered the hall alongside them are huge. I count at least fifty Dorii, female warriors of the federation. Their rank is clear by the silver pendants at their throats with an emerald cut into the symbol of their respective tribe. Thirty Bryshere, subservient male priests, have also traveled to Khanai to serve their Hearth Mothers and Dorii. The Dorii stand guard at the backs of their matriarchs much like we ten Praetorians in the hall do with the Tribunal Council, and the Bryshere fan out behind the Dorii. Like the Khanaians, Lytheians bear a coloring that's a conglomeration of browns. Unlike the Khanaians, the people of Lythe don't suffer insults.

So when Rossi and Caan turn derisive gazes on them, chagrined that the darker-skinned Lytheians—and women at that—occupy a head of the table while they're wedged in the center, all of Lythe's Hearth Mothers rake them with withering, cautioning looks that promise to nail their balls to the table if they give voice to whatever repulsive things their expressions make it evident they are thinking.

I like the Hearth Mothers. Grandfather did too.

Once Lythe's sizeable delegation is situated, small envoy groups from the scattering of Free Microstates that chose to send representatives file into seats on the long side of the table across from us Mareenians. The fact that not all of the microstates are present means it'll likely be the same situation with them during this second war that existed during the first war: some will fight alongside us, some will try to abstain from it altogether, and some will choose to oppose the Blood Emperor independently should he conquer Mareen, Khanai, and Lythe and then push northward where the microstates lie. The Tribunes regard them icily as well. As independent, small nations with only modest wealth, relatively small militaries, and ideologies that celebrate the cultural melting pots they've become, the microstates have never garnered much respect from the Tribunal.

The Khanaian delegation stands at the opposite head of the table from the Lytheians, in the place of honor as hosts. They arrived at the table first, and as a show of both respect and hospitality, they remain standing while the entirety of their guests take their seats. Only then do they sit too. The Khanaians' ever-courteous behavior presents a stark, visible, embarrassing contrast to our ill manners. It is evident the summit's attendees also take notice of it as stares travel between us and them. I inwardly curse. Already, we are repeating some of the earliest mistakes made during the first war. Every organized society on the Minor Continent needs to be united as one against the might of the Blood Emperor and his legions.

Yet while our cities are still being attacked, we continue to look down on and alienate the people we need help from. The Tribunes cannot have completely forgotten that Mareen needed Grandfather *and* the alliances he brokered to win the war.

Which, I realize with a start, only leaves one plausible answer for their actions: they feel that this time around they don't need either since they have iridium.

If that's the case, they're shortsighted fools. Maybe the iridium *will* do its job, and so Caan and Rossi find this all moot. But it seems unlikely it's going to be 100 percent effective. Or that we'll produce enough in time to fully prevent atrocity. In the briefing we got on the upcoming war, we were told that our Praetorian Trials in the Expanse and the Ice Wastes were meant to test the might of Mareen's best war tech against the might of blessings and curses proliferated by the gods.

We got our asses handed to us both times.

During the talks, something else is wrong too—we don't seem to be promoting the iridium as much as I would have thought. And it makes me wonder what Rhysien might be hiding about the so-called superweapon. He and the rest of the Tribunal are guiltless, vicious bastards and the fact that specifics were kept so secret even while disseminating information to us Praetorians makes me not trust something about it all. Namely, does iridium only harm the blood-gifted or does it poison *any* individual with a Pantheon blessing? Other gifts weren't quelled among the Khanaians, Lytheians, or a number of the Free Microstates following the Pantheon Age.

Is this all a ruse, then? Does Mareen really not *want* allies, like I thought before, and is *that* why their disdain for this summit is so open? If so, it again invites the question why come at all? Something is definitely not right.

If I was on alert before merely being a guard, now I'm practically jumping out of my skin.

What the hell is happening here? It's becoming my mantra.

The Grand Monarch asked for me to observe, and right now the only thing that's clear is Mareen clearly doesn't want to be at this table. The contempt Caan shows every time he speaks to someone in the Federation—no, scratch that: talks *at* one of the Hearth Mothers—makes my stomach turn.

And yet, it's all just gut reaction from me, not something I can necessarily tell the Khanians without betraying my oath to Mareen. Maybe I shouldn't care about it, but if I'm kicked out of the Praetorians, I can't do *anything*. So I'm caught between instinct, observation, and duty—to my grandfather, if no one else.

One thing that truly has me torn is that I think I could do something about all this if I can get close to Selene and compel everything she knows out of her. I suddenly wish I wouldn't have let the shock of impending war and my rushed orders to depart for the summit derail that. Selene stayed behind in Mareen with Epsilon to guard Krashen, so I can't get to her until after this is all over and we fly home. Which, judging from the proceedings, might be sooner than any of us were expecting.

"We will not tolerate being spoken down to with such disrespect!"

This snaps me out of my regret. One of Lythe's Hearth Mother's—a short woman with medium-brown skin and jet-black hair—shoots out of her seat. Her small hands are splayed on the table. She glares at Rossi, who—like Caan—has been talking to every head of state at the table who isn't Mareenian as if they're children, even the delegates who hail from the paler-skinned Free Microstates. At the Hearth Mother's justified ire, a cluster of Dorii behind her blow a hole through Rossi's head with their frigid stares.

I tense, and I can feel the rest of Gamma do the same. We're not going to have to fight, but we might have to fight, you know? It's an odd spot to be in when I really want to put a bullet through Rossi's head alongside the Dorii. The whole of Iludu would be better ten times over without men like Rossi polluting it.

"How can you stand to be in their disgusting presence?" At first, I'm startled because I think the Hearth Mother is speaking to me. But then I realize she's directing the question at Mustaph. "They don't behave as allies should," she tells him. "How can you trust someone to fight alongside you, whom you are therefore trusting with your life and the life of your people, if they do not even display that they consider your life as equal in value to theirs?" She returns her glower to Rossi. "Your porcelain skin doesn't make you better than me. It does not place you above me. But your hatred of me based upon it makes you filth that isn't fit to lie in the mud at my feet, not sit at a table in a room among other civilized people. You aren't civilized. You Mareenians have never been civilized toward those you call akulu. I don't know how Verne remained among you. He is the only reason Lythe agreed to an alliance last time. We trusted him. We fought beside him. He's not here, and you are proving to still be exactly the repugnant creatures you have shown yourselves to be throughout history. I don't trust the debased he-wolf or his little pup," she says, pointing at Caan. "He isn't fit to be an ally, for he will tear out your neck the second your death benefits him more than your life does. Lythe will not fight and die alongside anybody who holds themselves above us and who holds us undeserving of civility and common human decency." The Hearth Mother removes her hands from the table. At her pronouncement, the other five Hearth Mothers stand with her.

As they stride from the room, their Dorii and Bryshere march behind them.

"Lytheians are barbaric heathens. We don't need them," Caan mutters.

Enoch looks like he wants to use the ceremonial sword at his side to cleave every Tribunal Council man's head from his neck. So do most of the Khanaian army generals and Elders Senate representatives who are present. I have to school my face very hard not to appear the same.

For the first time during the talks, Mustaph's eyes flash with ire. "Your people have said that about Khanai too," he hisses. "Never mind that it has no basis or foundation other than its roots in prejudice and bigotry. You are guests in my kingdom and the Jade Palace, and you will remember that from this point forward. You will act accordingly and you will act with decency and with the *decorum* you Mareenians like to pretend you hold strict to. It is only out of necessity of this new war and a greater evil, and my wish to see my people protected, that I have invited you into my kingdom and home at all. It is only the mutual threat that I sit as an ally—no, *potential ally*—with men of a nation that once attempted to enslave my people and reduce us to chattel. Yes, Khanai may need Mareen and its war tech to win this war as we did the last one. But make no mistake about it, you need us as badly. The last war cleaved your population and your number of soldiers in half. The Blood Emperor launched an assault against all of us who stood against him, but he hit Mareen the hardest. Whether you wish to acknowledge it or not, you cannot win a war so soon after your civil war hobbled you and you have not completely recovered from it. You need our numbers in this fight. You need our resources. You need our wealth. You need our aviation tech. You need our production capabilities. And with Verne gone, you need us to be the middle ground between you and the rest of the Minor Continent you've perpetuated hatred against in the past. Because if Mareen is left on its own, Accacia will decimate you." He stares at Rossi. "You don't have Verne to save your asses this time around."

"We don't need Verne Amari." The condescension for Grandfather drips from Rossi's snarl. Reed, Dannica, and Haynes have got to be wrong. I can't believe he had nothing to do with his murder while he's sitting in the room oozing such extreme hate and venom at the mere mention of a dead man.

I look to Brock, who hasn't said a word during the entire exchange, and I can't help but feel disappointed by his silence. He is one of the Republic's leaders. He heads a major war house. He is equal in rank and power to Caan and has enough stature to treat with Rossi despite his title as Legatus. More, he has the ability to speak up. Yet, he did not during the talks and does not now. He showed Mustaph respect the other day. But now he does nothing.

His silence is echoing through the chamber for me.

"You can say that all you want, but without him, you have a lot of work ahead of you. Starting with making things right with the Hearth Mothers," Mustaph asserts to the Mareenian leaders. "I am not Verne. I will not do the necessary work for you to save your hide. You will make things right today because time is of the essence, and then we will resume these talks with better etiquette from everybody involved tomorrow. Rotten, despicable conduct will have no place at this summit."

The three men, even Brock, visibly chafe at being ordered what to do. They're the mighty Republic of Mareen's leaders. They helm a whole military force and control individual war houses. They do the ordering. It is never the other way around.

Rossi's face contorts into a very Caiman-like sneer. I think of all the nasty responses he's likely to cast Mustaph's way. "Yes, something is rotten and despicable," he seethes, "but I don't think it lies with Mareen." Out of all the things he could've said, that isn't something I'd imagined. It's so absurd, it's laughable.

But then Rossi and Caan share a very serious look.

"Leave it for now," Caan snaps. He pushes away from the table and stands. Brock does too. The Republic's leaders exit the room. We Praetorians fall in line behind them to escort them out. As I pass Mustaph, he lays a gentle hand against my arm. I don't look at him. I don't stare into the gaze that's steeped in sympathy for me being among such reprehensible men.

I'm in an impossible position, and he knows it.

And the truth of the world I live in just gets murkier and murkier.

31

"MAREEN SHOULD WALK!" LIIM RAGES. He, Chance, and Caiman were in the room for the morning's summit talk. The three of them stood directly at Haymus Rossi's back. "We don't need Khanai or Lythe. We don't need anyone. We have iridium. We can win this war without help."

"That's not the point," Enzo, who was also present, says. He sits beside me on the sofa. "The brass acted like asses today."

Dannica snorts. "Their default mode is asshole."

"You both have no respect," Liim says.

Dannica shrugs from where she leans against the wall. "Neither have they this entire time. They've been insulting dicks since we deplaned."

Haynes stands near her with arms folded across his chest, nodding in agreement. That earns him a look of disgust from Liim too.

"Enough," Reed says. "That's not why we're here." He cuts a grim look around his suite he summoned us to. Chance stands beside him, gleeful in a way I don't like. He's grinning like a demon straight from the hellpits.

"We've gotten new orders," Chance apprises us.

"Let me lead on this," Reed cuts in. "It needs to be communicated with care." His voice is gruff in a way that makes me study him for what's wrong. Whatever he's about to say, it isn't good.

Chance rolls his eyes. "Whatever. I forgot Gamma is made up of a bunch of sympathizers, bitch-mades, and undercover traitors."

A muscle in Reed's jaw ticks. "Not today," he says, clipped. His blue eyes swirl with agitation, and there is a churning violence to his demeanor that his usual coolness doesn't display.

Haynes, who's seated on the sofa next to me, and Dannica both notice his peculiar mood too. His second and third peer at him looking as puzzled and concerned as I am. Without acknowledging their pointed looks, Reed digs a small silver disc from his pocket, stalks to the nearest wall, stoops, and places it on the floor. As he rises, the disc casts a sound shield around the perimeter of the room. It's visible as an electric white net that clings to the wall like interlocking spider webs without gaps. The mood of the gathered Praetorians turns sober as Reed goes to stand in the center of the room again beside Chance. What they're about to impart is important enough that the Tribunal wants precautions taken so it isn't leaked—that silver disc is not standard kit.

A translucent holograph of Mustaph appears a few feet in front of Reed. He projects it from his Comm Unit. "Mustaph has become a kill target," he relays. "Our joint Gamma-Alpha team is no longer here to serve only as the Tribunal's Praetorian Guard. We're completing an assassination tonight."

Dannica explodes off the wall. She stabs a finger at the holograph. "Khanai is our ally! What the hell is wrong with the Tribunes?"

Haynes goes over to the projection of Mustaph and scrutinizes the Grand Monarch's face. "What's the strategy here in killing Gyidi at the start of a war? It makes no sense." His eyes take on the vacant gleam they get when he's deep in thought.

"It makes *perfect* sense," Chance spits. That's the reason the fucker is so gleeful. He gets to kill an akulu Grand Monarch, and he believes there's logic to it. "And what the hell is wrong with *you*, Dannica? These are orders from the Tribunal—that's all that should matter."

"And yet it doesn't," Dannica replies, acid dripping from her words.

"Because you don't care about the Republic. Well, *I* do. And because I do, I can see what you seem so blind to: Accacian forces invaded us in the east. Their legions are strictly attacking our fucking side of the *shared* border, and those Khanaian fucks haven't rendered aid. We've got men dying, and Khanai needs to host a forum and have *talks* first before they can do a damn thing."

"*Yet*," I say, rigid on the couch. "Khanai hasn't rendered aid *yet*." I stare at Mustaph's image, trying to wrap my head around seeing it paired with a kill order. I can't.

"Things are done differently in Khanai," Haynes adds. "The Grand Monarch has to give tonight's emergency address to his people first before the Elders Senate will back a war."

"Tonight's address and this whole summit is duplicitous," Chance states. "Khanai isn't fighting with us in the war. They made that much clear with their insults to us this morning."

Their insults? That's because the three men at the table haven't given Khanai the ability to do what needs to be done. They've deliberately sabotaged the meetings, and they've done so to kill Mustaph.

I still can't figure out *why*.

"Those are very cursory reasons to charge Khanai with treachery," I say with clenched fists.

But then I look to Reed, who isn't arguing against the points Chance is making. The resolute lines of his face make my stomach twist. It's going to be a lot harder to figure out how to avert this catastrophe if the Tribunal's got Reed believing the kill order holds merit too. I won't be fighting only Chance on this; I'll be fighting Reed and all of Gamma who will fall in step behind him if he presents any sort of logic that makes this seem like the right course. "What?" I say, dreading hearing it. But I need to know what I'm up against. "What do they think they have on Mustaph?"

For a second, his expression shifts to sympathy and something that's perhaps sorrow. It's a thing that's too fleeting to unravel. Detachment replaces it when he answers me. "Proof that's indisputable and that's been verified, Amari. We have decrypted communications between Mustaph and Accacian generals coordinating the discreet movement of Accacian troops through Khanaian territory while shielding their presence from the rest of the Minor Continent."

"No." It's the only word I can get out at first. Shock and confusion and outrage all crash into me and nearly suffocate me, making it hard to breathe. I spring from the couch and plant my feet on the ground, needing to do something other than sit. It's not intentional, but I assume a fighting stance. I shake my head furiously. Adamant . . . about what, I'm not sure. Just positive this is wrong.

"I don't care what they have or what you *think* has been verified. It's either been misconstrued or misrepresented. Why are you so sure? Why are you just accepting whatever the Tribunal fed you? They've clearly been trying to sabotage the summit since we arrived. They must have an agenda behind killing Mustaph—it's the only reason we're here, because it sure hasn't been to find allies. What that agenda is, I don't know. But they do. I expect Chance to be ignorant and blind to that, but you shouldn't be."

"K—*Ikenna*. Hold on here. You're directing your anger at the wrong person."

I shrug off the hand Dannica lays on my shoulder. "You're wrong. I am directing my fury at exactly the right person. He's Gamma's leader and he's believing this crap instead of speaking up or trying to figure out what the hell the Tribunal is really up to."

An above-reproach look settles on Reed's face, and it sends me careening toward the edge.

"If you're about to tell me I'm in breach of *anything*, I cannot be held accountable for what I do next," I warn him. I mean, I *can* be held accountable, but he won't be breathing to do it, and anybody else who has a problem with it is welcome to fucking try.

"This is how you run your cohort, Reed?" Chance jeers. "It's embarrassing and pathetic, even for you. Put the bitch in her place and dead the insubordination."

"You deal with your people the way you want, let me deal with mine," he tells Chance. "This is Gamma business. Stay out of it."

Chance steps closer to where Reed and I face off. "But that's the thing—it isn't just Gamma business. Not when she's questioning orders we have on a *joint* mission, and not when she's so close to the kill target. What happens if she flips? What happens if she decides to inform the Grand Monarch of the Tribunal's plans while we're still on Khanai's turf? That places all of us in a bad situation. I'm not fucking dying because you're too soft to keep her in line and because the Tribunes—for who knows what fucking reason—believe that you can, so—"

"If you finish that statement, it won't help things. What you think will happen might *just* happen. Let. Me. Handle. This."

I look between them, growing more pissed. "You can't fucking *handle* me," I tell Reed. "And that's not what this is about," I snarl at Chance. "This is about doing what is right and not letting the Tribunal murder an innocent man to carry out whatever perverse, self-serving scheme they're trying to execute." I won't stand aside while they murder a *second* innocent man. A second person who's close to me.

Then it hits me, and I stare at Reed, boggled why he hasn't seen it already, *ashamed it has taken me so long to see it*, and hoping what I'm about to say forces him to see it too.

"Rossi said himself he wanted to raise Mareenian flags over Accacia. He might not have wanted a war before, but now that one is here anyway, I can't imagine the *entire* Tribunal Council wouldn't unite behind that. Mareen has tried to expand its borders before. Before the last war with Accacia, we were always trying to reshape our boundaries. There were numerous skirmishes. You can't tell me the Tribunal wouldn't jump at the chance to be what Accacia is, to hold that kind of power. To be an empire instead of the contained Republic that the rest of the powers on the Minor Continent have jointly ensured we remain for so long. And we have the iridium now—which the Tribunes did not mention in this morning's summit talks, by the way. So, what if they figure we don't need Khanai or anybody else? What if we use this war to get rid of the Blood Emperor *and* destabilize every other nation on the Minor Continent with assassinations against their heads of state? Then the Tribunal sweeps in and raises Mareenian flags everywhere."

"What the fuck *if*," Chance asserts. "Taking issue with that possibility makes you a treacherous akulu whore in and of itself. Your allegiance is supposed to be to Mareen, *its Legatus and Tribunal*, and whatever agenda our government seeks."

I laugh. "Are you kidding me? That's rich coming from you. Where was your unwavering allegiance to the *Legatus* office when my grandfather was alive? You, the rest of Alpha, and a shit-ton of other folks did not hold strict to that sense of allegiance then. The way I see it, I'm within my right to question things here.

"*Think about it*," I say to Reed.

"I have," he says, evenly, and I blink.

"What do you mean *you have*? If that's so, why the hell are we having this conversation in the first place?"

He draws himself up taller. "Because one of the cohorts sent east to meet the Accacian threat *captured* a soldier in the Blood Emperor's army, Amari, and the interrogations of him returned the coded communications between Accacia and Gyidi that we then decrypted. And it left no room for any misinterpretation of their source. The messages had Gyidi's royal seal attached to them and it's been authenticated and verified several times over. This isn't a game. The Tribunal is well aware of the gross error we'll be perpetuating here if we misstep. I sat in on secure talks this morning that went on after the summit session between all fourteen Tribunes and Rossi while they debated our course of action. I'd think the same thing about this maybe being a ploy to expand Mareen's own borders in the end if I hadn't. But I *did*, and that's why I'm certain the reason for Mustaph's kill order isn't anything beyond what I've expressed."

"Authentication or not, it *doesn't make sense*. Khanai has as much to lose from Accacia gaining a foothold on our continent as we do. Us, them, and Lythe are the last remaining sizable nations that haven't been swallowed up into the Empire. If the Blood Emperor has taken up his Divine Expansion Campaign again, he will seek to conquer them too."

"That's true."

It's not a voice I was expecting to hear.

Caiman Rossi has stood up, and now speaks in a measured fashion that's as uncharacteristic as his agreement with me. "Yet how do you explain Accacian forces appearing in Mareenian territory so suddenly?"

Okay—so not in agreement with me. I grit my teeth.

He continues. "We are landlocked by Khanai in the northeast and Lythe in the southeast. The legions that attacked Rykos had to have traversed either Khanaian land or Khanaian airspace. Why weren't they intercepted? Why weren't we alerted with a call for reinforcements to halt their advance?"

When I spin around to turn my wrath his way, he holds up his hands. "You have to at least consider it. Your grandfather would. He was a guileful, calculating fucker, as much as any war house head is, I'll give him that. So you can't tell me that the formidable Verne Amari, who the world over either praises or fears for his supposedly genius strategic mind, *wouldn't* assess Khanai's guilt after extracting the evidence we did directly from an Accacian agent."

"He—"

Shit.

Grandfather absolutely would at least have given it some thought. Especially given the fact that it *is* prudent to ask why Mareen is being hit so heavily while the rest of the Minor Continent isn't. He'd note that Accacia contains its campaign to Mareen now.

I do not like where the line of thinking threatens to lead me.

But at least this isn't just blind faith like Chance has . . . or Reed. Though I'm no less sick for it.

"The Tribunal isn't mistaken. Khanai betrayed us." Keifer, an older Gamma Praetorian I haven't yet gotten to know well, asserts. He's scabrous in a way the younger ones among his cohort haven't yet come to be. He looks nearly to the age of forty, where he'd be awarded retirement outside of wartime. "*Krashna's Razor* applies here."

"I know *Krashna's Razor*," I say, detesting what I know he's about to say. The volume is the one artifact of Mareen's once-patron god that the Republic didn't abolish. Probably because there is no other body of text that explains the art of war so masterfully or so brilliantly.

"Then you shouldn't question our council's belief that Khanai betrayed us. '*For any conflict with multiple explanations, the simplest one is the correct one.*'" Keifer recites Krashna's First Principle verbatim.

"Even with everything that's been laid out, I'm still having a hard time digesting that Mustaph would turn on the Republic," I argue back. "Mustaph betraying the alliance with no cause doesn't reflect the sense of honor he holds strict to. He wouldn't allow the slaughter of thousands that came when Rykos fell if he could have somehow helped prevent it. And if we are applying *Krashna's Razor*, Khanai turning on us isn't the simplest explanation. How would it benefit them? How would it not ensure their ruin too?"

The looks Chance and most of his Alpha team keep giving me are withering.

"I'd agree with you if Legatus Amari were still around," Keifer says. "However, he isn't, and you're not thinking critically enough given that. People change. Loyalties shift. It could be that he was loyal to Verne Amari, not the Republic, and with Verne dead, he seeks a way to save his own hide from what we all knew was coming. What if he cut a deal? He facilitates access to us by allowing Accacia's passage across his lands and in turn the emperor spares Khanai? The Blood Emperor posed such a deal during the last war."

"And Mustaph turned them down," I stress to him *and* to myself because the evidence against Khanai is mounting.

"The Grand Monarch gave that offer much consideration before he declined and allied with us. The appeals of Legatus Amari, who isn't around to make them again, are what swayed him."

Keifer's words are wiser than I want to hear. They build a considerable case that Mareen's evidence might not be misconstrued. Still, I can't let it go just yet. Not until I've turned it over from every angle I can. The stakes and the consequences are too high not to. "Okay, but then why give an address at all then? And invite Mareen to it?"

Gods, Mustaph cannot have betrayed us.

And on another more personal level that I *will not* broach with anybody in the room, *Mustaph cannot have betrayed me and Grandfather like this.* He knows what the Blood Emperor had done to my mother and what he tried to do to me. I do not want to face what it means if Mustaph is working with Accacia.

But my arguments are growing weak even to my own ears.

"*Krashna's Razor.* The Second Principle says your enemy should never know they are an enemy until you've moved into position to strike. Perhaps Khanai and Accacia still have more maneuvering to do. Perhaps this is a trap."

Reed nods at Keifer. "That was discussed in this morning's meeting. It may be some type of trap, which is why it's crucial we strike at Khanai fast—and first—and then get out of here immediately."

"I can't believe Mustaph would turn on everything he and Grandfather worked to build." I say it like I can force the outcome I want to be true by sheer will alone. Horror, and anguish at the grim task before me, and the beginning feelings of gut-wrenching betrayal all wash over me. Nothing except pride keeps me standing where I am instead of plopping onto the couch engulfed in emotions too cutting and intense to adequately name.

I'd be an idiot to ever listen to anything Chance has to say, but the points Keifer made have a lot of merit. Mustaph's made his hostilities toward the Republic and its leaders very clear before the friendship sprung up between him and Grandfather. With Grandfather gone, there is nothing around to convince him to look beyond those old wounds and unforgivable aggressions for the greater good. It would be hard to blame him. If the Blood Emperor is courting Khanai to his side with promises of sparing it as he offered during the last war, Mustaph might be tempted to believe him this time around, tell Mareen to fuck off, and let us be razed.

Seeing the visible conflict I'm grappling with, Dannica moves closer to me in sympathy and support, *and I do not want it.* "Is there *any* possibility the Tribunal is acting on paranoia here and jumping the gun, Reed?" She has to be asking simply for my benefit when the former discussions have made it perfectly clear that can't be true. "Kenna sort of has one point: Khanai has been friendly to us for the last three decades. We've been the jerks."

"Precisely," Keifer says. "How much of that would any reasonable soul put up with? Sentimentality can have no place in war," Keifer tells me directly. "Heed the Third Principle and throw it away."

Chance smashes his fist into his palm. His smirk is nasty. "This entire useless discussion proves why those who aren't full Mareenian shouldn't be allowed to hold any combat rank—and especially not the Praetorian rank or the position of cohort leader. We were given a kill order. You shouldn't even be allowing these discussions among your crew unless your loyalties are divided and you want dissent." He launches that missile directly at Reed.

"That is not how Gamma does things," Reed says. "We are Praetorians because we passed the trials. Part of that means we are deemed smart enough to think with some independence. We're specifically given that independence as a check against the Tribunal overstepping. Gamma allows that independent thinking, and it allows discussions like this to take place, so when we move forward with orders as a team, to do what we are duty-bound and honor-bound to do, we do so together. It's better to get the doubt or the questions out of the way up front so there aren't any avoidable blips later. If the rest of the cohorts and the Tribunes took Legatus Amari's lead on that, you and your people would be involved in this discussion too, and all the cohorts would function for the better."

"That's giving Alpha too much credit," Haynes says, scowling at Chance.

"Is that really the reason?" Chance asks Reed, ignoring Haynes. "Or is it that you're a squeamish akulu trying to act like you're better than everyone, and—from everything I'm hearing—a disloyal one at that?" He cuts a scathing glance from Reed to me and then back to Reed. "Or maybe there's a third reason here. You're letting the akulu whore you selected for your cohort just to keep close by so you can keep conveniently fucking her make you lose the spine to do what needs to be done and these dragged-out *discussions* are nothing more than that.

"We have *orders*. Khanai let the Blood Empire through, and the only thing we should be talking about is *how* Mustaph is dying. But you haven't mentioned that to your bitch either. So don't tell me the time we've spent on this isn't in part about coddling her and being led by your dick."

Reed doesn't rise to the akulu insult or any of the others, but Haynes has no qualms getting in Chance's face. "You're a real shithead."

"And you're—"

"Shut up and fall back," Caiman tells Chance. "That's an order," he bellows when Chance bristles. "You're Alpha's lead, but I'm a war house heir and we are at war. I outrank you on this operation, and Reed is right—in some things. But key among them is that we don't need unnecessary friction among our joint team. This won't be an easy assignment. The palace will be crawling with royal guards in and out of uniform tonight because of all the individuals attending the emergency address in person. We're going to have to kill Khanai's head of state *and* get all our people out afterward in an incredibly hostile environment."

Like Chance did, he looks between me and Reed. Something is up, but I don't know what. But Caiman's gaze isn't contemptuous; it's empathetic, which is fucking bizarre. "I just got transmissions from my father about what's supposed to go down," he tells Reed. "I'm supposed to be the ears in this room and make sure things go how they're supposed to and the Tribunal doesn't need to intervene. Apparently, I have more confidence in Amari's ability to get over her shit, and quickly, to do what she has to do for her Republic. You should've ripped the gauze off up front. Chance stated it in a prick way, but he has a point and you know it. Stop stalling and tell her now if you want to be the one to do it, or else I will so we can get on with coordinating things."

I look between Caiman and Reed, who stiffens his shoulders.

"What the hell is going on?" I ask. "What else do I need to know?"

"I will tell her," Reed says.

There's an apology limning his face when he turns to me. It has the same intensity of the empathy Caiman threw my way. I brace for whatever new shitstorm is coming.

I'm not ready for what he says.

"The Tribunal has special orders for you. You have favor with the royal family. You're considered a friend and have been given unrestricted access to them. You're the only one who can get near enough to Gyidi to execute a kill, so your orders are to deliver the strike. The Tribunal wants us to take out Gyidi in a way that will cast guilt on Accacia and none of us Praetorians. They lifted a blood spike from the Accacian soldier they're holding; the weapon will be delivered here before

Mustaph's address for you to use. Make sure you leave it behind with Mustaph's body. Even if Accacia has proposed an alliance to Khanai, the Blood Emperor is notorious for his duplicity. So when the Crown Prince takes his father's throne, it'll be an easy thing for him to believe Accacia's guilt and he'll be furious. That should shatter any possible alliance with the Blood Emperor. Let me know if this is a task you can't do." He readjusts the Comm Unit strapped to his wrist. It's the one slip of calm, collectiveness, and control he allows. "We can't afford any screw-ups."

"I'm insulted for her," Caiman says. "There is no question of if she can do it. She *will* do it. She's a Mareenian first, and anything else second. Right, Amari?" Yes, the Ice Wastes are definitely melting at a vote of confidence coming from him.

I don't point out the inaccuracy or the reductivity in his statement because it was coming from a good place—this time—and I know what he meant. Mareen *is* my home. Mareen *is* my country. Mareen *is* an identity that's so intricately linked to me that what it means to be a Mareenian, or at least what it *should* mean, is fused to every cell of my body and coded into my DNA. Nineteen years of rearing and trainings and lessons from Grandfather made sure of it. Eleven years of schooling at a martial academy and then the trials only reinforced it.

Duty. Discipline. Endurance. Valor. Obedience. Honor.

I've lived that motto and that identity since I was born. But above that, what it truly means to me to be a Mareenian, what Grandfather taught me it *should* mean for everybody, is to stand for something and fight for something and pour your blood and sweat and all the strength that you've got into being a force to be reckoned with. And not simply to throw your weight around, but so that when you're faced with adversity, or war, or the unthinkable, you have the nerve, the resilience, the fortitude, the valor, and the honor already ingrained in you to stand in the face of *anything* and have the backbone, the fortitude, and the resolve to do what needs to be done. So Caiman is right about me, in that way.

But also . . . Grandfather would say Keifer's leaning on *Krashna's Razor* is wrong in regards to one thing: *sentimentality* has every place between kin, even in war. Mustaph is like my uncle, and Grandfather would not kill him without seeing the proof for himself. Which I haven't asked for yet—because maybe I was slipping back into the old Ikenna and didn't want it staring me in the face and leaving me unable to keep denying things. But I need to see it. It's the only way I can move forward. It's the only way Grandfather would even consider assassinating Mustaph, and it's the only way I'm going to consider doing it.

"The comms between Mustaph and the Accacian generals—I know you have them and I know the Tribunal gave you clearance to show them to me if I asked to see them." Regardless of how I feel about Brock at the moment and my not knowing where he stands where Grandfather is concerned, he knows what Grandfather instilled in me. So he knows that if the Tribunal wants me to deliver the strike to Mustaph, I would ultimately ask to see the proof.

"You shouldn't need to see them," Chance drawls.

I ignore him because the matter at hand is more important than addressing his bullshit statement.

Reed does as I ask. He projects the comms on the wall of his suite.

They consist of about a dozen messages, and like Reed said, they coordinate the concealed movement of Accacian forces through Khanai. All of the messages originating from Mustaph bear his signature and royal seal, authenticating them as coming directly from him. Numb, it is the seal that I study. The signature can easily be forged. The seal is an entirely other thing, and it reflects Mustaph's guilt without question. His royal seal, a holograph of entwined snowglories, is embedded in the bottom-right corner of each transmission. He uses two versions of it. One is for general head-of-state business. That's the one that is common knowledge, which anybody would recognize. Each of its snowglories has the accurate four white petals found on blooms. But the second seal he uses—the one for secure communications that validates his hand is the one that sent it—has one of its snowglories bearing only three blooms. I've seen that second one in communications between him and Grandfather before. Grandfather pointed the difference out to me for the same reason I have his access codes.

Just in case, Ikenna. It's wise to know these things.

I identify the second seal, the secure one, in each of Mustaph's messages, and it upends my entire world. It rips everything apart. It rips me apart. I just got the Gyidis back after believing I'd lost them as a second family when Grandfather died—and now I'm about to lose them again. Mustaph quite literally, and as for the others . . . after I carry out the kill order, there is no way I'll be able to face them. There's no way I *can* face them with any kind of a conscience and pretend like I didn't have a hand in executing him. Even if it is for a warranted reason. And it *is* warranted—I can see that now. Accacia cannot gain a footing on the Minor Continent. The war it has started cannot drag out, and Khanai allying with the Blood Emperor will lead to that. Thousands will die during the conflict, and when it's over, Accacia's past actions after it has conquered a land make it certain that the Blood Emperor will execute every soldier in every army that thought to oppose him. He likes spectacles, he likes to send messages drenched in gratuitous death, and he likes to force immediate subjugation. So thousands more will die after the war is over as well.

To save those thousands, Mustaph has to die instead.

I am furious at him for letting the Blood Emperor sway him. There's no excuse. There isn't one he could make for Grandfather, and there certainly isn't one he could make for me. There are many, many things I can forgive or overlook where the people I hold as kin are concerned, but aligning with the Blood Emperor is not one of them. Not with the very, very personal hate I have toward him. He sent men to slaughter my mother, an innocent pregnant woman, merely to shatter Grandfather. More than the reason he had her killed, the *way* he had her killed was heinous and vicious and debased. It doesn't take multiple men to kill one woman, nor does it take stabbing her thirteen times in her pregnant belly. It wasn't a *hit* he directed. It was a *butchering* of mother and child, and he did it simply as a tantrum over being bested.

And Mustaph has allied himself with that monster.

"I'll kill the Grand Monarch," I say. If Mustaph has found any reason to stand with the Blood Emperor as he perpetuates new atrocities, then there is no other answer I'd give.

He's betrayed Mareen.

He's betrayed the entire Minor Continent.

He's betrayed me.

32

THE STATE-OF-EMERGENCY ADDRESS THAT EVENING comes much too soon, and I wish I would've had one final moment with the Gyidis before I lose them. It isn't Mustaph himself that sends pangs of grief shooting through me whenever I think of the task I'll execute; on his death, I am set. But Enoch, and Akasha, and Nishia . . . I am dealing a devastating blow to them too. I'm about to do to them what those who killed Grandfather did to me, and it isn't something I can successfully shove away and not feel gutted about. *I can't let it change my course.* The repercussions are too severe if I do.

I steel myself toward fulfilling my assignment as I survey my surroundings of dark purple amethi rulizi floors, gold columns, skylight ceilings, and jade walls. Caiman sticks tight to Haymus Rossi's left side. Chance does the same on his right. Greysen, Liim, and another Alpha Praetorian guard his flank. Enzo, Reed, Haynes, Keifer, and I form the same tight arc around Caan. Dannica, two other Gamma members, and two Alpha men stick tight to Brock. It kills me to be trailing one of the men who I know took out my grandfather. I'd rather be burying a blood spike in Zephyr Caan tonight. But I have to *get through* tonight first before I can deal with that.

As we escort the brass across the grand ballroom, we weave through a crowd of Khanaians who have come to hear their Grand Monarch's address in person. The crowd is a mixture of government officials, nobility, and common citizens—though you couldn't surmise that from any difference in garb. All the Khanaians wear either jewel-toned kaffs or flowing dresses of the same finery. The difference between them and us rigid Mareenians in our stiff service uniforms is stark. But the similarities between my physical appearance and all of the brown faces around me stands out just as sharply too. If you consider it alone, I look like I belong among the Khanaians more than my Mareenian brethren. Enoch's offer squirms into my head. It makes me momentarily imagine a different, easier existence among people who would accept *all* of who I am. But I shake the delusion off. That was never a real option for me.

Besides, I've never needed *easier*. And I'm not about to jump at easier when so much is at stake. I'm tough enough to handle whatever strife because I never had *easier*.

I follow the Mareenian leaders to the dais, where the royal family is seated on thrones. Mustaph's is carved of a solid block of jade. His wife's, daughter's, and son's are made from amethi rulizi. Rossi, Caan, and Brock sit in the last three open seats reserved for guests of honor at the base of the dais. We Praetorians who escorted them there take up watch behind their seats. The rest of our joint Gamma-Alpha team is strategically positioned throughout the crowd. We all have nanomics wedged in our ears to communicate with one another so the team can act as my tactical backup when the time comes. Despite its compact size, mine is itchy and I scratch at it. *Your fidgeting has nothing to do with nerves—or guilt that shouldn't be trying to creep up*, I try to tell myself.

The Lytheians haven't departed Khanai yet. The federation's Hearth

Mothers occupy seats at the opposite end of the dais from where the three Tribunes were assigned to sit. Leaders from the Free Microstates have been seated between the Lytheians and Mareenians as obvious buffers. While Lythe turned chilly toward Mareen after the war, relations between it and Khanai remain warm, a thing underscored by the fact that the Hearth Mothers are here in attendance after the morning's debacle. It is no doubt only because of Mustaph. Which strikes me with another realization: if he has betrayed us, then he has betrayed Lythe too. The Lytheian Hearth Mothers would just as quickly bury a blade in Mustaph's heart for supporting the Blood Emperor's campaign. *Why would Mustaph be such a fool?* I get that aiding Accacia is probably some desperate attempt to shield his people from the brunt of the travesties that war with the Blood Emperor will bring, but what he's done isn't the way . . . and from what I know of the Blood Emperor, it is only a temporary fix at best.

Mustaph stands to address the crowd that has gathered in his palace and the millions of citizens who watch from their businesses and homes. Queen Akasha stands at his side. Their hands lace together, presenting a united royal pair. Enoch and Nishia remain seated. The last place I want to look is at the son and daughter and wife whom I'm about to rob of a father and husband by the end of the night. I also can't look away, though, because I wonder: do any of them know yet? Nishia would not. The princess is too young to be embroiled in such politics. But Enoch leads Khanai's armies, and Akasha is more than a consort to a king. The Grand Monarch and Queen rule Khanai as equals, and I can't imagine Mustaph making such a momentous decision and not consulting with his wife and son. The family's warm reception of me since I've arrived is immediately soured, as is Enoch's invitation to make a life in Khanai and among his court.

As I'm coming to this horrible realization, the Crown Prince locks eyes with me. He holds my gaze for the span of three rapid heartbeats that feel like the organ will explode out of my chest. For a wild moment,

I panic that he senses something is amiss. He's smart and astute, but I fend off the paranoid thought—there's no way he knows anything. If he did, he wouldn't be sitting on the dais looking undisturbed with one ankle hooked over a knee. He is the kingdom's Emrir now, its chief warrior and protector. If he had a glimmer of knowledge of my orders tonight, he'd be leaping off the dais, unsheathing the ceremonial sword at his side, and making every attempt to end my life. He'd set aside the fact that we're old friends—just as I'm doing tonight.

A scary prescience skirts down my spine. I don't have the Khanaian sight-gift, but I would swear I did from the strength of the sensation. I stare into that warrior's gleam in Enoch's brown eyes and know for sure that the Crown Prince will not accept anything he is told about his father's death that he does not confirm for himself. Which means this deception can only go so far, and the Tribunal shouldn't be so sure that killing Mustaph will sever Khanai's ties with the Blood Emperor. Then Mareen and the larger Minor Continent will still be fucked, and I will have gained an enemy who has become a king, with a dozen times more of a disposition toward violence and vengeance than his predecessor. It doesn't surprise me that they haven't thought this all the way through—they have proof, but they are also arrogant. It also doesn't change anything for me: Mustaph betrayed me, if nothing else, and for that, I will kill him. If Enoch doesn't automatically charge Accacia with Mustaph's death, I'll just have to deal with the blowback then.

"Khanai has stood strong for five hundred years," proclaims Mustaph at the start of his address. His regal voice commands the attention of everyone in the room, marking him as very much a king among men whom his subjects respect and revere a great deal. Even if the larger kingdom is unaware of his moves for the moment, his people will ultimately follow him to whatever end. "We hail from a people favored by the extraordinary Kissa," he continues. "She bestowed upon our ancestors and this land beauty, wealth, arts, grace, wisdom, foresight, community, and the unbreakable kinship of family. Those gifts to the very first of us helped Khanai blossom into the great nation it is today. I am proud to be a Khanaian. I wouldn't wish to hail from any other people. Khanaians are resilient and strong. Throughout history, some have tried to conquer us. Some have tried to break us. Some have tried to enslave us. Each time Khanai proved unconquerable. Unbreakable. We have thrived, and we will continue to thrive. We will continue to be the incredible kingdom that we are. We all mourn Verne Amari, a brother, friend, and Mareen's late Legatus Commander we were all confident we could trust. I know many of us fear what his death means for our future where covetous, tyrannical Accacia is concerned. I know many of us are afraid given the fact that Accacian forces have amassed in Mareen near our border. I assure you all that my Elders Senate and I are preparing to meet the threat that Accacia's returned presence to the Minor Continent presents. We are already in talks with our allies and will make decisions that are for the greater welfare of this kingdom. Khanai will persevere. Our people have always persevered." It's a laudable, flawless address. His speech rings true and free of deceit. As I listen to it, I wish to the gods it was everything it appears to be, and I come to loathe the Blood Emperor infinitely more than I already do. I detest him for Mustaph aligning with him even more than I hate Mustaph for it.

I hate the Blood Emperor because the Grand Monarch and all of the Gyidis represent even more family that godsdamned piece of shit has taken from me.

THE ADDRESS IS followed by a state dinner, in the Khanaian way of hospitality. It isn't some grand, glitzy party—that would be gauche in the face of war. It's a somber breaking of bread between supposed allies and important guests. Still, the food served is plentiful and there is bountiful honeywine from Khanai's southern vineyards and tinnu spirits from its northern agatru farms. I decline the clear tinnu a passing server offers me and the flutes of amber honeywine. I eat meagerly. The rest of my

Praetorian team, seated at the same long table as me, behaves the same. The Khanaians, Lytheians, and those from the Free Microstates at the tables around us indulge in the traditional dishes and drinks to their fancy. Their spirits are less grave than ours. Their moods less dark. I'm sure they see it as a function of our nation being the one currently under siege, while Accacia hasn't yet marched on their lands. But I know it's because we're about to escalate this war to an even greater height.

Grimly, I think perhaps the Blood Emperor learned from his past mistakes. With this new strategy, he could focus his legions on Mareen and decimate the Republic first, possibly keeping Lythe and a good portion of the Free Microstates from rushing to aid us until war is already at their doorstep. Out of spite, the rest of the continent could think to let Mareen drown in its own repugnant blood then unite to oppose the Blood Emperor afterward. Especially if Mareen hasn't relayed the information about iridium yet; our would-be allies have no additional compelling reason to look beyond old resentments and new insults. The Tribunal might not have fabricated Mustaph's guilt to further their aims at a Mareenian empire, but I still think they are playing a game of massive expansion—the secrecy about iridium and our behavior at the summit all point to that. The Tribunal's schemes may bite them, and all of Mareen, in the ass. If the Blood Emperor's plan is one of divide and conquer, we're playing right into it.

Then again, we did that the moment Grandfather died.

Rossi has left his seat to stand beside Mustaph. His hand rests on the back of the Grand Monarch's chair. He speaks with the stiff-backed Grand Monarch in hushed tones. It doesn't appear heated, but it doesn't appear amicable either. I shake my head. If the Tribunal Council was comprised of better men, things wouldn't be such a mess. A caustic smile twists my lips when I think of how precisely true that cutting fact is. If the Tribunal Council was comprised of better men, Grandfather wouldn't be dead and *everything* would be different in this moment.

Enoch stares at me in concern from his seat at the head table, catching the expression I stupidly let steal onto my face. I wipe it. The same uneasiness under his scrutiny that assaulted me earlier returns. His focus is pulled away by his father calling for his attention. Rossi steps away from Mustaph's side and Enoch replaces him. The Grand Monarch says something to Enoch, then stands, excuses himself from the table, and departs the ballroom. It is late enough in the dinner that it is acceptable for him to leave while guests remain in attendance if the Queen stays behind to host. Enoch turns back to me, and my face gives nothing away this time. He descends the dais and approaches my table.

"My father would like a word in private if you care to talk with him," he says into my ear. "Don't worry about the Mareenian leadership. It's been cleared." With impeccable Khanaian manners, he offers me his arm.

I nod. So that is what Mustaph and Rossi were speaking about. Of course Rossi obliged. I swallow past the lump in my throat because I know what comes next.

"Are you staying?" I ask Enoch, needing to figure out a way around the hurdle if he is. The eventuality may come, but I don't want to have to fight or harm him *this* night. Grappling with Mustaph is enough.

His eyes travel to his mother, who has a growing line of young women starting to crowd her side of the table. "No," he says, long-suffering. "My time is being hijacked for the remainder of the night."

Thank the gods for one small grace.

I stand and link my arm with Enoch's, stealing a moment to snuff out my anxiousness. I fail in my efforts. My head throbs in time with my hammering pulse. The stolen blood spike strapped to my hip grows weightier and turns searing, corrosive, and wrong against my bare skin.

Pull it together, I command myself. *Weave a flawless deception like you would if he were anyone else so you can get this job done.* I can do this. The academy trained me how to complete such an op. I paste a teasing smile on my face and slip into the less-morose Ikenna Enoch has known for years. I become the Ikenna who would tease him mercilessly and who had little worries. "Lead the way, *Your Highness.*"

"I don't think you've ever condescended to call me by any title a day in your life." He chuckles, brightening at the old version of me. His brown eyes dance and seem to say *I miss you.* I ignore it, as well as the guilt that threatens to trample me at letting him lead me away from the table and out of the ballroom so I can end his father's life.

Gods, why is tonight proving to be so hard to get through? My anger at Mustaph was supposed to make this easy. But anger is only carrying me so far; it is not the bastion of strength it normally is.

We're at war *with Accacia,* I remind myself. If my anger isn't enough, this fact should be. I use it to shake off any reservations about doing my damn job. I slip fully into the role of the longtime family friend that I need to exploit if I'm pulling this off.

"You're correct," I drawl. "But now that I'm a Praetorian, I absolutely insist you need to stop calling me Ikenna and call me *Praetorian Amari.* I enjoy the ring to it."

"You were always an immodest pain," he grumbles as we walk down halls I can navigate without him as a guide.

"And you always loved me for it." The bravado starts to come easier. "You're too humble, princeling. You should be more like me."

He feigns a shudder. "The world would implode if there were too many more people like you."

I jab my elbow into his side. "Watch it."

We turn a corner and come to a pair of aquamarine doors. I do not have another attack of conscience as Enoch pushes them open.

Mustaph stands in front of a throne identical to the jade one he sat atop at the address. "Go," he says to his son. "Leave us so we can speak."

Before he leaves, Enoch turns to me. "Consider my offer from yesterday," he urges. "You really can make a better life here in Khanai away from the pig's shit that is Mareen."

So that's what this is about. Mustaph seeks to sway me where his son did not.

"I will consider it."

Enoch smiles at my lie and leaves.

"Ikenna. Come. Embrace an old man and let us talk." Mustaph's voice retains its kingly quality. But it's also warmer, gentler, and more fatherly when addressing me in the intimacy of the throne room. He holds his arms out wide without a thought to me being a threat.

The blood spike at my hip grows cumbersome and accusingly heavy. I walk over to him and let him wrap his arms around me. He kisses my brow. "Kissa's Grace be upon you, child."

The blood spike is in my hand before Mustaph pulls back from me. His eyes flash with surprise, anguish, and crushing denial when he spies the lethal weapon. I'm a coward who diverts her gaze. I stare at the smooth skin of his neck instead. I slash the blood spike across his throat before he can shout in alarm.

Mustaph's death is quick. I pay him that kindness.

I also pay him the respect of stooping down to close his eyes before I leave his corpse sprawled on the throne room's floor. But as I kneel, the blood pouring from his slashed throat shimmers. It reverses direction, and it and all the blood that soaks the floor is sucked back into the wound. His body shimmers like the blood did, and Mustaph's form and face shifts into that of a stranger.

What the hell is going on?

33

SCATHING EYES THAT ARE LIGHT ochre instead of dark brown open, lips free of the lines of age curl back from teeth, and the unfamiliar man lying on the floor stands up.

I scramble backward. What I am witnessing can't be real. Only the most powerful blood-gifted can shift shape, and you don't find those types of individuals outside of Accacia.

"Who are you?" I whisper.

The stranger takes a step toward me. He moves with the fluid grace of a predator with prey caught in its crosshairs. Still on my ass, I scoot back more. "My name is Ajani, and I serve His Imperial Majesty of the Principal and Minor Continents, the Divine Blood Emperor of Iludu. The empire thanks you for your service, *Praetorian*. You've just won us a valuable ally and quite probably the war."

My brain refuses to process what I hear and see. My eyes rove over the tall man, whose face bears handsome features on the side of youth. He has a powerful build that skews lean. He's a shade lighter than me in complexion—his skin a medium-brown copper instead of dark copper—although that's a marking Accacians can't technically be identified by. The people of the empire display a broad spectrum of skin tones, from the porcelain and olive hues of Mareen to the ebonies and golden browns in Khanai and Lythe. It's the clothes he wears that brand him as indisputably Accacian. He no longer dons a Grand Monarch's garb. He sports a crisp uniform that's one ominous tide of black except for the neck-high scarlet collar. That notorious garment freezes my pulse. It's the uniform of the Blood Emperor's Red Order, his fiercely loyal inner circle of merciless warlords. There's seven of them, and next to the Blood Emperor himself they are the most powerful blood-gifted in Iludu. Their liege handpicked each of them to serve him because of that fact. There were several chilling instances during the last war where the seven of them leveled whole cities without needing the backup of a contingent of soldiers.

And now I'm alone with one.

Every drop of air is squeezed from the room. Undiluted terror drenches me.

"Get up," the warlord says. "Cowering on the floor like a dog is unbecoming of any blood-gifted."

I blink up at him, too shell-shocked to do anything else.

"Stand," he hisses. "If I have to tell you again, I won't afford you the respect of doing it on your own."

I stare at the floor where he lay with his throat slit appearing as Mustaph moments ago. There are only specks of blood on the gold marble now. Most of it flowed back into his throat. A throat whose flesh has knitted closed. The brown skin is smooth and completely unmarred. He healed a mortal wound in seconds.

"Dammit, I said stand." Pressure clamps around my mind, asserting a will upon me that isn't my own. Robbed of control, my body hauls itself to its feet without my conscious intent.

The bastard doesn't release the steel grip he has over my mind once he's made me do what he wants. His gaze cuts down the length of me, skewering. "That was too easy." His lips curl back in a snarl. "You're a disgrace to Amaka's gift. I shouldn't have been able to do that to you at all."

"Release me," I growl. He snorts at the demand, retaining absolute control over my muscles. But he's left me my thoughts, awareness of what's happening, and the ability to speak. It's a thing that takes skill and practice beyond what I've learned.

"Make me. Ah, that's right, you can't. You're a near fully evolved blood-gifted adult, and yet you have the power of an infant. Children in Accacia can block a bloodlink." He says it like he's giving me a lesson while chastising me for having to give it at all.

"Go to hell." Any fear is gone. Pissed-off rage replaces it. I'm staring at the enemy. A member of the pack of dogs the Blood Emperor sent to butcher my mother, who killed millions on the Minor Continent, and who are on their way to do so again. "What are you doing here?"

"I already told you that. Keep up. You are a trained soldier, Ikenna Amari. Are you not? Supposedly the best and most fearsome your Republic has to offer. You shouldn't need to reask questions you've already been handed the answer to."

I don't want to believe what he implies, and yet, all reason points to a single disastrous conclusion. "This was a setup. You wanted us to try to kill Mustaph."

"The Tribunal Council is full of imbeciles who had their own greedy reasons for wanting the Grand Monarch's death. While his Elders Senate understood that readily, Mustaph needed a bit more convincing." His smile is guileful. "The Grand Monarch hadn't allied with Accacia yet. In fact, his pesky principles turned *his* eventual assent into a tedious affair. He needed solid proof first that Mareen is the greater threat and that it would break faith with Khanai at first strife.

"And Mareen—through you—has kindly provided that."

The Elders Senate. That's who was in league with Accacia. That's who let the Blood Empire cross over into Mareen. Not Mustaph. The horrific truth leaves me nauseous and plunges me into a thousand hell-pits from guilt. The comms with Mustaph's seal . . . they were a plant. Mareen and I were able to authenticate them because Khanai's Elders Senate made sure they looked authentic. Mustaph was never at fault, and if this hadn't been a setup, I would've killed an innocent man.

The real Mustaph and Enoch sweep into the throne room with a dozen palace guards.

I flinch at the deeply wounded lines that crinkle both of their faces. The realization that I've been released from the bloodlink is eclipsed by the apology to Mustaph that sticks in my throat. It would be an insult to utter it now. It'd also be a joke. I've already carried out my orders to kill him. It just so happened it wasn't the real Mustaph whose throat I slit. On the heels of my shame comes indignation though—and a renewed sting of betrayal. "The Tribunal was partially right in their suspicions," I level at both father and son. "The two of you *did* help to set us up tonight." And evoking a much more personal hurt, they worked with the Blood Emperor's warlord to set me up. "*Gods*, how could you have even been entertaining thoughts of aligning with this *monster?*"

"This monster didn't try to slit my throat," Mustaph says.

"It's amazing how easily you believe their lies. You are half-Accacian, girl," the warlord says. "The Republic and Verne Amari have brainwashed you well."

"There was no brainwashing needed. History and the atrocities Accacia committed paint the necessary picture of what you are, not the words of the Republic."

"Why, Ikenna?" The soft probe comes from Mustaph. "Your actions are that of a woman I do not recognize. Why would you let the Republic use you to kill me? Verne would have never done such a thing so hastily. He had more principles than that. Principles he instilled in you."

I do not shrivel under the admonishment. In fact, I am getting sick of men admonishing me tonight. "As you said, you don't know the woman I've become. You have no idea who she is. All evidence pointed to the fact that you were guilty. So I made a decision and acted with expediency. Khanai might not be at war with Accacia, but Mareen is, and I did exactly what I should have done if the deception *you* allowed the Blood Empire to set up were really true."

"You should have come to me first," Mustaph responds. "I had hoped you would accept the offer of Khanaian citizenship and choose the alternative to the repugnant task the Republic handed you. I'd hoped you'd choose us over them." His eyes tighten in sorrow. "Why do you insist on remaining among those people with Verne gone? Be wiser, child. They don't deserve your loyalty or your service, and they didn't deserve his."

I don't truly owe him an explanation when he has an Accacian warlord standing in his throne room, but everything he says leaves my emotions rubbed raw and the wounds of losing Grandfather and everything that came afterward are ripped wide open, making the truth cascade out of me. "It's not about choosing sides. I stay in Mareen and I serve it—for now—*for* Grandfather. To avenge him. The Tribunal Council murdered him, and he deserves justice. Being a Praetorian gets me that."

"If you knew about Verne, and that is why you are still among Mareen's ranks, I wish you would've confided that in me too. You really needn't have stayed. We could've worked toward addressing the Tribunals grave offense together." The real Mustaph appears weary. Rundown. Tired. He looks to have aged a decade or two beyond his sixty-eight years.

"You couldn't have done a thing. You have no power in Mareen. Not for what I want. I want everybody with a hand in killing him dead."

He motions to the Blood Emperor's warlord. "I have more power on the Minor Continent than you think."

"So bloodthirsty," the warlord murmurs. "And eager for vengeance. That is your Accacian half," he says approvingly.

I don't respond to his taunt. I finish with the rest of what I have to say to Mustaph. "Since you brought up the subject of Grandfather and principles, *how is it principled* for you to stand aside and allow a man you two fought against together to gain a foothold on this continent? A man who will indiscriminately slaughter us? How is that honorable?"

"Khanai should've sided with us during the last war," the Accacian supplies. "The Republic tried to enslave the Grand Monarch's people. He should have never let Verne Amari sway his decision."

"Shut up!" I shout at the Accacian. I'm done hearing him speak. I turn to Mustaph.

"But Grandfather *did* convince you. Because he was right, and you know it. Just because he is dead, that doesn't mean you've forgotten why you chose to listen to him. Accacia knows no honor. Why would you give over your kingdom to a madman and a tyrant? Khanai did resist enslavement once. Your nation vowed to never see those conditions again. How is yielding your sovereignty to the Blood Emperor any different this time?"

"Because we are not relinquishing our sovereignty. The Blood Emperor has extended the same offer we were made before. Yes, Khanai will be a part of the empire, but it will be a tribute state that retains its independence and its own king, not an annexed territory."

"And you *believe* that? You question my actions and motivations, but now who is the one being naïve?" Mustaph flinches at the charge. I press on. "What is different this time? You turned it down once. It couldn't have been that appealing then if you did."

The weariness about Mustaph dies. Deep-seated anger replaces it. "I sided with Mareen because Verne offered up a vision of a tolerable and eventually better Republic. But then that Republic killed him and the Blood Emperor has carried proof that Mareen can never be what Verne envisioned. The Republic will always perpetrate harm against our people. It's been almost twenty years—can you honestly say relations between Mareen and Khanai have gotten any better? That the Republic thinks of us with any more respect than they did in the past?

Look at how your leaders acted these past few days—do you think that's something new? *They sent you to kill me.*" He shakes his head. "No. The only thing that's new is that Verne is now dead, and so any check on the Republic's disdain and aggression toward us is now gone."

Mustaph strides to stand in front of me. He cups my cheek. "I do not lay blame with you for what you attempted to do. The Republic is a cesspool. It corrupts as surely as it is rotten. Denounce it. If you want vengeance, then have it. But there is another way than remaining in that wretched place that never extended genuine love or acceptance to you or Verne. Consider how much it's taken you to be where you are today in Mareen: a dead grandfather and the horrors of the Praetorian Trials—oh yes, we know all about the rigors of that assassin factory. You joined them so you could find out who killed Verne. Haven't you done that? So why not join an army that will bring the Republic to its knees and see every Tribune General dead. Have your vengeance *that* way."

I back out of his embrace. "Because it still means joining the Blood Empire. And the whole Republic did not kill my grandfather. Not even all of the Tribune Generals did. I don't wish to see all of Mareen shattered and millions massacred for the crimes of a few. I want justice, not slaughter."

"Yet you would kill my father for the crimes of a few. How many millions do you think would have ended up dead because of that action?" Enoch asks as he lays a hand on Mustaph's arm. He steps between me and his father. Grief tangles with fury in his stare. "You were a friend of Khanai," he says to me. "A friend of this family." His hand grips the pommel of the ceremonial sword at his side. He unsheathes it to fulfill his duty as Emrir and execute me right there in the throne room for attempted murder against his king.

"No. She will live." Ajani's pronouncement is a command. The decree of a general used to having his word be undisputed law.

It surprises me. It surprises Enoch, too, because he doesn't immediately stand down.

"Your kingdom may have been granted sovereignty, but do not forget that you all fall under the Blood Emperor's authority when certain and specific matters necessitate him exercising it."

Enoch bristles at the cool reminder. "The deal was Khanai will govern itself."

"It will. However, the girl is blood-gifted and thus falls under my liege's dominion. That means she's under my dominion by extension. Her life is mine to spare or claim."

An old alarm fills me at hearing the secret I've kept all my life recited so plainly.

"How can you know that?" I ask the question I should've asked all along.

"Blood calls to blood," the warlord returns. "It's another facet of your gift you'd be aware of if you weren't so ignorant of its depths. Though I must admit there is a raw potency to what you possess that is staggering even in a dampened state." He looks me over without the rebuke of last time. There's a covetousness to his leer that makes my skin crawl. Without warning, the creepy reverence switches to rage. He lunges at me, and I brace for the assault. Instead of a blow, he seizes my shoulders and demands, "Tell me what the Mareenians are using to dilute your gift."

"I don't know what the hell you're talking about!" I struggle against his hold. "Let me the fuck go!"

"You're lying," he says, shaking me in anger. "We know they've developed a new weapon, and we know they're confident it works against the blood-gifted. I assume that confidence comes from you being the test case."

"Test case? How could I be a test case? Nobody knows about me." I wrench away, horrified and sick at the implications of his accusations. Grandfather and I were the only people in Mareen who knew of my gift.

Except . . . that's not true.

Selene knows, and when I told her, she wasn't as stunned or disturbed as it would have been normal for her to be. I was grateful and glad for it then because she was my best friend. I didn't think of it as suspicious. But what if the reason for Selene's easy acceptance is that she already knew? That, somehow, the Tribunal Council discerned my blood-gift, and they took advantage of having me within their grasp to test out iridium. I'd used it enough times for the lodestone to have detected it. Yet I was never called out.

If Rhysien had already discovered iridium's benefits, then he had the perfect reason to kill Grandfather and erase any opposition to the war he wanted. Mareenians are a warlike people. But they are also about status—power and wealth. I can't think of one Tribune General who would shy away from a confrontation they were positive Mareen could win. Nor can I see them enter into a battle where they might put all they have gained since the last war at risk. Furthermore, my grandfather would have then been the one guilty of treason, not his murderers, for harboring a blood-gifted granddaughter. The Tribunal would have eagerly wanted to remove him to get to me, and not one of them—Brock included, whose stance on the war clearly has changed—would have had qualms about executing him. Regardless of how close he and Grandfather were, Mareenian hatred of Accacians is too great for Brock to have looked beyond me being blood-gifted. Which means he *was* a part of the plot and it wasn't just a faction of the Tribunes who conspired to kill my grandfather. Likely all of the snakes sanctioned Grandfather's death, including Rossi. He might have wished to avoid a war under ordinary circumstances, but the Gamma team didn't know about iridium and me when they cleared him of guilt.

Yet it still doesn't answer Ajani's question. Because if they have given me iridium, I'm not aware of it, especially since I've been able to use my blood-gift numerous times. Then, there's the matter of Rossi being a part of it not adding up where I'm concerned if I really think about it. If the Tribunals' aim was for me to be a test case, why the hell would he instruct Caiman to kill me? Unless . . . the primary goal wasn't for me to die. The blood-gifted's staggering healing ability means you'd need to also test the bounds of how susceptible to harm but resistant to death an enemy combatant would be. That would be crucial data to have before iridium is used in warfare. The possibility makes me their lab rat in the truest sense. Humiliation rips through me.

Dissatisfied with my denial, Ajani hijacks my mind to pry answers from me. Under the compulsion, I divulge the things I know—iridium is the weapon Mareen seeks to use against Accacia via its release of poisonous vapors that pass into the blood. My info may be limited, but it's critical intel the empire didn't have before and can now use to figure out how to neutralize an attack.

"Bring me the Mareenian leaders," Ajani orders Enoch.

Enoch leaves and returns with more guards marching a detained Rossi, Caan, and Brock into the throne room.

Where are their guards?

I look at Enoch, who stands there impassively.

Of course—this was a trap. It takes me a second to remember that. Which means they were prepared to take the Tribunes, probably from the moment I walked away with Mustaph . . . I mean, Ajani.

Worry rips through me at the thought of my friends . . . and Alpha.

Again, I look at Enoch, and he gives away nothing.

As I consider my fellow Praetorians' fate, Ajani rips the full extent of iridium's effect as a bioweapon from his captives. His interrogation also confirms everything I've surmised. The whole Council has known about my gift since four months prior to Grandfather's death. Rhysien knew before that. He discerned it first and informed the rest.

I stare Brock down. "You helped kill him, then you manipulated me to take part in the trials." Nausea roils through me. I'm wounded, but I'm also fucking angry. He used me and exposed me to conditions where my life was constantly in danger and my blood-gift was activated in the presence of the iridium. And along with that, he used Grandfather against me, not telling me he'd been murdered until *after* I told Brock I wasn't entering the trials on Commencement Eve. Had I never told him that, I would've never known. But he needed to get me to change my mind, and that was a sure way to do it. I'm positive it's why he intimated that Reed was his chief suspect. Because Reed was also an officer for the trials, and Brock knew that naming him gave me a target for my grief and anger to immediately go after. He might've even known about Reed investigating him and figured he might get lucky and actually kill Reed and take care of that potential thorn.

No, not just a thorn. Or rather, not the only thorn. Because Reed has all of Gamma loyal to him, and that's a powerful weapon to want to render inoperable. But a good portion of the massive labourii class was upset over Grandfather's death, and that was a force that could have been rallied against the Tribunals too. If you throw me into the mix, I had the Khanaian royals on my side—so maybe Mustaph wasn't so far off base when he said he could've helped if I came to him about Grandfather.

But you know, hindsight is a bitch and a half and all that.

I focus once more on Brock in front of me, whose stare is vacant from Ajani having captured his mind and stolen his awareness. "Release him," I say. I want him free so he can face his treachery with full knowledge that I've found him out.

"Do as she asks," Mustaph prompts.

"No. I'm not finished with them. And I don't take orders from anyone but the Blood Emperor, let alone a little girl."

I rankle at that, and Mustaph does too—*so much for remaining sovereign, huh, Uncle?*—but Ajani nonchalantly compels me to ignore my own anger. I fight it enough to still be mad, but I say no more.

Mustaph turns to me with compassion that I don't deserve. "Do you see how corrupt the entire Republic is? It must be reduced to ashes. That is why Khanai stepped aside and allowed the empire passage onto the Minor Continent and over Mareen's borders. Yes, many will die. But many will also die if Mareen believes it has gained the upper hand with iridium. Its vapors may not only affect the blood-gifted. It may adversely affect all of the Pantheon-blessed. They may use the advantage it provides them to fight off the empire and then train their sights on Khanai once again. There was a time where the Republic sought to do what Accacia seeks. It wanted to annex the rest of us and install itself as the supreme power. Mareen has never afforded those they consider akulu or not pure-blooded a modicum of humanity. The Republic possesses a rot from the inside out that cannot simply be excised like Verne sought."

Mustaph doesn't lie, and everything he says confirms so many of my original doubts. The more I hear, the more I see the three men from the Tribunal spilling their secrets, the more I'm unable to curb the heinous thought that I *would* like to see the entire Republic reduced to ashes. It betrayed Grandfather. It betrayed me. It has used me against my knowledge as a lab rat, and would have just as easily killed me— either outcome was acceptable.

Because I am akulu, and in Mareen, that means I don't have worth.

"Ask them how they did it," Mustaph says to Ajani. "How were they able to use the iridium on Ikenna without her knowing?"

This time, Ajani obliges the request. But I answer the question before one of the Tribunal speaks. "They used Selene Rhysien, Sutton Rhysien's daughter and my best friend." I grasp the legacy pendant around my neck. I've worn it the entire time since Selene gave it to me at the start of the trials. I yank it off, my skin burning like a noose had been fitted around it. The pendant has to be the source. After the Accursed tore it off in the forest, my power that had been depleted flooded me again. The same thing happened the night of my fight with Chance after Reed took it off me.

Ajani snatches it from me before I can examine it closely. He palms it for mere seconds before his lips curl back in a snarl.

The confirmation of Selene's further guilt carves my insides apart. The anguish manifests as physical stabs of pain that make me clutch my abdomen.

"I imagine such a betrayal cuts deep," the Accacian bastard drawls. He watches me and drinks in the anguish I can't conceal.

I try to get it together to break down in private later, but the devastation is too much to stuff back inside.

"You seek vengeance," he says. "I can hand it to you." A blood spike forms in his right hand without him ever needing to cut himself. One minute the skin of his exposed palm is smooth. The next, a thin, red line appears across it and the blood that flows free hardens and shapes itself into the signature Accacian weapon. He hands it to me. I test its weight. "You can kill these three men if you like, and you can have the lives of the remaining eleven Tribunes. It will be easy with my aid. All of their lives were coming to an end soon anyway. It doesn't matter to me by whose hand they die."

The temptation is almost too great. I put myself through hell to get to this point. I'd been beaten, stabbed, shot, assaulted, almost eaten (a few times), *thrown off a cliff*, and called every racist slur those privileged idiots could come up with. My family was murdered and I was used as an experiment, all to end up here, in front of liars.

And now my enemy offers the exact thing I demanded from Brock. The thing I entered the trials for and swore I'd do whatever it took to achieve. Then Ajani adds the price: "Renounce the Republic. Pledge your allegiance to me. Fight with Accacia against Mareen. Amaka's gift in you is immense; you would be a valuable asset to the empire."

The offer should make me cringe. It should not be tempting one bit. Not after how greatly I condemned Mustaph for the same thing. I should spit in the Accacian warlord's face, then try my damnedest to kill him, choosing death at least while fighting. But . . .

"I need time," I say.

He looks at me oddly, as if not expecting that was an option. Maybe it's not, but I try for it anyway. Everything that is Mareenian in me rebels at the statement. But everything that makes me an akulu according to the Republic boils with rage, bitterness, and a howling need to avenge not only Grandfather but myself. I was already pissed and disillusioned with the Republic before. Now, I am fucking enraged. The same bloodlust I felt in the ring with Chance rampages through me. It warps my thoughts. It twists my anger into this hideous, misshapen thing that awakens some chilling version of me who gives consideration to what Ajani offers. I flicker between the Ikenna I know—the Ikenna I've always been—and the ghastly, monstrous form of myself I've long feared I might one day become. The latter Ikenna loathes the Blood Emperor but sees the advantage of allying with him to achieve the greater aim, to seize the violence she wishes to visit. I shudder, terrified by the threat of a shift in the fabric of who I am—of who Grandfather raised me to be.

For all that, though . . .

"I am done being a pawn," I tell Ajani. "I'm done being told things I'm just supposed to trust on faith and faith alone.

"You would make demands of me?" Ajani asks.

"I just ask that if I am to do this, I am to do it because it's real. Not some trick being played on me by their iridium or your compulsion or whatever the hell else there is that has been manipulating me. I want to do this because I'm the one who *can* do this. Who *should* do this."

I'm rambling, I know, but somehow, Ajani seems to understand the passion behind it.

"Release them from the compulsion," I demand of him. "I want them lucid and coherent, and I want them to stare down their deaths and see it coming." They deserve more. They deserve to be fucking tortured. They deserve for their deaths to be drawn out and messy. But I'll have to accept efficiency, and part of that is the fact that they need to know what is happening.

"As you wish, Daughter of Amaka."

I should wince when he calls me that, but in the moment, I don't.

The glassiness clouding the Mareenians' eyes vanishes.

Rossi's is replaced with lividness. "You," he snarls. "You are a soldier of the Republic. Your duty is to Mareen. You are a part of my Praetorian Guard. Get me out of this situation."

My laugh is hoarse. Venomous.

"How convenient of you to regard me as belonging to the Republic when it suits you. Yes, I am a soldier. Yes, I have a duty. Yes, I am a Praetorian—in training, at least. But my Republic is supposed to have a duty back to me. It is supposed to love me back. Accept me back. *Protect* me. Not use me and kill my grandfather." Under the haze of the bloodlust, I don't drive the blood spike into his chest. I use it to slash my own palm so I can form a spike of my own. His eyes widen as he sees my gift in full form. They widen more as I drive my blood spike into Rossi's heart, using the blood he and the Republic detests so much to kill him.

Caan begs for his life when I stand in front of him next. I have nothing to say as I slit his throat.

When it's Brock's turn, he hangs his head. "It was a matter of Mareen's best interest, Ikenna. Keeping such a secret about you was a liability. Verne should have divulged it as a true Mareenian. We quelled Pantheon blessings from our population for a reason. Verne threatened the stability of Mareen."

I drive the blood spike through Brock's right knee, and he stumbles to the ground.

"How's that for stability?"

"I-I hope you believe me when I say I always saw of you as one of my own daughters."

I stab him in the eye. He bleeds out slowly.

"Until you saw me for what I am."

He's weeping blood, a pitiful mess. He had all the control. More, he had my trust. In some ways, he even had some of my love, as a friend of Grandfather's.

And for all that love, I drive my blood spike through his heart.

"Three down, eleven left," Ajani croons. "Take my offer. It's a good one."

I hear his words, and fresh off the executions, I'm tempted once more. But a war is being waged within me. There are so many knotted, gnarled emotions that are impossible to unravel on the spot. The Tribunal might be reprehensible, and the Republic might be rotten, but I have friends in Mareen, and siding with Accacia and Khanai means I am siding against them. Enzo. Reed. Dannica. Haynes. The memories of Zayne and Dex and Bex. They serve the Republic and are bound to the Tribunal's will. They are the people I'd fight in a war. Then there's the matter of my mother. The Blood Empire murdered her. It tried to murder me as a fetus. Those actions it perpetrated make it no better than Mareen.

I'm not sure I can do it. What would it make me, what would I truly transform into, if I do take Ajani up on his offer in full and side with the man who will massacre a slew of others with the same brutality he directed at my family?

"Where is my team?" I ask, stricken by a fresh horror when considering the Blood Empire's ruthlessness. "Are they alive?" Rossi, Caan, and Brock had to be kept alive to interrogate about the iridium. There is no reason to have kept any of Gamma or Alpha alive, but I have to at least hope.

"They've been compelled to a holding cell by one of my people," says Ajani.

I breathe a little easier hearing that, but then dissect what he just said. "There's more of you here?"

"There's a few," he says with a noncommittal shrug. "We need a home base on the continent."

I turn to the Grand Monarch and Prince after receiving that bit of knowledge, shaking my head at their idiocy. "You don't even have the illusion of self-rule. You have occupation."

"You should be more worried about the team you asked after than my affairs," Enoch returns. "Because they will not get the same pardon you have been given for their collusion to kill my father. Their executions take place tonight."

"They were acting under orders," I say. "They are soldiers, just like me. They had no more will to go against the Tribunal Council than the tribunal members had when Ajani compelled them!"

Enoch's face is pitiless. "They chose their profession, and even crimes committed in times of war must be answered for."

I throw that righteous conviction back in his face. "Is the Blood Emperor going to answer for his crimes from the last war? You can't believe that principle so much if you so easily bend a knee for that murderer."

"How can you care to ask after them after all you have learned?"

"Because you are doing the same thing the Republic is doing: lumping everyone together as if living in a certain city or being a certain color is answer enough of their intent. I know, for one thing, that my team is different." Maybe I can't say the same about Alpha cohort, but Gamma cohort *is* different. Enzo would've frozen to death alongside me in an ice crevasse. Reed stepped into my bar fight with Radson, and he was the only person I could trust to patch me up after Chance shot me. Dannica and Haynes are different too.

"Maybe the young do not perpetuate certain prejudices of the old, but how different will they remain when they learn you are blood-gifted?" Enoch's question slices into me as if he's driven his ceremonial sword into my chest. I think I know the answer, and it leaves me destroyed. Selene found out about my blood-gift and only pretended to accept me. I have no assurances the others will be tolerant. Not with the horrors that blood-gifted legions inflicted upon Mareen.

However, they are still my team, and I don't want to see them die. I *will not* see them die. They did not walk into the throne room. I did. They did not slit the Grand Monarch's throat. I did. I'm the one who deserves to pay with my life for the crime. I won't let Ajani spare me while Enoch executes them.

"If my team dies, you lose me," I tell the man exercising so much effort to turn me to his side. *Amaka's gift in you is immense; you would be a valuable asset to the empire.* Although he threw that out casually enough, I saw the open lust and intent. His liege is notorious for collecting those with a strong blood-gift. He wants to present me as a prize to His Imperial Majesty.

"What makes you think that matters to me?"

I roll my eyes. "It's too late to bluff. You've already made your interest clear. If you want me, fine. You've got me. *If* my team is spared. I want full pardons issued to them by the Grand Monarch *and* the Crown Prince. Then I want them to get on a stealth jet and make it home to Mareen alive."

Ajani holds up a hand at Enoch's refusal. The Crown Prince grinds his teeth. He says nothing, however.

Ajani sighs. "You would have us send our enemy back so that they may try to kill us later."

"I ask that they do not die simply because of these three men here."

He shakes his head, as if my words are those of a child. "They will all die in the end, too, regardless of where they happen to be." Ajani shrugs. "But fine—I will oblige you in this roundabout way of getting to that end. I must say, though, that your tenderness for Mareenians is one we need to strip from you. To achieve that aim with expediency, I will grant your terms if you accept mine."

I brace for whatever is coming.

"First, you will swear allegiance to me at once. Then, you can set your team free and see them safely aboard a jet. As you're saving their lives, you must also deliver the news that their leaders are dead by your hand and that you bear Amaka's gift. Once they have been apprised of who you fully are, I assure you they will no longer harbor the love for you that you insist on retaining for them. Do we have a deal?"

I try hard not to let his words have their intended affect. It is a failed effort. Each one strikes me dead-center with debilitating force.

He is right about what will happen once they learn I am blood-gifted. But in this, I don't have a choice. I was trained as a killer, and yet I was trained to kill the enemy. My friends—for as long as that lasts—are not my enemy.

"We do."

34

ENOCH SHOWS ME TO THE Prisoners' Keep. The bars of my team's cell are the indigo blue of Khanaian steel that can't be breached, broken, or cracked.

"Blasters up." The twenty-four palace guards who escort us follow their Emrir's orders. "If the Mareenians twitch wrong," Enoch says, "shoot them all." He slashes a look at me. "If Ikenna gets caught in the crossfire . . . *accidents happen*. The emperor will have to understand. Please do something stupid," he says to my crew. "Give me a good reason to kill you and her." His words are glacial.

"Unlock the cell," I demand.

"How about you tell them your little secret first? That is the deal."

This callous facet of him is a version I've never seen. Then again, I never tried to kill his father before. If I wasn't clear on where I stood with him, I am glass clear now.

"Amari." The measured voice is Reed's. "What's going on? What secret?"

I turn away from Enoch and his rightful anger to face my team behind the bars. Reed's narrowed, distrustful gaze cuts me to the core. He isn't wrong for it. Neither are the other Praetorians who gaze at me in a similar fashion. They're behind bars while I've entered the keep free of restraints by my childhood friend's side. I'd be assuming betrayal too. "Mustaph is not dead," I inform them. "He didn't allow the Accacians to cross Khanai. His Elders Senate did. Accacia turned the senate to their side, and Mustaph was only considering allying with the empire. The soldier who got captured, the comms with Mustaph's seals—this whole night was a trap to help him make a decision. I did as I was ordered, but the Mustaph I killed wasn't the real Grand Monarch. It was an Accacian warlord wearing his face. They detained the brass. The warlord compelled everything they knew about iridium out of them."

I say this in a rush before anyone can stop me. If the Gamma-Alpha squad does make it out of the Jade Palace alive, they need to carry that info back to Mareen. The Tribunal is comprised of monsters, but the Blood Emperor of Accacia is the greater fiend—of that, I don't think I'll ever be convinced otherwise. He needs to be stopped first, and I can deal with them being monsters after that.

"What do you mean by they *detained* the brass?" Caiman steps to the front of the group. His hands wrap around the blue steel bars. "Where is my father? What did they do to him?"

"Yes, Ikenna," Enoch says smoothly, "what did *we* do to him?"

"He's dead," I say. "So are the other two." I don't relay further details just yet. If I confess to killing the Tribunal right now, it'll be more difficult to lead my fellow Praetorians out of the palace.

Chance spits through the bars, and the wad of saliva lands on my shoes. "I knew you were a good-for-nothing akulu whore. You're a traitor. I bet you alerted the Khanaians to the assassination and conspired with them to lure us into a trap."

Enoch reaches through and pulls Chance against the bars . . . and then punches him in the face. Bones crunch and blood flies.

"That is not a word we use here, Praetorian scum."

It's almost comical to see Enoch punch Chance over hearing the word "akulu." For a second, I think to clap him on the back and tell him thank you. But then I remember we're not friendly anymore and he'd like to punch me in the face too—or lop off my head altogether.

Chance spits again, and this time it's red. "I told you all—she's a traitor."

"Kenna wouldn't do that," Dannica says without thought. She'll regret rushing to defend me once she hears the rest, but I don't correct her about my name—now doesn't seem the right time.

Caiman only grips the bars harder after hearing his father is dead. "No," he finally says. "No!" he shouts at Enoch. "What game are you playing? Why did your new blood-gifted friend compel her to come to us and say that, you fuck?"

Enoch goes to the cell, towering over Caiman by a head. To Caiman's credit, he doesn't back down in the face of a glower that could fell armies. "I'm not the only one with a blood-gifted friend. You all have the honor also."

Caiman looks confused.

"Like hell we do," Chance says.

"Ikenna bears Amaka's gift too." The smile that follows the pronouncement is smug, and as much as I enjoyed him punching Chance, I want to claw any sign of happiness off Enoch's face now.

Hearing Enoch drop my secret so coldheartedly and so casually sends me spinning into another red haze. I am furious. "You bastard. That was *not* yours to tell. It was mine to relay in my own way."

"You tried to *kill my father.* You betrayed my trust, and you pretend to have the high moral ground? Fuck you, Ikenna." He sweeps a hand toward my team. "I can't kill you, so I needed some type of gratification, and witnessing how your supposed countryfolk regard you with such revulsion is almost good enough reparations. I know how much you love Mareen, and now you get to behold just how deeply it hates you."

I don't let his verbal strike get to me.

"Unlock their damn cell," I say through clenched teeth. "You were given orders from *your* new emperor's warlord. I'd hate to see how he treats those that betray *him*."

My counterstrike lands. He flinches before returning a look as vicious as the one I stare him down with. "You mean *our* new emperor, old friend. You swore a blood oath to his warlord in the throne room."

Reed punches the bars. His fist connects with the blue steel so hard that I swear I hear a crack. "What is going on, Amari? Tell me something that doesn't have you looking like a traitor."

"Yes, Ik—" Enoch begins.

"Shut the hell up," Reed yells at the Crown Prince. "I'm not talking to you. I'm talking to her."

Enoch's response is something unintelligible and guttural. He grips the lion's head atop his sword and unsheathes it. He slashes it down in an arc with power enough to cleave a man's head from his neck. It is angled to slip through a gap in the bars and bury into Reed's chest.

"No!" I shout. Before I realize what I'm doing, I'm flinging out my hand and a blood spike is flying from the barely healed cut on my palm. It embeds into Enoch's shoulder. His sword arm is knocked off course and the blow meant to kill Reed strikes against the cell's bars. The Khanaian steel striking Khanaian steel produces a deafening roar around the keep.

The first blaster shot from the royal guards rips into my stomach. Blood gushes from the hole. I brace for the onslaught of more rounds.

"We can't kill her like this!" Enoch cries out before the rest of the shots are squeezed off. "Accacia wants her to live." He yanks the blood spike out of his shoulder and hurls it to the ground. "However, kill her entire crew. I will deal with any fallout from that."

His order makes my heart stop. When it starts beating again, it is with a whoosh I hear that's as deafening as his sword's strike against the bars. It is thunderous and all-consuming and I now recognize the familiar reaction as my blood-gift surging. I can't fight Enoch and all his guards and win. So I do the only thing I can think of, sure that it won't work, but hoping upon hope I have enough power.

"Don't move! Stand down!"

I order them with every drop of my gift I can call forth. I dredge up every bit of it and throw it all behind the wide-scale compulsion attempt that is ludicrous and insane. I've only ever compelled one person at a time. I've never tried doing it to two dozen, and I've certainly never accomplished it without coming into contact with a subject's blood. But I am desperate enough to try anyway.

I also don't have a pendant around my neck shackling my gift anymore.

"Do not harm them."

The eyes of Enoch and his guards swirl with glassiness, their bodies jerk taut, and they lower their weapons. For a suspended moment, I reel in disbelief. Then I'm suddenly struggling to breathe and my skin blazes hot and clammy after the order. My whole body from my scalp down to the tips of my toes tingles from the power thrumming inside me.

Inside my head, I feel my hold on the minds of the twenty-four soldiers as tangibly as if I am holding them in my hand. It was easy to compel and hold a compulsion over Caiman and Chance. But holding it over a host of individuals leaves me sweating and trembling. A pounding explodes in my head. My skull feels like it's seconds from splitting open. Alongside that pounding, my blood continues to roar, producing the maddening whooshing in my ears. I double over and suck in gulps of air.

"Kenna." Dannica calls my name with twisted worry.

I don't respond right away. I need a couple more minutes to wrestle with the overwhelming, battering effects of using compulsion on such a huge scale. My grasp on Enoch and his guards is so tenuous I'm afraid it will snap without warning.

"I don't know how long I can hold them," I heave. I blink against the black dots swimming in and out of focus. "*Open their cell*," I say to Enoch.

He marches forward and does as I ask.

"Go," I tell my team. "Get out of here. A stealth jet should be waiting for pickup right outside the front gates of the palace. Your safe return to Mareen has been assured to me."

"You are holding men under compulsion." The disgust in Reed's statement is painfully clear. "You are blood-gifted."

Keifer regards me with the same contempt—and fear. "Most of you were born after the first war. I was five when it started, and my father was a Praetorian during it. The emperor's blood-gifted legions had hellish abilities, but wide-scale compulsion wasn't one of them. Only the emperor himself could do that. Why can you?"

"I don't know," I wheeze. My skin is even clammier and the black dots have ballooned in size. "And now isn't the time for a chat. Get out of here before my hold on the Crown Prince and his guards slips and they're free to carry out their orders to execute you."

Chance yanks a blaster from the hand of a Khanaian guard where it hangs limp at his side. "We should kill her before we go."

"*No.*" Dannica steps in front of me, using her body as a shield. "It doesn't matter what she is if she rescued us."

Chance trains the blaster between Dannica's eyes. "Move or you take a hit too."

Enzo steps up to Dannica's side. "Fuck you, Chance. You don't get a say in this. You've been against Ikenna from the start. Ikenna got us free. Ikenna is facilitating our passage home."

"Exactly," Chance says. "How did the bitch do all of that? How did she waltz down here free while we were locked up? What was she doing?"

"I was killing a man whose family I've been close to since I was a child for the Republic," I snap. "I was watching that man transform into one of the Blood Emperor's warlords and then Brock, Caan, and Rossi—*my supposed Tribunal*—got dragged in front of me, where I was made to stand and listen to them, the men I came here as Praetorian Guard to protect, admit that they and all the fucking Tribune Generals killed my grandfather because the Republic knew about my blood-gift and wanted to quietly test out iridium on me.

"That's why my grandfather died," I tell Reed and Dannica and Haynes, desperately hoping they understand, though I know they won't. "He would have refused. It's a secret he hid all my life to keep me alive. The Tribunal found a way around his refusal. They killed him, and Brock pushed me to become a Praetorian under the guise I was doing it to help solve a murder he was party to." My laugh is a bitter thing and I cut my own self down for how stupid I've been. The emotions I've been fighting to hold in check cascade out of me in an out-of-control storm. The pounding in my head from holding Enoch and the guards back intensifies with a savagery that makes me hiss in a breath. I fall to my knees.

Dannica drops down beside me. I flinch when she wraps an arm around me, because it's a gesture I don't expect. "You look really awful."

I tell her the truth. "I feel really awful. It feels like something is hacking away at my skull. You all can kill me. I wouldn't blame you if you did. I'd be gunning to kill myself if I were in your position. I wouldn't trust me, either, and I'd hate me too. But you can't. Doing so will break the compulsion. You have to keep me alive so you can get free. And the longer you wait around here, the less chance you have at escape."

Caiman, who has been strangely quiet up to this point on the matter, regards me in a way I can't discern. The face he's put on is wholly detached. "She is right," he says. "If we want out of here alive, we are forced to let her live. Let's go."

The fragile hold I have on the Khanaians snaps. "Too late," I whisper, scrambling to reestablish the bloodlinks. "You're out of time." My power is tapped out. When I reach for my blood-gift, I don't get so much as a smolder in response. The futile attempt drains me of the last energy reserves I have left. I go slack in Dannica's hold, too weak to support myself.

"Get them back in the cell!" Enoch thunders.

The guards rush to carry out the order, and the Mareenians and Khanians clash in a fight.

Reed goes straight for the Crown Prince, having marked him as the greatest threat. Enoch switches his sword to his uninjured arm and thrusts the blade forward, trying to spear him. Reed spins out of range, hammers a punch to the temple of a guard training a blaster on his head, and tears the gun from his grip. He ducks beneath another powerful swing of Enoch's sword and squeezes off three rounds. Enoch dodges each bullet, moving like there isn't a hole in his shoulder. He and Reed fight in a dizzying blur of Xzana strikes, sword thrusts, and bullet sprays. Enoch's sword bites into Reed's side. A bullet from Reed's blaster rips into Enoch's shoulder. They heave, both bleeding and injured, and squaring off again with each other. Reed's blaster is leveled at Enoch's chest. Enoch's sword is poised to take off his head. They don't immediately reengage. They assess each other, retaking each other's measure.

Enoch scrutinizes Reed. A muscle ticks in his jaw. "You are of my people. Do you acknowledge that half?"

"It isn't any of your business, but yes, *Prince*, I do."

"You are fighting for the wrong side, then, *Praetorian*, as Ikenna is."

Before Enoch can get out another word, Reed rushes him. Enoch throws down his sword, and Reed tosses his blaster. When the two collide again it is with offensive punches, kicks, and countermaneuvers that I'm barely able to track.

Enzo staves off two guards at once a few feet away. Chance trades UV blasts with the guard he fights, and Caiman knocks a guard out and snatches his blaster, finally arming himself.

I lie against Dannica useless and unable to help.

"Go fight," I tell her.

Her hold on me tightens.

"You're one more person they can use. They need you. Reed needs you."

That makes her let me go. She eases me to the ground, stands, and throws herself into the fray.

For a moment, there is hope that the Praetorians can actually fight their way out, and then more guards pour down the stairs. Keifer goes down, along with three other Gamma Praetorians and four Alpha Praetorians. Enzo takes a nasty blast to his gut.

Enoch will not call his men off until every last Mareenian is lying dead on his keep's floor. I see that absolute in the raging fire in his eyes as he fights Reed. We tried to kill his father. It doesn't matter what the Accacian warlord agreed to; Enoch wants us dead, and in this fight, he has the opportunity to achieve that and walk away, placing blame on me for starting it.

I have to do something. If I can only find the strength to peel myself off the floor. My team is dying around me and I'm spent. Any moment Enzo or Reed or Haynes or Dannica could be next. Every time I hear the thud of a body, I brace myself to glimpse the lifeless eyes of one of them when I look in the direction of the sound.

Dannica's gaze finds mine as she fights a guard. She tosses me a flippant smile that says *I know I am going to die down here.* Too sluggish, she fails to dodge her opponent's short sword. It slides into her stomach. Crimson drips from the portion of the blue blade that protrudes from her torso. Blood soaks the front of her maroon dress coat. At the same time, Enoch gains the upper hand with Reed, and his sword slices through Reed's thigh in a way that makes a dire amount of blood spurt from the wound. It bites into Reed's shoulder next. He deflects the strike meant for his neck. I scream his name. I scream Dannica's name and Enzo's name. At least, I think I scream their names. All sound other than sword strikes, blaster discharges, and bodies thudding to the ground is sucked from the room. My squad is dying. I'm losing people like I lost them in the Ice Wastes. My goal was to get the Gamma-Alpha team out of the Jade Palace *alive.* Instead, I'm lying on the ground watching as they go down in battle *doing nothing* because my energy is fucking sapped. I snarl at my damn blood-gift to flare back to life. I snarl at my body not to be useless. I need strength. I need power. I need whatever the hell I can get to haul my ass off the floor and save the rest of my people. Enzo isn't moving. I don't know if he's fainted from shock or is simply dead. Dannica lies on the floor near my feet, chillingly still as well.

Neither of them are dead, I tell myself. They can't be dead. I refuse to believe that they are dead.

Dannica's head turns. She finds me. That same flippant smile lights up her delicate face. She grimaces as blood trickles from her mouth. Not far from her, Reed is on his knees. Enoch stands over him with his sword buried in Reed's clavicle and a blaster pressed to Reed's temple. *Help them! Help me! Don't let them die too!* I don't know who I'm praying to—whoever or whatever the fuck is listening and might hear me. I do it in blind grief. In frenzied, frantic desperation. It's a slaughter around me, my friends are all next, and there is nothing I can do to snatch them back from death.

Evolve. Evolve and you can save them. The feminine voice is the same from my hallucinations in the lecture dome and during my Crossing. I'm not suffering a near heat stroke this time, and I haven't been shot up with fake venom. The desperate part of me that called for help latches on to the voice as if it's real.

"How?" I cry out loud. I pray that there is some force behind it that can help me, even though I know there is none. I'm shell-shocked, and my mind is dredging up a facsimile of hope. Of aid that won't come, simply as a way to cope.

Accept me as your patron goddess. Accept my favor. Accept your place as my Chosen. My Blood Daughter. Fully embrace your blood-gift and evolve, the feminine voice answers.

"I do," I say hoarse, too far gone to remember that I'm not speaking with a real person. Enoch hasn't yet struck the killing blow against

Reed. But Enzo is deathly still and Dannica's chest rises and falls with the shallowest of movements.

That's not good enough, the voice says. *Say the exact words. It's the only way it is binding. Then, you may have what you seek.*

"I accept you!" I yell. "I accept you as my patron goddess! I accept your favor! I accept my place as your Chosen! Whatever that means, whatever you want, I accept!"

Strength slams into me. So does the recharged thrum of my blood-gift. "*Stand aside and let us go!*" The compulsion behind the command tears out of me with a force that rattles the entire space. Enoch and his guards halt their assault. There is no pounding in my head this time. My hold over them is not tenuous either. I see it in my mind as rigid red filaments running from me to each of the Khanaians. The filaments look like steel cables instead of threads. They won't shatter. They won't snap. They'll endure as much strain and hold for as long as I want.

I stand. The amplified power makes me dizzy as I do. I place a hand on the wall to steady myself. "The wounded. Somebody help the wounded. Get them to the jet and patched-up." I'm struggling so much to reel in the thundering firestorm of my gift that's spilling out of my veins and flooding every sliver of my essence that I can't push myself off the wall and get to anybody myself. "Get out of the palace," I urge everyone. "Get to the jet. Get back to Mareen." An unintentional whip of compulsion arcs out of me when I say it. The Praetorians' eyes turn glassy. I stare at the effect, horrified.

I focus on the red filaments that connect them to me and concentrate on snapping them. At first they don't yield. They stay in place, and I panic that my power has surged so much that I've done something irrevocable. I concentrate harder on breaking the bloodlinks. On the fourth attempt, they give. The Gamma-Alpha team stares at me dazed, but without memory of the last few moments. "I'm sorry," I croak.

Reed lumbers to his feet, a hand pressed against the gash in his thigh. He limps to Dannica and lifts her into his arms. She just hangs on for a second, no strength in her grip. Then she groans, mumbles something, and squirms in Reed's hold. Haynes appears beside them. Reed sets Dannica on her feet, and the two of them help her stay upright.

"Let's get our people out of here while we can," Caiman says. "Amari, can you lead the way and keep any other hostiles off our asses?"

"Yeah. I can do that." This time my stinted breathing isn't about me rapidly losing energy or my gift dwindling. There is an eruption of scorching power raining inside me, and it feels like it's burning my insides to ash. It leaves me completely disoriented and overwhelmed as I grapple with control. I lean against the stone, letting its coolness kiss my neck and back. It doesn't help, and I start trembling. I push off the wall and lock my legs. I cannot fall down. People are depending on me.

We do not break. We do not bend. We do not yield. Under the crushing mountain of power, I must repeat Grandfather's mantra to remain upright. The room blazes red when I walk. I blink and catch myself against the wall again. I close my eyes just for a minute to steady myself and demand that the red go away. A firm touch grips my left elbow. A different one grips my right arm. I open my eyes to a red haze still overlaying my vision, but I see Caiman on my right and Greysen on my left. Instinctively, I jerk away from them. They must want to kill me for what I am.

"We are on the same side right now," Caiman says, reading my alarm. "Let me help you so you can help us." He gives me the same look we passed between each other when we made the pact to get our aspirant class off the mountain. I nod back, relaxing, and allow him and Greysen to keep hold of me.

"Why?" I ask as we ascend the keep's steps. "Why are you two doing this?"

"Selene and Drake aren't here. Enzo is injured. Your boyfriend has his hands full with Dannica. The rest of Alpha wants to kill you, and the rest of Gamma is too spooked to get close to you. We two are all you've got, and we owe you one for taking the blast meant for Greysen up on the mountain."

"I never said thank you for it," Greysen adds. "I guess this is it."

"You're welcome," I mumble.

We fall into silence as we push through an iron door at the top of the steps. We stand in the jade-lined corridor that Enoch and the contingent of guards marched me down to take me to my team. I point to my right. "That way. It'll get us to the throne room. I can get us to an exit from there."

Caiman doesn't start down the hall right away. "My father? Is he really dead?"

When I tell him yes, grief twists his features. Guilt riddles me. Caiman deserves to know the truth, that it was me who killed Haymus, but it isn't the right time to tell him.

"You're burning up," Caiman says after we get moving.

"I know" I say awkwardly. "It's a side effect when my blood-gift flares." He doesn't flinch when I say "blood-gift," which I'm grateful for. Of course, he has so many other things on his mind at the moment. And he literally has his hands full with me. My uniform becomes drenched with sweat while we walk.

As we approach the throne room, where the night turned into a catastrophe, I come to terms with what my new existence will be after we clear the palace. Gamma won't be my cohort anymore, Mareen won't be my home, and I'll be an enemy of the Republic. In a handful of hours I've lost everything—including Selene, the Gyidis . . . I even mourn the loss of Brock. With Grandfather and Zayne gone, too, I've got nothing and nobody left.

I'm really, truly, *achingly* alone.

35

THE ACCACIAN WARLORD STICKS TO his word, and we aren't accosted leaving the palace. When we clear its gates, a stealth jet awaits as he promised. I'm overjoyed *and* petrified by its presence. I pledged myself to Ajani, and once the Mareenians fly away, he'll be expecting me to return to him and fulfill my end of our bargain. I place grappling with that particular problem aside for the moment, though, to focus on the thing of immediate importance. First, I need to get the Mareenians in the air, and then I can worry about my deal with Ajani.

Only a few Praetorians—those with the gravest injuries, which includes Enzo, and those who hauled them out of the palace—immediately board the jet when we reach it. The rest face me. Chance, Liim, and the Alpha members beside them glare at me, ready to finish what Chance tried to do in the keep. Most of Gamma doesn't look at me with pure hatred; they look at me with something worse: weariness and grim determination that I'm a threat that needs to be put down.

The hurt behind the way I'm regarded is swift and brutal. I was prepared for this final standoff and yet it's still like being slammed by an armored transport after sacrificing so much to save all of them. I'm not looking for gratitude, but a little bit of not regarding me like some rabid animal they need to cull would be nice.

"Get on the jet," Reed orders Gamma. "I'll deal with Amari." Out of the six, Dannica and Haynes are the only two who don't obey their lead.

Dannica looks at me grief-stricken, while Haynes has a torn expression. Reed, he's burned away any sentiment toward me besides cool detachment.

"Get her on the jet," Reed tells Haynes, meaning Dannica, who is clutching a stomach wound that's leaking blood. "She needs to be patched up."

Dannica shakes her head stubbornly. "I'm not going anywhere. Whatever is happening is a decision we need to make as a team. You don't get to do it alone. I'm upright and conscious for the moment, so I've got some time while we sort this out."

"*Haynes,*" Reed says.

"Listen to our third. We all should get a say in this."

Reed clenches his jaw. "Fine. But if she bleeds out while this goes down, I'm kicking both of your asses." Then he looks at Caiman and Greysen, who still have a hold on me. "Do not release her." His eyes narrow on me in suspicion. And within them, I see his consideration of how things might play out. I see him weighing the question of killing me and how it might be achieved, and I muster a savage smile because it's the only thing I've got to hide the devastation that wrecks me.

"I'd love to see *you* try," I tell Reed. I glance pointedly at his right leg. "You're injured. Don't make me have to finish the death I've delivered you from." The bravado I reach for as a second shield is so fucking pathetically paper-thin. It threatens to crumble at any second, and if it does, I'll crumble too.

"You're blood-gifted," he says evenly, like that's the only explanation needed. And I get it, he lost both his parents in a skirmish with people like me. He and everybody else who is standing around watching him condemn me, despises people like me. I am and can only ever be the enemy for him and the others. Everything he says next drives home what I already know. "You've lied about it this whole time. You've been living among us this entire time. You know too much about Mareen, about how we operate, about our tactics. It'd be unwise and negligent to get on that jet and leave you behind in Khanai with our enemies."

I draw in a sharp breath. The unflinching judgment coming from Chance, or Caiman, or anybody else I could handle, but from him . . . so soon after I've just found out how much we're alike . . . how much we share . . . how intricately we're linked via Grandfather . . . it's ripping me to shreds.

"What exactly did you bargain for our release?" He takes several steps toward me, and though he's limping and favoring his uninjured leg, those steps are threaded with hostility that makes them nothing less than intimidating. "What exactly did you give them?" He takes another step. "It would've had to have been something extremely valuable, *so what did you betray, Amari?*"

Each word slices into me and cleaves me apart as cleanly as any blade.

"Fuck you," I say, embittered. "I didn't betray anything. I've been through hell tonight. Hell perpetrated mostly by Mareen. I should've betrayed *everything*, and yet instead I traded myself to save you all." I motion to the jet. "Get on the fucking way home I arranged for you, Reed, and take the rest of your crew to safety before you really piss me off. If you take things where you're trying to take them, I won't be held liable or feel bad for my actions when I defend myself, and trust me, nobody here *can* hold me liable for them or anything else you *think* I've done wrong tonight."

I easily break Caiman's and Greysen's hold, and this time, the massive influx of power buzzing around me isn't so new. It's settled enough that I'm able to stay upright on my own.

"Reed," Haynes says, stepping up beside him with Dannica in tow, "you're doing the same thing Chance did in the prison."

Reed doesn't take his eyes off me. "No. This is different. That was about him blindly hating Amari like he's always done. This isn't about that with me. This is about me remembering I have a duty and obligation to Mareen. Every last one of us does. We guard and protect it, and leaving her behind, here, with Khanai and Accacia, is counter to that. It's treason against the Republic on our parts, regardless of how we personally may feel about her. We might as well be handing our enemies the war after what we saw her do in the keep."

My eyes sting from tears I didn't even allow myself to cry when Grandfather died. I get it the fuck together and I do not allow them to fall. Reed doesn't get that satisfaction. None of the people around me who would stand aside and let him kill me do.

"But the Legatus—" Dannica says.

"The Legatus isn't here. He's dead. Like the gods are supposed to be dead." Reed stabs me with a glower that's a mix of horror and fear. "The gods are supposed to be dead and yet, we witnessed what looked a lot like an Old World communing where Amari accepted the gifts of a goddess then blasted what looked like god-level power around the place. How is any of that possible?" he asks me. "What precisely are you? Because from what I saw in the keep, it looks a hell of a lot more than simply being blood-gifted."

"I—" My voice is embarrassingly hoarse, and I hate it. In the face of his charges, I can't come up with anything to say except the truth. "I prayed to a goddess for help when you all were dying. I think . . . I think she answered. That's why I was able to do what I did in the cells." I catch myself trembling. I force my body still. I shove down the tide of emotions that want to crest the surface and crash out of me in a tidal wave. "*But that doesn't make me a threat.* Being different is not the pretext to war our history keeps making it out to be. That the Republic keeps trying to shove down our throats. Yes, I'm different, but I'm not your enemy.

"Do not make me have to fight you. Please just believe that I'm not on anybody's side except my own. The Blood Empire murdered my mother, too, remember? I feel as much hatred toward it as you do. Make no mistake about that."

"Then what do you plan to do once we leave?" Greysen asks.

The petulant, wounded part of me wants to refuse to answer. But I've already fought one set of people I should be on the same side as tonight. I don't have it in me to do it again. So I answer straight and hope it's enough to make them see I'm not their enemy and then get on the jet and go home.

"I've been thinking about that since learning Khanai and Accacia are bound to each other. Mustaph and Enoch are fools if they think the Blood Emperor will stick to his word and allow Khanai to remain un-accosted. The entire continent will drown in blood like it did during the first war. I swore an oath to the Accacian warlord who was assuming the form of Mustaph, but I don't intend to honor it. They were simply words I needed to say to get you all out of the Prisoners' Keep. The warlord said I'm ignorant of the depth of my blood-gift and that its power is vast. I don't think he was lying, and that means I could potentially be able to help fight off Accacia in a major way. So after you depart, I'm fleeing Khanai and the warlord who wants to use me too. Then, I plan to figure out the full extent of my gift. Once I do, I'm killing the Blood Emperor."

"So you're going rogue." Reed regards me with a little less hostility. Fuck him for what it took to get there.

"That's not a bad plan," Dannica remarks.

"It's a terrible plan. But it's also ballsy, Amari." Caiman huffs a laugh. "Nobody except you would think they could single-handedly take on the Blood Empire and win. But . . . perhaps nobody except you can.

You're arrogant enough to attempt it and you're self-righteous and brazen enough to maybe even get it done." He gives me a wholly assessing look. Then, he turns to the group, radiating all the authority of a war house head and Tribune General he technically now is. "We aren't killing her. We've cut enough allies loose. The Blood Empire needs to be stopped, and from what I saw in the palace Amari might be the one with the power to do it. We all saw her reduce a room full of guards to statues. That is a hell of a force to have on our side. It is a thing that can decide a war. The Republic needs her."

Chance steps forward. "Like hell it does. She just said she took an oath with an *Accacian* she's planning on breaking. And she's clearly already broken her oath to both the Praetorians and the Republic." There's a blaster in his hand. He hasn't raised it yet; it hangs at his side, but the threat is clear.

Caiman flicks a glance at it. "Don't be an idiot. If you try to shoot her, I'm not going to stop her from killing you. In fact, I might help her because you just defied a direct order from *your* new Tribune. With my father dead, I'm head of Rossi War House—and that means I steer Alpha cohort. Get your ass on the jet, Chance." He sweeps an uncompromising look at the rest of Alpha. "I'm staying behind, and I'm helping her take down the Blood Emperor. If you can manage to play by the terms of this new op that I set—and can deal with the fact that Amari is a part of that—stay on the ground. We can use all the good fighters we can get. If you can't do that, fly home."

"I'm with you on this," Greysen says, stepping away from my side and closer to Caiman's.

Chance rakes Caiman with a sneer. "You're *one* Tribune. When we get back, the rest will charge her, you, and anybody else who remains behind with treason. So know this isn't over. The Alpha team I take with me is coming back after you." The team he mentions follows him onto the jet when he marches up the ramp.

Yet two do remain.

"I was never leaving without you," Dannica says, directly to me. "Gamma takes care of its own *and* I wasn't abandoning a sister-in-arms. I was trying to wait for Reed to get it together before I said that, but he's taking too long. I'm all in for your rogue team. Let's fuck shit up."

"Count me in for the shindig too," Haynes drawls. "Sounds like a ball."

I look at them like they have all lost their minds, because they have. I'm set to argue and tell them they need to go home. If they stay with me, Chance is right. We won't just have Accacia to fight. We'll be hunted down by Mareen too. But a part of me stops to consider the heftiness of the task I'm undertaking and the extreme possibility that I won't succeed alone. If I go at things by myself, I will be one individual attempting to take on a tyrant who fancies himself a near god because of his level of might. It is wise to accept and use all the aid I can get. Also, if I'm being entirely honest with myself, underneath all the bravado I laid my plan out with, I am scared shitless. I'm relieved and grateful at the prospect of not having to face such a perilous course alone. "Okay," I say.

"There's one thing you should know though," I add, because they need to be aware of all I have planned if they're making the decision to stand with me. "My mission isn't just to topple the Blood Empire. I still have a debt to settle with the Tribunal. I want the sitting Tribunes dead for what they did to me and my grandfather. And then there's the matter of their expansion aims. Not straightaway—the Republic can't take that level of instability while we're at war, and the Blood Emperor is the primary threat. But after Accacia is dealt with, I'm dealing with their rot too." My battle is definitely a two-headed monster that needs to be slayed, and I'm going to do my godsdamned best to make sure I can create the world Grandfather always envisioned.

Maybe one that's even better.

"Those of us in Gamma were already doing that anyway," Haynes says, like I figured. The other Gammas stand a little straighter, and I'm strangely proud (considering what it all means) to be in their cohort.

I look to Caiman and Greysen, awaiting their reaction. They were not plotting with us before to go after Tribunes.

Caiman folds his arms over his chest. "I gave you my feelings about the Tribunal and how Mareen largely operates on the mountain. What I've learned in Khanai about them simply reinforces things. They dragged Mareen into a war for greed. They're willing to sacrifice us, when they're supposed to guard and protect us as much as we guard and protect them. I, you, and the rest of us took an oath to serve and guard the Republic—not the trash Tribunal. Let's take out the garbage, wipe the board clean, and give Mareen a reset."

"My support doesn't change," Greysen says. The two other Alphas who stayed behind also nod in agreement.

The only person left on the ground who hasn't verbally agreed they're with me is Reed. I raise my eyebrow at him questioningly. "You haven't moved to walk—or kill me—so I guess you're in?"

He passes me a curt nod. "I am." I think that's all I'm going to get from him, but then he clears his throat and says, "I acted like an ass back in the cells and out here at first. I committed the same nature of bigotry against you that I despise the Republic for so much. For what it's worth, I'm ashamed and I'm sorry. There's more I'd like to say but . . . later."

I return his nod. The wound is still raw, but the apology he offers has to be enough for now. "Yes, we can and we will hash everything else out later," I promise him, because there's no way in hell I'm letting him off the hook so easy. Not since we needed to stand around and have a conversation about whether I was worthy of existing.

"Let me go tell the rest of everyone to take off," he says, and limps past me. He ascends the jet's ramp and descends a few minutes later. He carries a trauma kit under his good arm. He sets to work patching Dannica's stomach wound up while the rest of us watch the stealth jet rise into the air. We track it until it disappears from view.

"Where do we go?" a bandaged Dannica asks.

"First, we should find a secure place to treat Reed's leg," I answer.

"We shouldn't linger outside the gates of the palace any more than we already have. Then, I was thinking one of the Free Microstates might be a good idea. We can have a safe haven there and plan how to execute things."

"And how are we supposed to get all the way there?" Greysen asks.

It's Reed who answers him. "I have a few contacts—and a specific microstate or two where we can lie low.

"Your grandfather," he supplies before I can ask how he has all this at his disposal. "He has well-positioned friends among the microstates. There are those who reside north who aren't as powerless as the Republic believes and take issue with things the Tribunal has perpetrated too."

"Right," I say, and want to laugh. "Of course Grandfather does."

We all agree on the Free Microstates. Although the path ahead is no less bleak, hazardous, or frightening with a squad surrounding me, the presence of the friends I've gained, the support I've gained, the wild, crazy rogue cohort I've gained brings nothing but a goofy albeit idiotic smile to my face. But we have a vision, and determination, and confidence to spare on our side. We also have nerve and resilience and a considerable combined strength. Our rogue cohort might just be able to take on both the Blood Empire and the Tribunal and win.

And then . . .

I'm done fighting for mere tolerance from the Republic. I want more than the illusion of power. I'm fighting for them, but I'm fighting for *me* even more. If we're making new rules and an Amari is saving the Republic's ass again, I want an Amari War House. I want a Tribunal seat. Not in several generations. Immediately.

Blood is my gift. And blood is what they'll get if anyone gets in my godsdamned way.

ACKNOWLEDGMENTS

I'VE NEVER DONE THIS BEFORE, and I'm not sure where to start. I also hope I don't leave anybody out. So, I guess I'll begin way back at the beginning.

To my best friend since ninth grade, my ride-or-die, my sister, and my forever cheerleader, Whitney, thank you, thank you, thank you times a billion. When I first started this writing journey and was terrified and thought it was a mad dream that would never come true, you kept me going. You were right there in my corner rooting for me and demanding I send the next book. You devoured each and every story I sent you. You gushed over the worlds and characters I was creating, and if it wasn't for you I would've never retained the confidence, strength, and determination to keep fighting for the dream.

To my sisters, Janee, Elana, and Lauren, thank y'all too! Thank you for reading drafts, sample pages, and messy chapters and talking through ideas with me. You all are the best sisters a girl could be blessed with.

To my mommy, Shelia, without your encouragement, support, guidance, and the belief you instilled in me since I was a baby that the sky is the limit, I wouldn't be here either. THANK YOU for that conviction.

To my dad, Don, Uncle Tony, Aunt Phyllis, and all the rest of my family that has always been nothing except absolutely supportive, thank you as well. Thank you for having a hand in raising me, nurturing me, and really being the village that made me who I am today.

To Granny, the first person who ever put a pencil and paper in my hand, thank you and I miss you. I wish you were here to see *The Blood Trials* be published and for us to laugh and look back on the time I was a little girl, back before I could read or write, when I sat at your kitchen table with you while you lesson-planned and scribbled wavy lines on a sheet of notebook paper. You asked me what I was writing, and I told you a story. Then I narrated the story for you that the scribbles were supposed to tell. That childhood story from a time I can't even remember is one of your greatest gifts to me. It's always stuck with me and has always let me know that God and the Ancestors blessed me with a gift for storytelling. It's why I've always wholeheartedly believed that I was placed on this earth to be an author. It helped me keep going when the going got tough.

Last, but certainly not least where my family is concerned, I want to thank the five most important people in my life: my spouse, Courtney, and our wonderful, magnificent kids, Carmen, Cydney, CJ, and Camaiya. Y'all are my cosmos, my universe, my world. Y'all make life worth living and amazing, and y'all challenge me every day to be the best possible version of myself. I love y'all to the sun and back.

To my amazing rock-star agent, Caitie Flum, thank you so much for believing in me, supporting me, and helping me build a brand and career that's in line with the vision of the kind of author I'd like to be. Thank you for all your edit notes, story chats, advice, and for putting up with my countless questions and messages about the million and one ideas I have all the time. Also, thank you for reigning my writer shenanigans in when the story I'm working on is about to go off the rails. 😊

David Pomerico and the whole Harper Voyager team, working with you is a dream. I'm still incredibly humbled and in awe to be collaborating with an editorial team who has published some of my favorite authors. David, thank you for seeing the vision behind *The Blood Trials*; believing in my fierce heroine, Ikenna; and helping me make her story shine. You have an incredible way of drilling down to the heart of a novel, and you helped me turn *The Blood Trials* into everything I imagined it to be and so much more.

To the Liza Dawson Associates team, thank you for your support of this book and everything you contributed to make it happen.

Now to my peeps Brent, L.D., DaVaun, Ebony, Andre, and the entire NSS crew—if I could gift each one of you a star in the sky I would, but you'd still outshine them all. Y'all are so dope and so supportive, and I'm so blessed to have a crew of Black science-fiction/fantasy creatives to go on this author journey with. Brent, thank you for reading countless drafts of *The Blood Trials*. Thank you for being there when I was in crisis mode while completing my first-ever huge revision post-acquisition and for being the sounding board and cheerleader I needed. L.D., thank you for being the pillar that always has fellow Black creatives' backs and for being always ready to lend your sword if need be. And of course, thank you for your notes on the early drafts of *The Blood Trials* too. DaVaun, thank you for the reads, critiques, spitballing of ideas, and all the time you've graciously and generously offered to help me on this journey. Andre, thank you for always being elated about whatever idea I'm working on and for always offering your perspective on things. Thank you for being a word magician when it comes to naming things! You're the best! Ebony, you rolled with me waaaaay back when during the story I wrote before *The Blood Trials*. Thank you for being an invaluable CP, thank you for rooting for me, and thank you for lending all your brilliance and wisdom on that manuscript. It helped make me a better writer going into writing *The Blood Trials*.

To Traci-Anne Canada and Ronni Davis, y'all are my girls! From the time we met at the Madcap writing retreat and drove back to Georgia together to now, y'all have been the literal wind beneath my wings (sorry for the corny phrasing). Y'all have been here to cry with me while I was in the query trenches, help calm my angst when *The Blood Trials* went on submission, and shout for joy with me when Ikenna's story was going to be published. THANK YOU!

To Jamar, whew! We both know it's been a ride to get here! You've been along for the journey so much of the way. Thank you for your reads, for talking with me through my ideas, and for believing in *The Blood Trials* and Ikenna from day one. Thank you for always putting things into perspective for me and helping to rein me in when I'm veering off into anxious, worrying hot-mess territory.

Raymond Sebastien, the cover art for *The Blood Trials* is nothing short of stunning. You truly have a gift. You brought Ikenna to life in such a vivid, gorgeous way, and I don't think I'll ever stop staring at her on the cover of *The Blood Trials*. In fact, I'm probably going to order an absurdly massive print and hang it in my house. ☺

Kwame, Jon, AJ, Melody, Liz, Yas: Y'all are the real MVPs. Seriously, thank you for all the chats, writer check-ins, sprints, jokes, laugh-my-ass-off moments, and craft talks.

Greg, you're the best! Thank you for being a cheerleader while I've been on this writing journey since the near beginning too. Thank you for always offering to read scenes or pages or whole manuscripts and for being so generous with your brilliant thoughts, feedback, and advice that is never not right on the money. Moreover, thank you for being a friend who I can always reach out to.

To Beverly Jenkins, author extraordinaire, romance queen, and titan with a pen: I owe you the HUGEST thank-you for being so open, kind, and generous with your support and advice. I appreciate it, and you're so dope and inspirational for the way you reach back and pull others up with you.

To Rachel Caine (RIP), who read the first manuscript I ever attempted to query with and told me she saw something special in my writing, thank you so much for that. They were words of encouragement that kept me pushing forward in a moment where I was thinking of giving up.

To Dhonielle Clayton, who is the epitome of Black Girl Magic, thank you for all the support you give writers of color and all the work you do to help ensure that our stories get told. On a personal note, thank you for believing in me and for critiquing sample pages of a work way back when and telling me also that you saw something special in the words. It was also a time of much needed encouragement that made me push forward and keep going.

If I missed anybody I am infinitely sorry. Please know that it wasn't intentional. To everyone who has helped me achieve my dream and make *The Blood Trials* possible: THANK YOU.

ABOUT THE AUTHOR

NIA "N. E." DAVENPORT is a science-fiction/fantasy author who has a penchant for blending science and magic. She possesses undergraduate degrees in biology and theatre, as well as master of arts degrees in secondary education and public health. When she isn't writing, she enjoys vacationing with her family, skiing, and being a huge foodie. You can find her online at nedavenport.com, on Twitter @nia_davenport, or on Instagram @nia.davenport, where she talks about bingeworthy TV, fun movies, and great books. She lives in Texas with her husband and kids.

Look for book two of the Blood Gift Duology, *The Blood Gift*, in Spring 2023.